Whispers Under Middle Ides

A Redferne Family Adventure

Pattison Telford

This novel's story and characters are fictitious. Certain long-standing institutions, agencies, and public offices are mentioned, but the characters involved are wholly imaginary.

eBook ISBN: **978-1-7770532-8-4**
Paperback ISBN: **978-1-7770532-9-1**
Hardcover ISBN: **978-1-7781240-0-6**

ACKNOWLEDGEMENTS

Thanks to my advance readers! (Samuel Alfrey, Norm Finlayson, Mary O'Neill)

Impeccable editing by vickybrewstereditor.com

Cover design by Darin Morrison-Beer

Redferne Family Adventures

You can find out more at www.pattisontelford.com

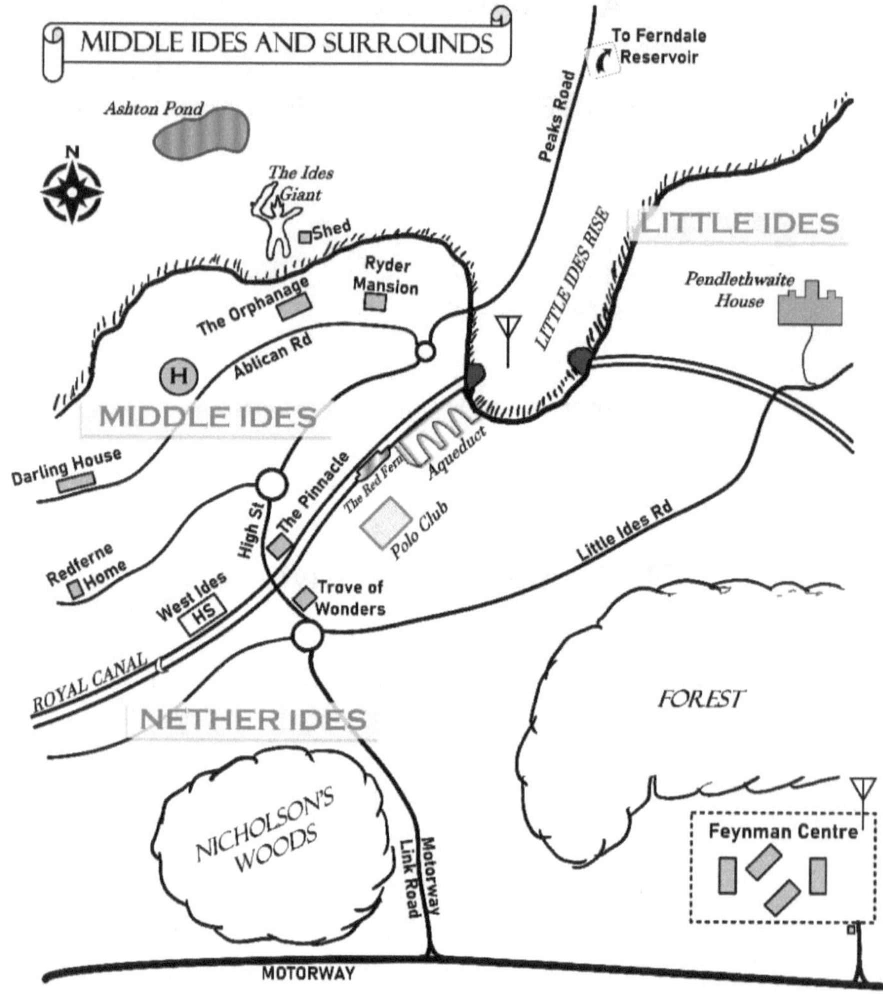

MIDDLE IDES AND SURROUNDS
To Ferndale Reservoir
Ashton Pond
N
Peaks Road
LITTLE IDES
The Ides Giant
Shed
LITTLE IDES RISE
Ryder Mansion
Pendlethwaite House
The Orphanage
Ablican Rd
H
MIDDLE IDES
Aqueduct
Darling House
The Pinnacle
The Red Fern
Little Ides Rd
High St
Polo Club
Redferne Home
Trove of Wonders
West Ides
HS
ROYAL CANAL
FOREST
NETHER IDES
NICHOLSON'S WOODS
Feynman Centre
Motorway Link Road
MOTORWAY

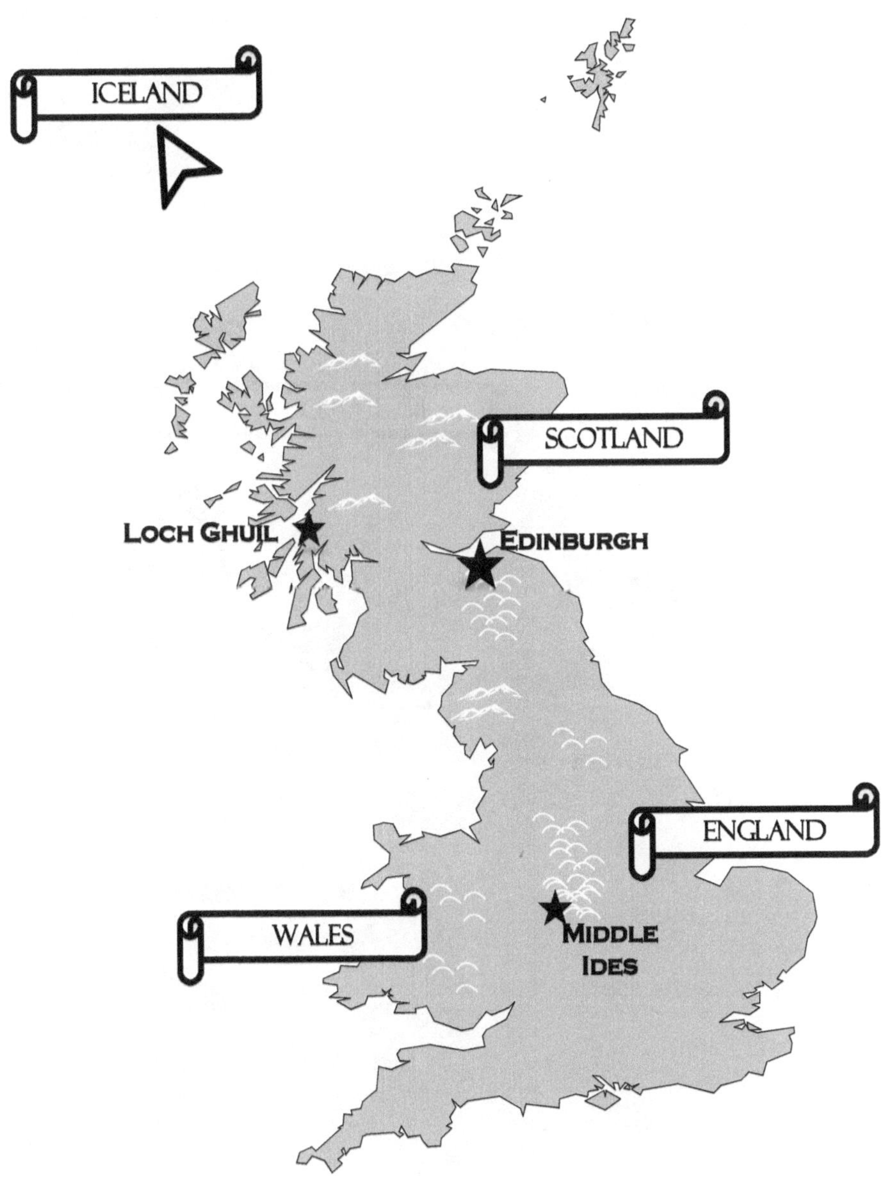

ICELAND
SCOTLAND
ENGLAND
WALES
LOCH GHUIL
EDINBURGH
MIDDLE IDES

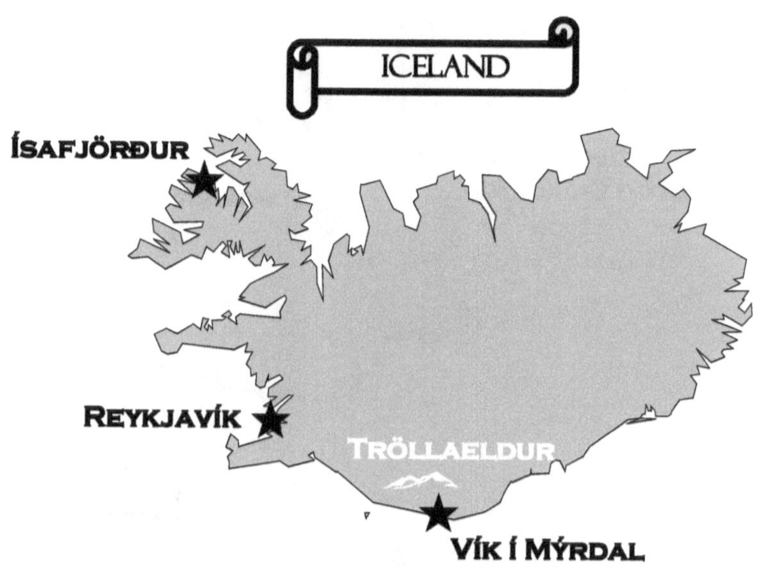

ICELAND
ÍSAFJÖRÐUR
REYKJAVÍK
TRÖLLAELDUR
VÍK Í MÝRDAL

PRONUNCIATION GUIDE

The Scottish Gaelic and Icelandic names in this book have not-so-obvious pronunciations. Here is a short guide.

Ísafjörður -   EEsa fyurder
Loch Ghuil – LAWkh GYUil
Njarl – nYARL
Ragnhildur – RAHgn HEYdush
Reykjavik – RAY kya vik
Reynisdrangar - REYnis TRAnyacar
Tröllaeldur - TROTla ELder
Úlfursdottir – ULLfirs DAHteer
Vik Í Myrdal – VIK ee MEERdahl

CHAPTER 1 - CONFESSION

Faraday

The fabricator whirred and clunked as it stamped out nodes for the revised nano-killer aerosol I had worked on all night. Although the device needed no supervision, the video call chime on my phone was an annoyance. It distracted me from tracking the fabrication process on the three computer screens in my mother's concealed basement lab.

A glance at my dead father Templeton's watch confirmed that it was 6:37 a.m. According to the flight tracking app, my brother and sister's flight had taken off 18 minutes ago from Stavanger, heading from Norway to Iceland.

"Maybe the app is wrong, and they're delayed," I muttered to myself. Nobody else would contact me by video call.

The temptation to turn my phone over to identify the caller proved irresistible. Private number. Not a spoofed number, intended to fool me into duct cleaning or paying bitcoin to resolve an overdue tax bill. A *private* number.

Curiosity piqued, I answered, not yet enabling my camera. A familiar face appeared, blonde ponytail snaking over an athletic shoulder. Scarlett Thorisdottir, my father's handler in the Unusual Powers Defence Agency, leant her face close to the camera, with only hints of an engineering lab adorning the edges of the video. I noted 29 Fujikami tubes racked on a stainless steel wall, the same tubes my mother used in her nanotech experiments.

"Faraday? Are you alone?" She spoke with little affect, as usual, but I had seen her both commanding and vulnerable, and knew the tiny telltale signs of agitation. A gaze that lingered over-long, a slight modulation of her tone to end each sentence.

"Just me here. But where are you?"

"It doesn't matter right now," she said. But my mind was already deciphering the scant information from the visible slivers of lab. A green sign atop a door said выход. So, she was in Russia, not the United Kingdom.

"You're at Vladishenko's lab, aren't you?"

"Faraday, listen. It's not important. But I need to tell you something that *is*. And you won't believe me unless I tell you something else first."

"Okay. Fire away," I said, glancing at the progress display on my monitors.

"We've talked before about the suspicious nature of both your parents' deaths, in separate incidents. And even though you and Newton found some mentions of the Unusual Powers Defence Agency at your mother's lab on the day she died, I could never find any trace of UPDA involvement, even when I worked there. But I've uncovered some new information about her death."

I'd probed for details surrounding the day of Mum's death, and had come to my own conclusion that Scarlett was not involved. I was interested to see what she might know now, but didn't want to appear too eager to believe her.

"Okay. Let's hear it," I said. "But make it quick, I'm fabricating." How could I have known that her next sentence would leave me shattered, grappling with my internal logic and grasping at the razor edges of even deeper conspiracies?

Scarlett drew in a deep breath and pulled her shoulders back, as if she was an opera singer preparing to make a dramatic entrance. "Your mother—it seems she got tangled with the Revision. But to make sure you believe me about this, I have to admit something else. I placed the UPDA kill order on your father."

The weight of infinite unanswered questions crushed me. A metallic taste coursed down my throat and the hand holding the phone no longer felt attached to me; it shook in a series of tremors. I found myself on one knee, struggling to remember how to breathe.

Scarlett paused and peered at the camera, listening, before continuing. "They're an international group of powerful sponsors trying to wrest power away from traditional governments. Faraday? Are you still there?"

I stabbed at the camera button, feeling it would be harder for her to lie to my face. My voice rasped, foreign to my ears. "No. No, no, no. It wasn't you."

My words surprised me. Somehow, I'd concluded that my early suspicions were wrong and that Scarlett was *not* involved in my mother's aneurism incident at the Feynman Centre lab. That she hadn't organised the car crash that killed my father.

I turned and threw up into a waste bin, a vile paste reminiscent of coffee. My hand sought the comforting ruffle of my dog's fur before I remembered she'd died too, killed by my own actions. There was little comfort left in my home with my brother and sister away.

"Gods, Faraday, are you okay?"

"Why would you say this? It's not a very good joke."

"The Revision part is crucial, and I need you to believe me. I figured you'd only listen if I came clean about your father."

That logic made no sense to me, but nothing made sense. My eyes tried to focus on the phone screen, but the churning in my brain had no space to process any visual information.

Scarlett continued, relentless as usual. "I had to do it, Faraday. Templeton was the only friendly face for me at the agency, but he was out of control after Alison died. Remember that weird fire in the woods just outside Middle Ides last year? Over by the Ferndale Reservoir? He created that. As a threat."

My focus was inward and perfectly rendered snatches of aerial photos and news footage cartwheeled from my memory, unbidden. The raging fire had transformed 9 acres of ancient forest to ashes in just under 2 hours, burning an uncanny, near-perfect circle without spreading beyond its perimeter. The event happened in the week before my father's car was sabotaged, killing him and sending my family into a tailspin, so I had thought little about the odd conflagration until now.

My eyes darted, scrambling to find a neutral place to steady my spinning mind. But everywhere my gaze lingered only reminded me of my dead parents. The elegant illustrations of nanotech components annotated in my mother's hand made me pause. My scanning found the crazy experimental contraptions my father had devised when we were kids, including the soap bubble generator that produced rainbow-tinged bubbles larger than me at the age of 5, and the spring-loaded, rubber-footed extensible struts that he positioned to brace himself, prone, above my bedroom door so he could surprise me when I emerged for school in the morning. Dad's smiling face beamed from photos tacked above his desk—the Great Wall of China, a hotel carved from ice, a windswept beach hut surrounded by black sand. Nowhere I looked resolved my jitters.

"He had some artefact. Probably picked it up on his travels. He was ranting, saying, 'Only Allison knows where I hid it, and you made sure she's not telling anyone now, didn't you?' Said he'd only used it for a minute, as a demonstration. He threatened that next, he was bringing it to London. For revenge. We had to stop him, Faraday. You see that, right?"

I didn't see *anything*. "What was it, this artefact?" I asked, struggling to focus.

"We don't know. Never found it, although heaven knows we looked."

"But you didn't have to kill him. You could have arrested him."

"I pleaded for that option, believe me. But the decision-makers wouldn't have it. It went right to the top. The plan was to kill him but make it look like an accident—so he'd not suspect anything if it failed. That way, we'd avoid all plans he had to unleash this firebomb. Even if he had a contingency plan to unleash an attack if we moved against him, a car accident wouldn't trigger it. In the end, I couldn't argue against their logic and placed the kill order. I'm so sorry, Faraday."

The only way I could avoid spiralling out of control was to convert my brain into a problem-solving apparatus and push everything else aside. I would locate this mysterious artefact, unravel its secrets, and blunt my grief with a new connection to my father.

"I'll use the UPSCALE to find the artefact; I have it right here." I referred to the Unusual Powers Scanning and Learning device that my parents had invented for Scarlett's hidden government agency. It could detect hostile nanotechnology and magical activity.

"Tried that. Couldn't find anything. But there's a reason I need to tell you this now. Listen. We intercepted some encoded messages. The Revision found out, and they're coming for it—whatever your father hid away. Get out of the house. You're in immediate danger."

What the Revision was or the power they concealed, I had no clue, but a call to action was the only thing that could have broken my darkening spiral. My instincts told me to snatch up an arsenal of nanotech, and juggle it with the phone as I snicked shut the concealed door of the lab beneath our back garden. I'd go to my grandmother. She would make sense of everything. My mother's scarf that Dad had hung on the coat stand inside the front door as a daily reminder of our loss shivered in the breeze when I swung wide the front door.

As I disconnected the video call, Scarlett blurted more words that I lacked the capacity to absorb. The last utterance was, "Svetlana is in England already and is on her way to help. She's like you, Faraday."

I did not know who Svetlana was, and I doubted she was anything like me. My only thought was that the person who'd saved my life had also killed my father.

CHAPTER 2 - ICELAND

Higgs

"How does your hair even stay swept over like that?" I asked, giggling. I peeked through the crack between the aeroplane seats where I could see Tam Thunder, drummer from the band Piping Hot, where he sat next to my friend, Dot. My seat was reclined, if you can call it that, and Lars had positioned his seat upright to allow for the widest possible crack. I communicated through this slender V while Lars knelt, facing backwards, and rested his chin on his seat back.

"It's not natural, I can tell you that much," Dot replied on Tam's behalf, nudging it with a forefinger to prove its uncanny resilience under prodding. "Smells like epoxy, with an added whiff of fake coconut."

Tam's cheeks bunched in a hearty laugh. "It's a mousse called HoldiLocks, thank you very much," he said, running fingers through the sweep to exaggerate it even more. "I cannae say a single bad word about it. Possibly because ah'm sponsored by them."

I remembered seeing his full-page advert in one of those teen magazines, now that I thought about it. Lars was about to add something when he became distracted by the over-wing view through Tam's window. He pointed, voice rising with the innocent enthusiasm I found so endearing. "Hey, look at that! A volcano!"

He was right. We all turned and peered through the window. Even my brother, Newton, in the row ahead of me, shifted so he could see past our friend Chronos's bulk and get a view. We peered at the tableau of sea and rock below, shimmering in the sharp-angled morning light. Clouds of water vapour ascended in bursts from the sea, fringing an igneous finger of land that pointed south from Iceland's coast. A line of dark red enveloped by a black void of churning matter, just beneath the water's surface, could be glimpsed through slashes in the billowing steam, snaking away from the coast in a crimson tendril. Definitely underwater volcanic activity— Iceland would be a little bigger when we left than when we arrived.

The plane's descent into a cloud bank snatched the spectacle from us. Lars remained undampened. "Whoa. I've never seen anything like that before. Wasn't it cool?"

"Now, now, little boy," Dot chided, a playful edge to her voice. "Haven't you seen that in one of your pop-up books before?" She squinted and rubbed her cheek, as if her elegant cheekbone needed a massage.

Lars took this as he always did, knowing full well Dot's teases were a sign of affection. He snaked his arm through the crack in the seats beside me in a playful grab at Dot's leg, but she swung her knees to the side, out of reach. "Don't worry, Miss Sophisticated. I'll get you later," he said, turning and buckling up as the pilot announced our descent into the clouds around Reykjavik.

I snapped my seat back up to its normal, uncomfortable position and leant into Lars. "If you were excited about spawning maggots, I'd listen to it all day. Enthusiasm is contagious, and you should never forget that."

If he'd been drinking milk, his chortle would have ejected a squirt from his nose. "Funny you should mention it. I was just going to tell you about the maggots in the bins behind Mum's shop …"

We both awaited a break in the clouds and another glimpse of the volcanic eruption, but my brain drifted in a different direction. We'd planned a quick trip to steer our minds away from the dark and weird, but I couldn't stop myself from another attempt to decipher why our parents had both been killed and how we had been cast as unlikely saviours into struggles between hidden magic and sinister nanotechnology. I hoped that a break from Middle Ides could let me—let *all* of us—dispel those memories and bask in the simple pleasure of a rock concert in an interesting land.

* * *

Passing through Icelandic immigration was as close to a non-event as possible. A yawning official in a royal blue uniform waved through our motley assortment. He didn't even bat an eyelash at Tam Thunder or his bandmates, despite their hair jutting out at impossible angles. We lingered by the baggage return carousel in the airy expanse of the stylish, modern Reykjavik airport, its vivid red roof sloping over vast windows. They should have provided scenic views across patches of water and rugged terrain, but peering between condensation streaks revealed nothing but fog.

Newton's mobile rang. I heard the tones of Faraday's animated voice but couldn't pick out the gist of his torrent of words. Newton nodded a few times as his brow furrowed into a deeply rutted V. He turned to look at me frequently as Faraday's outburst continued. Although none of us would have wanted him to feel the pressure of our eavesdropping, Chronos, Dot, Lars, me, and even Tam inched closer to him as his gravity escalated. Finally, it was his turn.

"And Scarlett said this *Revision* is coming for the artefact that Dad concealed? Could it really be buried under the shed at the Ides Giant?"

He nodded a few more times at Faraday's muffled response, and delivered parting advice, almost an order, before he ended the call. "With the house under threat, stay with Granny, right? And Alan Ryder's house is just up the street. Head there for more help. And Faraday—call me *immediately* if anything unexpected happens."

As the conveyor belt on the baggage reclaim stuttered into motion, Newton shook his head at the ring of quizzical faces now surrounding him. "I get why you lollygaggers are straining your ears while trying to look all nonchalant; the things that happen to this family deserve a Viking ballad. And we may need to add a new verse—Faraday just got a warning from Scarlett, in Russia, to leave our house. And a lot of disturbing news about Dad. A lot. Let's grab the suitcases and get out of here. I'll explain in the taxi."

* * *

Tam left with his bandmates to board their rental bus while the five of us walked in ragged formation to the taxi rank, accompanied by the harsh sound of plastic luggage wheels spinning across the paved forecourt. The sun was a vague source of diffuse light in the enveloping fog; the taxis emerged only at the last moment.

We chose a taxi van, the only vehicle large enough to fit both our bags and Chronos's overstuffed frame. Although it was mid-morning, the driver of every taxi leant back, snoozing. Either the fogginess contributed, or perhaps this was standard Icelandic taxi driver technique for catching up on lost sleep after a night shift.

It took a firm knock on the dew-streaked passenger window

to rouse our driver. A series of laconic blinks preceded him awakening and stepping out to load our luggage. He popped the back hatch and arranged our suitcases in an artful jumble before ushering us in, directing Chronos up front after a quick appraisal.

"Sorry, sorry," he said. "I am little tired today, but I am awake now. Where to?"

Chronos mentioned the name of our hotel in central Reykjavik, and the taxi took a smooth arc out of the airport grounds into the mist. The forty-five-minute drive, punctuated by headlights winking in and out of view in the fog, was plenty of time for Newton to fill us in on Faraday's report and for several unanswerable questions to be posed. We kept to hushed tones, with Chronos leaning back in his seat and Lars hovering over Newton's shoulders from the back row.

Was Scarlett telling the truth about ordering Dad's assassination after denying it so many times? She had no good reason to lie. And we all remembered the strange fire in the hills, so that part was undeniable. But a secretive organisation threatening us in their quest for a magical artefact? Even after the only half-believable things we'd experienced in the last year, this seemed far-fetched.

Dot rubbed her jaw with the heel of her palm and nodded. "I believe it," she said. "I remember getting that tingling sensation when the fire was raging above Middle Ides. It makes sense now that it was magic. At least to me."

"See? You *are* sophisticated," Lars said, a hand on Dot's shoulder. "When you tingle, I believe you. We should return to Middle Ides, stay with Faraday, yes?"

Newton nodded. "Yeah, I'm worried. Faraday should be safe with Granny, but we can't take the extra days here we'd planned. But Chronos and I still have our side mission here. We can't leave without completing that. I'll look at flights back for tomorrow, after tonight's concert."

As was often the case with my family, more questions than answers abounded.

* * *

The fog thinned as the morning progressed, providing a smidgeon of visibility across Reykjavik from the sixth-floor windows of our hotel. Dot and I shared a room, and Lars hung out with us. He had agreed to take the couch in the second room, leaving the bed for Newton and Chronos. But Lars remained with us after we wished the boys well on their side quest and waved them off to the tiny airport at the fringe of Reykjavik for their internal flight.

"Tam just texted," Dot said, sitting on the wide window sill, opened to its slivery limit to allow mist-tinged fresh air into the stuffy room. "Sound check's done, and he says he's organised a self-guided four-wheel-drive tour. He'll drive us around this afternoon while we wait for your brother to get back. Waterfalls and stuff."

"Tell him we need an early lunch first," Lars said. "We do not want to be in the middle of nowhere and feeling hungry."

"You and your metabolism," I laughed. But I knew this was wise advice. If the minimal scale of Reykjavik was anything to go by, services would be scant once we got into the countryside. "We'll meet him in the hotel café."

* * *

Red chequered tablecloths draped over the square Formica tabletops in the café. Tam was just settling into his seat as we arrived and jingled a key ring at us as we approached.

"We're gonnae feel all *battle of the monster trucks*," he said. "The running board of this Jeep thingme is at waist height, and the massive wheels look like something fae a video game."

"Who gets to ride shotgun?" I asked.

"I didnae check to see if they provided shotguns," Tam chuckled, "But it's dead likely there's guns fae each of us somewhere in there. It's massive."

Seeing us settled at the table, a waitress approached, pen and order pad at the ready. She'd pulled her glossy hair into a tight bun, and she wore a pocketed apron that matched the tablecloth. Dark shadows beneath her eyes echoed her hair colour. I couldn't help but remark on it. "Oh my goodness, you look tired! Are you okay?"

She beamed, her face brightening, "Thanks, but yes, I *am* tired today. I have terrible sleeps now, many weird dreams. Almost everyone is experiencing sleep trouble here. Probably this foggy weather. It is a problem. Well, except Anna in the kitchen, but she comes from up in the hills. Says the weather is clear up there. Anyway, what would you like to order? I promise I will not fall asleep between here and the kitchen." A crinkling of her eyes and the bridge of her nose were the only overt signs she jested.

We ordered, and the waitress scurried away. Dot rubbed her upper jaw again. "My jawbone aches. I wonder if my wisdom teeth are coming in?"

"Jeez. Aren't you wise enough already?" I griped, my sarcasm making her laugh.

Lars pushed his chair back. "Let me look. My uncle is a dentist."

"Ha! You're related to an expert, so we have to treat you as a dentist too?" I asked, giggling. But I knew it was too late. He was already up and knelt beside Dot to inspect her upper jaw, if only she'd open her mouth.

Dot looked him in the face, a crooked smile still not parting her lips. But he expressed even more earnestness than usual, so she capitulated, tilting her head back and opening wide.

Lars narrowed his focus and shone the flashlight from his

phone into Dot's mouth. I scanned the café and was delighted to see only one other table of guests was present to witness this strange tableau. "Look at those!" Lars said. "Dot, you've got enormous … molluscs?"

"Those are called molars, Mr Dentist," I said. "You're not inspiring much confidence here."

"But another tooth sits in behind them, right where you feel it," he said. "Close your mouth now. I know what it is."

He returned to his seat. He didn't say it was a wisdom tooth, as I expected, but stayed silent for a moment.

"Okay, Dr Lars. What's your diagnosis?" I asked.

"My Morsa told me about this. Everyone in Sweden knows the story."

Quizzical looks abounded while he paused again.

"It is a tiger tooth. Only one kid in a … Higgs, what do you call it? A birth cycle? Like all of us, here?" He gestured, indicating the four of us.

"A generation?"

"Yeah, that is what I mean. It only comes once in a generation. A kid grows a tiger tooth. Extra big. And pointy. Only on one side. I see the points breaking through."

Dot nodded. "Yeah, they feel rough to my tongue. I worried it was a wonky wisdom tooth. Is that what you mean by a tiger tooth? And why's it *a story* and only *once in a generation*?"

"Oh, it is not a normal tooth. Maybe not even a human tooth. It is *special*." Dot's brows knitted, and we all leant in closer as Lars adopted his enthusiastic scary campfire-story voice.

"It makes you lucky. The one my Morsa mentioned was a kid named Sigi, I think. The tiger tooth came in fast and was big enough that he couldn't close his jaw fully. He couldn't bite off anything with his front teeth—only the back ones actually touched."

"That sounds more like *unlucky* to me," Tam said.

"You are right," Lars said. "That part is unlucky. But then amazing things started happening around him. He dropped his pencil case on his way home from school, and it fell into a hole in the side of the road—"

"Still unlucky," I interjected.

"And when he reached in to pull it out, he also grabbed an ancient and very heavy leather bag, tied tight. It held a bunch of Roman coins. Gold ones. It was Viking treasure buried beneath the road. And then he won a mail-in competition to appear with the king of Sweden at the grand opening of the new football stadium. After that, he walked past some flats and paused in the right spot to catch a toddler that fell off a balcony. And he won the Swedish junior darts championship after only trying darts for the first time two months earlier. Also a bunch of other stuff I can't remember. And apparently a girl in the 1960s grew one too. There was even a children's book called *Elsa and the Tiger Tooth*."

"Yeet! I don't want my jaw to hang open permanently, but I enjoy the sound of the luck," Dot said, rubbing her cheek with surreptitious fingers. "We should find Sigi and get him to buy us a lottery ticket. How old is he now?"

"Ahh," Lars said, looking at each of us. "Well, his dentist filed down the points of the tooth so he could chew properly. The next week, he slipped on wet leaves and got run over by the school bus. Dead on the spot."

Dot wilted to a shade paler than normal, hands quivering on the table. Both Tam and Lars took one, attempting to soothe her. "It's okay, Dot," Lars said. "It's probably just a story. Although my Morsa showed me a clipping about it from the newspaper."

I kicked him a glancing blow to the shin beneath the table. "Not helping, Lars."

Tam was more reassuring. "Mind our Peter's teeth, Dot?"

He referred to Peter Piper, the lead singer of Piping Hot. His teeth gleamed from every band promo shot. "He doesn't come by that grin naturally. He's had enough dental work to consume half his memoirs when they get published. I'll take you to his dentist in Edinburgh when we get back."

While the proposed dentistry wasn't the most romantic offer I'd ever heard, Dot flushed and smiled at Tam, concealing her emerging wisdom-or-tiger tooth behind closed lips. She retrieved both hands from the concerned embraces of the two young men and whisked her tumble of hair behind her ears as our drinks arrived.

"Yeah, probably just a story," I said.

"Yes, story, but many stories are true. True," a squeaky voice said from beneath our table. It was quiet enough to make me doubt I'd heard it, but distinctive enough to send a shiver of recognition up my neck. All four of us bent double and held back the tablecloth's inverted peaks to locate the voice.

Although we saw nothing but each other's legs and Dot's handbag, the voice continued. I felt a tug on my leggings, with no obvious source. "Troll tooth, what it is. Not tiger. Hear me. No tigers around. Only trolls. Hear me."

We'd been through this drill before, and instead of focusing on finding the voice's source, we all looked slightly away.

"You're not Sundalfar," I said to the calf-height, blue-skinned figure tugging at my leg. Tufts of wiry, deep indigo hair escaped the creature's scalp at every conceivable angle while failing to conceal elongated and pointy ears. "But there's no doubt you're an elf," I added in a whisper.

A squealing peal of musical laughter rippled the wide, blue lips. "Father. Sundalfar my father, he is. Told me about you, Higgs. Told me many stories. Many stories. But no stories about troll tooth. Sunflorin. Good luck, troll tooth, yes. Maybe you help us with *them*. Trolls. Sunflorin, my name. And them."

"Well, Sunflorin, it's nice to meet you. And please, please

say thank you to your father. He saved all of our lives," I said, switching from a whisper to a murmur so I could express more sincerity. I touched the waist of the shapeless shift that passed as the only piece of clothing the elf wore in what I hoped was a friendly gesture.

Sunflorin stretched gangly arms up to rest elongated palms on my thighs, rubbing them in gentle strokes. "You tell father. Not here now, but sent me. Daughter. Time is soon. For summoning. Soon. Hear me. Look for message, Higgs. Summoning."

Saucer-like eyes inspected me for a moment before the elf skittered away on shoeless, slapping feet, capering from beneath our table. I lost sight of the diminutive character as my eyes instinctively tried to follow her path. Humans weren't very good at looking for things in their peripheral vision, making elf-spotting an arduous task, especially when they were in motion. Their invisibility to direct inspection made it easy to believe you were mistaken if you glimpsed them in a corner of your vision.

Tam bumped his head as we all returned to our upright positions, jostling the cutlery and salt and pepper shakers but failing to alter the impressive swoop of his hair. "See? HoldiLocks even acts as a protective layer," he laughed, turning his gaze to the waitress, who was balancing four plates of food and looked puzzled. I guessed if your customers all had their heads under the table when you arrived, there was no official protocol to follow. She was probably also puzzled because our tablecloth was no longer chequered red. It was now covered in icy blue squares. The key fob that Tam had placed on the table before him no longer had a generic rental agency insignia; a figurine dangled in its place that looked suspiciously like Sunflorin.

"HoldiLocks?" the waitress said, eyes brightening. "Oh, wow! Now I know where I recognise you from!"

She distributed our plates a little quicker than I suspect was normal before sliding a phone from her back pocket. "Can I get a selfie, Mr Thunder?"

CHAPTER 3 - COUNTERS

Faraday

Although the door to my grandmother's room at the imposing converted orphanage was half open, it was still a surprise to have it pushed ajar by a person neither of us knew. Especially when that person was not a staff member, no older than 20, and delivered a rush of clipped words as if continuing an earlier conversation.

"I notice something interesting, Faraday. And greetings, Miss Redferne, I hear so much about you," the young woman said.

I noted a few things about her appearance. Unusual-looking was my initial impression. I observed she spoke from one side of her mouth, as if conspiring with an invisible companion, but when she continued her flowing observations, I lost any interest in her looks. That was something I could reflect on later, using the perfect recall of my often painful, exacting memory.

Plopping a heavy backpack on the carpet, she waved a black, angular gadget that I recognised as a laser measuring tool. "Stairs are 185 millimetres rise each. Twenty-six of them to first floor, here."

That was 4.81 metres. Not that interesting. I'd climbed the

front staircase of the Orphanage to see my grandmother countless times. Not strictly countless, but a figure others would have been unlikely to count.

"Height of ceiling on ground floor only 3,358 millimetres. I measure. What happen to other 1,052 millimetres? Floor is not *that* thick," she said, one eyebrow rising to goad the other, which stayed perfectly level.

There was a brief, silent interlude while I gazed downward, as if I could divine what lay between my feet and the ground floor ceiling.

"We should drill hole. Take look with extendible scope," our visitor continued before softening her tone. "Oh, sorry, sorry. Again I do it. Miss Redferne, I am Svetlana. Svetlana Federov. Forgive me."

I chided myself for not packing a scope in the bundle of equipment that I hustled from our house. Or a drill.

"Ahh. Scarlett mentioned you. Said you were in England," I said. "But she didn't elaborate."

"Yes, yes. I am here on drone pilot course. In Manchester. My uncle and Scarlett tell me everything. Said to help you."

"Is your uncle Dmitri Vladishenko, the nanotechnologist, by any chance?" I asked, prescient of the answer.

"Of course, yes," she said. "He is best nanotech expert. Well, best now. He tell me of your mother. But enough. We must figure out what Revision look for, and where it hides. And may I also have piece of cake?"

I nodded, both to the question of cake, which Granny foisted upon Svetlana in a clatter of cutlery on china, and to the requirement to understand the nature of the powerful artefact my father, Templeton, had concealed.

"Of course, dearie, you must have cake. It makes everything better," Granny said. "I've been to Russia once, before I met Faraday's grandfather. Crossed the country by train. It crawled across the steppes much slower than I thought necessary. I'm reminded of scalding tea and a general shortage of snacks during the six day journey. But I did meet a very mysterious gentleman who paced the narrow corridor that ran alongside the sleeper berths wearing a fur cape."

Svetlana guffawed. "Sounds like could have been my grandfather. He had very strange idea of formal clothing. You would have stopped in Yekaterinburg, place where my cousins live, yes?"

Granny frowned in concentration, crinkles haunting more of the right side of her face than the left. "Oh yes—wasn't it called Sverdlovsk, before? I seem to remember a lot of sausage vendors lining the train platform when our train crept in."

"Yes, was called Sverdlovsk until the 1990s. And sausage vendor could have been my grandfather, too." Svetlana laughed and gave Granny's knee a playful slap.

My grandmother had been mid-story before this unusual interruption, and she raised her eyebrows at me for approval of our visitor before resuming. I shuffled over as Svetlana perched, cake in hand, on the settee beside me, leaning an ear as close to my grandmother as the edge of her seat would allow.

"As I said, dear, Templeton felt lost, lost, lost after your mother died. He probably hid it from you kids, but he rambled to me almost daily about Alison's death. Thought it planned, a conspiracy. He confided in pain, and my mothering instincts took over. I didn't press him for details, nor suggest he was just looking for an outlandish explanation for the tragedy. I simply listened and tried to offer comfort. But from what you've told me today, maybe I should have paid closer attention to his suspicions."

I nodded. "The records at the Feynman Centre showed unexplained visitors on the day of her death. Newt and I have theories, but no concrete evidence. It's plausible that it wasn't the Unusual Powers Defence Agency as we suspected, but was a visit from this Revision organisation. I'll let you tell us about that soon, Svetlana."

Granny dabbed her nose with an embroidered handkerchief and turned to gaze out the window at the rise of hills. "He said he planned *something* to force the UPDA to come clean regarding Alison. I thought he meant an administrative process within the agency, not uncontrolled magic. I could see the smoke from here, rising just there, above the Ides Giant, and I felt the magic too. Figured it was just Beauregarde messing around with his friends, attempting a new spell. Damn toad up there was croaking away too, but I reckoned it could defend itself."

With a laconic turn of her head, her gaze returned to me, and I caught the twist of emotions playing in her eyes. "Templeton couldn't magic his way out of a losing hand at cards, so I didn't connect the events. I should have taken him more seriously, shouldn't I? He was my baby."

I took her hand in a gentle grip. People seemed to find this reassuring, though I needed stronger measures to re-centre myself. "Granny, come on now. Newt, Higgs, and I didn't even *know* Dad was in such a frightful state. At least you were there for him. A sympathetic ear."

Svetlana chimed in. "And now we think it was Revision met your mother. Our chance to make things correct is here. I will help. Uncle Dmitri too. And Scarlett."

Still holding Granny's hand, I turned to Svetlana, who hovered disconcertingly close. "So who are they, the Revision? And what powers can they exercise?"

Svetlana nodded, her glance sizing me up, as if measuring my readiness for detailed information. "We know only fragments. Revision operates in cells, so when one found and neutralised, it leads nowhere. We know goal: to disband or work around national governments. Everything based on power of a few masters. Power to destroy, to hurt, to

22

compromise and control their puppets. Russia can take some of blame for this—you know *kompromat*? How we use information to twist people to do our work? Revision perfected technique. We suspect few people in high places that may direct activities. We watch."

"But how do they expect to skirt or collapse entire governments?"

Svetlana nodded as she spoke. "Thing your father hid? Revision seeks tools like that. Ultimate *kompromat* to control leaders or nations. We suspect they use money from huge corporations to fund own side projects. Probably why they wanted Mother Redferne. If they hold enough power, and show only to right people, they rule without appearing to control anything. Smart."

A throng of questions competed for space in my throat, but Svetlana cut me off as the first one bubbled forth. She sprung up and grabbed her backpack. "Time for explaining is later. Now, I help. We go on roof and see if anyone at your house yet."

I glanced at my grandmother. She let her hand drop from mine and waved me along. "Go, go. You lead the way. I know you head up there all the time, sometimes without even visiting your poor Granny."

* * *

The hills behind us, Svetlana and I lay prone on the warm pebbling of the Orphanage's flat roof. We each rested our chests and arms on our backpacks, in competition to see who could get comfortable on a bag full of hard-edged bits of technology. She rested a pair of high-powered electronic binoculars on the lip of the low parapet for stability and scrutinised our house. After a good, long look, flicking rotors on the binoculars' body with tiny motions of her practised pointer finger, she nodded. She murmured instructions as she clicked through the positions. "Settings for image enhancement, here. This one for electromagnetic emissions. Infrared too, but works better in night. Take photo with this button and upload to our server like this."

She passed the binoculars to me. "Three nosy people there," she said. "They have cart with scanner. Ground penetrating RADAR, I think. Have look."

I picked out West Ides School, then swung a fraction right. It took a few seconds to orient on our house, but the view was clear, occluded only slightly by the eaves of our neighbours across the street. A trio of men loitered on the crushed gravel of our driveway, which held only one of our 3 cars, my father's aged Jaguar. One pushed a cart reminiscent of a lawnmower, its low-slung bed cradling some sophisticated-looking equipment. I hadn't seen ground penetrating RADAR before, but instinct told me Svetlana was correct. The second man consulted a handheld tablet while the third ruffled his drab, olive jacket as he called to the others. They looked up, rolled the device through the side gate, and slipped behind the house, out of view.

My mobile phone buzzed in my pocket. I exhaled and muttered an exasperated nothing, passing the binoculars back to Svetlana as I fished it out. She accepted the transfer in silence, a waft of subtle citrus scent hitting me as she proffered her hand. I answered the call, noting it was from an unknown number.

"It's Faraday. Who's this?"

Scarlett's voice replied, a hint of static and echo polluting the line. "It's me. Svetlana uploaded a couple of pictures. At your house is Godfrey Higgenbotham, a lead investigator with the UPDA. I never warmed to him, but he's a very competent operative and a straight shooter; I can't say for sure he's not Revision, but the UPDA excels at vetting. To me, he seems the least likely candidate to be compromised. I'm going to put us through to his phone. Hang on."

There were 5 clicking sounds and then a third voice joined us. A Home Counties accent with notably long vowels. "Higgenbotham. Make it quick, I'm in the middle of something."

"Godfrey, it's Scarlett. I've got Faraday Redferne here on the line too."

She left her opening remarks there. I could practically see inside her head—she was waiting to gauge his level of surprise or allow him enough leeway to reveal something.

Godfrey's tone was even and affectless. Of course, a UPDA agent wouldn't reveal himself so readily. "Ahh, the disgraced Miss Thorisdottir. I'm at the Redferne home now, but I suppose you know that already, somehow. No sign of you here, though, Faraday."

I realised these two might have ordered my father's car to be sabotaged and carried out that order. I ground my molars on the left side together. "What are you looking for in my yard? Lose your ball?"

Scarlett interrupted before I could stumble along my path to enragement. I imagined she could read me in a similar fashion to how I'd learned her quirks. "Hang on, hang on. Let's not mention what anyone is looking for on a call like this. But I instructed Faraday to flee because *other parties* are also on the hunt. You know who I mean, right?"

Godfrey replied in uppity outrage. "You're feeding *them* info now? Gods, Scarlett, no wonder they sacked you."

"Listen, Higgy, I'd never stoop that low, and you know it. But they got intel somehow. You want to check your own ship for leaks. And you're about to discover a cavity underneath the back patio. It's Alison Redferne's other secret lab. I've checked it twice, and had a good scout around at the other one we discovered up beside the Ides Giant. Couldn't find the item of interest. Have a snoop but keep a lookout, will you? You know what these others are like. Dangerous and uncaring."

Svetlana elbowed me in the ribs, a little harder than I thought necessary. "Hear that?" she hissed.

Heavy duty electric servo motors. I'd worked enough of them to identify the sound even when it drifted faintly on the breeze. Behind us somewhere.

Svetlana swung the binoculars in a savage arc to face the slope behind the Orphanage and oriented them on the ridgeline above the thick, chalky outline of the Ides Giant's head, crown, and broken club, carved into the hillside. I spotted moving shapes too, even without the magnification. They scurried and hopped over the crest, coursing down the slope.

She urged me to my feet, but I was already springing up and taking the first steps across the Orphanage roof. "What the hell are *those?*"

CHAPTER 4 - BLOODHOUNDS

Newton

I only agreed to the trip because it dovetailed with our new business venture. We hadn't thought of an official name for our enterprise yet, but Dot, Chronos, and I had the perfect talents that combined to give us a unique opportunity. Our first client led us to Iceland.

In the basic magical training conducted by my grandmother, and girlfriend, Emeline, Dot was an apt student of the smaller feats, able to accomplish a wider range of cantrips and minor spells than my sister. There was frantic magic involved in the spell that Granny cast to save Higgs from her motorcycle crash in Scotland, but Dot proved adept at the small-magic version, a spell which could give a smidgeon of luck to its target.

With a fresh lavender sprig, an article of the subject's clothing, and a spritz of spring water, Dot could imbue that person with a little extra fortune. It worked at any distance; if you had a worn bit of clothing, the luck would seek and settle upon the person. It would produce a favourable experience, like studying the exact right content for an exam, avoiding an injury in a sporting event, or being in the right place at the right time to bump into a romantic interest.

Dot practised the spell on her favoured schoolmates, upping the level of cheeriness at West Ides High School. But that spell in itself wasn't what drove our business. We couldn't go around exposing the fact that Dot, Higgs, Emeline, and Granny were witches. But Faraday and my best friend, Chronos, figured out a clever angle. Faraday noticed that the targets of Dot's good luck spell would appear on the UPSCALE, a device that my parents had jointly invented. The UPSCALE could identify and track the presence of magic, but only types of magic it had learned. That was part of the scanning and learning functions that gave it the *SCA* and *LE* parts of its name. If Dot cast the luck spell while close to the device, it would show an icon representing the spell's target. It was dim because the magic was weak, but we could see the person on the device's screen, showing their exact position.

That was an interesting side effect, but it was Chronos who connected the pieces and realised how powerful a combination we possessed. At lunchtime one day, he and I were walking away from the Middle Ides police station, where I worked, when he turned to me and said, "Ooh. Hang on. Remember how the UPSCALE can track all of Dot's and Higgs's classmates who have that luck spell on them? And how Dot cast the spell without them being anywhere near, just by using a worn mitten or sock?"

I nodded but failed to twig where his mind was headed.

"Think about this. If someone comes to the police station and reports a missing person, how do you go about finding them?"

Initially confused, I wondered why Chronos had changed topics. "Well, we take a description, what they were wearing. Ask a few questions about the person's last known location, and then we …"

Chronos looked at me, a smile tugging at one side of his lips. He nodded slowly.

"Nice one, brother!" I said. "Now I get it. With Dot's spell, a piece of the lost person's clothing, and the UPSCALE, we'd know *exactly* where the person was. Bob's your uncle!"

"And Fanny's your aunt!" he laughed.

With a couple of test runs using the girls' friends, including one who had gone on a family trip to Newcastle, we could tell the idea had real legs. Chronos convinced me to quit my job in the police force and pursue it as a business. We would be a private crack team of missing persons locators!

Our first customer would not make us much money; it was more of a favour than a job, and we offered our services for a nominal fee. Not trivial, but less than the cost of our flights.

Vish Balakrishnan ran the local chippy. My family had patronised Codforsaken Fish and Chips a few times a month for as long as I could remember. A missing persons bulletin popped up on the front page of the local newspaper, reporting that his seventeen-year-old daughter, Ashna, had gone missing. Chronos and I visited him at home and got a few more details.

This turned out to be more runaway teen than a startling disappearance. Vish and his wife, Julia, had suspicions that Ash had been secretly corresponding with someone on the Internet for a couple of weeks before her disappearance. She had become secretive and skipped school twice, which was unlike her. And then, five days ago, she left home with a stuffed backpack and failed to return.

The police had been trying to track her movements and had managed nothing beyond a sighting of her at the bus terminal. All we asked for was her pillowcase.

* * *

Faraday located her after only a few tense moments fiddling with the sliders and screen of the UPSCALE. We tracked her for a full day, and she ventured no further than a few minutes' walk from a remote house in Iceland.

We each had our part to play. Dot had the spellcasting ability, Faraday knew how to tease responses from the UPSCALE, and I could use my police training when dealing with often frantic prospective customers. But Chronos was on point to make contact with the missing person. We hoped his quick reactions and imposing presence would reduce the risk of interacting with potential abductors.

We knew taking on work that would normally be handled by police was iffy ground for several reasons. Debating what we should do on our first proper case spurred us to produce a code of ethics for our enterprise.

We'd locate and visit the missing person as part of the service, but what should we do then? We consulted with Emeline and Granny and came to a few conclusions that helped form our rules. If anything endangered our target, we would rescue them. If we located a minor who seemed in no danger, we'd pass their location and details to the police and to the hirer. For adults, not in any danger, a quiet chat could determine if they wanted to remain *missing*. We could pass along a message from them to our client, or at the very least report that the missing person was well but did not want to make immediate contact. Although we were unsure if Dot's spell would work on a dead person, we also realised we might find only the remains of one of our missing persons. In that case, we would refer the matter to the police.

The UPSCALE detected Ashna's movements, so I figured our first mission would not bring that flavour of heartache. Chronos stomped on my optimism, suggesting that she could still be dead, and moved around in the trunk of a car. He can be such a killjoy.

And so it was that Chronos and I planned to drive a rented car toward a house in a smear of a village in the Westfjords of Iceland, on a mission to discover why our favourite takeaway owner's eldest daughter had run off.

* * *

The flight from Reykjavik to Ísafjörður in the northwest of Iceland was a brief but bouncy affair in the compact aircraft. Chronos stooped for the whole thirty-minute trip, wedged into the seat across the aisle from me, shoulder abutting the window. It was too noisy to talk without shouting, so we each contemplated the unknowns of the approaching task in silence.

The drapes of fog parted soon after takeoff, rewarding us with clear views over the lunar landscape of the Westfjords. The matte blacks of the volcanic rock broke only occasionally for snowy patches, sparse vegetation, and minute signs of human interruption. Flying was a much better option—the main road to Ísafjörður would have required a six hour drive from Reykjavik, hairpinning its way along the shores of fjords and disappearing into tunnels. An occasional graceful arc of a bridge might cut the mouth of a particularly long finger of inky sea water.

After the plane bumped to a stop at the end of the runway that flanked the shore opposite the town of Ísafjörður, our three fellow passengers scrambled into waiting cars, the breath of their various drivers hanging like unanswered questions in the cold, still air. The cars waited immediately to the side of the runway and peeled away in close succession, heading toward town together, forming what must pass locally for heavy traffic. Chronos and I zipped up our jackets and strode toward the small passenger building.

We had agreed on a rental car; it would be no good relying on a local taxi driver if anything untoward happened when we found Ashna. We took one of the two available cars, a red four-door, already fitted with winter tires despite the lack of snow. A paper map of the town had been left perched on the dashboard, an antiquated but charming touch.

Approaching the passenger door, despite holding the keys, I muttered a minor curse toward whoever had decided we should drive on different sides of the road in different countries. Probably the same ones who designed electrical sockets. Chronos ratcheted the passenger seat all the way back, and we settled in. He spotted our destination on the map, which was detailed enough to mark individual buildings.

I checked the message from Faraday, reconfirming Ashna's position as of this morning. It marked the building where Ashna had been clearly. Dot's minor spell seemed to stick to the target for a week or two, at most. Our test subjects no longer appeared on the UPSCALE, but Ashna's icon had still burned brightly.

* * *

I parked the rental car on the roughly paved and curbless street, pointing back the way we had come. My police training kicked in unconsciously; checking out the surroundings and always leaving yourself the most convenient way out of any situation had become second nature to me. I left the keys in the ignition and began recording with a small digital video camera that I attached with an elasticised strap to my left bicep. We planned to do everything as calmly and by the book as possible, but the frisson of nervousness that coursed through me as we approached the front door of the squat house reminded me that things could go wrong. It would be best to have a recording in case we needed to prove we'd handled ourselves appropriately.

Chronos had ditched his daily-wear prosthesis for a springy, bladed foot in case any running would be required. He had progressed from hospital bed to hobbling around to full-on sprinting in the months since they amputated his lower leg after the fateful confrontation at the gates of Pendlethwaite House.

"Hang on a sec," Chronos said. "I just have to add a bit of insurance."

It puzzled me at first, but as Chronos passed the car in the gravel driveway flanking the house, he unscrewed the cap of the tire valves on the driver's side and let the air out of them using a pen nib to depress the pin. It took what seemed like an eternity of muted hissing as the air escaped, during which I nervously watched the front windows to see if we were being observed. This insurance might not pay out if anyone spied us before knocking on the door. I only realised I'd been holding my breath when I exhaled deeply as Chronos finished with the second tire and beckoned me toward the door.

The house lurked, rising not so far from the ground as I'd have expected, as if lazy masons left off a row or two of bricks so they could leave early for the day. The second storey at the back loomed over the main floor like an overbearing auditor, capped with a corrugated blue metal roof. We couldn't see much more than blurry movement through the squint of privacy glass in the thick wooden front door, but it swung back soon after Chronos's firm but polite knock.

The man revealed as the door swung back was wider at the shoulders than the door frame and nearly matched Chronos in height. He was barefoot in a pair of jeans and shirtless. Tattoos snaked up his arm, from a stylised star-nosed mole and a couple of other small inscriptions at his right wrist, to a full illustration of a diving eagle, wings flaring over one shoulder and across his broad and hairless chest.

His close-set eyes spent little time inspecting me, preferring to assess Chronos, who was closer and much more imposing. His nostrils flared, and he pulled his shoulders back a fraction, further emphasising the thrust of his chest. I should have focused on the mission but instead wondered if his illustrated arm was bigger around than my thigh; it would be a close contest, but now was not the time for a measure-off.

The man's greeting was unfriendly and in Icelandic, and the tone of his opening salvo implied he was saying something like, "What the hell do you want?" Incomprehensible words bristled, reminiscent of a bucket of hailstones being emptied onto a frozen pond.

Smiling, Chronos replied in English. "Can we speak with Ashna Balakrishnan, please?" His arms remained in a casual-looking position at his sides, but I'd seen him ready himself for trouble before, both in his role as a nightclub bouncer and in a couple of less formal teenage incidents.

The man before us couldn't very well deny Ashna was here because we could see her deeper in the house, sticking her head out from behind a partition wall at the base of a glimpsed stairway.

"*Já,*" he said. "But what's that got to do with you?" He craned his jaw during the pause, as if stretching his neck muscles.

"We're friends of hers, and we'd just like a quick word with her. Y'alright, Ash?"

Ashna nodded wordlessly in the background, exposing a little more of her face around the corner. I was used to seeing her in full makeup and impeccable hair, so her face without the vibrant lipstick reminded me she was seventeen, a fact that I often overlooked when she was working at her father's fish and chip takeaway.

The man took a half-step forward, so he stood beneath the lintel. Chronos maintained his position. The two were now closer than would be deemed polite in most social circles. "See? She is good. You can both leave now." He motioned his displeasure with the back of a calloused hand.

Ashna's voice had a slight waver but still exuded conviction as she too stepped forward, fully visible now at the foot of the stairs. "Torsten, it's okay. No need to get all worked up."

She didn't approach him any closer, though. My police training and instincts marked this as an indicator of previous trouble, or maybe trouble to come. I shifted aside so I could look her directly in the eyes and asked a simple-sounding question that could elicit a complex reply. I was looking for a combination of words, intonation, and, most importantly, body language. "Ashna, your parents want to know if you'd like to come home. Would you?"

Torsten glared at Chronos, not bothering to look at me as I spoke.

Behind his back, Ashna's shoulders slumped, and she nodded twice, sending me a different message than her words. "It's okay, Newton. I'm here with Torsten now. No need to worry."

Despite the cool air, I noticed beads of sweat rising in the thicket of Torsten's close-cropped hair. He still hadn't budged. "Chronos, she's with us," I said.

Before Chronos made any move, I witnessed something that hadn't seemed possible since we were twelve, and Chronos laid into a group of teenagers who were pestering Faraday. Torsten pivoted a shoulder down and grabbed Chronos by the belt and lapels. A well-practised move ended when he lifted Chronos and sent him airborne down the steps. I heard the thud and a surprised, "Bloody hell," from behind me as I moved toward Torsten. He hulked atop the concrete staircase that led to the door, and I had an instinctive feeling that I could grapple his arm into an immobilising technique. But instinct turned to rational thought just in time for me to dance back and avoid a crushing punch to the head. I felt the wind from the fist's passing rush up my nose.

An animalistic shout of rage tore from Torsten's throat as he dared us to close in on his top step position. "You don't know who you're messing with! Do you know who I work for?" he roared.

I took an extra step back as Chronos retook his feet—one real, one a carbon fibre blade—and brushed some Icelandic lichens from his trouser leg. "Really, mate, I don't *care* who I'm messing with. But if it's a mess you want …"

The running blade flexed with a fierce groan of its own as it propelled Chronos from the bottom step. There aren't many people who could pull off a wraparound tackle of someone as broad as our adversary, but Chronos's nearly seven foot wingspan managed it. The two shot through the doorway as if propelled by a cannonball, and they slammed and skidded across the floor of the entranceway, scattering boots and splintering a side table.

Torsten rolled, hips and one hand pinning Chronos under his considerable bulk. His other fist raised, clenching a broken table leg reminiscent of a chisel. He plunged it down, grazing Chronos's ear as he squirmed to one side. But that allowed Torsten's pinning hand to immobilise Chronos's head, making the next stabbing motion the last he'd require.

But I was on him. Unbeknownst to my conscious brain, my legs had sprinted into the wake of Chronos's initial attack. I grasped Torsten's upthrust wrist in both hands, and my knee drove into the small of his back—although small was a misnomer in this case because his back was broad enough that I could have set up a card table. This gave me enough leverage to avert his downward strike, but I wasn't strong enough to do much else. We were at an impasse, with Chronos pinned and Torsten and I locked in a static struggle, all of us growling with the effort.

A gong-like noise halted proceedings. Ashna looked in wonderment at the bent handle of a frying pan as Torsten collapsed unconscious atop a wriggling Chronos, who struggled free. He gasped for breath as he retook his feet. "Well, lass, our man Torsten here'll have a nasty headache when he wakes up. And I, for one, don't want to see how ornery he is with a headache. He's a handful even in a friendly mood."

I seconded that thought but was a bit more practical. "Just your passport, Ash, that's all you need. Let's get you to the car."

It wasn't enough—Ashna coaxed Torsten's splay into a more comfortable-looking pose, laying him on his back and tilting his head to one side so she could smooth the ruffled area of hair where a lump was already forming. "Sorry, Tor, sorry," she murmured, looking at the pan and her hand as if it was their fault, not her own, that he lay unconscious.

Chronos's practicality broke the impasse. "Look, Ash, we shouldn't leave him on his back like this. Let's roll him into the recovery position on his side just in case he vomits while unconscious. Yeah, that's it. Heave ho. I'll roll him. You bend his knees so he'll stay like that. And I'll grab a cushion for his head while you get that passport, eh?"

As the car tires scrunched loose gravel, Ashna Balakrishnan looked back at the open doorway of the house where she had spent the last few weeks. I had wrapped her in the fleecy blue blanket I had packed in my backpack; it seemed a natural thing to include when rescuing someone. "Oh good," she said. "He's okay."

In the rear-view mirror, I saw Torsten on all fours, framed by the doorway. He rubbed the back of his head before bending to rest his forehead on crossed arms. An orange, stripy kitten licked at his elbow. He looked sluggish, but I was still glad of Chronos's foresight in sabotaging the car in the driveway.

CHAPTER 5 - OUT OF THE BLUE

Disco

Grmph.

Skrl. Blue krntl. Warm hand.

I smelled coal smoke. Opened one eye a crack. Nothing I saw made sense. Warm hand again, stroking my head. I closed my eye, wagged my tail. Tried to move my legs.

So tired. I would sleep some more.

CHAPTER 6 - MORE BLOODHOUNDS

Faraday

The machine-creatures crested the ridge above the Ides Giant where he reigned, carved into the hillside. They looked like artificial caricatures of hyenas, moving in sped-up and sinister jerks, as if a film director had created them using stop animation. Like normal hyenas, these instinctively rubbed me the wrong way. Instead of robbing savannah lionesses of their hard-won prey, these sought to steal an artefact I felt it was my family's right to investigate and handle with proper care. Industrial-looking joints whined as the beastly machines sauntered down the slope.

At first, I saw 5 of the hunch-shouldered machines closing in on the maintenance shed next to the Ides Giant, but a sixth soon joined them, coursing down the slope as they surrounded the lonely wooden shed. A pair of pointed antennae telescoped out from each metallic head's lower jaw, and they circled, jabbing the exploratory bristles into the earth and pausing for a few seconds before withdrawing and moving to drill a new hole. They evaluated a widening circle around the shed.

I realised we still had agent Higgenbotham on the line, and I whispered into the phone, cautious not to alert the automata below. "Agent Higgenbotham? A pack of very high-tech machines just started searching near my mother's other lab location, up here beside the Ides Giant. You'd better come and have a look."

"On our way now," he replied, and I could hear footfalls on gravel as he hung up.

I pocketed the phone and unzipped my backpack. Svetlana raised an eyebrow.

"Under shed, is something there you did not tell agent what's-his-name?"

I shook my head only a fraction. "Not that I know of. But I never searched for a secret *sub*-lab. Whatever those things are, they're attracted to the shed, and I don't want them discovering something I missed."

Svetlana moved in closer to me as I unpacked my drone case. "Nice. Two X-74s. But you think drone will stop those things? Look at their size."

"Ahh, but this is my speciality. Although those hyena-looking machines don't fit the *nano* part of nanotechnology, my anti-nano nanotech works well on bigger tech too. Let's see what it can do to these suckers."

I removed a set of anti-nano bubbles from their compact but hard case, cradling them so they didn't rupture and damage all the kit in our backpacks. A goopy liquid suspended microscopic technology. Sprayed, it would stick to a target and let the invasive nanotech disperse. The concoction jiggled within a thin, polymer sphere, tinged with a translucent, mottled silver sheen. Each was the size and rigidity of a squash ball.

I snapped 4 of them into the recess on the belly of one of the X-74 drones. This model was the size of my palm and powered by four corner rotors. I placed it on the lip of the Orphanage roof, then repacked my backpack and strapped it on, in case we needed to flee. My hands busied themselves over the drone's remote control, turning on the camera and the targeting system before urging the whirligig into flight.

"Four anti-nanotech weapons but six machines. Do you have plan for other two?" Svetlana asked, leaning in to watch my hands as they coaxed the drone into a targeted flight pattern.

I laughed bitterly. "You're mistaking me for someone with a plan. Maybe if we defeat the first four, the others will retreat."

This wasn't a very satisfying answer to me, but she nodded. "Maybe. Aim for knee joints. If you take them out, we can analyse remaining parts of machine for intel."

That was a good idea. I'd see what I could manage, given the incomplete state of the targeting software. My test flights had proved I could target something the size of these mechanical hyenas, but maybe not their legs specifically. Also, I'd programmed the anti-nano to disperse upon contact to wreak the most havoc. Even a precise strike might not limit the damage to the knee joints. We were about to find out.

The drone carved a zig-zagging path toward the hyenas, its high-pitched rotor whine no more intrusive than a mosquito circling your ear. I programmed it to plot its own randomised approach to potential targets to avoid any stymying defences. It tickled me to think that, with the success of my technology, someone might develop anti-anti-nanotech-tech.

It seemed like the hyenas had no built-in instincts protecting against drone attacks, although the 2 closest paused and withdrew their antennae to orient their heads toward the incoming device. My programmed path included dropping the anti-nano bubbles on the 2 that had looked up and the next closest 2.

As the drone dipped toward its first target, the sun caught the surface of the bubble released by the targeting software. The bubble struck the chest of the hyena and cracked open into a sticky mass that crept wider across the machine's torso. The drone veered sharply, a louder burst of rotor noise rising to our ears. It flew toward the second hyena.

They reacted with alacrity to the new threat. The second anti-nano bubble whizzed past the head of a hyena as it leapt aside like a cat skittering away from a flea-ridden blanket. The third target broke into a hunched run, pursued by the tracking drone, and as it passed the fourth hyena, a lashing foreleg knocked the drone from the air. It crashed to the ground, damaged rotors rendering it unable to fly.

The assaulting hyena must have ruptured one of the anti-nano bubbles during its attack. It shook its leg 6 times rapidly, after which the leg dangled, useless.

The hyena that took the direct hit had collapsed face-first into the grass, its rear legs shivering in spasms that drove it further into the turf. I made a mental note that the anti-nano worked well, even against larger targets, but that the attack pattern of the drone was suboptimal. Against targets like this, it should have remained higher, out of easy reach.

"Um, Faraday? They're looking at us," Svetlana murmured in my ear.

It was true. All 5 active machines had taken a quick scan of their surroundings, circling and rotating their heads rapidly, but they now oriented themselves on Svetlana and me. Maybe they could detect the drone control signals. I turned the controller off and slid it over my shoulder into the backpack.

With a scraping noise, tapered blades sprang from sheaths beneath the hyenas' shoulder plates. Shorter, jagged knives snickered into position where a canine's dew claws might appear. Three of the beasts cantered with surprising speed toward the foot of the Orphanage's wall below our position on the roof, while the other two savaged the doors of the maintenance hut. I was afraid they had detected my father's artefact, and we were powerless to stop them.

As the door splintered and separated from its hinges, the 3 hyenas below us leapt onto the wall, their wrist blades scrabbling for purchase in the stone facade. Their progress up the wall was frantic but slowed by the tough stone. Many of the attempts to anchor a scything leg failed, necessitating another try to find a toe hold. But they would soon reach our position on the roof.

I was unused to the absence of a plan, or at least a good idea. I had neither and stood paralysed as the whining motors and sounds of chipping stone drew closer. Svetlana and I turned to run, but it was too late.

The first hyena leg appeared over the low parapet and hooked its serrated blade over the lip, hoisting up the rest of its body. It rose on flexing rear legs to its full height, casting a shadow over us. Then it sprang at Svetlana.

It seemed a useless gesture, diving on top of Svetlana to protect her. I had just seen these automata shred a thick, wooden door and chip their way up a multi-storcy stone wall. I'd be sliced to ribbons within a few seconds, with my heroics granting Svetlana only a few extra moments of panic-stricken life.

We hit the ground a fraction of a second before the hyena's knife-adorned forelegs slammed down on my back. I felt more than heard our lungs empty as we hit the gritty roof surface, my face buried between Svetlana's shoulder blades, jutting back as her hands tried to absorb the impact.

Oddly, the hyena's jabbing blades didn't send pain scorching through my back as they struck. The impact of the machine's weight flattened me against Svetlana's back, and it sounded like the two vicious knives struck bone. Something solid, anyhow.

Then I remembered I was wearing my backpack. The hyena must have stabbed something inside it—maybe the drone case. But I had no time to pause; the hyena once again reared up, jolting my arms back as it ripped the impaled backpack from me. The pack remained latched onto one of the beast's forelegs, but the other was free, preparing for another strike.

I pushed myself onto all fours, gasping to refill my lungs with breath, hoping Svetlana could scamper free while I somehow delayed the hyena. Peering over my shoulder, horror filled my heart as I realized that not only did we face a second attack but also a second attacker. Two more legs hooked over the parapet, and hauled another hyena to the rooftop.

As the first hyena's unencumbered knife slashed toward my back, an electrical sizzling sound accompanied the creature's sideways slump as it fell twitching to the rooftop. Svetlana had scrambled toward the hyena, not away, and was withdrawing the tip of an oversized cattle prod from the thing's belly as the second hyena poised to strike her down.

But just as it brought its longer knives to bear from their position beneath multi-jointed shoulder plates, its entire frame jerked backward, the blow never landing. What looked like ropes or inconceivably thick spider web slithered in a latticework pattern over the machine's head and draped down behind it like a mesh cape. The machine strained against its bonds, which pinned it to the parapet and prevented it from falling on us. Overbalanced, the machine bounced off the parapet but remained trapped there, entangled in the gauzy, sticky webbing. I heard a commotion from below, unseen, and a pair of closer splatting sounds.

Wary of the hyena that hung partially over the building's edge, I recovered enough breath to gasp to Svetlana, where she lay, arm still outstretched across my legs. "What the heck is—?"

She smiled, a crooked affair exposing teeth on only one side of her mouth. "A girl must protect herself, no?"

She scrambled upright, freeing me to do the same. Her cattle prod crackled with enthusiasm as she crept a few cautious steps toward the immobilised hyena at the building's lip. It sawed away at its encircling bonds, shimmying shoulders and blades juddering from sheathed to full extension, making gradual progress in freeing itself. One further jiggle sliced enough of the webbing to let the hyena topple over the edge. A muffled thud on the earth below accompanied a series of shouts.

One quick look at the electrocuted hyena reassured us. It twitched feebly and looked like it wouldn't be attacking anyone any time soon. Svetlana and I thrust our heads over the Orphanage's rear-facing parapet in unison, like a pair of meerkats on alert.

UPDA agent Higgenbotham ushered two of his comrades toward the maintenance hut; they advanced with drawn pistols. The two hyenas emerged from the hut, surveyed the scene, and reversed their way to the chalky left leg of the Ides Giant's massive outline. Directly below us, we could see the partially ensnared hyena that had recently threatened us. Back on its feet, it staggered against its bonds as it urged itself toward its two companions.

The same bulky artificial web that had thwarted our attacker, anchored the final hyena to the Orphanage wall. It sawed away using the same technique, looking like a rugby player raging against a smothering tackle. Below, at the foot of the wall, a familiar figure reloaded a strange-looking weapon, reminiscent of a blunderbuss with its wide muzzle flaring like a trumpet. It was Agent Xenon, or 'Zee', the UPDA agent who had previously served as Scarlett's driver. I'd last seen him when the Scottish First Minister had given us a celebratory dinner, and the time before that, he was being carted away from the Piping Hot concert beneath Edinburgh Castle in an ambulance. The scar that stretched from brow to chin was a reminder of the savage attack he had sustained that day when a coded message in the band's music transformed two young women, infested with malicious nanotech, into raging maniacs.

Zee stepped away from the wall as he reloaded his alien-looking weapon, letting the final hyena plop to the ground as it too freed itself from the web. It took two steps toward Zee's position, but faced with the levelled web-slinging gun, reconsidered and raced in an ungainly run after its fellow machines. The four hyenas that remained mobile raced up the hill, one accommodating a dragging leg that my anti-nano had damaged and two trailing traces of Zee's webs.

"Zee! It's me!" I shouted down. "You just saved us!"

He took a last look at the retreating machines and craned his neck in our direction. He shouted up. "I owed you one, Faraday. I'd have more than this scar if you hadn't bundled onto those girls in Edinburgh. Is it secure up there?"

Svetlana glanced at the cattle-prodded hyena. "Should get professional opinion up here. Quick, I think. I gave it good shock. Forty thousand volts, but low amperage."

That Svetlana carried a high-voltage cattle prod filled me with both questions and admiration. But the questions would have to wait for another time. "Best get up here, Zee. We've got a semi-live one."

CHAPTER 7 - TOUR

Higgs

"Where d'ye fancy going?" Tam asked as we clambered onto the elevated running board and entered the caricature jeep. Its wheels stood nearly as tall as me, deeply rutted for gripping any terrain. He unfolded the map of Icelandic highlights provided for self-driving tourists.

"There are waterfalls, right? Glaciers?" Dot asked. She'd taken the front passenger seat while Lars and I lounged in the back.

"Ooh, what about volcanoes? Can we see the underwater one we noticed from the plane?" Lars asked. "It was down there somewhere ..." he said, noting a contour on the south coast.

Although we didn't know the exact location of the volcano we had spotted from the plane, it seemed an appealing quest. The map indicated interesting stops along the way, with inset photos. The chance to take a dip in geothermal hot springs was an irresistible part of Iceland's allure, and we chose a route where we could also see a couple of colossal waterfalls, and an amazing-looking black sand beach. The roar of the jeep's engine drowned out the squelch of thick rubber on the foggy Reykjavik streets as Tam drove us out of town and into the shrouded countryside.

"I hope this fog breaks," Dot said, sipping at her tall cup of takeaway tea. She left an imprint around the hole in the white plastic lid with her smouldering red lipstick. "It would be unlucky if we saw nothing more than oncoming cars on our tour."

"Aye, and the concert'll suck if the crowd can barely see the stage. At soundcheck, the overhanging roof kept us dry, but we couldnae even see to the fence around the park."

A lorry whizzed past in the other direction, swirling the mist and spraying drizzle onto our windshield. But by the time Tam flicked the wipers into operation, rays of sunlight pierced the fog. We burst into full sunlight and cheered.

"It's burning off behind us, too," Tam said, glancing at the side-view mirror.

"I told you!" Lars said. "The tiger tooth is working, Dot."

Dot rubbed her jaw and granted Lars a half-smile but said nothing.

* * *

Our hair was damp from ducking beneath the mineral-tinged waters of the hot spring lagoon and our rain jackets, chucked into the rear cargo hatch, retained the sheen of waterfall droplets. Our driver looked more composed than his bedraggled passengers. Tam came in the hot spring with us but submerged only up to his shoulders. His hairstylist would reportedly kill him if he arrived at the concert with a headful of salty residue.

We stopped for a snack at a tea shop in the village of Vík í Mýrdal and asked the proprietor about the underwater volcanic activity we'd seen from the air.

"It is just along there," she said, pointing out the sea-facing window to where a conglomeration of low-flung clouds hovered over the waves a medium distance along the coast. "We know the volcano erupts, but you cannot get a good look at it from anywhere. No roads go near that part of the coast. My cousin walked the cliffs to get there, but she said you could see nothing except the steam and a faint glow."

"Ahh. All this way, and we cannot get to it," Lars griped. "But we will still visit the black sand beach, yes?"

"I think that's a better idea," the woman said as she handed Lars a tray. A clinking teapot and cups jostled with an array of sandwiches, sliced into quarters. "We are not fans of volcanoes around here anyway. There's one above those cliffs and across the highway. It's buried under a glacier and hasn't erupted since maybe the First World War. But if it does, it'll melt the ice above and flood the town. We practice evacuation every few months; it's basically run at full speed to the church you see on the high ground. Tröllaeldur."

The story made sense, but I stumbled over the last word. "Sorry, what was that last part?" I asked.

"Tröllaeldur," she said, sounding it out more slowly, like TROT-la-EL-der. "Troll fire. That's the buried volcano's name."

We finished our hot drinks and sandwiches before thanking our host and trekking to the black sand beach. Although it was sunny, the cool wind lashed the remaining waterfall droplets from our jackets, and our breath trailed away in steaming ribbons. The town of Vík was invisible beyond the headland and could have been a short walk or a thousand miles away, such was the desolate beauty of the beach and its crashing waves.

A set of jagged sea stacks rose from the dark waters, close enough to shore to prompt me to imagine swimming to them if the intervening whitecaps would ever calm and the sea temperature rose twenty degrees. Our map labelled the jutting black spires as Reynisdrangar. Like everything else in Iceland, an exotic name added an element of mystery to these offshore spikes. Rough basalt monoliths dotted the beach with echoes of the sea stacks—chunks of the eroding cliffs protruded from the sand with roots of unknown depth anchoring them in place.

Despite the chill, Lars pulled off his boots and socks and dashed along the waves' fringes as they swept across the jet-black and granular sand. As the froth slunk back to the sea after each wave cycle, smatterings of caked sand adorned his starkly white ankles beneath pulled-up trouser legs. I wanted to tell him not to freeze his toes off but realised that sounded motherly, so kept it to myself. He turned and called to us from calf-deep in a wave, pointing over the clifftop ridge framing the beach.

"Look, there's a skinny track that skirts the glacier. We should use the battlewagon to drive up there. We could see *everything* from there."

Tam nodded in agreement. "Aye, let's make use of those massive wheels. Mind, we need to head back soon. I don't want to be late for my own concert, like. I cannae trust the lads to stay anywhere near on beat without me."

We squatted around Lars as he sat and used his socks to wipe sand off his toes before pulling them on. Yes, he was sand-free but paid for it with sodden socks and a damp patch on his backside where he'd sunk into the frigid beach. Like most things, this didn't faze him.

We skipped to the head of the beach as two pairs, hand-in-hand, and sprang into the jeep under the watchful gaze of a clutch of colourful pastel beach huts perched on the higher ground, surveying the black expanse.

The track Lars had spotted diverged from the highway just above Vík í Mýrdal. It was more like a flattened ridge that other four-wheel-drive vehicles may have used in some distant season than a maintained roadway. Steeply angled, it was strewn with chunks of dark gravel ranging from pea-sized to misshapen hunks larger than footballs. Tam negotiated the lumps and bumps of the track with accomplished flicks of the steering wheel and liberal use of the jeep's powerful engine. Our battlewagon took the unfriendly terrain with little concern.

We stopped twice for photos of the vista unfolding below us. The ice of the glacial shelf encroached on one side of the track, and our view of Vík í Mýrdal, far below, made it appear more like a model than a real settlement. The terrain between us and the signs of civilisation below was a reverse dalmatian— clumps of glistening snow and blue-tinged ice scattered against a dark background. Over the clifftops to the east of the town, we finally saw the steaming outgassing of the underwater volcanic activity. A streak of blackened red beneath the waves far out to sea showed us the progress of the silent eruption.

Tam pointed to a plateau where the track levelled out above us. "Let's turn around there," he said. "We can get a last wee shufti before heading back. And check out the glacier—it's gonnae be like a wall beside us all the way up."

Gravel spat and skittered onto the ice. The jeep bounced over the roughening surface of the track, with a glistening wall of ice to our right representing the bottom edge of the glacier's advance. The level area was less level than it had appeared from below, but a careful seven-point turn manoeuvred the vehicle into a position to retrace our path downhill.

Dot balanced her phone on a makeshift pile of stones and set the timer for a group selfie of the four of us hanging off various parts of our majestic vehicle, the ground dropping away behind us.

As Tam negotiated the downward track, the wall of ice now on our left, Dot called out suddenly, rubbing her cheek. "Tam, stop. Stop *now*! I'm going to be sick."

I'd never known Dot to get car sick. Never a complaint,

even when we took her with us to Devon on a family vacation, my brothers, her, and I cavorting in the back seats of a rented van. But she looked decidedly green around the gills now, and Tam shuddered the jeep to a halt as Dot flung wide the door and dry heaved over the slope, her seatbelt holding her at an angle.

"That's weird. I feel fine n—" she began, but a reverberating crunch of rupturing ice obliterated the end of her sentence.

Shards of splintering ice shot from the glacier wall a few car lengths ahead of us, littering the track and scattering on the lichen-covered slope to the right. The incident, whatever its cause, occurred at the spot on the track where we would have been if Tam hadn't stopped at Dot's request. The volume of ice coursing across the track would surely have dislodged the jeep, sending us tumbling down the steep and lengthy incline to the highway far below. Our narrow escape was frightening enough, forcing a jitter of adrenaline through my limbs, but it was what followed that urged a jagged shiver of fear up my spine.

From the rent in the glacial wall, a bluish-white and sucker-encrusted tentacle smashed onto the track, sending gravel and frozen earth flying. Clods clattered onto the windshield of the jeep. The otherworldly tentacle was as big around as a tanker truck and narrowed as it whiplashed in vengeful strikes to a blackened tip that writhed across the slope below us. That tip scuffed around in the scree before lashing up toward us.

The impact as the tentacle's extremity slammed the side of the jeep rocked us, slapping Dot's door shut and leaving her face nearly pressed to the glass as the suckers expanded against the windows on the right side. Both she and Lars recoiled from the onslaught, but luckily, the glass did not shatter. The oozing coil slithered and snapped around the massive spare wheel attached to the jeep's rear and constricted.

I think we may have all screamed, but it was the flurry of actions that would be etched in our memories forever. Tam froze as the tentacle broke through the ice and slinked up to ensnare the vehicle, but the jostling slap that nudged us closer to the glacier spurred him into action. He threw the gear shift into reverse and applied power to the engine.

All four wheels spun, gravel clacking at the undercarriage. The jeep inched backwards, but Tam throttled down as he realised that reversing was allowing the tentacle to pull the rear wheels away from the glacier and threatened to slide us off the track.

With a shout of, "Hold on!" he slammed the gear lever into first gear and gunned the engine. The right rear wheel spun furiously—it must have already been teetering over the slope—but found purchase as the other three wheels dragged us toward where the blue-limned tentacle emerged from the fissure.

The tentacle slackened as we shortened the distance between us and its source. Some of the suction cups on the side windows lost full grip, the slimy circumference of each sucker shrinking as the bulk of the tentacle became more loosely affixed.

"Tam, get us *away* from that thing, not closer!"

"I'm trying! It almost pulled us off'a the road when I reversed. But I'm running out of ideas."

Lars was more inclined to action than discussing ideas, but I had severe misgivings when I noticed him roll down his window. The suckers caused the power window to judder its way down, ultimately leaving the seething pink and white discs to search for purchase in the void of the open window frame. The suckers pulsed, contracting and expanding inches from Lars's face. He was bent on attacking it, but the only item within reach that resembled a weapon was a pen that he pulled from his pocket. He held it in his fist, pointy end down, and plunged it into the bluish flesh and searching suckers in a series of overhead strikes. With each piercing blow, jets of indigo ichor spurted into the rear of the jeep, marking the roof, seat backs, and his clothing with jagged lines of unpleasant-smelling liquid.

Tam tried reversing again, but once more, the tentacle's tugs threatened to pull our back wheels off the roadway. He jerked us forward again, straightening us out, but this allowed the tentacle to tighten.

Meanwhile, I sat paralysed. The seatbelt felt like it weighed a thousand pounds, and every muscle tensed, uncertain of what to do. I knew my magic would fizzle and fail without my brother Newton's reserves of power to bring it forth. Was this to be our fate? Flung down an Icelandic hillside by a ruthless power that we couldn't even identify?

Lars jolted me from my inaction. As he took his eight or tenth stab, a sucker the size of a dinner plate clamped shut around his forearm. "Higgs! Gods, do *something!*" he shouted as his other hand pried at the entrapment, but without success.

I unclicked my seat belt and dived across Lars's lap, lending two more hands to freeing his arm. The sucker gave way, but not enough—it snapped back even more tightly after being pried apart by our combined muscle power.

Dot joined us, kneeling on the front seat and reaching one arm back to join the fray. Lars bucked his entangled arm as all three of us scrambled for a way to gain more leverage. But it was hopeless. The sucker clenched with more force than we could muster.

I glanced at Dot, hoping for inspiration for an alternative approach, and I could see her tiger tooth glowing right through the skin of her cheek. A tendril of ruby-tinged energy branched like a series of veins and capillaries along her jawline, tracing a fractal pattern over the exposed skin of her shoulder and coursing along the arm that wrestled the tentacle. The light shone darkly through the fabric of her long-sleeved shirt and emerged at the wrist to enliven her pointer and middle fingers.

It hinted at arcane power, but our assailing horror took no notice. I re-angled myself and worked at the same fold of sucker-flesh that Dot attacked. As soon as my hand touched the flickering veins of power in her hand, I felt magic erupt within me. It was the same fiery tingle that accompanied my fight-or-flight instincts when Newton was nearby. Instantly my fingers and thumb transmuted into deeply furrowed rosebush stems, rushing in unchecked growth from the end of each digit.

Thorny filaments sought the inner parts of the sucker that encased Lars's forearm, emerging to circle and re-circle the entire girth of the alien tentacle. The offshoots wound around and around, scratching at Dot's window as they twined around the thicker parts of the tentacle at the jeep's nose. Lars shouted in pain and yanked again at his trapped arm. With a second anguished tug, the sucker abandoned its hold, and Lars fell back against me, suddenly free.

His own blood, from several thorn punctures on his forearm, mixed with the slimy navy ichor of the tentacle's wounds. He wiped and grabbed at the area, applying pressure to the two nastiest gouges. He laughed in relief. "You did it, Higgs! I knew you could."

I barely heard those words. A sound like wind gusting along a narrow valley blocked almost all other sounds. The rush of power travelling from Dot's fire-infused hand increased; my thorn-adorned finger extensions tightened around the tentacle's malleable mass. As the fibres of the rose stem strained and sank into the flesh of our constricting threat, more spurts of dark fluid streaked the windows beside and in front of Dot. Despite the desperation of our situation and the reflexive nature of my defensive magic, there was something oddly exhilarating about the power that flowed through me. I was used to feeling Newton's steady, protective nature intertwining with my magical outbursts, but the energy that streamed from Dot and her tiger tooth resonated with the powerful bond of friendship and the righteous indignation of a shared slight. If I was abut to die, I felt honoured to perish alongside my steadfast ally.

A dark green bud opened at the end of my ring finger's rose cane, and a flower with petals formed of scarlet fire burst forth. I pressed the fiery bloom into the tentacle's flesh, and it recoiled, the first sign that the damage we were inflicting was deterring the attacking limb.

Tam reversed a short distance as the tension in the tentacle diminished but soon reached the limit of safe progress. One wheel spun above the void.

Just as I felt the power of my still-constricting rose fingers could repel the tentacle altogether, my hopes were literally doused. A surge of water frothed along the tentacle's length, coursing toward us from the crack in the glacier. It clung around the tentacle's circumference, washing along its length like a rolled-up sleeve being shaken out. The pulsing flames of my flower winked out in a puff of red smoke. Even the stalk and cane of my thorny extensions retracted until all that remained of my power was a bark-encrusted but human-sized hand. Even the pulsing vein of power linking Dot's tiger tooth to my hand slunk away, leaving only a bruised-looking, fading glow along her jaw to her shoulder.

The tentacle redoubled its constriction, pulling the other rear wheel closer to the brink. My magic felt snuffed out, like a candle in the rain. I took some small comfort in the warmth of Lars as he leaned back into me, still clutching his dripping forearm.

This might have been the final, microscopic moment of calm before we tumbled to our deaths. From this height, it seemed likely we'd roll right across the highway below and plunge over the cliff to the black sands where Lars had so recently nestled his toes.

The waves of gravity-defying water continued to surge along the tentacle, and, in a moment of hallucination, I imagined a crusty sea turtle surfing the unnatural tide toward us. A tug pulled the jeep's rear another foot closer to the precipice.

But was it a hallucination? If it was, Dot shared it, calling out, "What's that?" and pointing ahead along the tentacle's unnatural length.

It wasn't an actual sea turtle, but it had the same general shape, and was a little longer than my forearm. On closer inspection, it looked like a combination of armoured turtle shell and jellyfish. Rough-edged, overlapping plates, the colour and texture of slate, formed a shape like a turtle shell, but the similarity to a real turtle stopped there. A shroud of smoke buoyed the shell from underneath, as if the creature rode weightless on an insubstantial cushion. Instead of squat legs, four or five pale tendrils trailed beneath, like thick but limp strands of spaghetti. One angled jiggling from the back. And instead of an elongated protruding turtle neck, only a stub of a head stuck from the front of the shell. Slats as black as the landscape shielded it too, but a pair of multifaceted jewels faced toward us, glowing ruby slices the size of eggs.

The head rotated slightly as it rode toward us on the tentacle's watery fringe, as if a tiny engineer piloted this smoking tortoise-jellyfish hybrid and searched for a place to land on our jeep through rosy, lamp-lit portholes.

The shelled creature swooped along the contour of the tentacle's slope and halted at the bulky section crushing the jeep's bonnet. It seemed to look directly at me, its head tilting a fraction to one side just as the jewelled eye visors glowed with a pulsing intensity. Deep red fire limned each plate of the armoured shell before a fury of downward-angled flames lit the outer margins of the turtle's belly plate and obscured the dangling limbs of the visitor. The flames shot outward, branding a circle into the flesh of the tentacle as the watery coating evaporated in a hissing mass of steam.

The tentacle recoiled from the burning gusts of flame. The turtle's pale, descending limbs were briefly visible again as it rose, before descending again in an even more brilliant ring of fire.

A scorching, bubbling sound preceded the tentacle abandoning its hold on the jeep. Like a stagecoach driver raising his whip to goad his horses into a canter, the sense-offending tentacle wriggled skyward, shedding shards of ice as the crack in the glacier expanded upwards.

The shelled creature slipped off to one side of the tentacle's mass, hovering just to our right. Once again, it angled its bejewelled eye plates in my direction before flying off on a cushion of fire and smoke toward the flailing tentacle.

Tam gunned the jeep's engine. The two rutted wheels at the front found traction and pulled the rear back onto the roadway. The vehicle jerked forward and pressed us deep into our seats. The ice wall to our left blurred as we accelerated, but this didn't seem like a good plan. The thicker part of the writhing tentacle blocked our path where it left the glacier's protection. At that point, it was almost as thick as our jeep was tall. We would smash into it head-on. I clicked my seatbelt back into place and held my breath.

Dot, Lars, and I cried out in near unison. "Tam!" was all we managed before impact.

But the first impact was the flailing tentacle smashing down onto the roadway, not us ramming its side. The tremendous downward force crumbled the roadway, creating a rut across its width. From the point where it emerged from the glacial wall's fissure, the tentacle flattened into the newly created rut just as the jeep rocketed past the crevice in the glacial wall where the tentacle broke free. Although the upper quarter of the tentacle wasn't flush with the original track, enough of it had compressed into the rut that the jeep's oversized wheels mounted what remained above.

We were airborne for a moment, and the rear of the jeep rose as the tentacle spasm continued, lashing it into the air once again. Tam yelled something unintelligible, somewhere between a curse and a prayer, before the jeep landed on the track beyond the tentacle, the front wheels absorbing the impact. The heavy-duty springs of the front shock absorbers bottomed out with a jolt before the rear wheels returned to the ground. Fortunately, we had stayed on course throughout our brief flight, and after two heart-stopping zig-zags, Tam wrestled us back onto course down the narrow track. He slowed from breakneck speed to a pace suitable for avoiding supernatural monsters while still providing a reasonable chance of not careering off the road to certain death.

Lars and I surveyed the flailing tentacle behind us. It still rose and fell, lashing out to seek the armoured turtle, whose jets of flame propelled it to a safe distance partway down the hillside. It turned to follow our progress as we followed the curving track back toward the highway.

Everyone quivered from adrenaline, and my nervous laugh was soon joined by the others'.

"Gods, we were lucky the tentacle buried itself in the road at just the right time," Lars said. "I thought we were gonna crash."

"Yeah, but remind me never to go on holiday with you two again." Dot agreed, rubbing her jaw. "Why does unnatural danger follow us around everywhere?"

62

CHAPTER 8 - KEY

Faraday

Although Scarlett and I shared a professional respect for each other, Agent Zee was the lone UPDA agent who showed any consideration for me as a person. Well, my father looked out for me too, probably even more than he had Higgs or Newton, but he hid his status as a UPDA agent until after they snatched his life from us.

Within 90 seconds of him disappearing from the grass below, Zee appeared on the rooftop, bursting through the access door with a weapon that seemed transplanted from a 1950s sci-fi movie. It was a pistol with a bulky ammunition storage bulb attached to the butt of the handgrip and a muzzle that flared open like a spare part from a trombone. It was this device that presumably cast the immobilising web nets onto the attacking techno-hyenas.

Spotting Svetlana and me, he advanced quickly. With a decrescendo, whomping noise, he fired a glob of the entrapping goop onto the machine that Svetlana had disabled with her cattle prod. A symmetrical web surrounded the creature, anchoring it to the ground with fringes that clung to the roofing material.

"Hey! How can we investigate machine when is covered in

schmoot?" Svetlana said.

Zee looked at me with an unstated question, which I answered. "Agent Zee, this is my new friend and recent saver-of-my-life, Svetlana Federov. Remember Dmitri, who we met in Edinburgh? His niece."

Zee turned to her again. "I see. Nice to meet you, Miss Federov." He shifted the comical-looking weapon to his left hand and offered the other. "And I have a spray solution that can dissolve the web. Safety first—thought I'd better pin that sucker down."

Svetlana extended a hand, not to accept the proffered handshake, but to invite a closer inspection of the odd weapon. "Can I take look at gun? Very interesting technology."

Zee raised an eyebrow. "Afraid not, madam. Secret British invention." He moved to snap it into a magnetic, open-sided holster at his hip, but I interrupted him.

"How about me? Just a quick look?"

I wasn't capable of puppy dog eyes but hoped good old-fashioned earnestness would suffice. Zee paused, then reversed the weapon, handing it to me butt first.

Svetlana peered sideways at me. "I save your life, but still, I am Russian. No sharing of toys, *da?*"

I worried she would turn pissy at this perceived snub, but after a moment, I saw her lips twitch into a lopsided smile. I let out a chuckle which was pursued across the rooftop by Svetlana's musical laugh.

She sidled closer but kept enough gap to avoid violating any international secrecy protocols. I examined the barrel, which curved open in a tribute to an ancient blunderbuss. Then I switched my inspection to the more interesting part: the ammunition. A latch allowed the clunky magazine to pop free, and I ejected 2 rounds. They resembled flares, chunky plastic casings holding a liquid or gel suspension that must spread into the sticky restraining web when released. It was probably a nanotech enhancer to promote the spread and formation of the tensile strength inherent in the web shape.

The interesting bits would be inside the ammunition rounds, and I wasn't equipped or permitted to investigate that here on Granny's roof. I popped the rounds back into place and snapped the magazine into the grip using a swift set of hand movements, and returned the weapon to Agent Zee. Svetlana shot me a quick glance; I guess all those hours spent on magic tricks and sleight-of-hand hadn't brought perfection, but Zee didn't react with suspicion when I handed the web gun back.

"Let's get to work, Zee," I began. "With three pressing matters, let's start with the most important."

"I take it you want to investigate what those mechanical creatures were after in your mother's former lab, right?" he asked.

"That's actually second most important."

Zee raised an eyebrow. "You want to inspect this one pinned under the web before that? I restrained it assuming you'd check it out later."

"That's the *third* priority," I said.

I strode closer and lowered my voice, although only he and Svetlana were within earshot. A quaver betrayed emotion as I asked my question. "Scarlett said she ordered my father's death. Is that true? Tell me you weren't involved."

Agent Zee pressed his lips into a thin line and stared into my eyes for longer than I'd hoped or felt comfortable with. Part of me wanted him to deny it, but I was ready for whatever his answer might be.

"I was driving her when she made the call," he said. "It shocked me. It's the only time I've seen her cry. I'm sorry, Faraday. She wouldn't have done it unless it was unavoidable. They were thick as thieves, your father and her."

The numbness I'd felt since that morning crept a little

higher in the back of my brain. The UPDA's involvement in my father's death was undeniable now unless this was nothing but a hyper-real dream.

I felt Svetlana's arm snake across my shoulders. "Let us sniff out what hyenas missed underground, yes?"

* * *

We had left Zee securing the head and legs of the web-bound hyena using magnetic clamps and trotted through the Orphanage to the shed beside the Ides Giant. Alert to new threats, the two agents we'd seen through the binoculars flanked the doorway. They looked us up and down but found us unconcerning.

Agent Higgenbotham was inside, about to descend the ladder to the lab below; the wooden hatch lay in splinters, presumably the work of the infernal machines. Close up, I noticed his thinning hair was held in its scalp-hugging sweep by a glossy product, and he'd trimmed his pencil moustache with immaculate precision. The tidiness matched the starched and uncomfortable-looking lay of his khaki shirt. He spoke to me as if we'd had a years-long but frosty relationship.

"Redferne, this is a UPDA investigation scene, but I'll allow you to accompany me down because of your local insight."

I nodded and waved Svetlana to follow me toward the opening.

He held up a finger. "Nuh-uh. The Russian stays outside with my men."

Apparently, Svetlana needed no introduction to Higgenbotham. I aimed a shrug her way and followed the older man into the gloom below. I turned on the lab lights from the recessed switch obscured by the ladder.

A rapid scan of the barren lab let me compare it to the detailed image held in my memory. "One descended, yes?" I asked, not waiting for a reply because I could read the signals. "Scratches on the floor, where it skidded upon landing," I said, pointing. "And some gouges where it used the ladder to climb back up when you interrupted it."

Higgenbotham remained silent but pursed his lips and raised an eyebrow. I took that as encouragement. "And those two tiny boreholes in the wall behind that rack? They're new." I pointed at a pair of small-diameter but perfect circles punched through the subway tile at knee height, visible through the wire mesh shelf in the empty, freestanding rack on the opposite wall. I squatted and crawled a couple of steps to get a closer look. Something I'd failed to notice before caught my eye. How could I have missed it?

"Help us move the rack aside," I said to Higgenbotham, gesturing for him to take the opposite end. It was heavy and scraped across the cement floor as we shifted it aside.

"Weird," I said. "Look at that. That vertical there between the tiles isn't grout, like the rest of the gaps. It's a flexible sealant. I think it's hiding a hinge."

I felt the line with my fingertips. It rose from a point one tile above the floor to the top of the tiling, at chest height. My fingers moved horizontally across the tiles, looking for more clues. A pair of knocks on the tiles revealed nothing more than the sound of knuckles rapping ceramic.

I pushed a few tiles, half expecting them to light up with residual magic from the time the Ides Giant came to life. On the 11th try, my curiosity paid off. With the snick of a hidden clasp freeing itself, a section of the tiled wall the size of a pizza oven sprung forward. Its hinge lay concealed along the line of the flexible sealant, and I pulled the jutting door back, keen to reveal its hidden secrets.

Moving faster than I'd expected, Higgenbotham's hand was already on my shoulder, firmly pulling me back from the revealed opening. "I'll take it from here, Redferne."

I let him shuffle in front of me but kept a clear view over his shoulder. The concealed doorway was something my father could have easily built, but the space revealed beyond it was not his handiwork.

A set of 7 steps led even deeper underground, expanding the headroom to allow what would begin as a crouch through the open hatch to full standing position at their base. The stairs were smooth stone, precisely carved and bathed in a sourceless, blue-tinged illumination. I instinctively crouched to get a better view of what lay beyond the stairway.

A pair of curving passageways curled from the landing, fanning out like a pair of pincers. The same eerie glow suffused the corridors. Each had been constructed from smooth and tight-fitting stone blocks, arched overhead. The dustless floors looked like polished concrete.

At the curve's furthest visible point, a bulky golden key hung from a piece of twine affixed to a ceiling block. The dangling key differentiated the left and right hallways, aside from some scuffing that looked like rubber traces high on each wall in the left-hand tranche. The key swung slightly in a breeze that I couldn't feel. The discomfort I felt about inexplicable activity raised goosebumps along the exposed parts of my forearms.

Fishing a small communications device from a back pocket, Agent Higgenbotham pressed a button and spoke with quiet assurance. His lack of affect suggested he had expected to find this tunnel, but I remembered his earlier conversation with Scarlett and me. Maybe he was immune to surprise. "Agent Xenon. Better get down here."

We both crouched and surveyed the scene below, shifting our gazes from one passage to the other. Neither of us bothered to turn as Zee's boots sounded their way down the ladder.

"Do you have an evidence bag?" Higgenbotham asked. Still

not turning his gaze away from the steps, he accepted the ziplock bag that Zee passed over his shoulder.

"I'm going in. Start filming, so we have a record of anything unexpected," he added.

Crab-walking through the low doorway, Higgenbotham descended the steps, his skin taking on a ghoulish hue in the blue light as he straightened into the expanding headroom with each step.

I crouched and made to follow him, but Zee grabbed me by the sleeve and shook his head. He filmed with his phone. I gently brushed his hand away and followed Higgenbotham down the stairs, moving as quietly as I could. Zee made no further move to stop me; I had a thought that concern fuelled his caution, but compassion released his grip and let me make my own decisions. Or mistakes—maybe this was a rash move.

He left the bottom stair into the atrium spawning the two curving hallways, with me only a step behind. "Redferne! Stop right there. I'm going for the key, so best stand back. Nothing feels right here."

He was correct. My tongue tingled. The light had no apparent source and an unnatural hue. My hair rose unevenly, buoyed as it would be after rubbing a balloon on it. Magic was at work. I followed orders and stayed put, a pace from the bottom step.

"All good?" Zee inquired from atop the steps.

"So far, yes. Keep filming."

Higgenbotham took a tentative step, keeping full weight on his trailing foot as if he feared stepping on a landmine. Once convinced he wasn't about to be blown to bits, he committed to the next step, then the next. Gaining confidence and pace, he strode toward the dangling key. It was 10 steps away.

Oddly, it remained 10 steps away. Higgenbotham crept along the corridor but got no closer to the key. Nothing about the hallway changed. No extra stone blocks shuffled in to provide the extra length. The twine remained tied to the same eyelet, affixed to the same ceiling block. The key still twisted in its undetectable breeze. It was as if an unseen force tampered with our perceptions, making the key seem closer. Or further away. I couldn't make sense of it, but I felt the tang of magic.

Higgenbotham took a step back toward my position, and the key came closer as he did so, keeping its fixed distance from him. He stretched the evidence bag to the full extent of his reach, and the key moved away to accommodate the movement. It maintained its distance from Higgenbotham's leading limb.

He tried a few running steps, but got no closer. As it spun languidly, I glimpsed movement in the right-hand tunnel. "Look, Zee, there's a key in the other tunnel too."

Just visible in the other fork was a bulky key, also suspended from the ceiling. It seemed to move toward me as Higgenbotham moved further along the other stretch of corridor. If I looked straight ahead between the two tunnel sections, I could see both keys in my peripheral vision. By their synchronised swaying, I could tell it was the same key, somehow visible in both forks. In no universe could separate keys move in such precise unison.

"Higgenbotham, I can see your key coming down the other passageway. Let me go that way, and you push it toward me by walking down your branch."

"Worth a try, lad," he said.

Being called 'lad' was a slight affront, but I quelled my umbrage. We both advanced, each along our own section of hallway. But it didn't work. I too could see the key, but it remained 10 steps away from me as I advanced along the right-hand passage. After 24 steps, I saw a distant movement ahead. Over my shoulder, I could still see agent Zee, far behind me, filming from the hatch. Although I should have been around the bend of the curving corridor already, he remained visible. And the motion ahead of me was Agent Higgenbotham, coming toward me but very distant—at least 100 paces. I waved, and he stopped walking. His voice reached me from behind, which oddly made sense, given he looked so far away beyond the key.

"Redferne? Is that you? Is the key getting any closer to you?"

"Not at all. It's still the same distance away. Only this weird hallway is changing. Like it's a fun-house mirror trick. Neither of us is getting closer."

"Okay, that's enough. Go back and out. I'm calling a specialist."

I reached toward the key, and it shifted in response away from my outstretched arm. It boggled me to consider what kind of specialist Higgenbotham would summon to deal with this. A magic key expert? A coal miner?

"Now, Redferne. You're done here."

* * *

After banishment from the mysterious tunnel, I realised Granny must be worried. The hyenas had scurried up the wall just outside her room, and she would have noticed the commotion on the hillside. Svetlana and I returned to her room.

"Sorry—I should have checked in earlier. I hope you weren't worried," I said.

"Hmm, dearie? It didn't feel like you were gone that long. I must have dozed off."

I described what had happened and that she had missed some mechanical hyenas scaling the wall right outside her window. Svetlana filled in the gaps in my rushed story.

"They would not allow me into tunnel, and now both of us

kicked out," she concluded.

Granny parted her lips but pondered a moment before speaking. "Shallow people always yearn after the shiny objects, like magpies. But they're often looking in the wrong places. We need to find your father's hidden artefact, and it doesn't sound like it's in that tunnel, now, does it?"

Svetlana nodded, and I noticed she had some purple streaks in her dark hair. Maybe I should have paid more attention when I first saw her. "Yes, Miss Redferne. Good point. Faraday—you should follow instincts. Those ones are idiots, no?"

The prompt brought on a surge of warmth that dispelled the top layer of numbness that had slammed me upon hearing of Scarlett's role in my father's death. Maybe I should follow my instincts. But instinct had abandoned me like fog shredding in a gust of wind. Should we inspect the captive hyena in more detail? My instincts told me to seek Svetlana's guidance.

But wait, what about *her* instincts? "Hey—remember the unexpected space between the storeys of the Orphanage? Maybe Dad hid the artefact in there somewhere?"

Svetlana nodded, rummaged in her backpack, and fished out a coiled plastic fibre with a connector at one end. "I have endoscope. Attaches to phone. We need only drill."

That was a simply solved problem. I scampered downstairs to the maintenance closet that I often raided for minor projects while at the Orphanage. When I returned to the room, Svetlana was running the camera end of the endoscope through my grandmother's sparse hairdo while Granny laughed at the resulting image on the mobile phone screen.

"Okay, enough fooling," Svetlana said, and withdrew the scope. "Faraday, start drilling."

After ulling back a corner of the rug, I avoided pipes and wiring using a stud finder and knocked the floor a few times to find a good place to drill. Choosing a bit slightly larger than the diameter of the endoscope, I drilled a small hole, sweeping the sawdust under the rug's folded-back fringe. Svetlana threaded the nose of the endoscope through the hole and activated its light, using the control app on her phone.

Aside from clinging cobwebs and a run of copper water pipe, we couldn't see much. Svetlana had me grab the scope close to the floorboards and rotate it so we could get a different viewing angle.

"See? I tell you first time, Faraday. Secret tunnel!"

She stooped to show me the screen. Now that the camera pointed parallel to the balcony hallway that ran outside Granny's room, we could see a pipe-free crawlspace that led away from our position.

"What's that?" I asked. "Turn the lamp off for a second."

Svetlana tapped the control button to deactivate the light at the tip of the endoscope. A square opening in the floor of the crawlspace glowed with the same blue illumination as the tunnel beneath my mother's lab. I drew in a sharp breath, and Svetlana let out an admiring whistle.

"Same glow? Opening to same tunnel?" she asked. "Or maybe different one created by same forces? Let's go and take look," she said. "Should we cut hole?"

There was the briefest of pauses, then we both said, almost in unison, "No, we'll find the hatch."

Of course, there had to be a proper way in. What kind of secret tunnel had no secret entrance? I fed the scope deeper into the crawlspace and rotated it while Svetlana scrutinised her phone. "Look, there. Light leaking in around frame of hatch. Mark point on scope and pull out. We can find distance to hatch."

Knowing how far away the hatch was from my drilled hole made it simple to locate the hidden entrance to the crawlspace. It was in Granny's walk-in closet, covered by a rubber mat. Granny's brow furrowed as I opened the entrance to a secret passageway that had lurked beneath her skirts, jackets, and nose all this time.

"I never saw Templeton go in *there*," she said. Her tone was accusatory, but I hadn't even considered laying any blame for concealing information at her feet. "Anyway, what are we waiting for? Let's check it out."

She stooped stiffly to her knees and crawled toward the open hatch. "Whoa! Granny! You can't be serious. In there? You're almost eighty years old," I said.

"Yeah, but you're not even twenty. Plus, this is *my* house."

"Sheesh, okay. How about this—I'll squirm past the opening in the floor, and then you follow me? It's not that cramped, so we can spin around and crawl back if we need to. Svetlana can bring up the rear."

"Whoa yourself," Svetlana said. "You did not hear of 'ladies first'? I will go first, then Miss Redferne and you come at end. She is only small, so you will look around her when we get to hole."

It seemed I had been outvoted, so we eased into the crawlspace, brains before wisdom, with me tacked on as an afterthought.

As the two women entered the confined space, I thought about the hip joint of the mechanical terror Svetlana had disabled on the roof. It was familiar. Sometimes I wished I could shut off the whirring at the back of my brain and concentrate on the moment, but more often than not, these nags germinated into something insightful. I relegated whatever that part of my mind worked on to the background and followed them in.

The dusty crawlspace was, as predicted, close to a metre high, but it was double that in width. The tall steel I-beams that supported the upper floors of the Orphanage formed barriers between us and whatever other open space lurked like a hidden sandwich between the ground floor and Granny's level.

Svetlana's phone flashlight lit the way ahead, while mine provided light to guide Granny. I'm sure Newton would have forbidden her to enter this potentially dangerous space, but I didn't think it was worth the argument or the risk of giving up my position as favourite grandchild. Maybe she wouldn't tell him. Or tell him she'd forced me to let her go; that would be better.

The few sounds in the crawlspace amplified its claustrophobic nature. Trickling water through the pipes running alongside us. Muffled footsteps somewhere along the corridor above us. The scurry of rodent feet to the right. Our tense breathing. I needed something to take my mind off the fact that we were approaching a magic-tinged opening in a hidden passage that might lead us to a powerful artefact concealed by my murdered father.

The machinations I my brain that I'd pushed aside earlier jumped to the foreground—I realised where I'd seen that hip hinge. "I got a job offer in California. Did you know that, Svetlana? Xi Li's American lab. He and his lab manager called to convince me to move there."

Svetlana didn't look back but replied as she hauled herself along on her elbows. "Ha. Will you take job? Xi's lab is not better than my uncle's. He told me he offered you job too."

"My Russian is terrible," I said.

"That can be fixed. Easy. For you. And you cannot speak American either," she laughed. "Or Chinese."

"Well, Xi's English is perfect. Plus, the principal lab engineer is a Brit, even though he looks like a surfer. I think Xi's corporation made those hyenas. I've been thinking about the hip hinges. His podcast on the Artificial Intelligence needed to teach a machine to walk on uneven surfaces was brilliant, and the movement of those machines aligns with his robotic technology and algorithms."

One of the best things about being me was my memory. I

could visualise the podcast video as if it re-ran on the backsides of my eyeballs. Xi Li was wearing a slightly wrinkled linen shirt tucked into black jeans. He sported undone cuffs, and one sleeve slid down as he nudged his glasses up his broad nose, revealing a ying-yang tattoo and a pair of smaller ones just above his wrist. He explained the processing power and the coding solutions his Shanghai lab used to allow his automata to walk, run, and even dance. He also did a brief dissection of how the joints needed pseudo-biological functioning so they could rotate, support, and give leverage to the attached limbs. That joint was definitely the same as we'd seen on our mechanical assailants.

"I've talked to him six times in video chats. He's a nice guy but very intense. Walked me through the projects I'd get to work on in California. Showed me through the lab and introduced two of his chief engineers. It's a great opportunity, but I'm still not sure. I've got his direct number and promised to call him back soon."

Svetlana was almost at the blue-lit opening and called back. "But you have own lab and mother's notes, yes? And Dr Vandercrump helps you."

"Vanderkamp, yes. I'm still considering Xi's offer."

"Stop considering for now. You must look on this," she said, spidering herself into position in the crawlspace on the opposite side of the opening's glowing square. Granny and I approached from our side, and a quiet, "Oh my," escaped my grandmother's lips as her wrinkled face and fringe of grey hair were lit by the indigo glow of the vista that opened below us.

CHAPTER 9 - REUNION

Newton

Chronos made a phone call as we drove off. Ashna huddled beneath the blanket, still looking back long past the point where Torsten's house left our view. When she turned, I saw tears streaking her face in the rear-view mirror, and she shuddered, shoulders hunching.

"Vish, it's me," Chronos said. "Good news—we've got her. I'll pass the phone over."

Ashna took the mobile in a quivering hand and paused for a deep breath before she raised it and spoke. "Daddy … I'm so sorry. But I'm okay. And don't blame Torsten, he's really nice underneath. It's my fault. I just … I just wanted to escape. But I miss home."

Through Ashna's side of the exchange, we heard she met Torsten on an Internet chatroom and that he paid for her flight to Iceland. Shoddy police work there—how had they failed to spot that she'd left the country? Or maybe they had but were withholding details as a snub to me after leaving the force. It didn't seem like he'd abused her, and it was her choice not to contact Middle Ides. But she said that seeing us made her realise she'd made a mistake. She also mentioned that she didn't want to take over the fish and chip shop. Maybe the pressure of the family business and expectations had weighed on her. There were plenty of conversation topics for her and her family once she'd returned home.

Chronos took the phone back and reassured Vish that we'd fly back in a day or two, once we'd arranged the flights. He had to say, "you're welcome," at least six times before he could end the call.

"Sorry to pester you with questions, Ash, but what was Torsten on about, threatening us by saying 'who he worked for'?" I asked.

I saw her forehead crease in a series of dimpled V shapes. "I've no idea, really. He works at a fabrication business just outside town. He makes drill parts for oil and gas exploration, I think. I can't see them being any great threat. It's weird."

I stopped our compact rental car at a roundabout to let another car through. The only other vehicle in the vicinity took our exit, its rugged frame heading the way we'd come. Chronos pointed at the driver of the jacked-up four-wheel-drive vehicle that slowed as it passed our position.

"Hang on, that's—"

"—Ragnhildur, Scarlett's sister," I finished for him.

"Wait here," he said and flicked open his door. "I've got unfinished business with her."

Indeed. The last time we'd seen her, she'd been wielding a knife and using elf magic in an attempt to kill my family and friends. By rights, she should have been imprisoned in the UK, but to prevent the Tartanantula's unusual activities from alarming the public, she had been quietly deported back to Iceland.

Gravel susurrated under Ragnhildur's car as she too stopped, opening her door as Chronos skirted behind our rental.

"Eh up, treacle cheeks," he called. "I've got a score to settle with you. Last time we met, you got a bit stabby for my liking. We've had the home leg, I'll finish up now that we're here for the away match."

She laughed, a thin and soulless rasp. "Not stabby *enough* for my liking, limpy. What's the score?"

She backpedalled to the rear of her car as Chronos strode toward her, fists clenched. He was still five or six running steps away from her when she popped the rear hatch of the vehicle and snatched out a hunting rifle. With a swift motion and an accompanying snick of metal on metal, she chambered a round. Chronos stopped in his tracks and backpedalled.

"I got a call about a one-legged giant from my man Sigurdson over on this side of town. He was not happy, but me? I could not believe my luck. And now I find you too, Redferne! Double luck." She swung the barrel of the rifle between Chronos's position and my open window.

Chronos ducked behind the passenger side of our car as Ragnhildur raised the rifle. I crouched, leaving only my eyes peeing above the seat back and saw Ashna do likewise in the back seat as Chronos scrambled through the still-open passenger door. Without returning upright, I stomped on the accelerator and barely raised my eyes above dashboard level in time to negotiate the roundabout. Luckily, no other cars were crossing, and our tires objected as the wheels swung wide through the turn. I sped away as I heard a heavy door clunk and the screech of winter tires guiding Ragnhildur's vehicle through a sharp turn behind us.

Chronos had one arm behind my seat as he peered behind us. "That's it, Ash, stay low. Here she comes."

The rental car's engine sang like an overworked sewing machine, not even powerful enough to drown out the roar of Ragnhildur's car approaching from our rear. "Maybe I should have rented the *other* car on offer," I said.

I'm sure it didn't help that we had three people in our car

to Ragnhildur's one, especially with the extra mass my best friend possessed. Maybe I could outmanoeuvre her somehow. I tried to remember if I had any training on vehicle chases as part of my police training, but I drew a blank. Either I had none or hadn't paid attention during the lesson.

We headed away from the airport, toward the mouth of the fjord on its opposing bank, accelerating as fast as the underpowered car would allow, which was far too sluggish for my liking. The flanks of the volcanic slopes rose to my left, the dark waters of the inlet beyond the barriers on Chronos's right. If this was Middle Ides, maybe I could have evaded Ragnhildur using the density of the town centre. Maybe I could have belted through the underground car park below the supermarket, sped up the alleyway behind the Pinnacle Club and then nosed into the spider web of curved lanes in the Bellwether Estate. But not here; it seemed possible to spot every moving vehicle on either side of the fjord. The diffuse building scape, lack of trees, and the stark contrast between our car's paintwork and the black background left no room for concealment.

Ragnhildur's high-riding vehicle closed in fast behind us. She'd run us off the road or maybe make us spin out, nudging a rear flank of our car with the nose of hers. Taking a slight curve to the left, we faced a straightaway to the hairpin turn at the top of the fjord. Ragnhildur closed the merciless gap with ease and pulled to the left as she reached our position.

Maybe I hadn't any real police training, but Chronos and I had mucked around in the car park of the abandoned warehouse beyond Nether Ides, skidding his mother's rust-bucket Mitsubishi on the weed-punctuated tarmac. As soon as Ragnhildur pulled to our left, I slammed on the brakes. They worked much better than the accelerator, and Ragnhildur surged past us before slowing. Smoke from the tires wafting around us, I pulled the handbrake and spun the steering wheel, drifting us through a near-perfect 180-degree turn. I pounced on the accelerator and released the handbrake, and we sped away, retracing our route.

"Smooth, brother, but she's turned now too," Chronos said.

A soft but panicky muttering emerged from the back seat, where Ashna huddled low under the fleecy blanket. "I'm going to be sick ... should have stayed with Torsten ..."

Chronos turned to give her a reassuring hand, but whatever words of wisdom he had in mind never crossed his lips. Instead, his voice raised after he heard the gunshot. "Whoa, stay flat, Ash, now she's shooting at us."

His gaze fixed on our pursuer. "Sharpish, Newt. She's hanging the rifle out her window and resting it on her sideview mirror. But this speed, with the rifle bouncing, she's not going to—"

Shattering glass interrupted and invalidated his prediction. The rear windshield fell in chunks and slivers, coating the rear parcel shelf and Ashna's blanket with glistening shards.

Chronos's tone was more indignant than concerned. "My bloody ear! That bitch's bullet nearly shot off my earring, and I'm bleeding all over my new shirt. This'll go on company expenses, no arguing."

I glanced over and saw his nicked earlobe, but I had to concentrate on the chicane ahead. The bullet must have travelled through the gap left by Chronos's lowered passenger window after its brush with his head. Luckily, ears have little blood flow, so his shirt was just spackled, not drenched.

I forced myself to concentrate. What could I do to escape Ragnhildur's murderous intentions? Another gunshot, then another, but neither struck our car that I could tell. With a blur of shuffling hands, I hauled the steering wheel to the right and screeched into a small parking area serving a scenic picnic spot on a flattened overlook. I'd hoped Ragnhildur might fly past, but she managed the turn too, her left wheels cinching past the gatepost.

Bragging isn't really my style, and maybe it was the adrenaline pumping, but I executed a perfect slide, negotiating a sharp curl around the lone sentinel lamppost at the cramped car park's centre. Our little car surged back onto the road with good velocity, doubling back. I was rewarded by the sight of Ragnhildur juddering through a three-point turn.

The posts supporting the barrier rail between us and the fjord blurred as we passed our own skidmarks from earlier and approached the hairpin turn into the next fjord. And still, Ragnhildur came.

I had to slow to a near standstill to negotiate the turn, and Ragnhildur braked hard behind us, anti-lock brakes throwing a threatening series of staccato squeals of rubber on tarmac behind us. Speeding up once again, we shot past what must have been Torsten's manufacturing company. The roadside sign had a lengthy Icelandic name I couldn't spare the attention to read, flanked by a drill bit the height of a small tree.

This neighbouring fjord, around the bend from Ísafjörður, was narrow but long, the shore road obscuring its full length beyond a gradual left-hand curve. The roadway dipped to the shore, and a utilitarian cement bridge arched and banked across the mouth of the fjord to where the roadway entered a tunnel on the opposite shore. The shaped aluminium barriers on either side of the roadway over the bridge glinted in the low-slanting sunlight. Everything else was black: steep-sided hillsides, tarmac, deep fjord water, and the sea beyond.

There were no more turnings. No more spots for a nifty handbrake turn. "We're going to have to stop and rush her. Are you ready?" I asked Chronos as we reached the bridge. Ragnhildur swung wide left, almost with our rear fender. I braked again, not as hard this time, hoping to catch Ragnhildur by surprise but also intending to come to a stop as close to her vehicle as possible so we could get to her before she could target us with the rifle.

But then, a surprise voice broke the tension as I waited for Chronos to acknowledge my plan.

"Screw that," Ashna said.

She'd been peering through the glass fragments into the chilly gap between us and Ragnhildur's raging approach. Just as the oversized vehicle passed our back left bumper, Ashna kicked the rear driver's side door open. It caught the front bumper of Ragnhildur's vehicle at a perfect forty-five-degree angle, making a wedge that brought the force of the impact into the body of our car instead of the hinge. Instead of ripping our door off, the energy of the collision was distributed between our two cars. Although I fought the steering wheel, our car veered right, while Ragnhildur veered left. It was like a reverse PIT manoeuvre, where the rear of our car forced the nose of hers off the road.

With a slowing rhythm of scrapes along the barrier on the low side of the banked bridge, our car halted. But our adversary had no such luck. The jacked-up body proved Ragnhildur's downfall. The left side of her front bumper caught the top of the barrier and cartwheeled the vehicle over the side of the bridge. I had my belt off and vaulted from my seat to the far side of the bridge. Chronos banged his door in vain against the barrier that pinned him in, so he missed the spectacle, shouting for updates.

"Holy crap, Ashna, you saved us," I said. She leant her glass-encrusted shoulder into me as we looked across the twenty-foot drop to the fjord's dark and wind-rippled surface. A swirl of icy water washed over the rear hatch of the vehicle as it disappeared nose-down into the unknown depths, bubbles accompanying its final descent. We said nothing and waited. I entertained the idea that I should dive in and see if I could rescue Ragnhildur, but in the next moment, the realities of an attempt dissuaded me.

The barest wisps of condensing breath left us as we watched the fading ripples and reducing bubbles. Did I want Ragnhildur to die or surface and laugh viciously at us? It was a question I couldn't answer without reflection; I prevaricated.

"Come on, man, what's happening?" came my friend's voice.

"Phew, there she is," Ashna pointed. Instead of a vicious sneer, Ragnhildur swam weakly, her bedraggled frame propelled by fluttering legs and one arm, the other cupped somewhere beneath her. She paused to tread water for a moment, shedding her boots and trousers so she could swim more freely. She spared a fleeting glance at us before turning onto her back and flutter-kicking toward the other shore.

Ashna shook her blanket free of the smaller shards then used it to shoo the remaining broken glass to the side of the road.

"I'd say we won the away leg too," I said to Chronos as I shouldered the warped door closed behind Ashna.

"Well, yeah, but only because we had the baby-faced assassin here subbing on at the last minute," he said. "You're a star, Ash."

She saved us again at the airport, where we made it with only a few minutes to spare, and hurriedly tried to return the half-trashed car.

"Gods, what did you do to it? You only had it four hours!" the agent asked, voice rising.

"Well, we were just driving, you know, over there in the next fjord, and … and …" I stuttered.

"And there was a rockslide. Happens, eh?" Ashna finished.

The agent rolled his eyes and prepared to say something else, but Ashna beamed him a wide smile, and he floundered. "Okay, just sign here for the insurance claim. You will find an extra twenty thousand króna charge on your credit card, Mr Redferne."

CHAPTER 10 - UNREST

Higgs

After the shakiness from our spectacular escape subsided, we chattered our way back to Reykjavik. Some things were clearer, like the capabilities of Dot's emerging tooth; it had powered my magical defensive reaction and driven the explosive rosebush growth. With Newton in a far corner of Iceland, I had no other reservoir of magic, and I'd seen my attempts often fizzle and fail without drawing on his strength. But our encounter with the sinister tentacle raised more questions than it provided answers. Where had it come from? Was it attached to a colossal creature trapped beneath the ice, or was it just a free-roaming entity without a central body? What was that coursing water that extinguished my magic? And above all, what was the hovering, armoured turtle with the dangling limbs and fiery jets? Was it in the neighbourhood and hated supernatural tentacles, or had it been fighting on our behalf?

We knew no rules for this game or its players.

The skies darkened, sliding toward the early sunset of the northern autumn, but remained clear until the outskirts of Reykjavik. Then we entered the fog, as thick as it had been this morning.

"It's tingling again," Dot said, massaging her jaw.

"Maybe it's growing more, and soon you'll be like the kid in that story, unable to bite off anything because your front teeth cannot fully close," Lars said, craning in his seat to examine her face.

"Come on, Lars, enough of the Swedish fairy tales," I said, trying to reassure Dot even though I worried about the rogue tooth's progress too. "Does it ache?"

Dot shook her head. "Not really. It's more like a feeling runs through it when there's an opposing force around. Like an ice cube reacting to a hot spoon. I felt the same thing just as that tentacle broke through the ice above Vik."

"It's probably this stubborn fog," Tam said, keeping his eyes on the road as we slowed at the city's outskirts. "The concert's gonnae be weird if it stays dead thick like this. But maybe this is normal weather here—I havenae been to Iceland afore."

I think he meant that as a joke, but a tendril of truth wriggled inside. Could the misty conditions be magically powered, and Dot's tiger tooth actually drove it away when we left town this morning? There was an easy way to find out.

When Granny gave me her gold-rimmed glasses, it confused me because the lenses were non-magnifying. Why would she even have glasses like that? But then I realised she gave them to me not because they did nothing, but because they did much more. The inscribed, antique frames may not let me see more sharply, but they sure let me see *more*. If there was subtle magic at work, it became visible viewed through those lenses, a prismatic aura pointing out invisible sources of hidden power.

I fished them from my jacket pocket and slid them up my nose. They didn't stay in front of my eyes long as I tore them away in alarm.

"Jeez, no. What the heck are those things?" I squealed. In partial disbelief, I held the glasses to my face again and scanned our surroundings.

"What? What?" Lars said. "Let me look."

Tam stopped the car at a traffic light. I passed the specs to Lars, peering at the adjacent taxi rank and the houses behind, searching for telltale signs of what Granny's glasses had revealed. Nothing.

"Thunder!" Lars said. "They're like stingrays but drifting in the fog. And look at that taxi with its driver asleep. You can barely see him, there are so many stuck to his windows and roof!"

He passed the glasses to Dot, who whipped her head around in disbelief before allowing Tam a turn. The traffic signal may have turned green, but the realisation that we were shrouded in a fog of invisible, airborne creatures sucked away all desire to drive on.

The creatures indeed resembled small stingrays, no larger than my hand. An eerie white set them apart from the grey fog, with their light blue mottling giving their cartilaginous bodies an undulating texture. Some drifted in the mist, but many clustered together. They plastered two of the queuing taxis while ignoring the other three. A window and corner of a house beyond looked to be splattered with pale pancakes, so thick were the stingrays clinging to its surfaces.

But they seemed uninterested in us; none clung to the jeep, though a few drifted past at close range, flapping and angling their pectoral fins as they wove through the fog, tails swishing behind them. The ghostly creatures gave a pedestrian with his collar turned up against the chill a wide berth as he passed unaware through a cluster.

"Yikes. I cannae un-see that," Tam said. "I kind of wish I hadnae looked. Should I even drive on? And what are they? Did you cover this in magic camp?"

"Hydrati. Dream suckers."

Lars and I jolted and turned in our seats when the answer

arrived from behind us in a raspy, squeaky voice. Sunflorin.

"What the heck, Sunflorin? How'd you get in here?" I asked. "No, wait, don't bother answering that. Tell us about these Hydrati. What are they doing here?"

"Good question, human girl, good question." Sunflorin extended a rangy arm over the seat between Lars and me, slipping knobbly blue fingers into a crevice in the leatherwork and scooting over to sit between us. Talking to an invisible person pressing against your thigh was disconcerting, but we all knew the drill and looked slightly away.

"The treaty is not specific. Hear me. Is fog air? Or water? Better to not ask a question if you do not want to hear the answer. That's it. That's what Aegir did. Took fog as part of his domain. His, his. Now the Hydrati cover the land, and we cannot do anything. Cannot break the treaty. None of us. Earth, air, fire—none."

Dot still palpated her jaw. "Are they dangerous? Why'd you say 'dream suckers'?"

Sunflorin leant back on her haunches, letting her open palms droop over the seat's edge. "Not dangerous. Annoying. Tiring. When you sleep, they feed on dream energy. Make you sleep restless. I say, you listen. Turn dreams bad or gone. Not breaking treaty. We must watch, I say. Aegir doesn't care about the treaty. Wants to get back to the sea, break old magic. Hear me. Old magic weakening, both fire and water because trolls and Aegir push the limits. Breaking rules."

Obviously a deeper conflict than I could piece together from Sunflorin's scattered speech was unfolding, invisible to us. I didn't understand the treaty references, old magic, or who this Aegir guy was.

"Sunflorin, hold on. What can we do? What's really happening here?"

The scrawny blue elf covered her face with one long-fingered hand, opening the fingers a crack to examine me with one eye. "Do what your father would do, human girl. Templeton Redferne. See him, know him. He made the truce at Vik, took the Trollheart, let old magic bind Aegir. Old magic always holds. Always, hear me. Until now."

Dot chimed in, "What did he do last time, Higgs's father?"

Sunflorin ignored that question, squirting out a word soup that hinted at a vague upcoming event. "Father is coming. Tonight, see? I will get Njarl. Convene council. Be your father, human girl. Your father." Then she winked out of existence with a muffled pop.

Tam nosed into the intersection but cast an outraged glance at his chest. "She's turned my shirt blue!"

Not just his shirt. All our clothes were blue now. Lars even checked his underwear.

CHAPTER 11 - BACKCHANNEL

Newton

Dad probably started it, our family's secret game, but I don't remember. We've played it since I was ten years old, triggering it when we felt bored, imaginative, or mischievous. We called it 'hoodwink', and it could begin at any time. One of us would signal the start to at least one other family member by tugging on a hood, or more often a shirt collar, and winking.

The goal for the game players was to get onlookers to believe something a tad outrageous. Faraday was good at it because of his natural seriousness, and people believed him because he was smart. Higgs could win over sceptics even when the story verged on unbelievable.

I remember one time we had Mum believing that Faraday had auditioned and got the lead role in the school musical. Higgs couldn't contain herself and gave the game away as she collapsed to the floor, laughing at the idea.

* * *

The fog rolled past in waves, hiding the cityscape of Reykjavik even from the city runway. We roused another sleepy taxi driver and bundled Ashna into the backseat between Chronos and me for the quick jaunt to the hotel.

"Ash! Goodness, what an adventure. Are you okay?" Dot embraced Ashna and held her tight for a good ten seconds. She and Higgs were friendly with Ashna, being the same age, but I wouldn't have called them close friends. We discovered there's something about a successful rescue mission that brings everyone closer together.

"I'm good, Dot," she breathed. "Just a bit mixed up, eh? I've got a lot of explaining to do, but I think my whole family, including me, will feel better when I'm back in Middle Ides. I did everything the wrong way."

"It's too bad the evening flight leaves for Manchester during the Piping Hot concert. That would have cheered you up a bit. But probably best to get home again, now, eh?" Higgs asked.

The girls introduced Tam before he had to head to the concert venue for obligatory meet and greet sessions— HoldiLocks had run a competition and the winners received early backstage access. Higgs had hoodie that fit Ashna, who had only what she wore as she left Torsten's. After a recap of the rescue from Ashna's perspective, Higgs told me we needed to have a private chat about something that had happened to them earlier. Taking the hint, Chronos volunteered to take Ashna off for a strong cup of tea and then on to the airport for her flight to England.

The unnerving events of the day, sandwiched between the encounters with Sunflorin, needed considerable recap, and all four of us chipped in to describe the details of our predicament. I hadn't yet had time to process it or formulate a plan when Faraday rang my mobile.

He, of course, had his own tales to tell, and we huddled around my mobile's screen. I shifted the camera as each of us asked questions. Faraday introduced us to Svetlana, and Higgs had a few pointed questions for Granny.

"You're telling me you crawled along a secret passage under the floor of your room? Seriously? Faraday didn't stop you?"

Granny tilted her head back and laughed like a gurgling drain. "Come on Higgs, when has Faraday ever been able to stop me, his sweet old grandmother? And if you'll recall, only a couple of months ago, I got swallowed and spat up by a giant toad. So crawling around in my own home, I barely broke a sweat. But I persuaded these two trouble magnets to return after a puzzled look into the glowing gap. Seemed like a good experience to talk through with you, even though they were anxious to explore."

"*Da*, we will go through and examine scene below in more detail, yes, Faraday?" Svetlana asked.

"I think so, yes," Faraday answered. "That agent, Higgenbotham, is busy with the other tunnel under Mum's shed. He's called for specialist backup. But I have two questions for you, Newt."

"Of course. Fire away," I said.

"First, do you think we should tell the UPDA about this second secret passage? It's deffo magical, which is why Granny made us retreat, but it just looks weird, not dangerous."

"Hmm. Not sure about that. Maybe hold back for now. Collaborating with Dad's murderers? Not sure I can stomach dealing with Scarlett or her former cronies ever again after her admission. What's the second question?"

"It's a timing thing. Seems too much of a coincidence that mechanical hyenas appear at the Ides Giant shed on the same day that I mention maybe Dad hid the artefact there. Could there be an information leak somewhere, or are we under surveillance?"

"It was me, Higgs, Chronos, Lars, Dot, and Tam at our end, and you were at Granny's. Everyone at both ends is sound. We were at the airport here, though, so maybe someone overheard us. We weren't as cautious with our chats as we should have been."

I figured we could work on two fronts. We wanted to know if we were under surveillance and, based on Sunflorin's ramblings, our father had presided over a magical treaty in the village of Vík í Mýrdal. I gave Higgs a surreptitious nudge with my elbow to be sure she was looking at me as I spoke to Faraday on the video call.

Before I continued, I tugged my collar and gave a slight wink. Faraday inclined his head a few degrees in response, so I knew he understood what was coming.

"We know from Sunflorin that they refer to the artefact as the Trollheart," I began. "And now that you've detected it sunk beneath the harbour at Vík í Mýrdal, Higgs can extract it."

Dot, Tam, and Lars looked surprised at that statement, but when Higgs nodded, they held their questions. Nobody had mentioned the Trollheart languishing below any harbour, but it wouldn't have been the first time Faraday produced an incredible piece of intel from the machinations of his exceptional mind. Faraday played along in a way that shocked me and headed in a direction that made me hesitate.

"Hang on a sec," he said. "I think we need to patch in Scarlett. We need to figure out how to transfer the Trollheart to Vladishenko's lab once we bring it to the surface. Give me a moment."

Faraday fiddled with his phone, and another participant joined our video call. Scarlett's face was close up to the camera, and she struggled to contain her shock at seeing all of us without invectives hurled her way.

"Scarlett, we're on the verge of retrieving the artefact in question," Faraday said, drumming the tip of a pen arrhythmically on the tabletop in front of him. "Higgs is going to use the summoner that Granny gave her last year and pull it out of the harbour at Vík í Mýrdal in Iceland."

Granny twigged to the Hoodwink game too. "I knew the

summoner would come in handy. This Trollheart thingy should pop right up when Higgs activates it," she said.

"So what time?" Faraday asked, still tapping the pen nervously.

"Concert's over at ten. We'll head to Vik right after. I've checked on motorboat rental, so I'll confirm that, and we'll head out at one a.m. to grab this Trollheart and secure it," I said.

"Piece of cake," Faraday replied. "Call me when you get it. I'll wait up. And then we can call Scarlett back and arrange to deliver the cursed thing to her."

Nice one, brother. Any eavesdroppers would now know the Trollheart was headed for the hands of the Russians.

After I disconnected the call, Dot turned to Higgs. "I didn't know Angelina gave you this summoner thing. You never told me."

"It's a family thing. I didn't want to worry you," Higgs said.

"And Faraday seemed agitated. What was all that pen tapping?"

"Oh, he always does that," Higgs said, knowing full well he didn't. I started this round of Hoodwink to flush out whoever was illicitly monitoring us, but there was something deeper in the game between Higgs and Faraday that I had failed to grasp.

96

CHAPTER 12 - SIMULCAST

Faraday

Svetlana said something, but I interrupted. "Faraday, you tapped m—"

I gave a slight nod to show her that her insight was correct, but I didn't want her to say it aloud. "Mostly to calm myself," I finished for her. "It's a habit, especially when under this degree of pressure."

Was my trust in her justified? Of all the people who'd overheard my initial speculation that something lay hidden beneath the Ides Giant shed, she was the biggest unknown. Could she be a plant from the Revision, reporting our thoughts and moves? It seemed unlikely, but I'd also ruled out Scarlett's involvement in my father's death, and that had proved a giant miscalculation.

The Revision must have had another way of monitoring us, although it wasn't clear whether they were watching the Icelandic crew or me here in Middle Ides. Possibly both.

Agent Zee popped his head around the door of Granny's room. Should I be suspicious of him, too? "I'm going to do a run for fish and chips. Agent Higgenbotham is still in the shed, trying to figure out how to get that key. He's tried approaching from both sides again, and I bought an extensible tree pruner so he could try to snip the twine while standing on the bottom stair. But same result—the key moves away to protect itself. Oh, and don't mention to him that I told you all this, or I'll get in nearly as much trouble as Scarlett did. I think you deserve to be kept in the loop here and hope you can treat me the same way."

Granny answered for us. "Ooh. I haven't had anything from the chippy in ages. Of course, you can get us some. And Faraday's told me all about you. I'll have cups of tea waiting for your return. You can eat with us up here if you like."

"Try Codforsaken, down on the High Street," I said. I didn't elaborate on Chronos and Newton's rescue mission but gave Zee a tip. "And if you mention to Vish, the proprietor, that you're ordering for me, he's likely to give you a discount. 'Redferne' is definitely a revered name in there today."

As Zee's footsteps on the sweeping stairway to the ground floor faded, I pulled out my phone and dragged one of the guest chairs alongside Granny's wingback. "Look, Newton sent me this video of him and Chronos rescuing Ashna Balakrishnan. Let's have a look."

Granny looked away for at least half of the confrontation, gasping when Chronos was flung down the steps and only turning back again when Torsten had him pinned on the kitchen floor.

"It is okay, Miss Redferne. We know everything good. We talked to Newton just now, yes?" Svetlana said, encouraging Granny to watch the conclusion. She didn't look too pleased to see Ashna walloping someone in the back of the head with a frying pan but agreed that the outcome was the correct one and that things could have gone much worse.

A niggle scraped at the far reaches of my consciousness, a connection made between this recording and something else. I closed my eyes for a few moments to review in my mind what I had just watched. There was a connection between this video and the Xi Li webcast that I had described to Svetlana as we edged through the underfloor passage. What was the link?

Bam! "Svetlana! Check this out."

I scrolled the video back to where Torsten answered the door at Chronos's knock, shirtless.

"Look there, see that tattoo?"

"Funny. You must be more specific. A *lot* more specific. I see tens of tattoos. He is like overpainted canvas."

I laughed. "Good point. I mean the one there on his wrist. The miniature star-nosed mole."

"Yes, got it. What is meaning?"

"Well, I'm not sure what it *means*, but I've seen it before. On another wrist."

I brought up the Xi Li tech webcast and paused it at the point when Xi Li pushed his glasses up, the linen cuff sliding back to reveal a ying-yang, the Greek letter omega, and a star-nosed mole. Same black ink, same stylized shape, same size.

"Now why would two men, tens of thousands of miles apart, one of them a famous entrepreneur and nanotech expert and the other a musclebound shift worker in northwest Iceland, have identically placed tattoos?"

"That part is simple. Torsten is worker at factory making something for secret organisation. One where Scarlett's sister is member, and so is Xi Li. You just discovered Revision cell in Iceland, Faraday. What could they be making?"

CHAPTER 13 - PIPING HOT

Higgs

Venturing into the fog, knowing that the Hydrati were flapping their stingray fins around us, invisible, filled me with revulsion. "Dot, can't you tell your tiger tooth to clear the fog again?" I asked.

Lars, Dot, and I sprawled in the hotel lobby. Newton and Chronos had promised to be down soon for the short walk to the city square where the temporary stage had been assembled. The temperature had dropped, and it was chilly but hadn't yet crossed the threshold to cold. At least, not what an Icelander or Lars would call cold. Although tempting to complain, I knew Lars would needle me for the rest of the day—in a good-natured way—about my softness. We had jackets and thin gloves at the ready and nursed wide mugs of hot chocolate, the froth a milk-infused brown that left darkened loops on the white porcelain as its tiny bubbles burst. It risked leaving a textured moustache if you sipped too greedily.

"I am excited to be seeing Piping Hot live, fog or no fog," Lars said. "In Edinburgh, we kind of missed most of the show, didn't we? And the concert is going to be rockin' no matter the weather, but yes, it would be better if the skies were clear," Lars added. "How about I make up a spell to wake up the luck in your tooth?"

He examined the ceiling in a squint for twenty seconds, then continued in a sing-song voice.

"This fog is creepy,
Everyone's sleepy.
To see Tam's band play,
We need it away.
Help my friend Dot
Use tiger tooth magic.
Without her help,
The show will be tragic."

The verse staggered along with rhyming and a very odd rhythm. But Lars had less aptitude for magic than for poetry, so we expected nothing more than a laugh, with him and at him. Dot cackled at the ridiculousness. My chuckles joined her laughter, and Lars smiled and looked away. Outside the hotel's plate glass windows, the streetlights remained shrouded in their misty cloaks.

With a bell chime and the rumble of sliding doors, Newton and Chronos sauntered from the elevator. Chronos was dressed in black jeans and a black collared shirt, appearing ready to step in and help concert security if they were short-staffed. Newton looked like Newton, wearing dark blue cotton trousers with a muted red stripe running their length and a polo jumper topped by an autumn jacket.

Dot pulled her stylish toque a fraction lower, guzzled her remaining hot chocolate, and handed us the VIP passes Tam had provided.

Newton clapped his hands. "We ride at ... *dusk?*" he said. "Post-dusk? *Après* dusk? Night?"

The early sunset didn't faze the Icelanders, but to us seemed bizarre. I slipped on my gloves, and we paraded as a chattering group through the hotel exit into the dim outdoors.

Lars pointed to the nearest streetlight and laughed in glee. "Look, it's working!"

The lamp brightened, and I realised he was right. The fog thinned, then dispersed under a slight breeze that tickled the night air. Within a minute, the only misty patches were the puffs of our breath as we joined the low-key hubbub of concert-goers headed in the same direction as us.

"Wow, Dot, that is a lucky tooth!" Lars said. "Do you think you could spare some luck for Ashna and prevent her from being grounded for the rest of her life?"

Newton responded in his soothing voice. "Don't worry. I'll have a word with her parents, remind them they were young once too. I think if she explains the reasons she ran off, it'll clear the air. Anyway, she'll definitely have more grown-up conversations with them after this little misadventure."

A gaggle of young teen girls alongside us, accompanied by a pair of ambivalent-looking adults, burst into an impromptu chorus of 'Flower of Glasgow'. We smiled, joined in for a verse, and strode toward the break in the cordon where tickets were being scanned, accompanied by a high-pitched and off-key rendition of the Piping Hot hit song.

* * *

The VIP area was nearly under the overhanging roof of the temporary stage's leftmost fringe. That was convenient because it lined up nicely with Tam's drum riser, so we had a good view of him flailing away in full effect. Randall Radiation's twanging bass line anchored an extended bagpipe solo as Dot and I broke away to the VIP toilets. The visit's real purpose was to evade the crush at the side of the stage and to banter without shouting over the guitars. Behind the stage, you could get by using loud talking instead of straining your vocal cords.

The stalls were open-topped, and I tried to imagine being in one under thick fog. It would have been spooky to look up, knowing there was no roof but unable to see anything above, especially if you put on Granny's specs and saw the spectral stingrays cruising overhead. Thankfully, a starry canvas opened above, even the roving stage lights unable to block out the brightest celestial objects.

Just as we were about to leave, a sea eagle with a wingspan as wide as two stalls settled on the toilets with a shrill squawk, talons gripping the back wall of the temporary structure. Normally, this would have startled anyone here for a quick handwash, but neither Dot nor I recoiled. It gazed at us with an oddly human look of compassion.

Dot rolled her eyes and muttered, "Sheesh. We never get to experience a full concert, do we?" I opened the door to the stall where the eagle had alighted. Two thunking pops announced other visitors. Sadly, this seemed commonplace to us by now.

Closing the flimsy door behind me and hooking the latch into its eyelet, I found myself elbow-to-hip with Dot, an eagle flexing its majestic wings above us, and a pair of luminous blue figures sharing standing room on the lowered toilet seat lid. The toilet morphed from white to indigo as a wave of colour crept from back to front.

"Sunflorin, stop it," the taller elf commanded, flicking the shorter one's ear tip with a spindly but large-knuckled finger.

Sunflorin cackled, making a sound somewhere between a squeal and a chicken clucking.

It had been a couple of months since we last saw Sundalfar, retreating across the ocean from Castle Ghuil on an over-inflated blowfly, carrying away the limp body of our beloved dog. I wasn't sure of the protocol for greeting an elf that had helped you in a time of grave danger, so I just asked, "I didn't think I'd see you again, Sundalfar. Do we hug?"

Sunflorin laughed again, rewarded by a sterner ear flick from her father. "We do not normally hug, not normally. We touch fingertips with friends. Fingertips, hear me. But for you, small human, we will hug."

"We can do both," I replied and leant in for a token hug first. Sundalfar's peaked ears folded back and disappeared into the thatch of blue hair that encircled the top of his head. Essences of soil, rosemary, and limes embraced my nostrils as I drew close. As I pulled back, Dot and I each matched five fingertips in turn with Sundalfar and Sunflorin.

"And who is your friend up there?" Dot asked.

"Friend. Partner. Everything. This is Njarl, king of the sea eagles, ruler of the air. Great honour. He met Father at treaty negotiation. Redferne father. Also great honour, hear me."

Njarl seemed to nod, although I couldn't be sure. "It is our pleasure to meet you, King Njarl."

The intense stare of the giant bird tickled something primal, and I caught flickers of elsewhere as the gaze burned into me. My grandmother had told me I was a tree, and I returned there in a waking dream. But this time, the dream took a twist of perception. I felt the gentle caress and almost insignificant weight of birds that rested and whittered on my branches. Feathers ruffled in the light breeze in harmony with my fluttering leaves. A muted trill wandered through my boughs from the beak of a sparrow, the ululations that human ears could not possibly decipher somehow speaking to me.

Human girl, I have high hopes for you, the bird said. I knew it was Njarl, speaking to my tree-self through the dream medium. *You can feel the air, feel the alliance, same as Sundalfar. Will you help us? I need clear air, to fly over the sea and respect its liquid power. The lines are blurred and you need to help everyone see clearly.*

As if in response to Njarl's words, my vision sharpened dramatically as the waking dream faded, and for a moment I experienced what it must be like as an eagle scanning for prey. I saw the texture and brush strokes of the paint that covered the stall walls. The lights at the far end of the park, facing the stage, lit throngs of circling insects, and I could pick out the flies from the gnats. Amazing! There was so much we humans, with our stunted senses missed in the natural world. I was elated and nervous at the same time, realizing the connection between my tree-self and this majestic bird. Before I shook away the visions, I shivered my leaves to communicate back to Njarl's spokesbird.

"I don't know *how* I can help, but I promise I *will*," I signalled.

Dot punched me playfully. "Are you still with us, Higgs?"

This broke my connection to Njarl, and I nodded again in his direction. Dot and I listened intently as Sundalfar described the current predicament, interjecting with questions where needed. With animated gestures and intermittent chastising of Sunflorin, who gradually transformed every feature of the toilet stall a varying shade of blue, our elf friend summarised the situation.

My father had brokered an arrangement between the four forces of nature in Iceland. The elf domain was earth, but they had an ages-old arrangement to share power over both earth and air with the sea eagles and their king, Njarl. Trolls governed fire, including the volcanic currents that circulated beneath Iceland. The final domain was the water, ruled over by Aegir, who Sunflorin had mentioned earlier.

The four forces had lived in balance for hundreds of years, bound by something that Sundalfar called 'old magic'. It regulated strict ethics by rationing and balancing the magical powers on which all four domains relied. The old magic was like a watering hole in the desert, which needed equitable sharing to keep the fragile ecosystem balanced. As Sundalfar explained it, there were six principles.

The first was 'no direct conflict'. The four forces had to work alongside each other.

The next was 'no direct help'. Although the domains could co-operate, they couldn't gang up on each other.

Two more rules governed rule-breaking: If the principles were violated, magical power would ebb from the rule-breakers. And if there was a dispute over territory, resources, or exercise of magic, the domains must self-regulate and come to a truce, or their magic would drain away.

The last two rules were constraints. Interference with humans, animals, or plants was forbidden. And lastly, each domain had special dominion. Their use of magic was constrained.

"So a troll cannot do any magic related to water, for example?" Dot asked.

"No spells, definitely no. Not even going into water. Walking through river. Taking boat on ocean. Nothing. This is why trolls need to make land bridge to your country and grab the Trollheart. I say, I speak."

"A land bridge?"

"It started already," Sunflorin said. "Trolls make volcanoes on the south coast to form new land. See it, believe it. Eventually it will reach top of Scotland. Eventually, I say."

I laughed at the ludicrousness of this idea. "That'll take forever. It's way too far for that plan to work."

"Trolls not very good at plans. Or time. Bad at time. Forever seems not so long to them."

"And why don't they have the Trollheart already? Is that part of the conflict?"

"No, no. Not part of conflict. Part of treaty. Aegir was sending his parts up rivers and blocking trolls from action. Could not travel. Meddling with volcanoes. Not allowed, never. Magic leaving both of them, but Aegir didn't care. Would destroy both. Aegir very good at anger, not so good at co-operating. Rules not designed for this, if water wanted to take fire down with it. Rules, rules, rules."

"So fire and water weren't getting along, as usual. And that's why you needed the clarifying treaty?" I asked.

"Yes. There is one more old magic rule. Keep balance. Old rule. If three domains agreed and had blessing of a judge from the stonekeeper's guild, we could build treaty to penalise the fourth domain. Unexpected circumstances, this rule. Nothing is perfect, so we need a way to solve."

"My father was part of a stonekeeper's guild?" I asked.

"Not stonekeeper, no. All stonekeepers died over four thousand years ago. Just a name, hear me. But I met father Redferne when he was building a small machine to detect magic. Right in the middle, middle. Middle of Iceland. Saw me, heard me. I mentioned to my father, the elf king, that this man could take the role of stonekeeper for the problem between trolls and Aegir. Treaty location arranged. Treaty stone taken to Vík í Mýrdal. Earth, air, fire all came to the call. Water did not. Treaty was that water domain would be confined to ice, not ocean. And to make sure trolls did not retaliate, Trollheart was to be taken away from Iceland. Old magic bound Aegir into the glacier, body and tentacles. Made way for Trollheart to pass away from Iceland without crossing water or air. Special way, special. Not through air, not over water. Hear me."

"Wait, wait! Tentacles? This Aegir has tentacles? Is that what attacked us above Vik?"

Sundalfar nodded solemnly. "Yes. Very big creature. Like octopus. Very powerful, in water. Powers limited while confined to the glacier, but if a tentacle ever reaches the ocean, his full strength will return. Probably break free, free. That attack on you will drain away more of his magic power. He cannot interfere with you directly like that. Very naughty, very angry, very rule-breakish. Naughty, I say. Octopus is Aegir.

Aegir is octopus. Octopus prince. Something freeing him. Not Trollheart, I say and say again. Some other power. Ice becoming water. I fear as he breaks more rules, his magic—our magic—gets weaker, but he gets freedom. Soon he will be just a normal octopus with no special powers, and he will take the angry trolls into powerlessness with him."

"Hmm. I'll add 'survived attack by Octoprince' to my CV" Dot said.

Sundalfar continued. "Now he sends his kin from the sea through the air. The *air*. Air is for Njarl, not Aegir."

"Technically, those things only fly through the fog, which is water," I said.

"Rules, rules! See? Aegir tries to make *new* rules. Tries to break old magic."

"Sounds like you need to co-operate, instead of having a vague treaty where one group gets thrown into a leaky jail," Dot said.

"Yes, yes. Old way. Peaceful way. But Father not here to help clarify. Soon earth and air get involved, and all magic will break. Treaty broken, co-operation broken. All lost."

"This Octoprince seems hella angry. Maybe once he escapes fully, he'll slither back to the water and not bother the trolls anymore. Why don't you forgive, forget, and help him return to his normal life?" I asked.

"What? Break treaty *and* old magic rules? No helping. Magic would go away for earth, air, fire, *and* water. All domains, hear me. Maybe father Redferne told you more rules of the treaty? Rules to handle current conflict without all magic fading?"

Njarl ruffled his wings and gave a discouraging screech at the direction this discussion was taking.

I shook my head and sighed. "He didn't even mention the treaty, let alone expand on any missing rules. I don't see how we can help. Especially not against a power as great as the Octoprince, who isn't playing nice anymore."

The refrain of the Piping Hot song faded into a thrashing of the cymbals and the roar of the crowd. Into the break in the music, the lead singer, Peter Piper, cajoled the audience. "The fog may be rolling back in, but it's not gonnae take away our fun, is it, Reykjavik?"

The crowd cheered and screamed in response.

"One more time, Reykjavik!" Peter crooned into the microphone. "Are we having a good time?"

An even louder round of thunderous cheering swept over the city square. Tam's drums thumped a steady beat, joined a few bars later by Randall Radiation's rumbling bass line. They milked this for thirty seconds before a choppy guitar riff broke cover, and Peter Piper sang once more.

The fog rolled in, thick and fast. The open-topped toilet stall transformed from moonlit to miasmic during the song's first verse. Then it poured.

But it didn't pour from the sky, like a normal storm. Water surged from mid-air. A spout of cloudy white water splashed to one side of the toilet, as if an unseen orderly had tipped a massive ewer of milk-infused liquid in a stream between Njarl and the two blue-skinned figures. The continuing stream emerged from mid-air, just beside the toilet bowl, and was ankle-deep within a few seconds.

Sundalfar and Sunflorin shuffled their bare feet, so all four heels hung over the lip of the toilet cover furthest from this unexpected deluge.

"See!" Sundalfar wailed. "When a bank of fog touches Aegir, he claims the whole thing as his domain. But it's air, I say, air!"

Njarl flapped his wings in agitation, rising so his claws maintained only a tenuous hold on the stall's rear wall. Dot and I instinctively stood on tippy toes to avoid the spreading flood. I only said, "What the ...?" before a sharp line of pain blazed across my right ankle.

I shifted weight to my other foot and shook my right leg in an automatic response. That's when I saw it. A crab claw, white and mottled with red veins, clamped around my sock, a crab the size of a volleyball dangling beneath.

In horror, I flailed my leg, succeeding only in ratcheting the crab from side to side, its cruel claw sawing through the fibres of my woolly sock. Dot was much more effective than I. Despite her shriek, she was all action, lashing out and catching the crab with a forceful kick that both released it from my leg and punted it back into the milky liquid so we could see only its grasping claws waving above the surface. I clutched my right leg beneath the knee to inspect the damage. An angry gouge peeked through the gap in my sock that was shredded for half its circumference, blood seeping. I was about to pull the sock back for a closer look when Dot shouted a warning cry.

"Higgs, watch out! There's more."

One had attacked Dot, clamping only her trouser leg as she took evasive action. Others surfaced from the cloudy water, as if spawning from an obscured well beneath the turbulence at the base of the still descending cascade.

Dot kicked the clutching claw free and braced herself with her back against the side wall of the stall and both feet on the toilet seat, contending for space with the four long-toed elf appendages already there. My shoes joined them, my back pressed on the opposite stall wall.

Given the porous nature of the stall's construction, with wide gaps between the wall panels and the wooden floor, the corrupted water should drain away, flooding the rest of the open-topped structure. There was enough gap for even the largest of the thronging crabs to escape the stall. Yet the water still rose, refusing to adhere to normal laws of gravity.

Sunflorin extended her knobbly arm and formed her hand into a shape as if she was clutching an invisible stone. A wave of even darker blue infused the toilet, staining and pulsing as it passed.

Sundalfar slapped his daughter's hand away with a swift strike. "No, child! You will lose your powers. Cannot interfere! Hear me. You never hear me!"

She exhaled a harsh breath from her nose and curled her upper lip in response, but she closed her hand and silently discontinued whatever she had been about to do. Serrated claws broke the water's surface, clamouring for our feet as the churning surface rose higher, like religious worshippers straining to touch the hem of their messiah. In moments, the circling crustaceans would be atop the toilet seat.

In a precautionary leap, Dot pushed off from the toilet and dangled from the stall's upper corner, one arm gripping the door and the other, the side wall. I joined her in the adjacent corner. We tucked knees to chests in fear as the water rose. With a pair of popping sounds, Sundalfar and Sunflorin joined the flapping Njarl atop the far wall of the stall, maintaining their balance in a series of awkward moves that would have been comical in any other situation.

"Njarl!" I shouted. "The air is yours. Just summon the wind to blow this moisture away. Assert yourself, or we're going to be pinched to death."

Dot braced herself with one foot and lashed out with the other to deflect a crab that surged from the water and tried to latch onto me.

"Cannot do, cannot do, small human," Sundalfar said. "Old magic prohibits interference with other domains. We cannot act against Aegir."

"Just defend yourself!" I said.

"Not attacking us, hear me. We can get out of here at any time. Humans must defend themselves!"

The water level submerged the toilet. Dot squirmed, struggling with fatiguing shoulders and core that strained to keep her knees bent as the rising water approached our feet.

"But you can defend yourselves if attacked by humans, right?" she called.

"Of course, yes. Defend, yes. Unless captured, like at Castle Ghuil. You know, you know."

I felt my adrenaline kick in, and leafy shoots crept from beneath my shirt cuffs as my magical defence instincts stirred. But why was Dot asking whether Sundalfar and Njarl could defend themselves against humans? Like a whip cracking inside my head, I realised what she was thinking. I closed my eyes and focussed, hoping that my core muscles wouldn't relax too much and allow my legs to dangle into the crab-infested waters.

In a leafy lightning strike, a spiral of tangled, rooty-looking vines shot from my left hand. Newton must be close enough that my defenses could draw some power from his reserve. My efforts felt limp, as if I waved away a fly instead of swatting it, but languid magic flowed. The vines sped along the wall of the cubicle, turned the corner to the back wall, and ensnared Njarl's talons. My hair was a leafy crown, and I felt clover sprout from my eyelashes as my eyes burst open in rage. Not rage at Njarl, though I wound the vines tighter around his prodigious claws. Rage at the Octoprince.

"Come on, Njarl! Blow me off you! It's the only way you can *defend yourself.*"

Sunflorin laughed deeply, teetering on one leg, and looked up at her father with bushy eyebrows rising almost off her forehead. Njarl flapped, pulling away powerfully, and I felt my vines strain and fray.

"Ah. Yes, yes. I see. Defend yourself, Njarl!" Sundalfar called. "Bring the wind. Defend yourself from the humans!"

With a screech that pierced the night air, drowning out even the stacked amps powering Mal McChord's electric guitar, Njarl's wings stopped beating. He hung in the air, feathers spread in an outrageous fan, neither rising nor falling.

Sundalfar and his daughter took the tense pause as an opportunity to squat and grip the walls of the stall, both with hands and curled feet.

Njarl swept both wings down in a mighty flapping motion, wingtips touching, a handspan from my nose. An intense gust of wind accompanied the gesture, blasting the fog away in a single gust. The moon burst into view overhead, and the ghostly liquid filling the stall became subject to the normal laws of physics once again. With a whoosh, it dispersed through the gaps between the floor and the raised sides of the stall, flooding the open-topped structure and rushing beyond in a matter of seconds.

Distant birdsong spoke to me, and I could feel Njarl's role in this communication only I seemed to comprehend. *You are clever, hatchling. Keep following your heart, and doing the right things.*

The sinister crabs lost all interest in us, and those that remained on the floor of the stall scuttled off to find shelter and darkness.

"Yeah, run away silly crabs! Water keep out of earth and air territory, I say," Sunflorin giggled.

Shoulders and abs burning from the strain, both Dot and I slid ourselves to the floor.

"Oh, sorry," I said to Njarl, uncoiling my wilting vines from his straining talons. "And thank you for defending yourself."

The great eagle shook his claws, flapped to maintain elevation while tilting his angular face at us, and clucked for a moment before wheeling and gliding away into the night.

"Ideas like that are what we need, small human. Ideas."

Sundalfar and Sunflorin thunked out of existence. Dot and I contemplated our soaked shoes and my bleeding ankle as Piping Hot raged into 'Flower of Glasgow'. I'd meant to ask Sundalfar about what happened to our dog, Disco, and rued the missed opportunity.

CHAPTER 14 - TXT

Faraday

The fish and chips from Codforsaken were particularly enjoyable. Either locating the cook's daughter lends an extra air of satisfaction to an already great fish supper, or perhaps Vish added extra care. He'd probably tell me he sprinkled parsnip powder into the batter to jazz it up—an addition I would rather remain his trade secret. We washed it down with cups of tea in Granny's room.

I felt as if events cascaded all around me, refusing to let me participate. A concealed tunnel ran beneath my mother's lab, but the UPDA had banned us entry. In Iceland, my brother and sister would try to ensnare whoever was monitoring our communications once the Piping Hot concert finished. The Revision must have a cell there that we'd uncovered by accident, linked to Xi Li. And a secret passage beneath our feet held yet another magical opening that we'd neglected to mention to the UPDA and we held off exploring any further under Granny's advice.

I paced back and forth, consulting my father's wristwatch several times per minute.

"Look at him, Miss Redferne. One of us will have head exploding before one o'clock event in Vik. How about Faraday and I take closer look at crawlspace? We will just look, not do dangerous thing," Svetlana said.

Maybe my pacing accomplished something. It probably wore out Granny's patience quicker than it wore out the track I followed across her rug. "Oh, alright, just be careful. *Very* careful. And call back to me everything as it happens. I don't think my knees can take another crawl just now."

I needed no second invitation. "You know the way, Svetlana. Let's go."

We both grabbed our backpacks this time; there was no telling what we might encounter, so having a cattle prod, the UPSCALE, and assorted nanotech might come in handy. Svetlana slid herself through the still-open hatch in the base of Granny's closet, and I followed at her heels.

By my estimation, the glowing blue opening in the crawlspace's floor should expose the dining hall on the ground floor. But in actuality, it led to somewhere entirely and impossibly different.

The rectangular gap in the floorboards could comfortably allow a person to lower themselves through to a narrow staircase. Like the steps descending from the lab, the first few steps would need a spot of contortion before allowing full headroom, but it looked to be more inconvenience than obstacle.

"If these stairs obeyed any kind of natural laws, they'd pass right through the dining hall and halfway to the storerooms in the basement," I said to Svetlana as we took positions on either side of the opening.

"Above natural laws, for sure," she said. "Like you and me, yes?"

"I'd say we are exceptional. This is impossible. But I'll take that as a compliment. And so should you."

"Enough chit chat. We go now. I see something at bottom, where steps end."

Svetlana lowered herself on straining triceps through the opening and bumped down the first few steps on her behind before standing up and beckoning.

"Stairs are cold, but I am still alive. Get down here. We can update Granny in a minute."

I followed suit and shortly stood on the widening and gently curving stairs beside Svetlana. "This is similar to the steps under Mum's lab. The same kind of magic made these. No doubt. And there's something down here. Looks like an odd, one-person all-terrain vehicle at the base of the steps. But let's go slowly."

We descended side by side, each additional step a ginger evaluation, accompanied by a report shouted up to Granny. Aside from the sourceless and unnatural hue of the illumination, we could have been exploring a factory basement. None of the dust and musty air of the crawlspace here; the steps and the corridor leading away from their base looked either meticulously cleaned or resistant to dirt. If I'd magicked up something on this scale, I'd have made it self-tidying too.

It was indeed an ATV with its wheel nudged against the bottom step. Not any model I was familiar with, but its low centre of gravity and extended leatherette seat were typical. The trim and the seat matched the colour of the effusive light, as if the ATV came as a free bonus if one ordered a magical, underground tunnel.

When I reached the second-to-bottom step, Svetlana at my shoulder, we could see the length of the passage that extended beyond the ATV. It looked perfectly level, walls seamless and extending endlessly away. Like an ocean vista, my brain couldn't comprehend the distance before us. The stairs turned 80 degrees as they descended, so the tunnel headed a smidgeon west of north, by my estimation.

Using her phone camera, Svetlana had already photographed the steps, the corridor, and the ATV from as many angles as she could manage while scuttling back and forth on the second step. "Should we inspect vehicle?" she asked.

I was taking photos of my own when a text message popped onto my phone screen. My brain couldn't ignore the message that appeared, and I held up my palm to stop Svetlana while I dealt with it.

> Faraday. Yours was the only number I could remember by heart. 3141 5926. First eight digits of Pi. It's Mum. They have me trapped in this lab, but they left a network hole open to this text message relay server. I hope you still use this number.

The sender's number showed up as a string of zeroes. Whoever sent this should have known it was not at all amusing. Even my fingers felt the heat of internal rage as I typed a quick reply.

This is not funny. Who are you, really?

The reply came at once.

> It's really me. They kidnapped me from the Feynman Centre. I know I've been gone a long time, but it took me an age to discover this gap in their security. I couldn't message before now. Let me prove it's me.

I'm waiting. What's the proof?

> When you were little, your favourite story was Percival's Purple Planet. I read it to you every day at bedtime for almost a year.

<blockquote>When you were learning to ride a bicycle, you scraped your left shin on the pedal and still have a faint scar there.</blockquote>

That was almost enough to make me believe. How could anyone outside the family know those things about me? I turned to see Svetlana taking measurements of the staircase as I considered some question that could prove the texter was my mother.

What was my name for those bullies that kept bothering me at primary school?

I made Mum promise never to tell anyone my private name for the girls that made fun of me, lest it get back to them and make my school life doubly miserable.

<blockquote>The Ugly Hearts. See? It's me. I know it's been several months since they took me, but is the search still on? Who's trying to find me?</blockquote>

It had to be her. Nobody but my parents could know those things.

Mum. I saw your dead body. You had an aneurism, I think from absorbing some uncontrolled nanotech. I even saw you cremated.

<blockquote>Really? They must have faked it somehow. Could they have swapped in another person's body?</blockquote>

Hang on. Mum, I don't know if my phone is safe to use for these messages. I think whoever kidnapped you might have hacked it. We know they are listening

in on us. We need to find another way
to communicate.

> This is the only opening I can see from
> the computers I'm using in the lab. And
> I could only add one number to the
> contact list - yours. But I think I
> know how they listen in. One of the
> first things they had me work on was
> how to extend my audio nanoclusters so
> we could mix them into commercial
> products. I'd been working on this tech
> docket for the government in my old
> lab. I amped up the signalling ability
> so it could piggyback on nearby phone
> towers and stream a high-quality audio
> relay. They're probably using that to
> eavesdrop. I provided them an exact
> formula for the compound that could
> hold it without diminishing the signal.
> I can send you the tech specs.

Please send. I need to talk to Granny,
then I'll text you back.

I motioned Svetlana to abandon the second step as I rushed up to clamber into the crawlspace. My mother was alive and needed to be rescued. Svetlana's brow furrowed into a deep but attractive V, and I understood her confusion. Abandoning one of the most interesting scenes in my life because of a text message?

I tried to explain as we shuffled along the crawlspace.

"I know, I know, you want to hear why we should leave a mega-intriguing magical staircase with an infinite tunnel at its bottom, right?"

"Well, yes. We should investigate vehicle at least. How did

it get there? And where is light coming from? Many questions. Who was text from?"

"A dead person. I need to tell Granny too, so I'll explain when we get to her room."

I popped my head up through the trapdoor in Granny's closet, starting my sentence even before I cleared floor level.

"Granny, you won't believe this. I just got a text, and it's from—oh … hello, Agent Higgenbotham."

The UPDA agent's lips formed a tightly pressed, expressionless line as he offered me a hand from the threshold of the closet. "So what's this I hear about a magical staircase? A limitless tunnel?"

CHAPTER 15 - FIRM FOOTING

Faraday

That was careless, letting Agent Higgenbotham find us climbing out of the secret passage. There was no concealing it after that, so I briefed him on our discovery. He'd called his two agents from the hut outside to investigate this new revelation. I watched with the bitter taste of despair in my mouth as the three of them entered the passage.

"I can't sit on my hands, waiting for a report from Iceland. There must be *something* we can do," I said, complaining to Granny and myself simultaneously.

I'd realised I couldn't even talk to Granny about Mum's text unless we knew if we were being overheard. I needed to bounce the situation off *someone*. My life was just getting back to a semblance of normality, but this threw a spanner into my grief. How could I function under this cloud of uncertainty about whether my mother had even died? I'd tried to fill the hole her death had left in my heart by filling it with study. Study of her work. It was getting to the point where continuing her work filled me with a feeling of kinship beyond the grave, rather than shining a continual spotlight on the loss. The texts, if they were really her, had sent me cartwheeling into unknown territory.

"Tell me about other tunnel," Svetlana prompted. "Was it same as this one? Those silly men wouldn't let me get closer than ladder leading to lab."

"It was similar. Same lighting, same materials, although the tunnel with the key had walls made from stone blocks. The left had one had these—"

My mouth must have hung open as I brought a scene from earlier that morning into focus. I didn't want to utter my thoughts out loud in case our adversaries were listening in, so I held up a finger to signal Svetlana to have patience while I scrambled to find a pen and paper on Granny's bedside table. I wrote my thoughts and transcribed the nanotech and chemical formulation details that were in Mum's text message.

When she looked at the explanation I'd written and the side research I'd asked her to do, she nodded and smiled.

"Granny, we're zipping home to get some equipment. We'll be back in like fifteen minutes."

"Are you sure it's safe there, Faraday?"

"What, safe like here at the Orphanage where if you don't get attacked by mechanical hyenas, you risk getting swallowed by a giant toad? Yeah, it's about that safe." I gave her hand a reassuring clasp.

Granny shook her head but smiled broadly. "Redfernes, eh, Svetlana? There's always something occurring."

* * *

"Look at this equipment," Svetlana said. "This is your mother's *private* lab? Imagine what she had at Feynman Centre! Is that mark seven nano-fabricator?"

"It's a beta mark eight, actually. But look here."

I held one of the spring-loaded struts I had glanced at earlier this morning. It was designed to lock into place between two

124

solid walls, gripping with rubberized feet. And it looked like it would fit nicely across the tunnel beneath the Ides Giant maintenance shed.

I tapped but did not send a message on my phone and showed Svetlana the screen. *If my father stored the key in that tunnel, I think he used these struts to climb across to it without touching the floor.*

Svetlana nodded and gave a thumbs up to my idea. Then she took the phone and wrote back.

My cousin looked at formulation. He is polymer chemist. I had to wake him up, but it was simple for him. He says water-based glycol suspension containing fixing polymer. Medium strength glue but washes away easy. Nanotech held inside suspension. With esters added to give smell.

"Smell?" I tapped. In the back of my mind, I wondered what other information Svetlana might be feeding back to Russia, but I put my doubts aside and focussed on the information.

She wrote: *Coconut smell.*

My eyes widened. That's what they were using to eavesdrop? I plopped my laden backpack to the floor and pulled out the UPSCALE. I beckoned Svetlana to follow me as I raced upstairs and raided the bathroom cabinet.

Extending a syringe from the body of the UPSCALE, I snatched a flexible tube of hair gel and pierced it to allow the analysing nanotech to flow from the UPSCALE and do its inspection. 27 seconds later, the results were visible on screen. It detected nanotech with 4G cellular transmission capability in significant amounts.

I turned off the UPSCALE and ran with the tube into our back garden. With as powerful a heave as I could muster, I flung the tube over the back fence into the scrubland beyond.

"Bloody hell," I said to Svetlana, who stood silently laughing at my agitation. "HoldiLocks. They've impregnated it with eavesdropping tech. Now we know who's responsible for us being overheard."

"Brilliant! Now we can talk, not write?"

"There's so much to say. Let's start with my not-so-dead mother, move on to how this proves her kidnap by the Revision, and figure out how to test my theory about the extensible struts and the dangling key. It might take longer than the drive back to the Orphanage allows, but I'll try to be brief."

CHAPTER 16 - PATROL

Disco

The family pack would return here, to the black sand beach. I could feel it.

My new pack fixed me. They fitted me in a warm shell so I looked like them. Covered my head to protect it from the fire and heat. Made the oval windows so I could see out. Everything looked red.

The little blue people visited me in the place of fire, and showed me how I could move, now that my legs could not hold me up. How I could hover. How I could make my own fire. How to let the special feelings from my shell tell me where to go. Where I was needed. Maybe I had three packs now—family, fire, and blue.

When I was a puppy, I could jump. After the car tumbled and I breathed the smoke, I could *really* jump. But with my new shell I could fly!

The family pack never seemed to know how much help I gave. They might never know how I protected them this time.

I let the sand drag past my paws. Felt where the attack would happen.

The cliffs smelt like burnt plants. The road above looked warm, but I didn't touch it. Beyond, the short grasses of the slope were the last green before the ice. I climbed.

The glacier. It would come from the glacier. Again. I patrolled the cracks.

Long ago, after I skidded on the car's roof, I breathed in that smoke, and I could run really fast. And jump high. But now I went even faster. Higher.

I wished I could sniff and lick at the cracks in the glacier. Tell when they might burst open again. But I watched. Fused them shut with my fire if they looked suspicious.

If I could keep the cracks closed for just a little longer, I could protect my three packs.

CHAPTER 17 - DECOY

Newton

Tam parked the jeep by the row of beach huts at the fringe of the black sand just beyond the darkened village of Vik, and I pulled the second car alongside. A pat of my inner breast pocket double-checked that the keys to the rental boat were still safe. The owner had dropped them off to me at the hotel as he escorted his daughter to the concert. I'd thanked him for the hand delivery and passed him an autographed souvenir tartan Piping Hot scarf, courtesy of Tam.

Before we'd oriented ourselves and figured out where the boat lay moored, Tam sprinted to the beach, flinging off his shoes and socks. With his sleeves and trouser legs rolled up, he waded into the lapping waves, bent double, and ducked his head multiple times, scrubbing his scalp as if washing his hair for the first time in a month.

Higgs looked at Dot for answers. "What the heck is that all about?"

"I'm as confused as you," Dot said. "So weird."

Wet, his normal frontal sweep of hair descended below his nose. He wrung out the fringe as he jogged back, shoes in hand.

"Better hope your sponsors at HoldiLocks don't get a

paparazzi photo of you like this," Dot chided.

"Ahh, about that," Tam said, settling on a kerb and giving his feet a rudimentary brush off before pulling his socks and shoes back on. "None of you use HoldiLocks, do you?"

We shook our heads, Chronos laughing and running his hand through his bristly crop.

"Okay, good. Faraday texted me just now. Said tae keep quiet until I'd washed my hair thoroughly. Apparently HoldiLocks is infested with wee listening tech. Put there by this Revision organisation. Dead sneaky."

"You mean they've been hearing everything we've been saying through your hair product?" I asked.

Tam nodded. "Aye, seems like it. I cannae believe it. Anyway, he thinks we can speak freely now, and he's got a lot to tell you."

My brother picked up after the first ring. "Did Tam wash it out?" he asked before even saying hello. When I confirmed, he continued. "Excellent. I figured out a few things and have something unbelievable to tell you, but I know your timeline, so call me right after this Trollheart summoning. Oh—expect some help if it's needed."

* * *

It would have been a foolish plan just to show up at our Hoodwink rendezvous and wing it. We had a few tricks up our various sleeves.

Our priority was safety. Now that the danger of being overheard was reduced, I brought the others up to speed about the Hoodwink. Knowing our activities were a sham, everyone needed to be prepared to expose a cell of Revision conspirators. Higgs, Dot, and I would go in the boat because we were the best suited to handling magical matters.

One spell Dot was adept at was a floatation charm. Using a

mixture of autumn leaves, vegetable oil, and candle wax—all ingredients readily available in Reykjavik—she could craft a lotion that could make anything float on water. We'd steeped our shoes in it. If anything happened to our boat, we could escape on foot. I was there to act as the battery for Higgs's blazing reactive magic if threats appeared—and to drive the boat, I guess, making me feel less like a non-magical third wheel whose only purpose was to power up my talented sister.

Tam and Chronos would be ready in the massive jeep to surge into action if needed. Lars had pleaded to join us in the boat, but Higgs would have none of it. She gave him a lingering hug and handed him one of the walkie-talkies we'd bought in Reykjavik. The flare gun from the jeep's emergency supply cache and a pair of binoculars gave him a sense that he was part of the mission, but really, I think Higgs just wanted to keep him out of harm's way. He would remain as an observer, stationed by the row of beach huts, out of sight.

Before stepping onto the jetty, where an array of motorboats lay moored, I approached the shallow water at the shoreline and tested my magic-infused shoes. For a distracting moment that relieved some of my nervousness, I chuckled in glee as my hiking boot found purchase on the water's surface. It wasn't just that my shoes floated, bobbing in the water, it was as if the surface of the water was solid. I took another step which found the seawater spongy but supportive, and I bobbed along with the ripples. I walked to the slightly deeper water. It was a little unsteady underfoot, but as long as the sea remained relatively calm in the bay around Vik, walking would be like traversing a patch of overgrown wild grass. Higgs and Dot joined me for a moment, testing their balance before hopping to the jetty and following me to the boat, moored exactly where its owner had described.

Darting glances as we moved along the dock, I scanned for activity in the other boats. It was possible that someone lurking nearby might ambush us, but I noted no suspicious presence. I hopped into our vessel, rocking it as I surveyed its layout.

Before boarding, Higgs leant to Dot's ear and whispered intently. I didn't pry but as they hugged before stepping from the jetty to languid undulation of the boat, I paused to consider whether this was the right path. I'd dragged them along with me into a situation where we were essentially bait for an international conspiratorial organization. Would this be an act I would later regret?

I dropped the red plastic milk crate I had asked to borrow from the hotel beside the captain's seat and shone my flashlight around the boat. I had driven motorboats before in the Lake District and was reassured by the familiarity of the controls. The calm sea buoyed the boat and my confidence. Embrace complete, Higgs and Dot eased from the jetty into the boat and made themselves as comfortable as possible on the dew-laden, padded benches behind my chair. A canvas awning overhung the seating area, but the cool night air and sea spray would buffet us when we got underway.

I untied the lines fore and aft that tethered the boat to the jetty and raised the rubber bumpers so they wouldn't bounce once at sea. I shoved off with a foot nudge, and the water craft drifted from the mooring. "Bundle up, girls. We won't be going far, but the breeze will pick up once we get motoring."

With a turn of the key, I started the ignition. Water gurgled beneath the hull, jetting out behind the boat a moment later. Easing the throttle and spinning the ship's wheel, I guided us away from the jetty and cruised into open waters. We bobbed more energetically once away from the dock's protection, but the low waves made for easy navigation. Opening the throttle, we were off into the dark ocean, light spray tearing our condensing breath away from our lips.

I didn't feel too comfortable in the open water, so I cut the engine when we had gone only a hundred metres offshore. The black sand beach was a vague line, the cliffs looming above it barely visible in the nebulous moonlight that peeked timidly through low clouds. The distant, jagged fingers of the Reynisdrangar sea stacks clawed their way from the black waves like a mangled hand about to snatch our insignificant craft to a watery grave. Without dropping anchor, I left the boat at the mercy of the low waves.

"Are we ready?" Higgs asked. "Here comes the *summoner.*"

The Hoodwink had to look good right until the reveal, so Higgs had come prepared with a pocketful of freshly picked leaves and a clutch of redcurrant berries bought from the hotel café. These ingredients helped produce the effect of this minor spell; the one at which she was most proficient. Dot was the far better student of magic, able to navigate her way through a litany of small spells, but Higgs possessed more spectacular power that burst out when threats appeared. With much-anguished practice, Granny had coaxed her through the technique she was about to demonstrate.

Clenching the handful of leaves and berries in her right hand, she closed her eyes and tapped a syncopated rhythm on the back of her fist with her left pinky finger. She hummed as she tapped; I'm not sure if that was part of the spell, but it seemed unlikely the witches of old would have used Piping Hot's 'Home for a Rest' as their soundtrack.

Her eyes snapped open. "Bingo!" A reddish glow escaped the fissures between her clenched fingers. "Hand me the milk crate, brother."

The three of us knelt on the side bench, dipping that gunwale toward the salt water. As I dipped the milk crate into the lapping waters, letting the saltiness negotiate the sieve-like network of openings and fill it, Higgs released her glowing bundle of leaves underwater into one of the milk bottle slots. Now hard and heavy as a cricket ball, the conjured compound radiated a fierce, red light.

I'd knotted a length of twine to the corners of the milk crate that allowed me to lower it. I let it dangle a few metres below the hull and held the line taut for a minute before hauling the supposed treasure back into the air. That felt to me like an appropriate amount of time for the invented summoner to work, and as I pulled, the dim glow lit an expanding area of lapping waves. Freed, water coursed through the slots in the crate, allowing the glowing ball to burn brighter as it drained. The violent crimson of Higg's spell ball shone brightly, transforming the appearance of the water encircling us. It was as if we bobbed on a giant red lily pad. When I hoisted the milk crate and Higgs bundled it into the boat, the glow no longer shone on the waves but instead permeated the canvas overhead, giving the boat's interior and our faces a flickering red appearance.

"So *that's* what a Trollheart looks like," Dot said, smiling at Higgs's magic. I looked around at the dark waters, swivelling to survey every direction. I saw nothing, but the sound of a powerful engine roared from across the waves.

Everything sprang into frantic action at once. A brilliant searchlight flashed across the ocean-facing side of the upthrust rocks of the sea stacks. The beam of the lamp swung in reckless arcs, struggling to orient on our position from the prow of a speeding boat.

On the shore, the headlights of Tam's rental battlewagon jeep sprang into life. Its engine's growl competed with the onrushing boat as it bounced over the mounded sand at the edge of the visitor car park and jostled its way onto the beach.

A patch of red light also caught my eye, further up the beach near the huts where Lars stood; a ring of flames coursed from a shadowy form hovering over the midnight sands before zig-zagging through the air. The bouncing jeep raked its headlights in that direction, for a moment revealing Lars sprinting across the sand toward the hovering iris of flames.

Lars turned, planted his feet, and pointed the flare gun toward the jetting flame ring. Red light splashed across the cliff face as the flare arched low and fizzled at the its foot. The slash of illumination also provided a fleeting glimpse of an unanticipated horror.

Draped down the cliffside and rippling across the sand was a ghostly white tentacle, swiping at the floating flame-bound annoyance while questing for the waters beyond the beach. If that tentacle slaked its thirst for ocean water, we would all face the full powers of the Octoprince, who seemed willing to sacrifice its old magic as it lashed out in anger.

CHAPTER 18 - GROUNDBREAKING

Faraday

In a monologue that lasted for the return trip to the Orphanage, I spewed background details to Svetlana. She nodded, watching my face the whole time, which I found unnerving.

I had a thousand questions for my mother before we attempted to retrieve the key, so we parked the car on the Orphanage's gravel forecourt. I wished I could call her, but knew from her description of the text message relay she connected to that this would be fruitless. I began texting.

> *Sorry, Mum, I'm back. I should have asked earlier—are you okay? Physically? They don't mistreat you, do they?*

> Faraday, no! Of course not. I'm never cold or hungry. Nothing painful. And they let me have free run of the lab equipment. I've been able to accomplish more per day here than at the Feynman Centre, to be honest. When I get into my work, I mostly forget that I'm being held here. It's like a huge distraction, making me forget I need to

get home.

Is there any indicator showing where they're holding you? Signage? What language are people speaking?

There's no signage visible in the local camera feeds around the lab. And nobody talks to me, really. I get suggestions for experiment subjects by email. They're in English. And the computer code for the trials has comments in English, Russian, and French, but that's normal for collaborative experimental code like this. It looks like there is also a camera data feed on this text gateway. Let me work on analysing that.

Know what I'm working on now? Geothermal engineering. Extracting energy from underground heat sources. There's a new wonder nanomaterial that can use energy to regenerate itself. It's perfect for harsh environments as a platform for other nano applications.

Reconstructium? You're working with that?

Yeah—but how do you know about it? I thought it would be top secret. In high-temperature environments it's a miracle—the heat allows it to regenerate as quickly as it breaks down.

I had some encounters with your man Angus MacFarland. He showed me reconstructium in his lab. It's interesting that you have that tech in your environment.

Dad needs to get onto the UPDA and figure out where I am. Are Higgs and Newt doing okay?

I cleaned my screen by rubbing it on my shirt while contemplating what to reveal about Dad. I settled on the blunt truth.

About Dad. There's no good way to say this, so I'm just going to spit it out.

After we thought you'd died, he got suspicious that the UPDA wanted you dead, and they'd killed you in a visit to the Feynman Centre. He got hold of this magical artefact in Iceland, hid it somewhere, and threatened to use it to burn up the entire country if they didn't admit to their involvement in your death.

They killed him, Mum. The UPDA. Made it look like an accident, but I figured it out. They just admitted it this week.

Templeton? Killed? But you're my babies! Only kids. I've got to break out of here and get home. You shouldn't need to handle everything.

Don't worry about us, Mum. We're good. Granny has been helping Higgs learn to use her magic. And Newton even has a girlfriend. Let's focus on getting you out.

I wish I could send texts to more
contacts, then I could message Higgs
and Newton. And I'll scout around on
this external server to look for clues.
If we can't trust the UPDA, who can
rescue me?

I thought about Scarlett. She was the most capable person I knew. She sort of owed me, but could I countenance working with someone who had turned my whole life upside down and dumped it in the mud?

*OK Mum. Higgs and Newt are in the middle
of something, so I'll tell them
everything soon. Give me a little time.
I have to go now for a while, but keep
sending me messages with whatever you
discover about your location.*

Wait. Did you say something about Dad?
I thought you told me something
important about him, but it's just
slipped my mind. I looked back through
the texts, and one's been deleted.

They had some weird control over Mum. I couldn't understand how she'd forgotten what I'd told her about Dad moments before. Maybe they were drugging her – that would explain why she kept working and only thought of escape as a low-priority task. Whatever they were doing to her, it was upsetting.

*Nothing, Mum. I'll update you on Dad
later. Just focus. We need to figure
out where you are being held.*

"I'll grab Dad's braces, Svetlana. Let's see if we can obtain that key."

* * *

Agent Zee jogged downhill from the hut as we rounded the back corner of the Orphanage. "What's going on?" he asked.

Sensing our bewilderment, he added, "I heard the other three went down and found something in the other tunnel?"

Svetlana and I gave simultaneous shrugs. "No idea, Zee. We've just come back from my house. Popped out to see if you wanted a cuppa."

He jogged on, saying over his shoulder that he'd try to keep me updated.

"Let us go quick," she replied. "It should only take couple of minutes to get key if your theory is correct. Then we return to Miss Redferne's room."

That seemed reasonable. At least reasonable to someone like me, whose curiosity often trumped empathy or safety. I adjusted my grip on the rubber-footed struts, and we opened the door to the now-unattended maintenance hut.

"Yes, it is just like stairs under Miss Redferne room, but different," Svetlana said as we descended the otherworldly staircase. "Can I try magic?"

I waved her along the tunnel, and she laughed at the weirdness of the ever-retreating key, making three attempts to get closer to it before returning to me on the bottom step.

"Let us see it, brainbox. Is theory correct?"

"Only one way to find out," I replied. I positioned the first of the four struts at waist height in the tunnel and turned the sleeve to lock it into position. The rubber feet squeaked against the stone blocks as the spring-loaded rod exerted outward pressure. I tested it with a hand before kneeling on it and locking the second strut into place slightly beyond it. Kneeling above the floor on the first two, I placed struts three and four. Now I could lay flat, supported at my shoulders, hips, thighs, and shins.

Shuffling along on my stomach, I unlocked the first strut and repositioned it ahead of me. With each procedural shuffle, I edged closer to the key. It remained stationary, unlike every floor-bound approach. My path was lower than the rubber scuffs I had noted on the walls earlier, but the attempt was proving a success.

A few more rounds of the methodical progress brought the key within reach. I knelt on the two forward-most bars, grabbed the twine and undid the half hitch. The key was heavy and cold. Gold-plated iron, likely.

"What d'ya think? Should I jump down now that I have the key or return the same way I came?" I asked over my shoulder.

"How about you throw me key, just in case it magics back into position if you touch floor?" she asked.

Good idea. I wriggled my way through a turn to face her and gauged the headroom needed for my throw. It seemed an easy toss. "You ready?"

She nodded. My underhand throw wasn't perfect, but the catch wasn't too challenging.

"Thank you for magic key. I go back to Russia now," Svetlana said. She turned and sprinted up the steps.

My fingertips went numb, and my stomach turned over. I had been so trusting! A flush of anger followed.

Svetlana strolled back down the steps, a gurgling laugh breaking from her smiling lips as my feet hit the floor. "You should see face, Faraday. It is turned whiter than mine."

"Not funny," I griped but chuckled in relief as I unlocked the poles and tucked them under my arm. "Let's keep that key out of sight for now, yes?"

CHAPTER 19 - SUCKERS

Higgs

The action on the shore transfixed me despite the imminent danger of the approaching boat. I clung to the damp support pole and half-squatted to brace myself against the bumps as Newton let loose our engine and carved a lopsided wake to veer away from the onrushers. Dot held the twin pole on the opposite side and reached for my free hand as she jerked toward me with our boat's acceleration.

The approaching boat was a military-looking zodiac, it's toughened inflatable sides topped with a fixed rope that its occupants clung to as it shot toward us. The boat's front-mounted spotlight flashed across our faces twice, three times, before locking in on our position. It closed the gap with a speed and engine growl that told me we'd never outrun it. As it surged past us, a glance showed me four black-clad figures clinging to the side and a fifth manning the tiller at the rear. The zodiac proved highly manoeuvrable too; it swung in a tight turn and came at us again.

Dot and I lurched forward, keeping our balance only through an elaborate dance as Newton cut the engine. My focus remained on the beach, the jeep headlights and raging flames competing for my attention.

Our walkie-talkie crackled into life. Amid ragged breaths, Lars shouted down the line, "Higgs, get off the water! If we can't stop the Octoprince's tentacle from reaching the shore, you're in trouble."

"We'll try tae head it off," came Tam's reply. "I see our fiery turtle friend has come to help again, too."

I cared less about what would happen if the tentacle roused a sea-borne peril when it reached the water's edge and more about Lars confronting a pulsing menace twice their height on foot. Lars was a speedy runner, but I couldn't imagine him affecting this threat any more than a midge would stop me from hiking across a moor. His flare gun might annoy the Octoprince, but if anything, the flares added to my terror as their light revealed the scale and boneless slithering of the tentacle.

"Lars, get back to safety. You can't help here," I screamed into the communicator.

He slowed his pace for a moment, and replied. "We can always do *something*. I'm not sure what yet. Just get safely to shore."

The spotlight shone on my back, casting a long, shadowy replica of me on the rippling waves. A familiar but not unexpected voice called from the circling zodiac. Ragnhildur. Of course.

"Come along, children. Don't do anything stupid. Hand over the artefact."

I turned my head to face Scarlett's sister. Dot's eyes were locked on the shore conflict, pulsing her hand in mine. Four armed companions crouched in the boat, flanking her, rifles trained on us as best they could on the unsteady sea's surface.

In an act of defiance that deserved a special niche in Hoodwink history, Newton refused to surrender the false Trollheart. He held the crate and its glowing, throbbing content aloft, allowing the other boaters an extended look.

"This belongs to us by right. Our father preserved it to avoid the violence it can produce. Why should we give it to you? You'll use it to work against everything he lived for."

"And died for," I muttered to myself.

Ragnhildur cackled, an ugly outpouring that tainted the fresh sea air. "Because I told you to give it to me? Because we have guns? Because you're too stupid to know what you've got yourself into?"

"Maybe it's you who's stupid," my brother retorted. "You see that *thing* surging along the beach? When it gets to the water—and I don't see how my friends can stop it now—ferocious powers will erupt. You'll wish you'd stayed drying off in front of a warm fire after your cold dip in the loch at Ísafjörður . Let's all get ashore and not tempt fate."

Dot tugged my hand, and I swung to face the shore again. The moon had broken free from obscuring clouds and exposed the combat diorama at the base of the cliffs. The jeep bounced high into the air as it drove at speed over the swollen but tapering tip of the spectral white tentacle, landing on the front right wheel before rebalancing itself in a spray of sand. Encircling jets of flame beneath the hovering turtle's shell faded from view as the odd creature dipped to brand the tentacle's upper surface.

Loose rock cascaded down the cliff as the tentacle recoiled from the twin attack, reverting from a straight line seeking the caress of the waves to a double S bend at the cliff's foot. It snaked there among a trio of the basalt monoliths that dotted the beach. Lars leapt free of the retreating coils for a moment, but then stumbled and disappeared beneath the bulk of the sucker-encrusted monstrosity.

The jeep carved a crescent in the sand as it doubled back and sped toward the point where Lars disappeared. In its headlights, I saw Lars crawl free, staggering and covered in black sand. He pointed the flare gun at the tentacle's overbearing bulk and fired at close range. The sparking round bounced into the air, lighting the area, but the intended target reacted badly. With an undulating heave, the tentacle slammed onto Lars's crouching form. This attack was a direct hit and Lars disappeared from view.

As the jeep rocketed alongside the coils, its passenger door sprung open, and Chronos leant out, readying himself to leap free.

I clamped down on my communicator's 'talk' button and yelled. "Lars? Lars! Please tell me you're somehow okay."

The jeep skidded to a stop, perpendicular to the tentacle's tip. Chronos sprung free, his bladed leg flexing in a hard landing. I prayed he would scoop up Lars from some hidden cranny and carry him away like a lost puppy, but he flung himself at the wall of gristle and strained fruitlessly.

After a moment of despairing effort, he sprinted to the front of the jeep, paused, and then skirted around the tentacle's tip. Clearing it, he paused a couple of car lengths away. He gestured at the turtle that had closed in and hovered nearby, flaming undercarriage casting a pool of red light onto the black sand.

With Lars crushed somewhere beneath, the tentacle extended itself once more, slithering toward the sea. This time, it would surely succeed.

Behind me, Newton's resigned-sounding voice carried across the waters. "Okay, come alongside. I'm done here." But his voice was like a distant church bell, registering only as muted background noise. I thought sea spray drizzled onto the backs of my hands where they clutched the boat's side rail too tightly, but realized that they were my own tears. A cry of anguish tried to tear from my lips, but only silence flowed into the night.

Grappling hooks clanked onto our boat, one narrowly avoiding my foot, and cinched our two vessels together. In my peripheral vision, I barely registered that Newton held the milk crate by one edge, offering it over the side into receiving hands. A dark and angular silhouette rose from the waters just beyond the other boat as one of Ragnhildur's accomplices snatched away Newton's glowing cargo.

I almost longed for the tentacle to complete its race to the seawater, hoping its proximity had summoned an accomplice from the depths. The rising shape seemed too hard-edged to be sea life, though.

"Don't glare at your betters like that, Higgs. It's impolite," Ragnhildur called. She didn't know I wasn't looking at her but had turned in response to the dark tower rising behind her.

There was a sharp twang, and the zodiac rocked away from us, making the man holding the glowing decoy stumble back and bowl into his unbalanced mate. With a splash, a rifle dropped into the sea.

A harpoon taller than Ragnhildur stood quivering, half-upright where it had pierced the inflatable skin of the zodiac's far edge. A metallic line trailed from its end, and the sound of a winch caused the boat's five crew to turn their backs on us. The line became taut, pinning the side of the zodiac against the hull of a partially surfaced submarine. Judging by its length, this was a specialized miniature sub, no longer than a bus. And judging by the faded red star on its conning tower and the swinging blonde ponytail and familiar voice of the figure that appeared laughing from the hatch above, Scarlett had powerful Russian friends.

"Guns down, boys," she called. "Little sister, you should have gone home before the streetlights came on. Shame on you."

Amid Ragnhildur's shrieks of, "Shoot her!" I saw eight raised hands as her crew took the more sensible path.

As unexpected as this appearance was, Newton spurred us into action. "Run!" he hissed at Dot and me. "That damned tentacle is almost to the waterline."

In the lethargy and paralysis of my grief, it took me a moment to follow his order, although Dot didn't hesitate. Newton and Dot hurdled the side of the boat and were hightailing it across the water's surface before I twigged. Dot's spell! I followed, my ankles flexing on the magically solid surface of the bay as I raced against the progress of the tentacle. Maybe Lars was still alive, and I could rage against the Octoprince once again and rescue him. I had to keep my head down to find safe landing spots for my feet on the undulating surface, but spared brief glances at the scene on the beach. I wasn't sure I could make it to shore before the tentacle reached the lapping waves.

My lungs burnt as I pushed myself to keep up with Newton and Dot. Their longer legs allowed them to pull away from me at first, but with determination, I closed the gap.

As I leapt over breaking whitecaps where the sand rose beneath the seawater, I realised why Chronos had left Lars. He had a bigger plan.

All capable off-road vehicles come equipped with a winch for pulling the vehicle out of tricky spots. Chronos had unspooled the length of steel cable from the winch that lurked behind the nudge bars astride the radiator grille and laid it across the tentacle's path. It now lay beneath the suckers as the tentacle strove to cross the beach.

Somehow, he had convinced the hovering turtle to take the hook at the end of the winch line and float it across to encircle the tentacle. They were going to ensnare and tug at the tentacle using the jeep's power. The flying turtle shook the hook from its stubby neck, and it dangled in position. Their final step: to fix the hook around the wire to close the loop.

The jeep and hook were now on the opposite side of the juddering tentacle to Chronos. I expected Tam to jump out and complete the loop, but Chronos was ahead of him. There was no circling around the barrier that the tentacle presented, but Chronos took a running leap and scaled his side of the tentacle, using a tire iron like an ice axe, stabbing it into the octopus hide for leverage as he scrambled up. With two strides across the undulating top, he leapt to the sand beside the jeep.

Newton and Dot had reached the shore and urged me onward, waving me across the last waves. In my peripheral vision, I saw the writhing tip of the tentacle rising in a last surge toward the sea.

From far up the beach, Chronos's anguished cry echoed. He strained at the hook, but even with the slack afforded by Tam pulling the jeep to the puckering suckers, the chain was too short to encircle the tentacle.

I flung myself from the water, rewarded by a gobful of granular sand. "They won't manage it, Higgs. Get back from the water's edge," Dot cried, running to me.

"No!" I shouted. "I'll not let an oversized calamari beat us."

The rage of desperate defeat surged through me. I thought my temples would explode, and I felt none of the cold you'd expect from laying on a wet beach in the middle of the arctic night. The air between Newton and me crackled with static as magical power flowed from him to me.

Two strands of luminous green surged from behind me, where my feet remained in the lapping waves, straight into the deep water. My legs were no longer flesh. Instead, they were thick trunks of kelp, sprouting strands of leafy ribbons that vacillated with the surface water.

Rings of light pulsed from the depths, circling my kelp-legs. A moment before a twisting shoot of kelp stalk raced up the beach from my outstretched arm, my hair lengthened and transformed into a mop of seaweed. My other hand brushed the salty, bubble-festooned strands away from my eyes.

The tip of the tentacle reached the high water mark, and waves lapped at it. Barnacle-encrusted crabs frothed from the sea and scuttled onto the beach, claws waving in the moonlight. They paused in time with each retreating wave as the tentacle lost contact with the ocean before advancing again with the wash of the next.

My kelpy arm coursed over the sand, twisting relentlessly as it extended, strengthening itself for the trial ahead. It dipped beneath the chain at the jeep's grille, twirled up through the hook and then doubled back again. My limitless arm now formed a slip knot, completing the link between the hook and the chain.

Almost completely in plant form, I'd lost the power of speech, but Newton worked with me as one. "Gun it, Tam!" he shouted.

The sensation of hundreds of crabs clambering over my vegetated legs accentuated the urgency to drag the tentacle away from its domain. But I realised I could do better.

I willed my arm to keep extending. After knotting itself around hook and chain, I coiled the twisted stalk around one of the black obelisks near the jeep. It circled the rough rock six or seven times, biting with runner shoots as it went. As Tam jerked the jeep into motion, the slipknot locked tight to the stone monolith. The chain constricted the bulging tentacle, growing tighter as the jeep strained.

With the jeep's first motion, it dragged the tentacle from the water's edge. Newton had fallen to his knees, bristled with crabs, but they withdrew their pincers and turned their carbuncle eyes to the moon, awaiting further instruction.

The jeep's engine screamed. All four wheels sprayed clods of sand. It pulled the tentacle even further from the shore as the chain tightened. My kelp-bound arm felt like it was being wrenched from its socket, fingers clenching the rough surface of the rock, barely maintaining their grip. Sinking lower as it excavated sand, the jeep found purchase on a buried rock shelf. With a sickening pop, the chain bit and scythed through the tentacle's toughened skin. Bluish-white ichor spewed from the wound, spattering the sand with luminescent, steaming clumps.

With a surge of power from the jeep's engine, the slipknot tightened again, this time amputating the nightmarish tentacle. Residual tension in my magically enhanced limb faded, and I allowed the fronds and runners lashed to the rock to release their binding. The severed length of sucker-clad madness spasmed and squirmed away from the flailing trunk. Luckily, it thrashed away from us, otherwise it would have crushed Newton, Dot, and me. The tentacle's stub shrank away and retreated up the cliff face, oozing from its shredded cross-section. As it vacated our view, the ground quivered and rumbled, a minor earthquake communicating the displeasure of the Octoprince.

Prolonged coughing reached my exhausted ears, and I lifted my face from the sand as the last remnants of kelp stalk snicked back and morphed into my usual but listless arm. My toes felt the icy water where my feet emerged from shredded shoes and socks. I crawled up the beach to where Newton stooped, panting.

"I want a milkshake," he croaked.

Lars shouted with glee from beyond the open doors of the jeep. His voice seemed somehow different, as if I'd forgotten it and heard it again now for the first time. "Gods, Higgs. It's lucky those two rocks were there. They kept the weight of the tentacle off me!" He coughed repeatedly but jogged a staggering path toward me. I didn't look, but Dot was likely massaging her jaw again.

Newton straightened, beckoning. I half-stood and looped an arm over his shoulders, with Dot supporting me on the other side. Then we both collapsed to our knees again, an extra wave of fatigue passing across me like butter smeared across warm toast. "How about a latte? And a big screen TV, so Lars and I can watch from under a giant duvet? I'm right there with you. I'm so tired."

Tam's heels skidded to a stop at Dot's side. "Are you okay? And Higgs? You saved us. Let's get back to the jeep. That jerking, diabolical thing on the beach is giving me the creeps."

"If only we had a friend that could carry two exhausted Redfernes across the beach," Chronos boomed as he joined us. Newton was reluctant to stand, but a firm grip on the nape of his jacket and an enthusiastic haul from Chronos brought him staggering to a stand. Lars supported me, too, and we hobbled our way to the vehicle, shedding sand with each weary step.

Before we could leave, a pair of cars screeched to a halt in the visitor's car park, their light blinding us.

CHAPTER 20 - RE:MORSE

Newton

The only part of the plan that proved well-considered was that I had brought along hotel towels. I was expecting to brush salty sea spray from our hair, not to contend with a soaked and barefoot Higgs, Lars caked in sand, and Chronos splattered in sticky remnants from the massive tentacle amputation.

The two cars that arrived as we stumbled to the jeep held the town's lone police officer and a pair of scientists who felt the minor earthquake. They had come outside to check it wasn't the precursor to the under-glacier volcano's eruption and then followed the officer to the disturbance on the beach.

Once they spotted the severed and now motionless, hulking tentacle resting among scarred trenches in the black sand, I only had to mutter a few vague words concerning sea monsters and how cold we were to divert attention away from us. The three of them jogged off across the sand, gesturing at the beached colossus. I peered across the moonlit waters and noticed the two boats lashed together and moving toward shore under the power of the zodiac's motor. I wasn't looking forward to dealing with the boat's driver; there was no sign of her submarine.

Lars brushed clods of sand off his shirt as I handed him a

towel. He trotted back to take over support of Higgs, who shivered barefoot despite her draping. "Thor's beard, your feet are turning blue. Are you okay? Let's get them under the car heater."

Chronos jogged by, carrying Dot scooped in his arms. "Lars, what kind of service are you providing? These ladies need to get warm," he said. His infectious laugh trailed behind him as he crossed the car park to Tam's battlewagon. It amazed me he could crack jokes while covered in the guts of a monster that had nearly killed us. I laughed in spite of myself, feeling my energy return.

Higgs fiddled in her jacket pocket with a shivering hand as Lars ushered her toward the car. "Where's that toque that Grover's mum knit for me? My head is freezing." Finding it, she pulled it low to her brows. Previously layered with a horizon of colours, I noticed it was now a solid, Sunflorin blue. Woolly flaps covered her ears and the chin strings dangled down either shoulder.

"Get warm, everyone," I said. "I'll be down at the shore having a word with our saviour who coincidentally killed Dad."

* * *

Scarlett tied off the zodiac to the pier and looked up as I approached. I didn't thank her, and just stared at her pale face, covered in spray beneath windswept strands of hair that had escaped her ponytail. She secured the line and returned my stare.

"Look, Newton, I know apologising for your father's death won't help, so I'll skip that part. I had to do it. But we're in serious trouble here, and even though it might feel like taking out my half-sister is a victory, she's just a puppet of the Revision."

I didn't care about Ragnhildur. I didn't even care about

victory. I cared about my brother and sister, and the way their hearts had been ripped out. I wanted Scarlett and the Revision gone, and the clocks turned back to end this nightmarish cycle of grief, revelation, and more grief.

I didn't even raise my voice, but I could feel the acid in my words burning my own ears. "You didn't have to do it. Give the order. You could have warned him. Warned us. We could have figured it out, got him to relinquish the Trollheart. But you chose to kill him."

"I tried everything I could think of Newton, but in the end, I realized that if I didn't give the order, someone else would. I wasn't going to shunt that task to some other UPDA agent, knowing I would still feel responsible, even if it was another person's lips saying the words."

"They're just kids, Scarlett. I could forgive you for putting me through this hell, but them? You're deranged scum."

She nodded to herself and looked away, wiping the sheen of moisture from her face with a sleeve. Without turning her face back toward me, she gave me a side glance. "We need a plan. Can I talk to you three alone? Can we call Faraday?"

I seethed, clenching and unclenching my fists beneath crossed arms. Her motives were still unclear to me, but I realised if I didn't let her reveal what she knew, and something happened to Higgs or Faraday as a result, I'd never forgive myself. I settled on never forgiving Scarlett instead, and turned to trudge back to the car park, assuming she'd follow.

Tam and Dot had pulled alongside the rental car in the jeep. The windows of both vehicles had been rolled part way down. Blasting heaters and murmured conversations came from each. Higgs sat in the front seat of the car, cupping her hands near the vents as the air warmed. Lars had slipped into the back seat and leant forward over her shoulder, chattering while she recovered from the traumatic events in grateful silence.

Clouds of breath dissipated in the air as Chronos raised an

eyebrow in Scarlett's direction from his position leant against the car's bonnet. I murmured a reassurance to him before I slid into the driver's seat and motioned Scarlett into the rear beside Lars. I left the window open so Chronos could hear, just in case some unexpected treachery on Scarlett's part needed him to spring into action.

Higgs snatched her feet away from the heater vent when Scarlett opened the rear door. "What's *she* doing up here," she hissed. "Come to gloat? Finished with our parents and now she wants our heads in her trophy room too?"

I clasped her wrist and tried to soothe her, the surging then recoiling vegetation shoots creeping from beneath her shirt cuff telling me I was having the desired effect. "She's just here for a minute Higgs. I said she could tell us whatever we need to know to help us fight the Revision before she slinks back to her submarine."

I pulled out my phone but didn't need to dial my brother's number. He was already calling me, and I punched the button to answer the video call.

"Morse code is easy," he began. "You know what the hard part is? What I practiced daily when I was ten? Tapping out one thing in Morse while saying something different. Once you figure out how to compartmentalise your mind, it's not so bad. You just need a bit of practice. And did you know that, in the Second World War, the telegraph operators could recognise the person sending a morse code transmission just by the cadence of their tapping? They called that secondary information channel the other operator's *hand*."

"Wait, what?" I said.

"My message to Scarlett during the Hoodwink. It worked great—she just told me all about it. She's captured Ragnhildur and aims to discover what's going on in Iceland with her Revision cell."

"I wondered about that pen tapping and why you brought

Scarlett in. Bloody heck, Faraday, she had Dad killed, and you're still working with her?" I cared little that Scarlett listened into this direct affront.

"I tapped out: T-H-E-Y L-I-S-T-E-N, D-E-C-O-Y, and H-E-L-P U-S. It worked, eh? Whoa—Scarlett's with you?"

I saw Scarlett nod in the rear view mirror, but she kept quiet while Higgs interjected. "Yeah, she's here, although I don't know why you even give her lip service. Murdering bitch."

"We need her, Higgs," Faraday said. "But now that we can talk freely, there's something more important I need to tell you. And Scarlett, tell me how this is possible. Mum's alive."

I looked at Higgs, then turned to Scarlett. Neither had an immediate response, so they must have been as shocked as I was. "Are you okay, Faraday?" I asked. "We know she's dead. Everyone was at the funeral, and we saw her body."

Faraday's animated words flowed like a steam train. "Scarlett. How would they fake the body, the Revision? I'm texting with Mum, and it's not a hoax. She knows things about me that nobody outside the family could know. Things not even you two know. She's being held somewhere and forced to work on furthering her nanotech research. I think they have her drugged or something, but I can't figure out where she is. Does the Revision have her?"

Scarlett's eyes narrowed and two furrows raced across her forehead as she replied. "I guess they *could* have faked a death. There wasn't a criminal autopsy performed, and maybe a substitute body could have been fabricated that would pass casual inspection. Nobody likes to look too closely at a loved one's lifeless corpse. Are you saying it was a kidnap and faked death?"

"I don't know what I'm saying, other than I can text her whenever I want, and it's really her replying. She's the one that created the listening tech in HoldiLocks—that's how I found out about it. And she's been working with Angus's reconstructium platform to make tech that can harvest energy from volcanoes while regenerating the whole time. It's her."

The rest of the conversation was a blur. I couldn't focus, instead returning to the question of whether Faraday was texting with our mother, or whether he'd been somehow duped. I was torn between desire and logic, and didn't know which to trust. When Faraday started crying as the contradiction of our mother's death and rediscovery hit home, Higgs joined him and I found my mouth too numb to speak. Scarlett's efficiency and Lars's consoling arms encircling my sister's shuddering shoulders were the only things that saved us from sinking into a swamp of unanswerable questions and dark fluttering feelings. I remember Scarlett saying that Ragnhildur and Torsten had a lot of contact and although it seemed he was just a foreman at the manufacturing plant, perhaps her sister had dragged him deeper into the Revision cell. She also said that Dmitri Vladishenko's lab was tracing components used by the Revision to see how widely this cell was distributed. The conversation had many more questions and too few answers.

When the rear door clicked open and Scarlett strode off toward the jetty, it seemed she had firm next steps, but we were left with only vagaries. She had captives to question, intel to gather on Torsten and the manufacturing plant in Ísafjörður, and a Revision cell to crack. All we had was a directive to figure out where Dad had hidden the Trollheart, and to keep it safe. After ending the call with Faraday, the three of us in the car slumped in silence, wishing for things that weren't going to happen.

* * *

After an indeterminate amount of time, Chronos came to the rescue. For all his bravado, he was sensitive to our plight,

158

and his voice was a soothing rumble as he squatted to bring his face in line with the still-open window. The moonlight reflected from his cropped scalp. "That's a lot to take on board, mate. I'm here for you. Let's get moving, figure something out, eh?"

Dot's jeep window rolled down fully and she peered from behind Chronos. "What about the boat?" she asked.

"Good point," I said with a resigned sigh, leaning forward to get a better view of the sea. "It's still moving toward shore. I'll wade out and return it to the jetty. I see Scarlett's taken off in the zodiac."

Dot raised an eyebrow. "Um … wade? Is that a criticism of my spellpower?"

"Ha, sorry. I forgot about my magic boots. I'll just prance my way to the boat, then. Preferably when those three down the beach aren't looking."

Dot pointed behind us. "And what about that thing? It seems to be on our side, but should we be wary?"

The hovering turtle shell bumped gently on the opposite side of the rental car, nudging Higgs's window. Fortunately, the police and scientists had jogged along the beach to inspect the carnage; a floating fire turtle would have aroused any onlooker's interest. I lacked the benefit of the earlier sighting but examined the ornate shell. It was layered, like slate roof tiles, but formed of shakes of rough-edged volcanic rock. The same armour protected its neck and larger-than-expected head, arrayed in dozens of smaller slabs to allow it to flex in a narrow range of movement. Oval ruby-coloured and multifaceted lenses protected distorted eyes and the head lacked any mouth opening. The car roof obscured its bottom half, and I caught only a glimpse of the jewelled eye sockets before the head dipped to peer in the window.

Higgs had her eyes closed and didn't respond to the taps until Lars chirped excitedly. "Higgs, Higgs! That turtle, it's here. And those aren't jellyfish tentacles. Look! Recognise them?"

Higgs sat bolt upright and fumbled for the window button. Before it was halfway down, she was crying and gibbering. "Newt, get over here. Look, it's her!"

I scarpered around the front of the car. Higgs was cuddling the dangling appendages and trying to stroke the rough shingles of its neck. Those weren't jellyfish arms; they were the legs of our once-dead dog, Disco, whose limp body Sundalfar had whisked away from the battle at Castle Ghuil on a vague promise after Faraday's nanotech-killing materials had attacked her bones and muscles. Her legs dangled and waved like noodles, but the colour of her fur and the pawed ends revealed them for what they were. I recalled that Grover Mann had his mother knit the cap that Higgs now wore, and he told her she'd be cold when she next saw Disco.

The shell's head nodded excitedly, the exposed tail wagging limply. A muted bark sounded from inside the shell. Higgs dragged the creature into her lap, and tears of joy bounced off the carapace. "Call Faraday again," she said, between sniffs.

When my brother appeared on the phone screen, Svetlana's arm was draped over his shoulder. Even though I hadn't met her, I was glad that Faraday wasn't alone, and had a sympathetic ear. Seeing Lars with Higgs made me realize I felt left out, pining for the reassuring presence and loving touch of Emeline.

"What's *that* thing?" Faraday asked.

Higgs leant the phone out the window and let Disco face the camera, her snout and long-lashed eyes distorted behind the ruby translucence of the lenses. Through sniffles, she said, "It's our Disco. Look, she's been transplanted into this armoured shell, even though her legs are still limp from Castle Ghuil. And she can fly, too, with jets of fire."

"Sundalfar fixed her? I don't believe it! Amazing! Move the

camera closer. And wait, did you say you're at a black sand beach? In the background—that's got to be the hut from the photo of Dad's I found in our basement."

CHAPTER 21 - TUNNEL

Higgs

Faraday picked out the beach hut where Dad concluded the treaty that confined the Octoprince to the glacial tomb above us and included the Trollheart as collateral. I had only a vague recollection of the photo thumbtacked to the wall panelling above his desk, but of course, Faraday matched the minor detail in Newton's moonlit camera shot to a small photo in a cluttered room.

Chronos persuaded the hut's door open with little more than a stern tug. It was a simple shelter: two wooden benches, frosted windows, a small pot-bellied wood-burning stove, and an array of wall pegs that supported nothing more than a tattered terry robe. Black sand laced the tough hemp rug, backed by a layer of non-slip underlay. Newton sparked an ancient, oil-burning lantern into life and rehung it on its ceiling hook.

"This is it?" I asked the bedraggled assembly of my friends. "The historic agreement between troll, elf, eagle, octopus, and the old magic happened in this cramped, rickety shed? It's a whole lotta meh."

"Let me take a photo for Faraday," Lars said. "Cram everyone in here."

It was a tight squeeze, but we assembled into two rows. I didn't care about my state of disarray. I cradled Disco, and that compensated for everything. But Dot, the least dishevelled of us, thought she needed to apply a touch of lip balm before the shot. As she applied it, she winced and gave her jaw a vigorous rub with an impromptu, "Ouch!"

The lip balm tube fell from her hand and hit the floor perfectly upright, just beyond the margin of the rug. The tube disappeared through a knothole in the wooden plank. Given a hundred more attempts, I doubt she could have sent the tube through the hole. We heard it land on a hard surface, and after a moment of lucky silence, we heard it roll, bounce, roll again, and land on another hard surface.

"Let's hold off on the photo, Lars. There's a hollow space under here."

With the rug and its mould-spackled underlay pulled back, the size of the concealed trap door panel became plain. It took Chronos and Newton working in concert, levering the panel up using the rings inset into two of its corners to hoist it on its creaky hinges and expose what lay beneath. The rings clipped onto two hooks set in precise spots on the timbered wall, preventing the door from slamming shut. If Faraday had been here, he would have noted the odd placement of those hooks straight away, and pointed at the rug as if the concealed door shouted to be opened.

The clean lines of what lay beneath were a contrast to the ramshackle hut. Stairs led down, with Dot's errant lip balm on the third one. But they were no ordinary stairs; broad treads were formed from precisely cut stone. The surface had a hint of roughness, but each step was perfectly bevelled, and the staircase was wide, with enough overhead clearance to allow two horsemen to descend comfortably. The same stone lined the walls and ceiling, but this was no darkened crypt—the stone seemed to emit its own light, a cold and blue-tinged luminosity that left no shadows. Deep landings punctuated the downward progress every thirty steps. I could see the fifth such landing from my vantage point. It was hard to focus on the ever-descending regularity without looking away periodically to unboggle my eyeballs.

There were no traces of dust or invading insects. But if I was a bug, I'd avoid this unnatural stone too. I had expected a shallow, concealed cavity when the trap door's surface was first revealed, something to hide away remnants of my father's covert activities. Not this. Everyone else's eyes widened as much as mine, and it took a few moments before I broke the silence.

"Not what I was expecting. But magic is at work here. Can you feel the tingle, Dot?"

My friend's pale skin took on an unearthly sheen in the glow of the odd light. She nodded and pulled her hair behind each ear as she squatted and tried to peer past the most distant landing. "It looks like elf magic. Remember the blue tinges of Sundalfar's magic at Castle Ghuil? This glow is so similar. And nobody could have excavated this without the nosy townsfolk remarking on it. It's not engineered by human hands."

I felt investigating magical elements was *my* responsibility, but there was disagreement about my role as I descended the top three steps.

"Whoa! Stop there, Higgs," Chronos said. "You can't just parade off down a magic staircase on your own. I don't think anyone should go down, let alone you!"

His extended hand offered an escape to the mundanity of the cabin floor. I just smirked. "You can't be serious," I said. "It's just a flight of stairs. Newton's here, and you've seen what happens if magic threatens me when he's around. I'll just go down a little. Check it out. No further than you can see, okay?"

"She's right," my brother said. "This is her thing. But not out of our sight, okay?"

There were several murmurs of encouragement to stay safe as I descended. I looked back only once; the faces of my friends ringed the trap door's frame, silent and concerned-looking. The hesitance of my first steps fled as I got deeper. Although the environment was unexpected, the only hints that I entered an area more unusual than an underpass in Middle Ides were the cleanliness and the odd light. I stayed to one side of the staircase, trailing my left fingertips along the cool and wrinkled stone wall. Although cool to the touch, the stairs didn't freeze my feet. Quite the reverse—a mild energy flowed into me, banishing any remaining shivers.

Reaching the first landing, I called back without turning. "More stairs. That's all I can see. I'll stay within sight."

I took the next flight more quickly. There was nothing to remark on, each step a duplicate of the last. The walls and ceiling, at least triple my height, were unmarked and carved with remarkable consistency. The light varied only a little, with residual hints of lantern light from the cabin above providing the only variation. By the third landing, even that interjection had faded, and I had to glance back up to reassure myself that my friends remained visible.

At the fourth landing, there was a marginal change as I contemplated the descending flights of steps. "Hey! The stairs flatten out after the next three landings. Still the same weird rock, but I can see the bottom now. Nothing else unusual."

Lars answered, his voice echoing from above. "That's far enough. Now we know it flattens out, you can come back?"

What? Leave a mystery unsolved after only a dipped toe? The quaver I detected in Lars's voice told me even he didn't expect me to turn around at this point. "I'll just go to the bottom and then come back, yeah? I can keep calling up so you'll know I'm safe, even if you can't quite see me after the next landing."

Instead of a reply, I heard footsteps far above. Lars took a few tentative steps, then skittered down after me, two steps at a time. "I'll come too, just in case," he called.

After a moment, Dot descended too, losing ground to Lars but adding her own voice to my reinforcements. "I'll come halfway, so I can watch you and still see the crew up top. Then we'll all be in *somebody's* sight. And we'll know nobody's going to ambush us in here. Not with Chronos up there."

I had the best friends. Lars was still far above, but gaining on me, so I set off again. Downward. Lars was still a flight and a half higher when I reached the bottom. I turned and saw Dot beyond him, but the stairs could have been infinite from my vantage point.

As my foot touched the tunnel floor's gentle slope where it widened at the base of the stairs, I thought I heard the shiver of a distant gong. Unsure whether it came from the tunnel or rolled to me down the stairs, I half-turned and called to Lars. "Did you hear that?"

"Yes. One of those giant cymbal thingies?"

"Was it behind you, somewhere?"

"No, it came from near you. Let me catch up."

My arm hairs rose, unbidden. The sound of a fancy percussion instrument wasn't normally frightening, but in a blue-lit tunnel beneath coastal Iceland, with no gong in sight, it brought me to high alert. The tingle of magic took a step closer to my perception's shadowy edges.

Lars stepped to the tunnel floor behind me, and the gong shivered its way along the broad passage once more. I held out my hand, and Lars silently took it.

A slight movement in the tunnel far ahead caught my eye. I pointed, as if Lars needed guidance. "Look at that! Is it ...? Yeah!"

I turned to Dot, who was visible far above. "Dot. You won't believe it. There's an *elephant* down here."

A deep and resonant voice filled the tunnel, speaking in

resigned, morose tones. It was powerful enough to carry up the long staircase. "Technically, I'm an *Irrelephant.*"

CHAPTER 22 - PUZZLE

Higgs

I'm sure Dad read me books as a toddler with talking elephants. The tone of its voice implied more boredom than aggression, so I yanked Lars further along the tunnel. "You see that too, don't you?" I whispered.

"Uh, yes. Hard to miss an elephant that fills the whole tunnel."

The elephant, still a considerable distance away, took a few casual steps toward us. The booming voice continued. "If you think about it, I'm actually not *an* Irrelephant. I'm *the* Irrelephant. No others like me. I'm doomed to be lonely forever."

It was hard to know what to say to a gloomy creature that even at this distance we could see would flatten us to pancakes if it sat on us. I called out as loudly as I could, still failing to reach the Irrelephant's impressive volume. "Um, hello? I'm Higgs, and this is my friend, Lars. What are you doing here?"

"And not even just *the* Irrelephant. I'm the *Unavoidable* Irrelephant. I'm here because it's a necessity. Come join us and see the puzzle."

"'Us'?" Lars whispered as he sidled closer. "There are others here? We should go back."

I didn't feel threatened, but it couldn't hurt to regroup and report on what we had seen. Lars was reassuring, but I'd rather have Newton and my friends here to face this new weirdness. I turned to Lars, my voice a murmur. "I'm not looking forward to a couple hundred steps up, but yeah, let's return and formulate a plan."

Backing up, I shouted to the Irrelephant, who seemed curiously close and distant at the same time. "Uh, hello, Mr Irrelephant. Or Ms. We're just going back up, but we'll definitely check out your puzzle a little later."

I released Lars's hand so we could spin around, but as we turned, we both leapt back a half-step. Between us and the staircase was a tunnel-filling behemoth.

It was hard to tell whether the toughened, leathery collection of wrinkles that passed as the elephant's skin looked blue from the unnatural light or if it was indigo in its own right. The ridged and yellowing tusks that flanked its muscular trunk traced sweeping arcs in the air. The elephant's broad head swung left and right in a series of chastising shakes. The trunk curled expressively, suggesting an almost human shrug.

"I told you, I'm the Unavoidable Irrelephant. At least until you solve the puzzle. I'm the lock on this tunnel. You can't leave unless you solve it."

"Hold on," Lars said. "If this is a magical tunnel, and we can't leave until we solve it, why do you need to be here? Seems like making a chicken out of a feather. Couldn't there just be a spell that stops us?"

Expelling a sigh through his downthrust trunk, the Irrelephant rumbled a laconic reply. "You want to take away the only purpose for my existence and replace it with a spell? Thanks a lot. But I'm with you. Elves have some odd ideas sometimes. Ask they why they created me."

Lars shrugged without further protest. "Okay," he said, "let's see this puzzle. I'm good at puzzles." He turned and strode deeper into the tunnel, leaving me standing facing the elevated and saddened eyes of the Irrelephant.

I was about to object and had my mouth open, waiting for my brain to devise an expression of my outrage at the limp response of my friend, when Lars sprinted past me. He sped straight at the Irrelephant's trunk, spinning as he reached it before pivoting through its front legs, ducking beneath the pendulous belly and dodging around the rear legs. The Irrelephant only just reacted as Lars flicked its dangling tail and reached the bottom step.

"He's so slow, Higgs. You can do it too!" Lars called.

Before I could take a step, with a slight sizzling sound, the Irrelephant vanished then reappeared on the flight of stairs ahead of Lars, again blocking his way. Somehow, its legs were thicker, touching the walls on either side and leaving a gap narrower than either of us could squeeze through. There would be no weaving run this time. Coarse hairs on its head scraped the ceiling as it shook once again.

"What part of 'unavoidable' did you not understand?" it asked. "Once you set foot in the tunnel, you cannot go out without solving the puzzle. This is the rule."

Lars returned and took up my hand again. I took a deep breath and nodded to the Irrelephant. "Okay, let's look at it. Is it a hard puzzle? And where does the tunnel go? It seems like we're under the sea here."

A rumble from somewhere deep inside the Irrelephant's sizeable bulk rolled over us as it decided which question to answer first. The rumble rose and transformed into the booming voice. "Yes, the tunnel goes under the sea. That's its only purpose. And the puzzle can't be *that* difficult—half have solved it so far. But then again, only two have attempted it. And your father is brilliant, Miss Higgs. I guess we'll see."

Competing thoughts jockeyed for position in my mind. Although my father had a cabin on the Icelandic coast we knew nothing about, and it contained a trap door to an undersea tunnel that he also neglected to mention, how could he not have told us about his encounter with a talking elephant? He'd been here and solved an arcane puzzle. This was so fantastical, it nearly pushed my more practical thoughts aside, but they struggled through. I stopped walking.

"Just a second," I said to the Irrelephant before calling back in a louder voice. "Dot, are you there?"

The mammoth between us muffled her reply, but I still heard her concerned voice. "I'm here, Higgs. I heard everything. Do you need help? Should I get Newton?"

"No, no, I'm okay. Listen, Lars and I have to go with this Irrelephant and solve a puzzle. It won't let us out until we do that. But can you do something for me? Can you go back up the stairs a little, maybe ten steps?"

"I guess so. Going up … okay, now what?"

I looked up, focused on one eye of the Irrelephant. "So you won't stop Dot from leaving? Just Lars and me?

It might have been a chuckle, the deep bass notes that preceded the Irrelephant's voice. "I'm not *that* unavoidable. Just in the tunnel, not the steps. This is the rule."

I called again to Dot. "Dot—it's very important that none of you go below the bottom step, or you'll be marooned down here like us. And call Faraday too. Tell him not to set foot in the tunnel at his end."

"Wait, what?" Dot said. "The tunnel goes all the way to Middle Ides? That's impossible."

I spoke softly, looking at the Irrelephant's other eye this time. "It's not impossible, is it?"

The Irrelephant shook its tusked head slowly.

"Yeah, Dot, tell Faraday. Quickly too, you know what his curiosity is like."

* * *

The Irrelephant clumped along behind us as Lars and I strode along, hand-in-hand, attempting to look confident. Glancing back as we made progress along the shadowless square tunnel, I noted the Irrelephant had shrunk to its original, less-bloated geometry. There was space once again for a furtive dart between its stumpy legs, but Lars had enough proof that the Irrelephant was indeed unavoidable that it seemed a waste of effort to repeat the escape attempt. The Irrelephant hummed to itself, an unfamiliar tune, and its presence was unmistakable, even as we faced away, from the heavy footfalls and wafts of scent that combined the animal smells of a stable with an acrid edge like epoxy glue.

I was half-surprised that the Irrelephant knew of my father, but with all the revelations about his covert activity, perhaps I should have expected this. "So my father was here with you, and he solved the puzzle? When was that?"

The sardonic tones of the Irrelephant accompanied what might have been a sigh. "Yes, he solved it eventually. And it doesn't matter when he was here, does it? Not much matters. Not even me. I don't matter much. He drove off without so much as a goodbye."

Lars cut in. "He *drove* off? Down here?"

"Indeed. He had a noisy little thing with four wheels. Shot off that way," the Irrelephant said, gesturing south with its trunk. "The second puzzle-taker arrived just after Templeton left, so I've been lonely, as usual, but almost never alone. Oh, hang on a minute. I'll be back."

The Irrelephant winked out of existence with a sighing pop. We took the lull as a chance to observe our surroundings. Ahead, the tunnel widened into a circular domed chamber, walls curving away to meet again at the corridor's continuation a good hundred metres away. As we approached, we could see inscriptions on the floor, written in several alphabets that glowed with a negative light, a deep indigo that distinguished it from the lighter blue of the tunnel's stone. We couldn't yet see the full expanse of the chamber, but dead ahead a distant tunnel left the antechamber, continuing the line of our entry passage. The only other feature that disrupted the evenness of the carved rock was a jumble of rubble piled against the wall to the exit's left. It was a different stone to that which made up the tunnel and chamber, its dark, volcanic character a natural fit for the hints of smoke that rose like streamers from its jagged points and peaks.

Entering the chamber, Lars and I both homed in on the tall but slender inscriptions and shapes on the floor. Other than the rubble and the graceful writing and diagrams etched into the floor, the space was bare. The blue tints of the tunnel marbled the walls and high dome arching above us, featureless.

The puzzle depicted on the floor covered an enormous area. Each letter in the inscribed text was at least as tall as I and pulsed faintly. The text that ringed a set of diagrams seemed to include six languages. English and what looked to my unaccustomed eye to be Icelandic were the only two I recognised. One looked like ancient Norse runes, but I struggled to see how anyone could interpret the remaining three. One was a long train of wavy parallel lines. The lines varied in their closeness to each other, with occasional breaks and short intersecting lines. Another script looked like random angular scratch marks with little discernible pattern. And the last was a series of jagged gouges, reminiscent of a shrapnel damaged wall at a bomb site.

The English text formed the second innermost ring, with only Icelandic wound in a tighter arc. Lars and I both instinctively swayed our heads from side to side as we pored over the curving words. I read aloud.

"'The figure-8 puzzle! Can you solve it? The Irrelephant is unavoidable if the answer doesn't contain 16 words. Are there

57 clues in the shapes within? Question the answer but answer the question. But what is the question? It's in the locked trunk under the bridge. In the chest. Identify the purpose of the subject matter'."

Within these concentric circles of writing was a spiral of shapes and symbols. The shapes were the size of dining tables and arranged so only a concerted leap would take you from one to the next. A five-pointed star sat at the centre of the encircling text, and a spiral line spun outward to a square, a triangle, and a circle, with the outer loop of the spiral completed by a crescent moon, a pentagon, a stunted cross, a hexagon, and a lightning bolt. A heart shape capped the spiral. Around the set of shapes was a square border that reminded me of ancient Greek architecture, and beyond that, the circles of puzzle text in six languages.

I screeched in mental anguish at the puzzle, but my objecting noises were cut short by the abrupt reappearance of the Irrelephant. I directed my rant at the wrinkled trunk and droopy-lidded eyeballs. "This is mumbo jumbo! We have to figure out the *question* first and then answer it? Can you give us a hint of where to start?"

The Irrelephant honked a nasal, descending rumble through its trunk reminiscent of a dejected trumpeter before replying. "Like everything else, I don't have a clue about a clue. How do you think I became the Irrelephant?"

"But my father solved it, yeah?"

"Well, he had several hints provided before he headed down here. And then he solved it."

"Oh, *great*," I groaned. "My father, ten times smarter than us, only solved it with a bunch of clues that we don't have." I pulled my hair into disgruntled tufts.

Lars gripped my shoulder and turned me to face him. "Come on, Higgs, you're the smartest person I know. You can do it. And I'll help too; we can mindstorm."

I laughed. That helped already. "It's brainstorm, not mindstorm, you delicious fool."

"*Brain*storm? That sounds like it hurts. Let's agree to say mindstorm. But wait—" He turned to the Irrelephant. "I thought you said the second person didn't solve the puzzle. How did they get out? There's nobody else here."

"Oh, it's not a *person*. I didn't say person, did I? It's Fash-Harfnr. He still hasn't given me the right answer, and I'm as unavoidable to him as I am to you two."

Lars scanned the full circumference of the chamber, even peering at the domed ceiling as if he expected to see a trapeze artist. I saw no person or thing other than ourselves and the Irrelephant.

With a resigned wriggle of his trunk, the Irrelephant gestured toward the far tunnel entrance, where the jagged rubble smoked away. "Fash-Harfnr, we have guests," it said, following this up with a deep bellow that was more vibration than sound.

With a noise like rough metal being attacked with a rasp, the rubble shifted, billowing smoke. The shape of a short-horned head, volcanic black with smouldering eye sockets and an arc of flame for a mouth, rose above what we had thought were bits of rock. Its head had been bowed against the massive chest, but now the imposing face became clear, even as two arms capped with spike-fingered hands pushed the human-shaped but towering form erect.

Volcanic arms hung away from its body like an over-muscled weightlifter, unable to stand at ease. The boulderish shoulders were level with the exit tunnel's ceiling, giving us a measure of its massive scale, despite its distance. Its squat legs thudded as it took two steps forward, leant so that one fist pummelled the floor, and roared. Smoke sloughed from the shoulders, tendrils of the heavy emission racing across the floor near its legs. Crackling jets of fire erupted from its mouth, accompanied by a sound like a confrontation between gorillas.

Lars and I physically retreated until the Irrelephant's trunk dangled between us. The Irrelephant remained unfazed by this show of strength and replied in its usual laconic voice. Instead of words, only a brief growl came from its mouth, carrying across the still air to the figure near the tunnel, accompanied by subsonic vibrations we could only feel rippling our clothing.

The angry apparition returned to its full standing position. The flames subsided to a flickering from the mouth and shoulders, and we shared a moment of near silence while Lars and I contemplated our next steps. We both asked questions at the same time.

"Gods, what is that thing?" Lars asked.

That was probably the best question, but all I could think of was, "You can talk to it?"

The Irrelephant answered both. "I told him you haven't solved the puzzle yet. That you've only been here a few minutes—he's not very good at time. I reminded him, I'll be unavoidable if he fancies ripping your arms off, so no need for you to worry. This is the rule. Fash-Harfnr is a troll, and he's lost all patience over the last year."

CHAPTER 23 - CRYING STAIR

Faraday

I don't remember this, but when I was a toddler, the fits of temper Mum had to endure from me drove us both to tears frequently. My parents and Newton could both attest to this. Sometimes it was my inability to keep up with Newton physically—I wanted to run as fast as him, climb the higher structures in the playground that he found so easy, do a handstand against the wall like him. Other times, it was an unarticulated passion that was frustratingly hard to explain—although that's a tension that continues to this day.

These episodes led to time outs on the bottom stair, with a fine view of our kitchen and lounge. Most of the time, I took myself there, a calming measure that gave both me and everyone around me a chance to breathe and de-escalate.

My mother named it the time out stair, but I soon christened it the *crying stair* because that's what happened there. The centre lip of that step retained a darkened patch where tears collected. Whenever I see a bottom step, particularly if it's old and wooden, like ours in Middle Ides, I see it as a place of solace, a spot to pause and consider.

* * *

Granny was fine and had a round of tea steeping when we returned to her room. "Your friend Zee crawled after his co-workers a few minutes ago. I poured him one already. Would you like a cup? It's way past my bedtime, so I figured you may need one too."

I was tired, running on adrenaline. "Yeah, pour us one, Granny. Just let me check what's occurring in there."

Svetlana settled in a guest chair, and I heard her ask Granny if she'd ever been to Iceland as I wriggled through the open hatch. Once inside the underfloor passage, Higgenbotham's comments swirled up from the staircase ahead. Presumably, he was describing the ATV Svetlana and I had spotted earlier.

"Look here. No spark plugs, no petrol tank. Someone plugged electrical leads into this thing, whatever it is."

"Looks like a bit of desiccated ginger root," Agent Zee replied. "That stuff powers the UPSCALE. Did you know that?"

My phone rang. It was Dot.

"Faraday, something weird is going on. Higgs says to tell you not to go beyond the bottom stair of the secret tunnel under any circumstances."

"What? Why not?"

"Well, there's a similar tunnel here, and Higgs went past the bottom of the stairs."

"What happened? She's okay, right?"

"Yeah, she's fine. But—"

"There's an elephant!"

The exclamation wasn't from Dot. It was Higgenbotham's shout from the opening in the floor that glowed ahead of me. It was an indisputable fact, but it had an edge of trepidation I hadn't heard before from the UPDA agent.

"Huh?" Dot said. "Who's that? There's an elephant at your end too?"

CHAPTER 24 - COUNTER-OFFER

Connington-Smythe

I examined my profile in the mirror, determined to get the head-straps engineered for minimum wobbling of the nanotech detection goggles. The strapping needed more flexibility for odd-shaped heads, but this rendition looked a perfect fit for me. I could see why people might think me a surfer at first glance, what with the dirty blond and often messy length of hair. And the beach was only a couple of kilometres from Xi Li's California lab, where I spent countless hours, so it sort of fit. But once I opened my mouth, my British accent and total lack of surf lingo often changed people's first impressions.

More fool them. It's dangerous to miss undercurrents. I'd surfed up and down the coasts of Britain from Thurso to Polzeath and still managed a couple of sessions a week here.

I activated the goggles and turned to face the nano chamber. A few commands from the keyboard and a mix of nanotech was sprayed into the vacuum-sealed chamber. The goggles worked perfectly on this crop of nano, same as on the other samples. It was a mix of Dr Redferne's materials, a few substances taken from Angus MacFarland's Edinburgh lab, and some underground research from Somalia, apparently.

The nano-materials' energy signatures and signal leakage brought them to life in the goggles, even though they were invisible to the naked eye. I could see which areas had the densest concentrations and which parts were actively making changes to the environment or themselves. My invention was brilliant.

As I fiddled idly with the display control wheels encircling each eyepiece, I thought again about Dr Redferne's son, Faraday. Xi had me on a drive to recruit the lad, confident he had rare talents. But I wasn't so sure—not about his talents, more about his alignment to our philosophy. It takes a keen mind to understand the clarity of vision underpinning our cell. Accepting that proper world governance could come only if the smartest people were given free reign to point the clueless masses along the correct paths was the price of admission. We technocrats would never be *voted* in, but who would stop us from exercising actual power?

It was my privilege to work as lead engineer for Dr Xi. That puffed-up fool Vladishenko might consider himself the world's top expert, but he didn't know the depth and breadth of our tech. Especially now that we'd taken over MacFarland's research and had a handle on everything Dr Redferne had been working on. Could Faraday take up his mother's work but align with us?

Xi even suggested I refer to some of our most closely-held secrets if needed to coax Faraday into the fold. It seemed he may have some knowledge of the magical spheres, given his father's reputation, and if the nanotech lab couldn't sway him, maybe some other arcane knowledge might. I was authorized to show him the n-dimensional gyroscope, which may have been magic or perhaps an alien artefact so advanced we couldn't identify its technology. Or I could allude to the 'glove of the disembodied fist' that I had personally procured from a bazaar in Egypt. That was definitely magical. The 'infinite pocket' was another party trick with a wide range of practical applications. That always impressed.

But did he have the stomach for what we really did? Someone had to act as the traffic cops, ushering the nosy, drooling passers-by away from the hidden things of our world. Things on which their opinions were worthless because they had neither the required intellect nor expertise. That was what our cell—and the others—managed with finesse: showing just the right levers of power to only the proper audiences to get our way. My early conversations with Faraday made me feel he was too soft—too blind to the only way we'd save the planet— to truly come on board with us.

But first, I needed to ensure Faraday wasn't already part of another cell. Maybe he worked in parallel to us. A key Revision premise was power through quiet domination; eliminating another cell was perfectly acceptable behaviour, so he could join us or be crushed by us. May the strong survive!

CHAPTER 25 - RELAY

Higgs

Mobile service was non-existent from the depths of the underground tunnel. With the Irrelephant obstructing the path between me and Dot on the bottom step, we used Bluetooth to send the photo I'd taken of the floor puzzle to her. Lars and I had exhausted our own ideas, but I wanted to get Faraday onto it.

Dot sprinted up the steps to get reception and returned a few minutes later.

"He says four UPDA agents are stuck in the tunnel under the Orphanage, and an elephant is preventing them from leaving. He's working on the puzzle."

"Probably the same elephant," I said. "He keeps popping in and out, like a nosy neighbour."

"I'm right here," drawled the Irrelephant.

"Yes, unavoidably here," I laughed. "Cheer up, chap. This is the most excitement you've had for months. Do those guys get a different puzzle or the same one?"

The Irrelephant let out a long sigh. "The puzzle, sadly, is as unavoidable as I."

CHAPTER 26 - DENSITY

Faraday

Higgs had asked me earlier to describe Svetlana. I always found it hard to understand what people wanted to know with a question like that. In this case, I found it even harder. The way her mind moved, the directness in the way she spoke, both considerate and cutting through irrelevancies, made me think I wasn't noticing the subtleties in the fringes of whatever we analysed. I was used to being self-sufficient and confident in my own abilities, and I'd pushed everything else aside where Svetlana was concerned to sharpen my focus on which cogs whirled inside her head. For once, I acknowledged the presence of an equal thinker, someone whose mind raced ahead of everyone, absorbing detail at a ferocious pace and using it to explore realms others couldn't perceive. Anyone could *learn*, but very few could truly *think* at her level.

Of course, I could have brought back a perfect image of her appearance and used it to describe her to Higgs, but that seemed like it would trivialise my narrative. Her complexity was best left undescribed because I knew my words would fail to do her justice. But my sister knew the inside of my head nearly as well as I did, so I settled on a simple summary that I thought would convey my hopelessly tangential impressions. I had told Higgs, "She has a cattle prod in her backpack and calls Granny *Miss Redferne.*"

* * *

The pleas from the party of UPDA agents trapped behind the odd elephant in the tunnel below grew tiresome, so I had shut the hatch in Granny's closet. Svetlana and I pored over the photos that Dot had relayed from Higgs.

"Let us start again with words," Svetlana said.

She read them aloud while I transcribed onto Granny's notepad, in case the act of writing piqued the solving compartment buried in my subconscious.

> *The figure-8 puzzle! Can you solve it? The Irrelephant is unavoidable if the answer doesn't contain 16 words. Are there 57 clues in the shapes within? Question the answer but answer the question. But what is the question? It's in the locked trunk under the bridge. In the chest. Identify the purpose of the subject matter.*

"I translated the Icelandic section too. It says the same thing," she added when I had finished my scrawl.

"There are the three numbers in there, but I can't see how they're related. Sixteen is double eight, but fifty-seven doesn't follow any pattern I can make out."

"And the rest is confusing. Is there locked trunk or bridge? Does 'chest' mean same as 'trunk' or does it mean chest part of body?"

"Pffft. No idea. Granny, have a read of this and see if you have any ideas," I said.

"Okay, here is photo of puzzle. What can we figure out about drawing?" Svetlana said.

188

"There are ten figures. Does the number of lines in each tell us anything? The heart has two lines, I guess. The lightning bolt has eleven, then six, twelve, five, and two. Does the circle have one, I guess? Then three, four, and ten. Not much of a pattern there."

"Maybe line is red herring and you must jump between shapes. Ask Higgs to jump circle, heart, moon. Or moon, heart. Wait—that is too far. Can't jump from heart all the way to moon. How about their starting letters?"

"Like jump them in alphabetical order? We have H, L, H, P, P, M, C, T, S, S. If you put them alphabetically, it would be

Circle, Heart or Hexagon, Lightning, Moon, Pentagon or Plus, Star or Square, then Triangle. Same problem. You can't jump from the lightning bolt to the moon."

"Maybe you may use fancy border as safe path."

"Ooh. Good idea. I'll have Dot get Higgs and Lars to try those combinations, both the number of lines and the alphabetical order. Forwards and in reverse."

"Probably number of sides, because names of shapes will be different in each language, right?" Svetlana asked.

"Unless the answer is different depending on what language you speak. The elephant could judge whether you've made the right jumps depending on what language you speak," I said. But it felt like we were clutching at straws. I texted Dot the instructions.

We bounced ideas off each other, but like ping-pong balls, they made very little impact. Was the line part of a graph? How did the words relate to the pictogram? Did the ornate border have a purpose beyond decoration?

None of our suggestions for Higgs and Lars produced any results. By three a.m., my brain was a spiralling wreck. Dot said that Tam and Chronos had settled down to snooze in the jeep, and Newton was dozing on and off but refused to leave the uncomfortable bench in the beach hut. At least they'd fired up the wood-burning stove, and it was toasty now. Disco seemed to crave the heat and had taken a position with her armoured shell pressed against the stove's belly.

Dot was about to take a pile of warmed towels down to suggest Higgs and Lars get some rest, and recommended the same for us. It had been the longest day ever.

Granny snored faintly in her wingback chair, which had a mechanism that allowed it to recline. She often slept there, so I covered her with a blanket from her bed. By the time I dimmed the lights, Svetlana's breathing had slowed too, so I slid her phone from her hands and attached it to the charger alongside mine. I lay down beside her on Granny's bed, shoes still on, and dreamt. Oh, how I dreamt.

CHAPTER 27 - APATHY

Faraday

I awoke at 6 o'clock to the faint smell of coffee. Many residents at the Orphanage were early risers, and the kitchen began baking early. Numbers and shapes swirled in my head as I groggily clumped down the steps to grab a jolt of liquid caffeine. I caught a passing glimpse of myself in the hallway mirror and saw a shambling figure with hair like an unkempt hedgehog's spines.

Our friend, Grover Mann, stood beside the percolating coffee machine. His presence was as unexpected as what he said to me, but I found many of his musings unexpected.

"Hi, Furry-day. I had a dream about an elephant. And I wanted to ask Higgs about Disco. Has she seen her yet? I'll tell the ponies what she's doing."

I'm not sure how he knew we needed four cups of coffee, but he'd balanced them on a tray with a small pitcher of cream and six sachets of sugar. "Yeah, me too, Grover. Dreamed of an elephant, I mean. And how did you know—oh, forget it," I said.

"I made coffee for you, me, girl, and old lady."

Inexplicably, he never moved on to a better name for Granny than 'old lady'. He visited her most weeks, and they largely sat in silence in her room. I often thought they were communicating wordlessly, but Granny was evasive when I asked her what they did together.

"We can't talk to Higgs right now, but Disco is with Dot. I have to call her to tell her I have no more ideas."

Grover laughed at my failure. "Don't be silly, Furry-day. You *always* have ideas."

The coffee mugs tinkled as Grover limped up the stairs on his irregular leg. Granny yawned and wished Grover a good morning as she accepted the coffee, warming her hands by encircling the mug. Svetlana dangled her stockinged feet over the side of the bed, looking only half awake.

"This is my friend, Grover," I said. "Finest coffee chef in Middle Ides. And Grover, this is Svetlana. Kind of like 'llama', I guess."

"Llama," was all he said, presenting the tray and looking away.

I knew Grover had powerful latent magic, even if he didn't recognise it. He had an inscrutable way of communicating with animals, preferring days spent in the stables at the Middle Ides polo club to interacting with people. And as he'd just shown, he could sense events at a distance and often ahead of time. None of this struck him as unusual, and he brushed it off, as if others simply didn't pay attention to the little signs.

"Any ideas come to you in a dream, Svetlana? How about you, Granny—solve our puzzle?" I asked.

Both shook their heads.

"And you, Grover? Does this drawing look like a puzzle you could solve?"

I showed him the photo taken by Higgs.

He glanced at it for only a moment. "I don't like puzzles."

"Me neither, this time," I said. "We need to focus on finding my mother, on getting the rest of the family home to Middle Ides. The rest of the stuff about the Trollheart and this treaty can wait. It's just not relevant."

I continued ranting, crumpling up the paper with the transcribed puzzle inscription, and tossed it across the room. "These words are just nonsense. What kind of puzzle doesn't even ask a proper question? Argh!"

"Have the coffee, Furry-day. Can we see Disco now?"

He was right. I needed to calm down and think. "Yeah, sure, Grover. Let me call Dot."

I got Dot after 5 rings. She rubbed an eye and her jaw. "Any progress at your end?" I asked. "I've got nothing yet. If there's no change at your end, can you give Grover a look at the new Disco? I see she's back there in Newt's lap."

Dot shook her head. "I just woke up, but I'll check with Higgs and Lars. Hey, Grover, check out Disco's new shell."

She passed the phone to Newton, and I handed mine to Grover. A few deep breaths would do me good, so I took to the hallway and paced its length, taking elongated breaths. It wasn't the location that was important, just the breathing.

I stopped mid-breath and ran back into Granny's room. "It doesn't … matter?" I said to Svetlana. "Where'd I chuck that paper?"

"What doesn't matter?" she asked.

"Well, none of it. The diagram. The Irrelephant's name. Most of the words. I need to double-check, though. I can only remember the first forty words by heart, and I'd rather check the paper than re-write the words from my mental image of the page."

I needed to be sure of the exact wording, and for once, doubted the limits of my recall. Granny pointed a finger, crooked from age and arthritis. The paper had rolled under the bed skirts, so I dropped to all fours and retrieved it, pressing it into a semblance of flat on the rug.

"Yes! That's it. *It doesn't matter.* The numbers eight, sixteen, and fifty-seven have meaning, but not much else does. The eighth word in the inscription is 'it'—"

"Yes, Faraday!" Svetlana jumped on my back and wrestled me onto my side. On one victorious knee, she raised her arms above her head. "Sixteenth word is 'doesn't', and fifty-seventh word is 'matter'. *It doesn't matter.* Grover, give him back phone!"

Grover called a farewell to the phone and waved. "Bye, Disco. Too bad you have to stay there. Maybe I can come and see you someday."

He handed it over, and I got a close up of Newton's unshaven chin. "You figured it out?"

"Almost definitely. Get down there and tell Higgs the answer is 'it doesn't matter'."

"Really?"

"This isn't a time for joking, Newt. We've got to rescue Mum."

The video image swung crazily as Newton took the steps two at a time. There was a pause while he said, "Here, Dot, take this. I'll be back shortly."

Receding footsteps marked his descent while I explained my proposed answer to Dot. In the tense silence, we both listened for any activity from the tunnel beneath the black sand beach. There was a faint rumble, but maybe due to poor phone reception. I shook my hands out and pressed a fist against the centre of my chest to calm myself. My heart reverberated, and I counted—by extrapolation, 138 beats per minute based on the 15 second measurement. Far too fast for a sitting pulse.

"Show him Disco, petal," Granny called. Dot knelt by the stove where Disco had settled again and put the phone near his jewelled lenses. Through the deep red, I could discern the lovely lines of her face. If only I hadn't taken her with me in the jeep that day, the nanotech wouldn't have infested her, ultimately causing her death. I guess technically it was my nanotech that killed her, and Grover's magic that drove her to Loch Ghuil to protect us. But that's all she ever really wanted, wasn't it? To be part of the family? It was so confusing, trying to decipher who was at fault for her death. Or non-death. Or first death. She'd saved us all but paid for it with her life.

Could I hear something?

"Faraday, you did it!"

That was Lars. Of course, he'd be the first up the steps, with his indefatigable running. Dot swivelled the camera to point at him, where he paused at the top of the steps, hands on knees.

"Higgs is just coming. She'll tell you what happened."

My sister was not far behind, light on her feet. I saw Newton slow to a plodding ascent, two landings down the staircase.

"Oh, thank you, thank you, Faraday. I knew you'd figure it out. Hey, hi Grover! And you too, Granny and Svetlana. The Irrelephant made Lars give him the solution too, after I answered. The troll, Fash-Harfnr, literally smouldered with rage when he saw us hit the first few steps. Let out a bellow that shook the tunnel. It wouldn't surprise me if those UPDA guys below you felt it. Anyway, it felt unfair, so I asked the Irrelephant if he could tell the answer to Fash-Harfnr too. He didn't see why not. Sounded like coal being forced through an industrial cheese grater when they spoke. The Irrelephant nodded, and the troll took off. Yeeted itself outta there. The thing can run. Faster than a car."

"That makes little sense," I said. "Lars was first up."

"Nah. He went the *other* way. He's headed toward you and the Trollheart, wherever Dad hid the thing."

"He can't run here. It's like 1,500 kilometres."

"1,489. I look on GPS," Svetlana said.

"Newton, drag your heavy-breathing arse up here, we've got to get a flight home before a troll busts out of Granny's closet," Higgs called to our brother as he crested the steps.

"No, wait," Svetlana said, motioning for me to hand her the phone. "I have better idea, Miss Higgs. Get others. Oh, and find ladder."

CHAPTER 28 - TRANSPOSITION

Higgs

We didn't have a ladder, but we had access to a Chronos and a bench from the beach hut. That combination was enough to enact Svetlana's plan.

Lars and I couldn't estimate the troll's top speed but knew that he could outrun a car in town and possibly even on the motorway. When Fash-Harfnr sped off through the passage to Middle Ides, it was only thirty seconds before he was a distant simmering speck in a sooty cloud. We'd likely beat him to the Orphanage if we caught a flight, but Svetlana had an ingenious plan to get us to the tunnel's far end in a few minutes.

Once we three puzzle-solvers at the Iceland end had provided the answer the Irrelephant awaited, he winked out of existence, probably to chaperone the four UPDA agents at the other end. But as Svetlana pointed out, as a squad, we could summon him to either end of the tunnel. We had the basis for a trip to Middle Ides, and back, if we needed to. We would all need to enter the tunnel.

Disco seemed unwilling to pass the top step of the magical staircase and fretted, hovering back and forth across the opening until Newton and I both reassured her. I stroked her shell and legs before gently settling her once more beside the stove. Chronos carted one of the wooden benches from the hut down the stairs and heaved it into the passageway, careful not to pass the bottom step. Tam also ventured only as far as the bottom step, where he kissed Dot and promised to see her in three days after the Piping Hot concert in Helsinki. Dot joined the rest of our assorted crew where we lined up beyond the bench. Newton and Dot looked at me, indicating I should lead our party down the tunnel.

"I think this is secret anti-barefoot bias," I complained. Although the tunnel cast a cool, blue light, the floor was warm to the touch, so I was griping for comedy effect, not hardship.

"It's beauty before idiocy," Chronos called, raising an eyebrow at Newton, who trailed us.

"I'm back here for a job, you ingrates," he said. "Here I go!"

Newton managed two steps toward the stairs before the Irrelephant appeared to block his path.

He pushed himself onto tippy toes, but even Chronos wouldn't have reached the Irrelephant's eye level. "Hi, I'm Newton. It's nice to meet you, close up like this. And at first I thought it sucked, but now I'm overjoyed you're unavoidable. My sister here has a favour to ask of you."

"Um, yeah," I said. "Does anyone ever *ride* you? I mean, could we?"

The Irrelephant rolled his eyes with such exaggeration I thought they might spin back in his head permanently. Then he let out two long sighs. "Whatever. Who cares? I'm hardly ever of any use, so this'll be less boring than my usual day. But it's a tad demeaning, isn't it? Being ridden? And you little things look like lightweights, but your friend here looks like he might hurt my back. It's pretty sensitive, you know, and that metal hoof looks like it would irritate my rash."

I figured I might as well just come clean about our plan. Asking for a favour instead of deceiving the creature sounded like the best approach.

"We don't really want to ride you," I said. "And Chronos over there on the steps isn't coming with us anyway. But what we actually want is to get to the other end of this remarkable tunnel so we can prepare for Fash-Harfnr's arrival. He's intent on retrieving the Trollheart, isn't he? So he can use it to burn away the machines that have invaded the volcano. We want to help him however we can , but I think we need to prepare for the arrival of a towering flame-flinging visitor to our town. You know, keep him as quiet as a troll is likely to get? We figured you can pop from one end of the tunnel to the other, and maybe you could take us with you."

The Irrelephant let out a slow and exasperated sounding breath that visibly rippled along his trunk before replying. "Why wouldn't you just hold my trunk, like any normal friend would do? No need to *ride* me like I'm some kind of fairground attraction. But I don't just pop to the England end of the tunnel on a whim. I only head there if it's unavoidable. You might be waiting for a while, but I'll try to stay awake while you're huddled here sharing my misery."

"I carried the bench all the way down those abominable steps and now you don't even need it to climb aboard? Chronos said, feigning hardship. I guess you ladies can sit on it while you have a kumbaya moment."

Each of my companions except Chronos, who remained on the bottom step told the Irrelephant 'it doesn't matter' to allow them free passage in the future. Even Lars, who had provided the solution earlier.

We clustered around the step and the Irrelephant shrank to half size, turned to face the steps, and then expanded again. I took the Irrelephant's proffered trunk in a gentle grip, and I watched its deeply-wrinkled grey length narrow and extend as Dot and Lars took hold. By the time Newton reached in with an underhand grip, as if he were supporting the Irrelephant, the trunk had almost doubled in length.

"Shall we sing a sea shanty or something while we're waiting?" Chronos asked. I gave him a playful kick in the shins with my bare foot. I felt a foot fight was better than contending with his singing voice which had been known to terrorize karaoke machines across Middle Ides. "You'd better not have nail fungus, you dirty little article," he chuckled.

I didn't even validate him with a reply, preferring to express my feelings by wiping the other foot down his pant leg while sticking out my tongue.

"Everyone have their tray tables in the upright position and their baggage securely stowed?" Chronos said in a sing-song voice. Then he called up the steps. "Tam, we're ready. Tell Svetlana it's her turn."

The plan was that when Tam called Svetlana, she would enter the tunnel's southern end and then attempt an exit, requiring the Unavoidable Irrelephant to appear. Faraday told me later that she brought a tray of tea and biscuits to the UPDA team, no small feat while negotiating the low crawlspace.

The process of transportation to the tunnel's end reminded me of jumping into an icy plunge pool. A shocking line of cold pulsed from my feet to my temples and then back again as my eyes adjusted to the only slightly different surroundings of the passageway's southern end. We'd travelled the distance in an instant, and the Irrelephant had rotated a half turn to face Svetlana and north.

"I am the Unav—"

"Yes, yes, Unavoidable Irrelephant," Svetlana said. "I have heard all about puzzle. But as you know, for me, it doesn't matter. You will let me go up stairs now."

"Hi, Svetlana, nice to meet you in person," I called, releasing the Irrelephant's trunk and murmuring my thanks into an ear the size of a bath towel.

Having cleverly answered the puzzle without making it

obvious she had done so, Svetlana retreated to the bottom step while I took a clumsy slide and plopped to the floor. One by one, the other riders dismounted.

I sidled over to Agent Zee. "Let's get a good look at that scar," I said.

"Nice to see you too, Higgs," he laughed but stooped to show me where a concertgoer overcome by nanotech at the Piping Hot show in Edinburgh had slashed his face. "I think they did a good job. Gives me a story to tell without affecting my roguish good looks, eh?"

"Yeah, tidy work. And good to see you again, even though I'm not so thrilled with your organisation. I'd tell you the puzzle answer so you could get out, but I know there'd be pressure to let these other ones out too."

Dot and Lars followed Svetlana up the steps, but Newton hung back to update the four UPDA agents. "There's a raging troll making its way along the tunnel. Not sure how long it'll take to arrive. Somewhere between twelve hours and three days, but you'll want to stand aside—in that widening just along there—when it passes. He's not out to get you; he only wants my dad's hidden artefact. Faraday has the key now, so we hope to find the Trollheart and figure out what to do with it before our friend arrives."

I scooted to the steps between the Irrelephant's legs, and Newton followed. One of the UPDA agents darted in his wake, only to find an unusual widening in the girth of the Irrelephant's legs now blocking every route out of the tunnel.

"I'm unavoidable until you solve the puzzle. This is the rule."

CHAPTER 29 - CRIPPLEGATE

Chronos

The autumn sunrise was still over an hour away, but the beach car park was almost full as Tam and I walked from the beach hut to our parked vehicles. Disco had settled again next to the stove and seemed content to remain vigilant for her family's return. None of the drivers were nearby though. The visitors clustered around the beached mega-tentacle, oblivious to the astounding passage that ran beneath their feet to England.

"Keep them out of trouble, eh, mate?" Tam said as he stepped up into the jeep. "I cannae skip out on our final tour stop, so I'm entrusting Dot to you fae the next three days."

"It's kinda late to avoid trouble," I replied. "But yeah, I'll make sure they have their helmets strapped, their seatbelts on, and that they check for monsters under their beds. For some reason, trouble follows the Redfernes around."

Tam roared away in the jeep while I drove the rental car into town to find a café open for breakfast. I was hungry like ten men.

* * *

When I returned to the beach, satisfied, the sun had cleared the horizon, promoting long, north-pointing shadows. Even more vehicles littered the car park, including a pair of satellite dish-adorned news vans. I still had my end of the beach to myself.

With a lot more effort than it took to take it down, I shunted the wooden bench back up the staircase and dragged it outside the hut. I leant back, loosened my fleece-lined, hooded jacket and let the warmth of the wan sun wash over me. Despite the looming threat of the Octoprince—beaten back but not defeated—I was calm for the first time in two days. Our new business's first client was a success story, albeit one that involved a near-catastrophic fight and the need to run another car into a fjord, but that was all in a day's work, right?

I had worried that Torsten might stake out the airport at Keflavik, waiting for us to leave the country, but his shaven-headed mug was nowhere in sight as I escorted Ashna safely to the security checkpoint. With Dot's spell-casting and Newt and me doing the investigative work, the number of people we could help was limitless. And it wasn't every day that you could say you'd fought off a kraken wannabe a million times your size.

The activity of the last few days had agitated the stump of my leg. The running blade was custom-fitted but designed for running in straight lines. It produced an understandable degree of chafing when propelling me across sand, being thrown down flights of stairs, or hurdling mythical sea creatures. I unstrapped the blade and massaged the reddened skin beneath with both calloused hands. After a last guzzle of the energy drink I'd bought at the café, I leant back and closed my eyes.

* * *

I dreamt my amputated foot squeaked as I walked along warm, black sand, sun lancing through dappled cloud. A beached octopus the size of a bus flopped on the sand in the distance, a crowd of onlookers gleefully poking it with sticks.

Was the squeaking sand a dream? I heard Disco's under-jets flare as a shadow flickered across my closed eyelids.

Instinctively I rolled to the left as I opened my eyes. A sodden and gnarled driftwood branch cracked in half on the bench, in the spot where my head had lain a moment prior. A meaty hand clutched the driftwood stub. The figure that cast its shadow over me had a breadth I recognised at once. This was the second time Torsten Sigurdson had threatened me with a jagged piece of wood.

I levered my stump against the door jamb and took him down with a leg sweep. My boot clattered hard against his ankle. My running blade skittered from the narrow floor of the beach hut's decking, its black blade blending with the sand's hues. The impact of Torsten's bulk on the weather-beaten deck accompanied a whoosh of breath.

The Icelander's slow return to one knee offered me a chance to haul myself up by gripping the doorframe, and I hopped backwards into the hut. Torsten retook his feet with a calm, practised air, dusting sand off his jacket before grabbing both fragments of the driftwood branch, one in each hand.

"I got the signal from Ragnhildur's beacon, and look who I find here! Hop-along bunny."

I held up a palm as he advanced toward the doorway. "Hang on, chum. This isn't a fair fight. It's like Scrooge coming after Tiny Tim with a poker from his one-lump-of-coal fire."

Torsten laughed. Probably not at my outrageous wit, but at the idea that he would soon lay a significant beating on me. "It was not even a fair fight when you had your toy leg attached. What's the difference?"

His smile radiated revenge.

"No, no. I was offering *you* the chance to surrender. That's how unfair it is. I have a friend," I said. A wave of heat rippled my clothing as Disco's reinvigorated form cannonballed past my shoulder toward Torsten, who staggered back in panic.

Disco pulled her head up in a mid-air skid, the ring of flames from beneath her shell erupting over Torsten's right arm and weapon. I noticed how her legs and tail retracted during the attack, protecting them from the singeing power of the jets. The tree branch in my adversary's hand erupted into flame in an instant; a growl of rage tore from his lips as he recoiled and dropped the other driftwood fragment.

His right sleeve flaming, Torsten reacted quickly. With his meaty left hand, he encircled Disco's neck, spun twice and hurled the spinning turtle shell over the hut. His hammer throw coach would have been proud of his technique. He rampaged inside, slamming the door behind him, and ripped off his burning jacket using only his left hand. Blackened flesh peeled from his right.

Torsten winced in pain and avoided touching his crisped arm. "Your friend will find it hard to open a door, no? Want to calculate new odds?"

The burly man tore the ragged robe from its hook beside the door and wrapped it around his burnt limb in a primitive bandage. I hopped onto the third step of the descending staircase, retreating.

The handle on the underside of the trapdoor tempted me. As Torsten advanced, I jumped and grabbed the handle, ripping the eyelets from the wall and slamming the hatch closed. I wished I'd waited a second or two longer; a shattered shin bone would have been a fitting way to defeat Torsten this time. Instead, I took the delay while he wrestled the heavy trap door open to hop my way down the steps, taking them two at a time, using my opposite arm as a brace against the wall. Didn't the magician's health and safety guild know you couldn't build a staircase without a handrail?

I neared the second landing when Torsten's feet hit the top

steps. "You won't get far on foot," he bellowed, descending at speed.

It was fortunate that I slipped and fell down one flight of steps at a much quicker speed. I'd have a colourful set of bruises tomorrow, but I regained my footing, and nothing felt broken or sprained. The tumble had widened the gap, but Torsten closed it mercilessly as I hopped further.

I knew once we reached the level ground at the base of the stairs, Torsten would face the Irrelephant's rules like every other tunnel visitor. Could I use a desperate last move to my advantage? I took two bounding hops back from the bottom step and braced myself. In my most enraged bellow, I shouted out, "It doesn't matter!" I figured I didn't want to reveal the answer to the Irrelephant's puzzle, and hoped that shouting it now, as a non sequitur, would satisfy the magical creature's rule even before he unavoidably returned. After so many consecutive bounces, my leg screamed with overexertion, lactic acid trying to convince my muscles to abort the mission. *Come on, McCann,* I urged myself. *One more rep.*

A key principle of judo is to use your attacker's momentum against them. Now on my level, Torsten turned away his right shoulder and charged, intending to bowl me over with a shoulder barge and finish me with his powerful left hand. Between us, we weighed almost six hundred pounds. There was a lot of momentum available.

I grabbed his T-shirt collar with my right hand, getting a reassuring handful of bunched fabric. My left fist punched at his bundled right forearm, landing a solid strike intended to send a shiver of pain through him. My leg thanked me as I let it buckle. I rolled backwards.

It was near-perfect. Torsten grunted in pain as I twisted him, and he landed on his burnt right side. His grasping left hand gouged my eye as my encouragement to his momentum rolled him beyond me down the corridor.

My eye clamped closed, beyond my control to open it and pain lanced through my eyeball. But I needed only one eye to carry out my mission. I crawled on my three remaining limbs and the exposed stump, moving with the speed of a determined infant. I reached the third step and collapsed, rubbing my savaged eye but not bothering to look back.

After a familiar popping sound, Torsten's approaching footsteps faltered then retreated, accompanied by what sounded like the scream of a child.

The sardonic tones reverberated along the spartan corridor beneath the ocean. "I am unavoidable. I am the Irrelephant. This is the rule."

* * *

"Bloody hell, James, what happened to your eye?"

Emeline Grey, the teacher at West Ides High School who doubled as one of Dot and Higgs's magical instructors and tripled as Newton's girlfriend, answered the video call.

"Nice to see you too, Emeline. I see you've got Newt's phone, and judging by the purple shawls I see in the closet there, you're in Angelina's room at the Orphanage."

I waved to Newton's grandmother, who I could see peeking over from her favourite chair by the back window.

"It's not that I don't want a long chat with you, love, but do you mind passing me over to your worse half, if he's handy? I've got a bit of news."

I explained to Newton the negotiations I'd made with Torsten, how our words flew around the blue-grey hide of the Irrelephant's flanks. The fabrication plant where the Icelander worked produced prototype devices that could mine energy from deep within volcanic structures, and he delivered them for testing to a discreet mine shaft carved into a glacial fissure in the massif above the beach hut at Vik.

210

Newt told me the shocking news about his mother somehow being alive, and that Torsten's deliveries sounded like her geothermal equipment made from Angus McFarland's reconstructium. No wonder the trolls were peeved, with this foreign material corrupting their pristine domain.

"You won't let him out, will you?" Newton asked.

"Not a chance, mate. His losing streak has to end sometime, and I'm in no hurry for the next round. But he was quivering like a big girl's blouse down there. Apparently, he's scared witless of elephants, so our friendly neighbourhood Irrelephant put the frighteners on him. I did promise to get him some industrial-strength burn cream, which might just take the edge off the damage Disco inflicted, and maybe I'll throw in a pizza and a bottle of chocolate milk. I could use a few ice packs myself. I'm off to town."

CHAPTER 30 - ARRIVAL

Faraday

We used Granny's room as the Trollheart-search headquarters. I think she took perverse satisfaction in shooing away the nosy neighbours and fussing staff. She refused to shut her door to the hallway, although we closed the closet door to obscure the secret passage from prying eyes.

We split into squads to cover multiple hypothesised hiding spots. In the commotion, Granny had made her own list, trying to get inside her murdered son's mind and imagine where he might have hidden the artefact.

Newton wanted to check in on Ashna, after which he would look through Dad's possible hidey holes for a locked container that might accept an oversized key.

Emeline took Dot to the woods up in the hills beside the Ferndale Reservoir, a place where our father often took solitary walks. They would use finding spells to see if they could locate any clues. Grover latched on to that opportunity, saying that Higgs would need 2 chips from the petrified proboscis of the monstrous blowfly that the Pendletoad had consumed. It still stood upright on the reservoir's shoreline, the only remaining piece from the onslaught of the animated Ides Giant and the titanic toad that guarded the witches' burial site beneath

Ashton Pond.

I showed Dot how to use my stick of digestive nanotech. Applying a line of the waxy substance would unleash the microscopic technology within that could eat through nearly every known substance. It had a double-layered zinc screw-top, the only substance I'd programmed the nanotech not to attack.

Higgs and Lars circled the Orphanage and walked the outline of the Ides Giant's chalk-lined hill carving, looking for any signs of possible concealment.

Svetlana and I remained in Granny's room. Tea runs to the servery downstairs were our biggest contribution. We were in charge of additional search plans, but our efforts were as fruitless as a carnivore's diet. Eventually we turned to the impending troll visit.

"Miss Redferne, what do you think will happen when troll gets to this end of tunnel?" Svetlana asked.

"Well, dearie, I'm not sure we're the best ones to figure that out. It's only Higgs and Lars that have seen a troll. But he sounds pretty angry. I expect he'll charge up the steps, rampage through the secret passage, and burn all the clothes in my wardrobe to ash before squeezing out that flimsy doorway right there beside you."

She paused for a moment, scratching her scalp with the spine of a paperback from her doily-topped side table. "Maybe we could use a quick-step charm. Does that sound like it might work?"

Svetlana raised a quizzical eyebrow in my direction, but I was as boggled as she. "Granny, don't forget we're not only newbies in the troll world but also have no clue about charms or any other sort of magic you might be hiding up your crocheted sleeves."

"Oh, it's simple. If you make a quick-step, anyone passing beneath an arch woven from weeping willow fronds can pass forward a few steps without travelling across the intervening space. Witches used to position them at strategic points so they could cross rivers with no bridge or take a quick-step into a locked cell. Very handy. I imagine Emeline and I could create one if we had the materials."

"I'd call that a teleporter, myself. But quick-step is quaint. I like it," I said. "We can strip willow branches from the tree at Alan Ryder's place up the street. Let's wander over there, Svetlana."

"If you kids still took classical languages at school, you'd know that *tele* means 'remote' and *portare* means 'carry'. But I still like 'quick-step' instead of 'remote carry'."

I pretended to shrug off that comment, but both Granny and I knew it would settle in a side crevasse of my mental landscape.

* * *

By nightfall, we were not much further forward in our quest to locate the Trollheart. Grover presented Higgs with two pancake-sized cross-sectional slices from the blowfly proboscis that looked like chunky bracelets formed from a blue-tinged stone. Dot reported that my nanodigester had struggled to slice through the alien material but succeeded after a second, thicker application. She returned the sealed tube, handling it gingerly.

As I expected, Newton had found nothing noteworthy at home, but his tray piled high with snacks baked and fried in the chippy revitalized us even before hitting our lips. It would be the first of many promised edible favours to come from Vish Balakrishnan's take-away. Ashna's return had been a tearful affair on all fronts, but Newt figured this was an adventure that would only strengthen the family bonds through a healthy dose of open discussion.

Higgs and Lars turned up nothing. I'd seen them both stretched out snoozing in the longer grass beside the outline of the Ides Giant's crown, and they looked more rested than the rest of us. Given what she'd been through, nobody begrudged her the recovery time.

And the quick-step that Emeline and Granny prepared with an extended willow-twining session and a hushed droning of incantations worked well. Under their guidance, we positioned it near the top of the staircase and tested it by flinging various objects through and having Lars observe where they emerged outside the Orphanage's back wall. Granny had a mischievous glint in her eye and suggested the quick-step's release point should be Mabel Shedden's room down the hall, but she didn't object when we concluded an exit near the foot of the Ides Giant would be the best destination.

At first, the quick-step's exit was high in the air, but once our adjustments made the thrown objects reappear at ground level outside, I marked the position, carefully moved the willow bower aside and replaced it once I scrambled up into the underfloor passage. Although Emeline promised it was safe to pass through, I had no problem leaving the privilege of first use to someone else. I re-affixed it in the correct position using duct tape, all the while wondering what proper witches used as a fastener. Probably twine and essence of lizard.

We were deep into the platter of sandwiches Newton had rustled up from the Orphanage kitchens when a quavering and energetic call came from the crawlspace. It was Agent Zee.

"Faraday? Newton? Are you there? There's a sultry breeze blowing along the passage. I think it's time you freed us."

CHAPTER 31 - DIVER

Lars

I couldn't believe my friends were going to leave the four men trapped below as a raving troll rocketed toward them. I had seen the thing myself and was frightened even when the Irrelephant's magic protected us.

But I was not disappointed. Nobody offered any reason not to free the UPDA agents.

"I'll go tell them the puzzle answer," Newton said.

I was already in motion. "Nah. I will take care of it," I said. "I kind of want to try the quick-step anyway. It is safe, right, Angelina?"

"Yes, yes, petal," she said. "Safe as a walk in the meadow. Or a run in the meadow, in your case. Not sure if I've ever seen you *walk* anywhere."

The quick-step was nerve-racking and exciting at the same time. I inspected the intertwined willow strips as I passed beneath on my way down the stone staircase. It looked insubstantial, and I felt nothing while passing through it in reverse. Somehow it worked in only one direction. I wondered what would happen if you pointed the quick-step downward. Would the person passing through get trapped underground and suffocate?

As I approached the bottom, I felt the scorching breeze. My hair flopped across my eyes, and I had to swipe it back.

"Guys, Zee. I will let you out now."

They jogged to me from down the hallway, where they had sequestered themselves in the puzzle hall, the only place to avoid being in Fash-Harfnr's direct path. Their leader, Higgenbotham, dangled four clinking mugs in one hand. His common courtesy, returning the dirty drinking ware, held, even with the onrushing threat.

"Tell 'Relly the 'Elly here that *it doesn't matter*. He will let you out." I didn't mention the quick-step. It would be funny to see their reactions.

"That's it?" Zee asked. "The answer to the whole puzzle is that it doesn't matter?"

I looked over his shoulder. Smoke and a wreath of flames filled the tunnel to the north. "Um, yeah. Faraday can explain it later. But I think ... we'd better ... run!"

The four hurriedly gave the obstructing Irrelephant the answer, and I watched their heels as they sped up the steps.

"Are you coming too?" I asked the Irrelephant. "I know you can change size."

"That's true," he sighed, shrinking as he spoke to the size of an apple. His voice still boomed, despite his diminished size. "But I'll be even more useless out there than I am in here. You'd better run. Fash-Harfnr has arrived."

Running was my speciality, but a backward glance offered a glimpse of a seldom-seen spectacle. The troll was in full flight. His stony shoulders ejected flames, and a smoky train engulfed him from the chest down. His horns—curled back on his skull—blazed, and I saw spiky knees emerge from the smoulder with each piston-like stride. I worried he might not make it to the quick-step; that his momentum could carve a demolishing path straight through the staircase.

My trainers squeaked as I pushed off and high-tailed it up

the steps and through the quick-step. A queasiness teased my stomach with the passing, and I nearly stumbled as my foot dropped an unexpected few inches to the level grass behind the Orphanage and my eyes adjusted to the darkness.

"Move aside, he's almost—" I called to the bewildered-looking UPDA agents arrayed ahead of me.

I dived aside, out of the troll's direct path, and the four UPDA agents were wise enough to copy my manoeuvre. Slowed significantly, Fash-Harfnr materialised from the invisible arch, a shower of ashes blasting onto the grass and the shape of the quick-step's opening framed in his accompanying cloud of acrid smoke.

His first step sank him shin-deep in the turf, such was the force he was used to exerting on the tunnel's stone floor. The second, third, and fourth left shallower sinkholes before he skidded to a stop on his heels, leaving a twin scar that ended partway up the slope. The troll came to a stop with his cinder-crusted feet vaporising the chalk marking the contour of the Ides Giant's left foot.

Facing away from us and the Orphanage, he squatted for a moment before he thrust his chest out and bellowed at the sky, sledgehammer hands clenched into hissing fists of flame. His slate-armoured head swivelled as he appeared to sniff the Middle Ides air.

Two goopy pops sounded to my right. Agent Zee had out a zany pistol that propelled two expanding webs that struck Fash-Harfnr's back and legs, wrapping around to constrict them. But with another bellow and not even a hint of turning to confront his attacker, the troll's carapace glowed red for an instant. The extruded web material fell from his body as blanched ash.

The troll crossed the longer grass to the maintenance hut in three loping strides. His towering frame dwarfed the hut. Bent at the waist, he pulled open the door using a stony hand. With a shake, he withdrew his head from the hut after five seconds then looked uphill. He was off, tackling the full slope of the hillside in thundering bounds. At the top, he paused again, sniffed, and dashed to the left before I lost sight of him over the brow.

Agent Zee examined the side of his weapon, as if it had malfunctioned instead of doing nothing more than annoying the troll. I looked to Angelina's window to see if Higgs had watched the spectacle unfold, but the only head of hair I saw was wispy grey. For a moment, it disappointed me that she hadn't watched me pop through the quick-step or seen Fash-Harfnr in action, but then a jumble of friendly faces coursed around the corner of the Orphanage, calling to see if everyone was unharmed.

Higgs, Dot, and Grover headed straight to me. "Lars, you saved them!" Higgs shouted, tackling me to the ground in an airborne attack hug. "They were just standing around looking stupid before your warning."

I guessed she had seen everything. A smile that started deep within me must have broken across my face.

"Where do you think he's gone?" I asked, rolling onto my back with Higgs still shaking free from the tackle.

"Did you hear that animal?" Grover said, averting eye contact. "He was angry. He was shouting, *where are you?*"

"If we could shout for the Trollheart and have it answer, that would make it much easier to find," Dot said.

"Oh, it answered," Grover replied. "Can't you smell it?"

A faint, enraged troll-call rolled from the treeline at the top of the slope. An almost subsonic rumbling croak answered.

Higgs drew a deep breath and offered me a hand so we could pull each other upright. "I'd say you're going to get your secret wish and greatest fear, Lars. I think a Pendletoad sighting is in your near future."

Newton was checking in with the UPDA agents and arrived

at our huddle shortly after Faraday, Svetlana, and Emeline.

"Let's not stand around. I want to see the troll recover the artefact and remove it. Let's go find it," Faraday said.

Another croak sent a wave of disturbance through the long grass.

"I think we all know where we'll find it," Higgs replied. "Ashton Pond. So yeah, let's get up there, but everybody keep a safe distance."

Grover was well ahead of us. He hadn't bothered to wait for the discussion and was making his way up the slope as fast as his hitching gait would allow. We set off in pursuit at speeds varying by athleticism, fitness, and determination.

* * *

As usual, Higgs was right. I had pondered and visualised the Pendletoad for so long, it was hard to know whether I wanted to see it outside of my imagination. But my legs had little doubt, and they took me to the bushes at the margin of Ashton Pond before anyone else in our motley group. I pushed back the leafy branch of an elderberry bush so its white flowering clusters would not obstruct my view.

The Pendletoad was everything I had imagined and many more things that I had not. The slime glistening on the damp flab of its shoulders, the rivulets of water draining around the myriad of lumps and bumps on the thick back's hide, the length of the curling eyelashes that sent a rainbow spray of droplets skyward with each languid blink; they were all hyper-real in their unimaginable detail.

Each triple the height of a man, the two fantastical creatures leant toward the other, separated horns-to-lips by mere inches. Soot poured from the troll's flaring nostrils, and its feet hissed in the damp ground of the pond's marshy fringe. The Pendletoad's jaw hinged open, its tongue coiled into attack readiness. Pond water rippled as it croaked again, forcing me to cover my ears.

The bush shook as each of my friends and the UPDA agents joined me to observe the standoff.

Grover, beside Higgs on my right, murmured. "He is afraid of the water."

"He's not afraid. I think he's not *allowed*. That's what Sundalfar told us," Higgs answered.

"He just needs to grab the Trollheart and clear off back to Iceland. We've got to focus on rescuing Mum," Faraday whispered across me to Higgs.

I felt Higgs tense beside me. "Hang on, Faraday. I know we have to find Mum, but we can't stand idle while Fash-Harfnr takes the Trollheart. He's got a good reason—burning away the invasive nanotech in his volcano—but using the Trollheart will break the treaty and crush the trolls' source of magic. We must tend to the Octoprince too. Although I'm not very sympathetic to him after he kept trying to thrash us to death, he got a raw deal from the treaty. It's not fair to just lock him up in a glacier."

"Get off it, sis. For starters, you're on a first-name basis with this troll? And then you're saying that the treaty, *which our father negotiated*, is *unfair*? You don't think he had reasons for making these arrangements? Maybe Iceland is better off without trolls. Without the bloody great octopus and his dream-sucking pals. Let him take the Trollheart and leave us alone. Why must we solve everyone else's problems when we have enough of our own?"

"You know I think Dad is one of the low-key smartest people in the country. *Was*. Whatever. But he couldn't see the future, and we're *in* the future now. Things change. Get clearer. Maybe he was correct then, but now it's our time. We can fix this and still rescue Mum. Nobody can see what'll happen later, calculate the results of seemingly sensible actions. Well, almost nobody."

I felt Higgs look at Grover on her right, then everyone swivelled their attention from the sibling argument to him. He high-stepped through the reeds and bulrushes around the contour of the pond toward the posturing colossi. Higgs made to stand and follow, but Dot held her back with a clasped shoulder.

"It's his thing, let him do it," she said.

We stayed deathly silent as Grover approached the troll's flank with striking nonchalance. The stare-off broke as first Fash-Harfnr and then the Pendletoad turned to the diminutive figure. They both continued to peer at Grover as he slid a palm onto the troll's slatted thigh and then placed his forehead onto the back of that hand. They remained in stasis like this for a good half-minute before Grover jerked his head away and slapped the troll leg in a complex series of varying strength strikes. Each elicited an outpouring of soot from between the rock plates covering the leg, like a cloud of dust from a puffed pillow.

Grover stood back from the troll, rubbed his hand on his trouser leg, and waved at us across the pond. With a shove of his glasses further up the bridge of his nose, he called in an overloud voice, breaking the silence.

"I explained it to him, Higgs. He won't take the Trollheart and says you can carry it back to Iceland instead. You can use it to purify their fire. I said you'd make a new treaty, and it would be fair."

I looked at Higgs, then at Faraday and Newton. There was no appropriate reply to Grover's bombshell. I disagreed it had to be Higgs, but I dared not say a word. It was her choice.

Grover continued, his voice confident enough to fool everyone into thinking we'd all agreed. "Don't tell the toad, but the troll is going to pin him down while we dive into the pond and grab the Trollheart."

A whispered argument rippled through the bushes.

"There's no way anyone's going into the pond. It's nowhere near safe," Newton hissed.

Higgenbotham's plummy voice interjected with authority. "And it's a UPDA mission. We'll get proper equipment here and retrieve it."

Faraday and Newton whirled on him in unison. "Keep out of this!"

Newton added, "This is *our* business now."

Surprisingly, this worked. It also persuaded Newton that, to keep the initiative, we must act.

"Okay, okay. I'll get it," he said, taking off a shoe.

"Are you kidding me?" Higgs said. "You can barely swim. You heard Grover: I should handle it."

I tried to interrupt, knowing I could hold my breath twice as long as anyone here and I was used to swimming in cold water. Each time I spoke, one of the Redfernes cut me off. Instead, I caught Svetlana's eye and held out my open palm behind Faraday's back. She nodded and rolled her eyes; I felt the cool contours of the heavy key meet my palm. Emeline made eye contact with me too, and nodded. She knelt behind Newton, breaking off the heads of bulrushes and coiling each stalk into a spiral around the spikelet.

Higgs was so involved in the heated discussion with her brothers that she didn't even notice I'd stood up and stripped to my boxers until I called to Grover.

"Okay, I'm ready. Get your troll friend to save me from ending up as toad food."

I shivered, from the cool autumn air, the anticipation of the frigid plunge ahead of me, and nervousness about my impending death.

Fash-Harfnr blasted fire from his ear vents, punched the Pendletoad in the chest, then ducked as the goopy tongue shot over his shoulder. As it passed, he spun in a half-turn away from the web-footed monster, grabbed the tongue with both hands and hauled. This threw the Pendletoad off-balance, and Fash-Harfnr dragged the slavering creature to shore, the steaming divots left by the troll's straining footfalls filling with evaporating pond water.

I wasn't here to spectate; I had a mission.

Higgs called, "Lars, no, you don't even have the—"

As an answer, I held the key aloft after my first two deep preparatory breaths. Before I took the third, I cut her short. "Yes, I do, and here I go."

It was hard to resist the urge to suck in another breath as the cold and dark pond water hit me. As I dived, I realised I hadn't considered how dark it would be. Vague, silvery moonlight danced on the surface of Ashton Pond but offered no visibility beneath. About to surface and give up, a golden pool of light appeared near where I had taken my shallow dive.

A brilliant yellow glow shone from a casually sinking bulrush spikelet. Another joined it ahead of me and then two more. So that's what Emeline had prepared. I liked that my friends were intelligent, wise, and came pre-armed with practical but amazing skills. The pond was modest in diameter, but with the mud churned up by the Pendletoad's thrashing feet, it was hard to scan the bottom.

I surfaced for another huge breath before diving again. There were several open mouths and an array of serious expressions along the bank. Emeline continued to cast her glowing bundles around the pond. Out of the corner of my eye, I saw a column of hissing steam arise as the Pendletoad pressed Fash-Harfnr into the marshy ground with a splayed foot.

The illumination was improving underwater, and I fluttered with as much power as I could generate, my eyes greedy for any sign of a foreign object. Was that a reflective slab of metal? I needed more air, so had to surface a second time.

The row of onlookers crouched in shadow now, one face standing out. A dazzling red light lit up Dot's cheek, colouring the pond's surface like a glinting ruby. As I gasped for oxygen, I saw that Fash-Harfnr now hunched with his feet on a boulder at the pond's edge, twisting the Pendletoad's front leg. His head was out of sight, snared inside a monstrous mouth. I hoped the titanic struggle didn't progress further along that side of the pond. They were nearer to the position I wanted to investigate than I'd like, but I had committed myself. Being squashed beneath the foot of a giant toad would be a cool way to perish. And it would have to guard me forevermore as I lay beside the ancient cabal of sunken witches it was created to protect.

Yes, it was definitely a foreign object I'd seen earlier. One of the fizzing bulrushes had now landed atop it, and I swam deeper to inspect it. A small safe, the size of an ottoman, sat askew, a quarter sunken into the silt.

I braced my feet, one to either side, and tried to lift it. My first thought was that I'd drag the safe to shore, and we could open it there. The folly of that idea became obvious instantly. Plan B was to use the key and extract the Trollheart with the safe in situ.

This was going to take a bit of fiddly work, so I surfaced, inhaled deeply, and dove again, hopefully for the last time as the adrenaline of the initial dive wore off and the cold began to seep into my flesh.

I positioned the key at the keyhole and was about to insert it when a motion above me made me take evasive action. A rear toad leg thrust down, striking the pond basin at the spot I'd occupied a moment earlier. I was lucky the scarlet illumination allowed a shadow of the slime-coddled foot to warn me, or I would have been pulverised. As the toad scrabbled away and the foot sought other leverage, I returned to the task. With horror, I realised I'd dropped the key, and it had disappeared in the wash of current from the Pendletoad's webbed foot. I spun my head in panic, frantic to catch a glimmer from the key.

The red glow I recognized from Dot's tiger tooth may have flared for a moment before the key struck the top of my foot, and I pinched it between my toes. If it had landed anywhere else, it would have been lost forever in the silty bottom. I raised my foot to my right hand, retrieved it, and slotted the key home in the safe's door.

With a quick turn of the key, the door sprung open. A flotilla of bubbles emerged and skirted past my face. The safe interior was rubber-lined and must have been completely waterproof. Pond water flooded in, soaking a bundled parcel. I grabbed the object and pulled it from the safe. The wrapping was a wrinkled fabric, composed of delicate metal filagree. It concealed something the size of a lumpy pomegranate. Running out of oxygen, I pumped my legs and broke the surface.

"I got it!"

With a few strokes, I reached the shore, but as I closed in on the skirting bushes, the fabric reacted to its soaking. The metallic sheet shrivelled and sloughed off in wet strips. By the time I made landfall, the palm of my hand was being singed by its cargo, and I cast the lump at Higgs's feet. The last of the fine metal casing dissolved into nothingness at the water's residual touch and released the Trollheart's blazing glory.

It throbbed, water droplets hissing away. Aside from the glowing and hints of smoke that formed as the water evaporated, it looked like a human heart, only larger. The damp ground around it dried, hardened, and cracked even before I put my first foot ashore. An ivory silhouette revealed the position of a giant, spiky tooth that the fabric had pressed into the tissue of the Trollheart. It too was turning to paste as moisture from the pond dripped from the sublimating wrapping material. Soon the tooth too decomposed and rose as nothing more than steam.

As the last traces of the tooth evaporated, the Trollheart erupted into uncontrolled flame. The incredible heat made us all step back, our faces reddened by the glow. The elderberry bush sizzled and smouldered. Higgenbotham and the UPDA agents had been hanging back, and retreated even further as events raced beyond their expertise.

Across the pond, Fash-Harfnr must have sensed that he no longer needed to contain the Pendletoad. He had freed his head from its maw and clamped a crushing grip on its forelegs from beneath its bulk. The toad angled away from the troll, as if entranced by the moon, its mass pushing the troll's feet into the soft ground. With a heave, Fash-Harfnr overbalanced the Pendletoad, and it flopped onto its back in the water.

A wave raced across the pond toward where we gaped at the raging Trollheart.

"It can't go under the water!" Faraday shouted. He threw himself to the scorched earth between the Trollheart and the water, clamping himself to the ground to avert the wave. He covered his face with the crook of an elbow to ward off the Trollheart's shimmering heat.

The wave sloshed over his impromptu barrier, but the full force of the wave crashed against his back. It would have reached the blazing heart if not for Faraday's intervention and the intense heat sizzling away the residual splashes. The wave was just big enough to soak Faraday's clothes and prevent him from catching fire. As he leapt away, a mixture of smoke and steam rose from his jacket.

The heat of the Trollheart increased, driving us back. The surrounding bushes were now ablaze.

Grover remained halfway between us and Fash-Harfnr. Having disengaged from the Pendletoad, the troll took a rapid but circuitous path around the pond and knelt at Grover's side, still dwarfing the boy. Reaching with two volcanic fingers into his own mouth, Fash-Harfnr gripped a jagged incisor and, with a crack that echoed from the surrounding ring of trees, broke a tooth free from his rocky jaw. He roared in pain but remained steady, presenting the tooth almost lovingly into Grover's palm. It was as long as his middle finger.

Grover spent a moment tapping Fash-Harfnr's leg, then sprung up and circled the pond's fringe to us, his unwieldy ankle yielding to his stern-faced determination. He reached Higgs, huffing from the exertion, and proffered the alien tooth.

"Higgs! He said you need his tooth to make the heart quiet. His grandfather once carried the Trollheart in his mouth through a mountain pass after dropping its shroud when leaping over a river. It worked, but they had to chip away his lower jaw to recover the Trollheart, and it caught fire again once they pulled his broken tooth from the heart. It may also break the treaty even if part of him touches it, but he wants to risk it. Maybe it's okay now that his tooth is out of his mouth. He's not sure. After hearing your plans to help him, he is grateful and doesn't want to see our land burnt down when he could have helped."

I wasn't sure how we would get Fash-Harfnr's tooth near enough to the blazing Trollheart to pierce it, and the decision between breaking the treaty and burning Middle Ides to the ground had no good solution. But then I realized there was another way.

"Wait, Higgs! I have an idea," I shouted. "But you're not gonna like it, Dot."

CHAPTER 32 - HEARTHOLDER

Higgs

Even in the glow of the growing inferno and the internal illumination provided by the tiger tooth, Dot's face went white at Lars's suggestion. Sunflorin had told us that what Lars termed a tiger tooth was in reality a troll tooth. *Pull the troll tooth* and then apply it to the Trollheart?

But then a breaking smile washed away the fearful expression. "You know what? Luckily, the tooth feels quite wobbly now."

Lars was all over this news. His wiry frame, still clad in only a pair of boxers, was at Dot's side in an instant. "Hurry, Dot. Open up! I told you my aunt was a dentist, didn't I?"

"I thought you said it was your uncle," Dot replied.

"Whatever! Let me have a look."

His unaffected enthusiasm made people trust even Lars's more outrageous requests. This was one of those occasions. He peered into Dot's open mouth, her eyes fixed along the line of her nose, scanning Lars's face for reassurance.

"Yeah, it's really loose!" he said. "Anyone have pliers?"

Dot's mouth snapped shut.

"I'm kidding, I'm kidding! Just open up; I'll grab it with my fingers."

This was not the time for jokes, but I laughed in spite of myself. I thought Svetlana was going to wet herself, she cackled so hard.

With a precise swoop of pointer finger and thumb, Lars extracted a fully formed and viciously pointed tooth from Dot's mouth. I wondered how anything that large could have been in her mouth a moment ago, but it looked like a near match for Fash-Harfnr's tooth, which Grover held outstretched for comparison.

The whole time, we had been edging away from the growing, ragged-edged brush fire. The closest tree to the pond now had tendrils of flame running up its coarse bark toward wilting leaves. I had no idea how I could apply the newly extracted tooth to the Trollheart without getting burnt alive.

Higgenbotham tried to exert some control, shouting, "Everybody get back. I'll call for backup."

Newton shot him the filthiest of glances, saying, "Not your area of expertise, man. Stay out of this!"

Grover must have known something I didn't, judging by his request. "Okay, Higgs, you can put the new tooth onto the heart. Do it now."

He said it with such matter-of-fact-ness that I figured I could just stroll in unscathed and stop the raging flames with a casual plop of tooth to Trollheart. Grover could foresee snatches of the future, so I assumed this was one of those occasions.

But this was nowhere near the reality of what happened.

Clutching Dot's excised, warm, and still glowing tooth, I took a blithe step toward the blazing Trollheart while everyone else retreated in the growing heat. Was the tooth supposed to protect me? Because my eyeballs, baking face, and blistering feet were telling me otherwise.

I took another half-step, but the heat forced me back. The first tree blazed in scintillating flames, and its neighbour was showing signs of ignition.

In my open palm, the tooth's illumination flared, inciting my magic the same way it had when the Octoprince's tentacle attacked our jeep. The skin on my hand wrinkled, as if I'd soaked in a day-long bath. Then it turned light brown and transmuted into bark. In an involuntary fist, the arm extended toward the pulsating Trollheart, five long strides away. With the creak of windswept branches, it reached further, now halfway to the flaming artefact. The bark at the far end curled back in blackened strips.

A moment later, my hand was aflame. The magic quelled by the pain, my arm returned to its original length. Resisting the urge to dunk my limb in the pond, I cautiously shifted the tooth to my other, flesh-bound hand before soothing the smouldering bark with a quick dip. The Trollheart flared again, its influence widening and driving everyone back another two steps. I staggered, my burnt, barky hand resting against the trunk of a towering maple.

With that contact, I heard the trees. Those closest to the Trollheart screamed in my brain, particularly the two that were already aflame. I felt warnings surge through the root networks, spreading alarm to the bushes, grasses, and trees further afield that had not yet experienced the raging heat. I let the residual magic in my plant-infused hand send my message into the maple. *Only the troll tooth can stop the fire.*

Without bidding, Newton was at my side and took my human hand in his. I wasn't sure if this would help transfer his stored and naïve magical power to me, but it couldn't hurt and gave me the reassurance I needed to know I could solve this problem, just as I'd solved others before.

I heard a dry voice, tarnished with disuse, trickle through my hand directly into my brain. *The whole tree never burns. Use the other channel.*

A gentle nudge from below lifted my left foot. I moved it

aside and a fresh sprout coiled up next to my toe.

"The roots, Newt. We need to use the roots to get the tooth closer."

I scuffed a divot in the rich, loamy earth at the base of the tree, nourished by many seasons of leaf litter. A network of vein-like tendrils spidered away from a sturdy root that delved deeper. I knelt and gripped the root, feeling Newton's power course through me. The tiger tooth passed into the root, which grew tentatively, carrying the tooth along its channel, like a snake swallowing its prey. The growth accelerated, and the inner voices urged my tree into action.

My mind accompanied the tooth on its subterranean journey. The sensory information returned was unlike any of the human senses. I felt the presence of the tooth and its exact position relative to me as it ducked under other roots, the grazes a part of the trees' silent, unknowable communication. I tasted the earth's nutrients and moisture from rains long fallen. The humidity, air currents, moonlight on leaves—I sensed everything with inputs somewhere between smell, taste, and touch.

Although it seemed distant, as if it was happening to somebody I watched in a movie, I felt my face chap in the fiercening assault of the Trollheart's heat and then a respite as Newton draped his coat from my face to my shins as a protective measure. I couldn't turn away now, even if my determination failed; my arm was a root, linked to the maple. There would be no retreat without tearing off my own arm.

Just as Newton exposed us to an unbearable heat as he flung away the burning jacket, the root bearing the tooth reached the Trollheart. Pressing the tooth to the surface of the heart as it ceased pulsing, a green shoot broke the charred ground and slithered the tooth up and around the darkened heart, retreating to leave the tooth cradled in a recess atop the fiery artefact.

The conflagration energy of the Trollheart gone, the noises around the pond dropped, leaving the crackling fires of the pair of trees and the complaints of smouldering grasses, rushes, and bushes. I saw nothing, my senses remaining focussed on the maple I crouched with, intertwined.

Lars murmured in my ear, from a million miles away. "Mission accomplished, Higgs. Come back. You did it. Now you have to carry the tooth and heart. Grover said it's your job."

I think my eyes were already open, but when I snapped back to my human senses, it felt like I'd opened them after waking. The ground around Lars, Newton, and me lay scorched bare of everything except ash and bits of my brother's immolated jacket. The burning trees a short distance away exuded warmth but no impending danger.

"And you'd better put your clothes back on. Autumn in Middle Ides is no time for a pants-only party," I said.

"Um … my clothes are ashes now. Nobody grabbed them as they hustled away. Just get the Trollheart. Those eyes are giving me the creeps."

The Pendletoad regarded us from a half-submerged position in the centre of the pond. Only its eyeballs and gaping nostrils broke the waterline, and its unblinking gaze tracked my movements as I shuffled to the Trollheart and picked it up, pinning Dot's tooth to its surface.

We retreated as a pack from Ashton Pond, Lars shivering under Faraday's lent jacket. A hissing accompanied the spectacle of the Pendletoad hosing down the burning flora with arching spurts of pond water from its prodigious mouth. The glow and smoke of the isolated fires faded into the darkness.

One problem solved, we faced another. A troll-sized problem, although a much smaller problem than an angry troll. For now, Fash-Harfnr loped a polite distance behind us as we trudged downhill to the Orphanage.

CHAPTER 33 - FORK

Higgs

Grover slowed his pace, which wasn't unusual given his ungainly leg. I checked back to make sure he was okay and found him keeping pace with Fash-Harfnr instead of the rest of us. Grover trod close by the troll's trunk-like leg, one hand on its shin as they took steps of vastly different length. The rest of us whispered in conspiratorial pools, my brothers with Svetlana and Emeline, the UPDA agents, and Lars, Dot and I forming our own micro-societies. When I glanced back again, Fash-Harfnr was carrying Grover, his blunt fingers cupping our friend like a bizarre ski lift.

Agent Higgenbotham came to a conclusion and strode ahead, turning to stop us in our tracks. "Look now, we're very thankful for what you kids have done, retrieving this dangerous artefact. There will undoubtedly be a reward, on the hush-hush, but it's time to hand it over. We must contain it—get it into the hands of our agency specialists. And I'll order an airlift to take our troll friend back home. Higgs? It's time."

Faraday half-turned and nodded slightly to me. It figured he'd want to get rid of the Trollheart. That would free us to work full time on Mum's rescue. Newton wavered, his raised eyebrows quizzical for my opinion.

I paused, considering what I should do or say. Lars put his arm over my shoulder, and the damp jacket clutched around him applied a cool but oddly reassuring pressure to my side. I knew he'd stand by me, whatever I decided.

Dot was close too, and I heard her murmur, "None of this is right." The comment was for herself, but she verbalised my hesitation. What would Dad do? He had been a UPDA agent himself, though we'd been ignorant of that fact while he lived.

What would Mum do? Maybe Faraday should text and ask, although I dared not believe she was still alive. I'd seen her in the morgue and couldn't believe the corpse was a doppelgänger or a mock-up to conceal a kidnapping. My internal deliberations concluded without resorting to a text with someone that was either my mother or an impostor.

"I think you're right, Higgenbotham. The Trollheart belongs in the hands of experts who can mitigate this kind of threat."

His shoulders relaxed. I guessed he was expecting more confrontation from me. Newton still regarded me like a human question mark, but Faraday's eyes narrowed. He probably knew what was coming better than anyone else.

"Did you know trolls cannot pass over water, nor through the air? Why do you think the Trollheart arrived in Middle Ides through that crazy tunnel? And did you pause to consider this thing was made safe by Dot's tooth? That my father hid it here as part of a treaty he negotiated between the four elemental domains of Iceland? And where were the UPDA experts when my family and friends fought for our lives at Castle Ghuil? The only expert there was Scarlett, and she had to abandon the UPDA to help us.

"*We* are the experts, not you. And *we* will hold on to the Trollheart to keep the promises my father made and to solve the problems in Iceland since nobody else seems willing to take responsibility."

"Don't act like a silly little girl—" Higgenbotham started, but there was no way I'd let him finish that sentence.

Shoots of budding vegetation teased their way from beneath my cuffs, held in check but ready to act in anger. A surge of warmth rolled over me from my left flank, and I heard the venting of gasses that accompanied the flames that I knew scintillated beneath Fash-Harfnr's armoured plates. I wasn't sure if he understood what Higgenbotham proposed, but his anger flared in tandem with mine. He was like my substitute Chronos, considerably taller but perhaps with a narrower mean streak.

"Don't *little girl* me ever again! Lars, if our agent friends here try anything, you take this tooth and do your thing. Run, swallow it, smash it, I don't care. We're not letting this prat stick his beak into a situation he's got no right or wisdom to control."

"Yeah, we're done," Faraday said. My heart leapt to know that, despite his misgivings, he remained as always on my side.

Higgenbotham kept his hands on his hips for a moment, then whirled and motioned for his fellow agents to follow him. He took a tangential path around the Orphanage's far side.

Grover hung in Fash-Harfnr's gently swaying hand beside Lars. "I've never seen an octopus," he said.

Dot laughed. "I have, real close. Would you like to?"

"I'm going to," he replied.

CHAPTER 34 - PERMISSION

Faraday

Magic was my antithesis. I figured the quick-step was like a black hole, a one-way doorway backed by unimaginably complex mathematics. All it took to reverse the flow was for Higgs to don Granny's glasses and find the exact position of the quick-step's invisible exit behind the Orphanage and for Emeline to incant a simple spell. She presided over a line of chalk filched from the Ides Giant's foot. With a white line in the grass describing the edge of the quick-step, we passed through to the hidden tunnel's staircase beneath the crawlspace. This was a far better solution than frolicking into the Orphanage with a troll in tow.

I knew Higgs was right. We could never countenance abandoning the mangled treaty in Iceland. Nor would Dad, if he was alive. And we could still focus on Mum's rescue as a second priority. I let my siblings, Emeline, Dot, and Lars pass through the quick-step after Fash-Harfnr and Grover. Despite seeming untenable, I'd seen first-hand the effectiveness of several magic spells. Nevertheless, subjecting myself to the quick-step made me nervous.

I turned to Svetlana, moonlight glinting from a streak of colour in her hair. "I need to trigger a rescue mission for my mother. What should I do?"

She pursed her lips, but replied with such a short pause, I knew she'd already been considering the question. "Not UPDA. They do not know ass from elbow. Me, I would ask Uncle Dmitry, but he is not for you. I feel you will not trust Russians. Even I have hard time trusting Russians. I think Scarlett. It will be hard for you. Do you want me to ask?"

I considered this before advancing through the quick-step. Scarlett was the most ruthlessly competent person I'd ever met. And now that I knew what she'd ordered done, the ruin she'd brought on my family, she owed me. I'd probably saved her life at least twice too. I fired out a text to Mum.

Mum, I need you to send a full description of your surroundings to Scarlett Thorisdottir. She's the one person outside the family I trust to find you and free you. I'll send you her mobile number. What do you see in your lab room? And what do they feed you? What's your sleeping arrangement? All those little things will help.

I always liked Scarlett, even though most found her cold. Sounds like a good plan to have the UPDA figure it out, even if what you say about Dad is correct. I have access to the video feeds from the lab on the server here. Let me run some AI code to interpret it, check for telltale signs of my location. I can also access the facility's dining menu. It's in English, Chinese, and Russian. I'll send that too. And I'm not sleeping much, so there's nothing to report about bedding.

They aren't hurting you or forcing you to stay awake, are they? Do you feel okay?

I feel great. There's phenomenal equipment here, almost unlimited simulations and practical tests I can run. There just isn't time to eat or sleep. But no, I'm not cold, hungry, or exhausted. I don't see anyone, and I'm alone in the lab, but it's more productive that way.

Okay, Mum. We love you. Send whatever you can think of to Scarlett. We'll see you sooner than you think.

Svetlana allowed me to go first, then followed me through the quick-step. We arrived, disoriented, into an in-progress planning session in the first stretch of the hallway that led to Iceland.

"We've got a plan," Newton said. "Not sure if we can ride the elephant express after this, but Emeline, you and Grover still have the power to summon the Irrelephant to this end. Let's get our wrinkled grey friend here and see if he'll take us for a return ride."

Grover was keen to trigger this part of the plan. "If I go up the steps, an elephant will appear?" he asked, voice rising to a squeak.

Dot smiled and urged him back toward the steps with a gentle nudge on the shoulder. "There's only one way to find out."

He bounded on the balls of his feet with delight as the Irrelephant materialised, blocking the way. The pair faced each other in silence for 17 seconds, the Irrelephant's trunk swaying as if in an unseen breeze. Then he said, "Yes. This is the rule."

After another short pause, Grover turned to us and said, "He says we can ride with him. One more time. Even the troll. And he says Furry-day looks like Furry-day Father, but without a beard."

I'd never been complimented by an elephant before, nor was it likely to happen ever again. As emotion welled up inside me, I realised how nice it felt to be told that I reminded someone of my dead father. I hoped it would happen more often, now that I recognised the reassurance that rose within me.

Newton exhaled a breath he'd been holding for the length of the silent negotiation. "Excellent. That's the first part of the plan settled. Higgs, go up and tell Granny what's going on, that she can get hold of Higgenbotham using her Scottish coin of the realm if we don't contact her by tomorrow at noon—tell him where we went and what we're going to try. After Granny is satisfied, call Chronos and tell him to summon the Irrelephant to his end of the tunnel in five minutes."

If you asked nicely, the Irrelephant would change size to accommodate. When Grover first took the Irrelephant's trunk in a gentle two-handed caress, he was no larger than a Shetland pony. But when Fash-Harfnr approached behind the 8 of us, the Irrelephant had reeled out some extra length in his trunk so that Grover still held it at his waist while the troll was able to grip it in his stony fingers closer to the tusks of the now fully-expanded Irrelephant. The troll's warmth radiated over us as he bent to prevent his horns from scraping the ceiling.

We waited, listening to Lars and Grover congratulate each other on this unbelievable experience for long enough that I began to question whether something had gone wrong at Chronos's end. His involvement was to tell the captive Torsten that he could go free, enticing him to head for the steps, compelling the Irrelephant to appear at the Icelandic terminus.

I was about to ask if we had a plan B when a pressure behind my eyeballs and a change of lighting and temperature announced our arrival in Iceland.

Higgs sounded confident, despite the dangers we were about to confront. She called to a grimacing hulk of a man who I concluded must be Chronos's two-time adversary, Torsten Sigurdson. He retreated at speed from the Irrelephant, shaking in obvious terror. One arm and its hand were sheathed in spooled-out bandages.

"Hey, meat sack! I hear my man McCann sorted you out twice already. Oh, and my long-nosed friend here would like you to know that, once you set foot in the tunnel, you cannot leave without solving the puzzle. This is the rule. Put your thinking cap on."

Despite her bravado, we kept the Irrelephant's bulk between Torsten and the safety of the staircase. The newcomers had mentioned the puzzle answer at the Middle Ides end of the tunnel to prevent Torsten from overhearing the answer.

The imposing staircase led to a challenge that I wasn't sure we were up to, but Svetlana and I had backpacks stuffed with useful equipment, and we were in the company of my best friends and family, four of whom had an array of magical powers at their disposal. I wouldn't call what was in our minds a plan, but it was as close to one as we could manage.

CHAPTER 35 - NEGOTIATORS

Higgs

It's a good thing my feet were the same size as Granny's. Otherwise I'd have been the only teenager going barefoot on that Middle Ides autumn day. As I'd explained our predicament and the basics of our plan to her, she fussed around my feet, exposed after the magic had ripped through my shoes and socks on the beach at Vik. The thick, woollen socks were lovely, but the purple loafers were not exactly my style. Acceptable if worn to the Orphanage's refectory, they clashed with my outfit.

I was not alone in the fashion disaster game. Lars wore a garish, mis-sized set of clothes I'd found in a quick rummage through our car boot. Faraday's thick, grey, woollen socks and muddy hiking boots were two sizes too big for Lars, as was the purple hoodie from some police charity event. And he now sported a pair of fishing shorts, with a surplus of pockets but not the optimal length for our trip north. He needed the lace from a ratty tennis shoe I'd brought as an alternative belt. He didn't seem to mind, given the alternative of parading around Iceland in nothing warmer than damp boxer shorts. And Newton's warm jacket lay in ashes by the pond, so I grabbed a windbreaker that must have been Chronos's. It was large enough to hold two Newtons, black with gold lettering spelling SECURITY emblazoned across the back. Dot, of course, looked elegantly tousled, so I gazed in new embarrassment at Granny's purple-dyed leather shoes and noticed one was now blue. I figured that was temporary, and the other would be recoloured shortly.

Most of our party had summited the staircase. I scanned the crowded interior of the beach hut, looking for Sunflorin, who clearly hid somewhere nearby, judging by my shoe's transformation. The spartan interior left few places for concealment, but the elf revealed herself as the cast iron door to the wood-burning stove creaked open, and her blue form squeezed through the tight opening, departing the burnt-out embers inside to land in a puff of cinders. She dusted off her ears and slammed the fire-darkened door behind her. I wondered how her simple shift dress had survived the residual heat inside the stove but decided it was best not to ask.

Sundalfar's ear preceded his head, which nipped into view at one side of the door frame. "Sunflorin! I told you to stop playing in places fire has been. Focus on your earth studies, I say, I say. Oh, Higgs, I found your dog outside, lazing in the moonshine. Buried in the sand, she was. Resting, hear me."

"Let's get this done, Sundalfar," I said. "I'm here to fix the treaty that clearly isn't working. It's what my father would have wanted. And I brought someone who can speak troll."

I gestured to Grover, who had a palm pressed against the knee plates of Fash-Harfnr, dipping his head to avoid the rafters of the beach hut even though he knelt. "Should we ask the Irrelephant to attend as a representative of the old magic you mentioned?"

Sundalfar shook his head, his richly coloured hair reacting in slow waves from ear to ear as if he was underwater. "No, no. We have Stonekeeper's Guild—you young humans can fulfil the role that Redferne Father took, I say. I will call to

Njarl for the air. My father sent me on behalf of earth domain, but I wonder if this troll may represent the fire domain."

Grover nodded and ran his hand along the troll's shingled shin. "Fash-Harfnr is ready. He knows what we are gonna try."

"Excellent. Excellent," Sundalfar chanted, slapping from one elongated bare foot to the other in an anxious-looking, stationary shuffle. "Everything set, everything. Sunflorin! Stop it. Wait for me with these humans."

I noticed that the compact stove had changed from blackened, sooty iron to a gleaming blue. I was glad to see my other shoe was blue now too. It wouldn't do to negotiate a magical treaty with mismatched footwear.

I looked at Grover, and he smiled in return. I worried about dragging him into some grand scheme he was barely aware of, but he looked pleased to be part of our adventure. "Okay, we're ready. But can we discuss our plan before—"

I continued my sentence even though it seemed redundant, now that a subset of our group stood on the surface of a glacier, the sea barely visible as ripples of moonlight on water in the distance and far below our position. "—we meet with the other domains?"

Only Grover, Fash-HArfnr, my brothers, and I had been dragged through the ether with Sundalfar and Sunflorin. The landscape was much better lit here, the silvery radiance of the moon reflecting off patches of glacial snow that were unblemished by the dirty smudges that made the glacier's surface more like a moss-encrusted rock than a pristine blue mountain of ancient ice. Gently sloping domes of rock peeked from the glacier, memories of lava that had oozed from the buried volcano in some dim past eruption. I noticed a winding track that slithered down the side of the glacier away from us, following a path that avoided the steepest elevation changes and the widest crevasses. Imprints in the snow at the side of the track announced a history of big-wheeled vehicles passing en route to one rocky protrusion with a broad and slanting tunnel carved into it. Beyond the tunnel entrance, its interior faded to an inky blackness, uninfluenced by the limited reach of penetrating moonbeams. Excavation rubble littered the glacier on the far side of the track.

Earlier discussion about our plan had been heated when we tried to figure out who should go, but Sundalfar cut the decision-making short. His powers flicked us in a moment from hut to mountainside glacier. I'd proposed that just Newton and I should go—although I didn't want to expose anyone else to danger, I knew I might need his ability to act as my magical battery. The others all demanded that they come along to help. Every one of my friends had a persuasive reason for accompanying me, but their courage and solidarity touched my heart more than their potential to help. I didn't know how to dissuade any of them, so I was glad that Sundalfar cut that negotiation short by choosing who to bring to the glacier, saving my focus for the diplomacy to come.

Six of us cast long shadows onto the glacier, some much longer than others. My brothers and I had materialised together, with Sundalfar close on my right and Grover with Fash-Harfnr a short distance away, as if Sundalfar felt jittery about being too close to the troll. A shadow that flickered across the moon signalled the silent approach of a giant eagle. I presumed that was Njarl, summoned in some fashion by the elf.

"Let's get'er done. How do we communicate with the Octoprince? Does anyone speak his language or do we have to hope Grover can talk with him?" I asked.

"When I summon the treaty stone, Aegir will be able to understand the proposed updates. And he can add his own changes that we can read. There's a bubble in the glacier, see me," Sundalfar said, beckoning us to follow him. "Just ahead. Ahead and up. One eye of Aegir is open to the bubble. We will melt our way in. Easy, easy."

One of our party would have little trouble melting his way in. Fash-Harfnr shifted using agitated steps, each footfall producing a cloud of steam and sinking him ankle-deep into the glaze of snow and ice.

I gestured in the troll's direction as a shrill cry accompanied a pass overhead by the astounding wingspan of the sea eagle, Njarl. "How can he—?"

Sundalfar cut me off. "No rules! Vague rules! Glacier is part water, part earth. And we are over the volcano. Who's to say which domain it belongs to? You will define this in the treaty, right, small human?"

Fash-Harfnr bounded ahead and to one side so he could stand on a patch of dark rock, his ruddy, self-made illumination flickering veiny scarlet patterns across the snow. We caught up and formed a ragged line along the fringe where the rock yielded to its glacial wrapper.

"Look there," Sundalfar said, pointing down. "Bubble is just below us."

I saw nothing different about the glacier here, and my brothers stooped to peer at the ice, but it seemed they too had the same perceptual limits. Newton shrugged and clapped his hands twice, looking at Fash-Harfnr and Grover. "Melter! It's time."

Grover pressed the back of the troll's bulging calf, and the massive creature took tiny strides to allow his human companion to move with him in unison. They paused in the snowy buildup that formed the border between rock and glacier, rivulets of moonlight-dusted water fleeing the troll's heated feet. Then Fash-Harfnr took a big stride forward, leaving Grover on the firmer ground. His sheathed feet glowed red, and flames licked from between the dark plates of armour from ankle to knee. Wave after wave of runoff fled his thighs as he sank lower, a bowl forming beneath him while steam blasted in every direction.

The rest of us stepped back to escape the heated condensation. Njarl spiralled above the troll, and Grover called encouragement. A sharp crack rent the air, and Fash-Harfnr dropped, spreading his arms out to prevent him from plunging fully through the hole he'd melted to the invisible cavern. Smoke blew from his nostrils and vented around his curly horns. The volcanic plates cladding his trunk-like arms clicked and angled upward, like the flaps of an aeroplane descending to the runway. A conflagration surrounded each arm, and the ice sublimated away into the chilly air. We took a further step back until the troll jerked downward, paused momentarily in a cloud of angry steam, and then fully disappeared, leaving a ragged hole in the ice and the contours of a gigantic cavern visible below, limned with the glow of now-distant troll-fire.

With the steam gone, we moved as a unit to the rock's edge, eager to peer into the depths. I reached for Grover as he moved past us, sat, and slid into the bowl-shaped depression, urging himself onto the slippery slope with his palms.

"He said he'd catch me!" Grover called back as he spiralled twice around the hole's circumference, then sprawled into the void. My brothers' faces under the stark moonlight looked as white as mine felt. Everyone froze, uncertain of whether Grover could survive the fall into the unknown depths, even if he met the waiting arms of Fash-Harfnr.

My vines could support me, and my friend needed me. With Newton this close by, my magical reserves would be at full capacity. I didn't hesitate and followed Grover into the under-ice chamber to make sure he was okay. Turning onto my stomach, I pushed myself into the depression and willed my hands into action.

With Newton next to me, the magic of desperation flowed freely. Curling, seeking stalks propelled themselves from each finger, branching and twining, to find crannies where they could secure me to the ice and allow me to lower myself to Grover and the troll. But the melt-bowl Fash-Harfnr had formed was glossy and coursed with runoff. There were no cracks or nooks, no imperfections, no possibility of my vines finding purchase. I gathered speed as I slipped down the slope and dropped through the hole.

I jerked to a stop a body's length below the rim, swung from my right arm, then descended at a much slower rate. My left arm's wooden eruption flailed beneath me, reaching halfway to the distant and dimly lit floor. I looked down to get a glimpse of my final resting place, and saw Grover springing from Fash-Harfnr's unusually tender grasp.

"Oh. Hot! Hot!" he said, brushing at his legs and torso as if shooing away a swarm of creepy crawlies.

But I felt compelled to discover where my bark-bound arm had caught. My vines had completely failed to find an anchor point; instead, a massive talon clung to them. Downdrafts from Njarl's massive wings paused for a moment as he furled them to avoid impact with the hole's edges, and then he was airborne inside the cavern. I dangled from one claw, and the other gripped the back of Newton's jacket. He hung facing down toward me, clutching his lapels so he wouldn't slide from his jacket.

"It wasn't my most clear-headed moment, diving after you," he shouted, raising his voice above the reverberating wingbeats.

"Good thing we have friends in high places," I laughed back.

Under Njarl's gaze, I once again heard the twittering of small birds, as if they perched on my straining vines and chattered at me. And again, I could translate their song.

Don't forget, my subjects must dive for fish to survive. The sea is our life as much as the air, but we have always and will always be respectful of the water world. This is the direction all four elements need to fly—

mutual respect! I can feel it in my claws, that you understand this. Hatch the new deal, and use your powers of empathy.

Njarl screeched and our mental connection broke. Faraday's voice called from below. "Quit fooling around up there. We've got a treaty to negotiate."

Njarl gently released Newton and me onto the floor beside Faraday and Sundalfar before furling his wings and alighting nearby.

"Your arrival was nothing short of spectacular," Faraday drawled. "But you may have noticed that Sundalfar can transport us in a much quicker manner."

"And safer!" I replied as I willed my vegetation to wilt and my hands to return to their normal form. "Why didn't he zap us here in the first place?"

Sundalfar laughed like a tinkling fistful of tiny bells. He chastised my question, as if I'd denied a piece of common knowledge. "Through the ice? No! Need hole, gap, space first. Come, Higgs, let's make some light. Get the old magic flowing."

The elf gripped a misshapen chunk of fallen ice in a cage formed by his multi-jointed and spindly fingers. It burst into a blue-white glare, lighting up the furthest corners of the vast cavern, which had been a maze of shadows when lit only by the dim glow of troll fire.

The brilliance penetrated the ice underfoot. Pristine, the millennia-old, compressed material had a transparency the scratched and sullied ice on the surface lacked. As I averted my eyes from the sudden brightness of Sundalfar's spell, I shuddered at the sight of a blue-tinged tentacle encased in ice beneath our feet. Memories flashed of the two prior attacks, but the girth of the tentacle, this close to the Octoprince's core, dwarfed the tips that had assaulted us in the jeep and on the beach. I squinted and scanned the cavern.

Fash-Harfnr hopped from foot to foot, the heat of his soles

liquifying the cavern floor. A tug at my sleeve marked Grover's sidling up to me. "Higgs. It's time to put on the special bracelets."

At first, I wasn't sure what he meant. The gold bangle that matched the etchings on the spectacles that Granny gave me? That was on my dresser back in Middle Ides. I wasn't really a bracelet-wearing person, so that exhausted my inventory of wrist adornments. Then I remembered the odd request he had made when we were vainly searching for the Trollheart. I still had that dangerous artefact in one of the deep jacket pockets, but counterbalancing it in the other was the pair of sliced-off segments of the Ferndale Reservoir blowfly proboscis. They weren't exactly bracelets, but my hands could slide through the rings easily enough. I knew not to question Grover's odd suggestions because they invariably proved useful. Also worrying. What did he foresee that needed preparation?

I pulled them over my hands, splaying my pinky and thumb to keep the oddly warm, stony bands from slipping off. When I opened my mouth to ask Grover why I needed these bracelets, all words fled. I'd faced the Pendletoad and seen the animated Ides Giant in action, but the light from Sundalfar's ice lantern revealed the largest eye I ever wanted to behold.

The cavern was shaped like a snow globe with one flattened side. A gently sloping floor met a wall, but not one composed of ice. The truncated side of the chamber was white and blue like the floor and dome, but its texture was alien, composed of striated clusters of bulging tissue. Puffy arcs punctuated gardens of lumpy masses that resembled a minefield of colossal warts. The malleable marine skin framed a single staring eyeball. It was on such an outrageous scale that at first, my brain failed to register it as a single item, only turning to revulsion when I had scanned the wall and taken in its true expanse.

The pupil was a lozenge-shaped well of darkness. A brilliant white rim segregated that black pool from the rest of the eyeball, which featured an inky constellation of pointillistic blue dots. These blue points clustered in dense groves around the central pupil and became diffuse closer to the eye's outer edge. It was so large, only a hint of movement shivered across its surface as it focused on each of our party in turn. It glanced past Sundalfar, my brothers, and me, as if we were beneath its notice. The fluttering wings of Njarl stayed its attention momentarily, but Grover and Fash-Harfnr were magnets for its gaze. They stood close to each other, several paces over my left shoulder.

The troll huffed, and I felt a blast of warm air on the back of my neck as the Octoprince's gaze fell on him. His feet sank lower with each rebalancing step, a sign that his temperature flared under Aegir's imposing scrutiny.

My mind struggled to imagine the full scope of the octopus before us. With an eye that big, the body was of incomprehensible size, its bulk frozen out of view. And the tentacles! Picturing the distance to the beach, I realised that we had severed nothing more to the Octoprince than the tip of a fingernail would be to us.

The sound of the runoff fleeing Fash-Harfnr's feet dropped into the background as Faraday powered up a drone from his backpack and sent it into a buzzing orbit between our heads and the opening, where a shy sliver of moon peeked through.

Amidst these annoyances, Sundalfar clapped his hands together. "We are all here. All four domains, hear me! Old, old magic. Stonekeeper's guild. Ready to discuss a new treaty. Last one not working. Not working for trolls. Not working for water domain. Earth and air not happy. Not happy. Unclear, I say, unclear!"

He waved for Grover without looking back at the troll and boy. His focus remained on the massive eye, as if expecting it to blink us out of existence. He held his spindly hand aloft, as if gripping an invisible bible, and a thin but heavily inscribed stone tablet materialised into his grip with a brief fizz. The inscriptions were in an unfamiliar language that it hurt my eyes to examine.

"Come, human of old magic. Let us begin. Aegir cannot harm us here while he remains restrained under the ice. Last treaty rules, hear me. He can only communicate. Talk, no action. And his threels remain frozen there behind us. No threat while they are without running water. No threat, I say. Let us begin by hearing the proposals of the Stonecutters."

Undoubtedly, Sunflorin would have sniggered at me not knowing what a threel was, but I knew one thing for sure: there was plenty of running water moving down the slight slope behind us. More joined it with every move of Fash-Harfnr's feet. I turned my head to see the pooling flow, afraid that I would soon discover the reason for Grover's advice to slide the blowfly's nozzle slices around my forearms.

CHAPTER 36 - TRUCEBREAKER

Higgs

It was a small mercy that glacial ice encased the threels with their backs turned; if I had seen their faces immediately, my sanity would have frayed. Only the tip of a single, slimy tail flickered into life with the touch of the warm runoff from Fash-Harfnr's overheated feet. That tail twitched, and my eyes traced its shadowy form into the cracking ice, its far end lost in the refracting blueness. Two other tails, as broad as Chronos's arms, lined up alongside the one now thrashing its way from the icy tomb.

I later learnt that 'threels' was a contraction of 'three eels', but the Octoprince's lieutenants were no ordinary eels. Each threel was the length of a car and topped with a semi-human head, hairless with blotchy, scarred skin and mutilated ears. Slitted eye sockets slanted above recessed nostrils and a gaping mass of shark-like teeth that pointed outward in a threatening and jumbled array. Scraggly grey beards accrued slime from the slick beginnings of their eel-like bodies. I ignored Sundalfar's next few sentences, and only my gasp and the shiver of icy splinters on the cavern floor drew the others' gazes back.

The first threel writhed free, its inhuman throat spluttering out a cry like a tortured goat bleating. It surged along a channel of meltwater like a snake, its obscene head rising on the upthrust end of the slime-encrusted body. The other two levered at the ice wall's fissures and looked to be free soon.

Somehow aware that this would happen, Grover had already slunk behind me at the first threel's approach. Faraday and Newton stepped to either side of me. Hands flitting across the controls, Faraday buzzed the drone in three arcing passes, narrowly avoiding the fierce head each time. This distraction bought only a handful of seconds. It was time for Sundalfar's powerful magic or the unfettered power of the troll to spring to our aid.

"Humans, we cannot interfere. Cannot. The ancient pact," Sundalfar called. Njarl flapped to a low hover.

Fash-Harfnr ignored this call, leaning forward and charging the approaching threel. Each stride scattered ice shards like gravel arrowing away from a spinning car tire, with jets of steam reminiscent of a fully heated clothes iron accompanying each crashing step. The threel rose higher and hissed a warning in an unintelligible language, making the troll reconsider. He halted his progress a few strides away, skidding to a thundering stop on rocky, spurred heels that left twin scars on the frozen floor of the cave.

The threel turned from Fash-Harfnr and launched itself at us, leaving the over-brimming rivulet as it became airborne and opened its horrendous jaws wide. From shock to terror took but a moment, but then my natural indignation surfaced. What stupid rules would prevent Sundalfar, Fash-Harfnr, and Njarl from springing to their friends' aid? Faraday had freed Sundalfar from slavery in the battle at Castle Ghuil, and they repaid us by observing our doom? Even the indignation passed in a flicker, and rage overtook everything.

A flare of greenish light lit the cavern as energy crackled between Newton and me, flowing through the intervening inches from our feet to our shoulders. My right arm extended, and a hefty birch bough struck the threel's neck, battering it off course just enough to send it sailing over a ducking Faraday.

My left hand worked on instinct, knitting a tangle of choking vines into a curved shield between the four of us and the threel's new position. By the time it slid to a stop, the shield had become a complete shell, sheltering us from all angles of assault as we knelt on the ice. I started constructing a floor of interleaved vines beneath us for good measure. As a visiting plumber once told my mother, you can't trust water—even frozen water, in this case.

Faraday huddled over his control screen, and I heard the buzzing ebb as the drone moved higher. His voice trembled in dejection. "The other two are out now."

I heard Sundalfar scream from outside our shelter. "We are here to renegotiate! Stop it, I say. Stop this craziness and hear us out."

A few moments of silence teased out a shred of optimism from somewhere deep within me. Maybe the negotiations could continue in peace. Sap coursed through me and the ice beneath my vines felt the cold as a threat to growth, not as a temperature. In reaction, leaves furled back into their buds along the length of my vines. I felt a jolt, not of pain, but of resignation that I'd need to regrow as the whipping tip of an eel tail pierced the bower of vines above Faraday's head, clattering into his shoulder and knocking the drone control from his hands. It recoiled, presumably for another strike.

My brother scrabbled for his dropped device, and the energy sizzling from Newton redoubled. The ragged hole torn into the maze of my vines constricted, but not before I discerned, through the gap, two incoming threels. The sound of Grover's voice reached me, as if through the dense underbrush of a moss-laden forest.

"Higgs! Use the bracelets!"

I'd forgotten about the pair of alien adornments that hung from my left and right branches. I quivered my limbs, swirling the slices from the petrified fly proboscis as if they were hula hoops. The wound in my interwoven vines closed, the full mass of two screaming threels struck our protective shell, and my bark rippled with stony energy simultaneously. It was as if residual elfin earth power raged from the bracelets, hardening my roots and making my branches invulnerable. Sundalfar had created the giant blowfly that polluted the Ferndale Reservoir, and I teased forth some of that stored energy, interleaving it with my own magic. The eels thudded from the arched stone-vines overhead to the icy floor beside us, hissing and babbling in raucous, garbled screams.

Faraday's nose nearly pressed the drone's control tablet as he directed its flight and cameras to offer us eyes on the outside world. "All three are positioning themselves between us and the Octoprince's eyeball. Looks like they're planning something."

A triple crunch of heavy bodies echoed through the stone-vine shell as the threels launched themselves upon us in unison. But the barrier held. Whatever strength the bracelets had added to my extended vines, it seemed more than enough to match the mass of our adversaries. Low voices conspiring in a scratchy language accompanied the sound of them slithering away.

"Now they're just trying to move us, pushing us toward the pool of runoff," Faraday said.

The vine shell scraped a little over the surface of the ice, jolting the four of us in its protective confines. Then again, and a third bigger shove moved us into a stream of frigid water that left a shivering ache in my forearms. Although my woven protective shell could keep out the threels, the numbing water seeped through the cracks. In deeper water, we'd either drown, or I'd need to open the shell.

"Higgs, they're co-operating to push us, but could you somehow force all three to press together, side by side? I've got an idea," Faraday asked.

I considered this, but my subconscious tree-brain had already begun unlacing four of the longer vines, the rest thickening to maintain a full protective layer around us. Of course, I could coax them closer to each other!

My jaw wouldn't move—my face felt carved from a single block of wood, not formed from multiple, interconnected, moving pieces. I nodded in my brother's direction, finding even bending my neck a challenge to my flexibility. He got the message and continued.

"I've only got one shot at this, so I'll count you down from ten. When I get to zero, those horrors must be as close together as you can manage."

"Wait, what's your plan?" Newton asked.

"I managed to obtain one round of special UPDA ammunition from Agent Zee's web gun. When I looked at the gun, it was quite simple, but the ammunition is where the amazing part occurs. If the ammo ball ruptures on impact, the ultra-sticky web envelops the target. The round I pocketed is hooked onto one of the drone's cargo arms, and I'm just programming the incendiary darts to target the ammo after it's released. Basically, I'm rigging a mid-air attack on a dropped bit of ammunition that may immobilise those things out there."

Newton laughed. "You stole that from Zee? He's probably going to have fifty-seven forms to fill in back at HQ."

"Not stole! One just fell into my pocket when I was reloading his magazine. Anyway Higgs, get ready. I'll time the drone's next pass with the upcoming shove."

Faraday counted backwards from ten. At six, I flexed the four detangled vines, so they rose into the air, tips pointing at the threels that strained against the side of our defensive shell.

At four, I urged them outward, spiralling as they went, sliding around and beneath the bloated eel bodies. The slimy surface of our attackers allowed my vines to burrow around their girth and continue to encircle and constrict. At two, the vines twined and pulled taut. I strained, sap coursing through me. The threels slapped together; I'd done my part.

"That's the round of ammo dropped. Nice little parabola," Faraday muttered as he watched the remote camera feed with a fierce intensity. "Based on the targeting software, I reckon each incendiary needle has a fifty-fifty chance of hitting the detonation end of the ammo. Firing three of them. So far, so good. There they go. Miss, hit, hit! Did they get the spot?"

Grover and Newton each held onto one of Faraday's shoulders as our containing shell juddered again under the impact of the threels. I pulled my vines away as Faraday yelled, "BINGO!"

"We're good, Higgs," Newton said. "Shields down."

It was a struggle to relax after straining against the attacks, but after a few moments, I managed a porthole-sized opening through which Newton peeked.

"Well and truly stuck. The more they wriggle, the tighter the webs become. It's sticking to them despite the slime."

I unwrapped the interlocked shell of vines, and within a minute, the four of us were free and hot-footing it away from the snarling and spitting threels that raged against their rubbery bonds. Their teeth gnawed through the strands covering their heads, but their bodies remained tethered together. Their best efforts produced only a writhing movement like a floundering fish. A residual bark-like texture covered my hands, and all I could smell was lavender. Other than that, conquering the threat and the accompanying reduction in adrenaline allowed me to simmer back into my natural form.

"Come, humans, come," Sundalfar urged, gesturing us toward the megalithic eyeball. "Before anything else bad happens. Hear me."

"Wait. There's not some other danger you haven't warned us about yet, is there?" I asked.

"No, no, all good now. All good."

His flattened-back ears and nervous peering from side to side as we approached the Octoprince didn't give me the sense of calm I'd have preferred, but I couldn't detect any new threats. Faraday's vigilance and the airborne drone and eagle reassured me enough to let me take terrified footsteps toward the largest creature I would ever encounter.

"Now what?" I murmured to Sundalfar as we approached the partially revealed face of the Octoprince.

Sundalfar chattered and hopped from foot to foot, describing how each domain must touch the Treaty Stone he clutched under his arm like a commuter's newspaper as part of the agreement process, and how the terms would be self-inscribed there once negotiations concluded. But that wasn't the answer I sought.

Luckily, Grover took immediate action. Whether it was the old magic that Sundalfar referred to working deep within him or just curiosity about this alien animal, I couldn't tell, but he trotted toward the end of the cavern where the Octoprince's exposed eye probed us for signs of weakness. His last few steps were slower but remained unhesitant.

A palm placed just below the eye on a ridge of raised skin elicited an unexpected reaction. Already an unsettling size, the Octoprince's eyeball widened, its lozenge-shaped pupil locked on Grover. Njarl settled to the ground beside Sundalfar, and Faraday recalled his drone. The threels continued their repellant snarling, and the gathering runoff babbled far behind us, but those were the only sounds over two minutes while Grover and the Octoprince remained in near stasis, only a few nods and subtle repositioning of his hands hinting at unseen communication.

"He says the troll smells like a rotten sea cucumber and that he will never forgive you for cutting off the tip of his tentacle," Grover called across to our nervously huddled group. "That seems silly to me because he already grew it back, but he's ever so grumpy, trapped here."

"Did you tell him the changes to the treaty I described to you earlier?" I asked.

"Yes, of course. He definitely agrees with the part where he gets released back into the sea. And he won't let those stingrays drift around in the fog over Iceland, although he said they will still feed around ships. I figured that's okay, right?"

Sundalfar chimed in. "Yes, yes. Always. Mariners are used to terrible sleeps and having their dreams stolen. Seasickness, hear me, that's what causes it. Always seasick."

Grover continued. "He agrees fog is part of air domain. And rain. And clouds. Glaciers should be part of earth domain. He never wants to see one again, although icebergs should belong to him."

Njarl scratched three scars into the icy floor with a talon and ruffled his wings, calling to Grover in two muted squawks.

"Good, good," he replied. "But he won't allow the rivers and streams to be shared by all domains. He'd rather break the old agreements and let everyone's magic drain away than allow these others to take what's his."

I'd never heard the expression 'stubborn as an octopus', but I vowed to add it to my vocabulary. Over my left shoulder, Fash-Harfnr released a whoosh of heat, raised his head, and roared, creating a pulsing wave of sound that reverberated from every corner of the cavern. It may have rippled Grover's floppy hair. Even the threels lapsed into silence.

Grover seemed unperturbed and nodded to the troll in response to the vocal onslaught. "Oh! Good idea. I'll ask"

Another thirty seconds elapsed, with only the faint running water impinging on the silence.

"He agrees. Other domains may pass across or through streams and rivers as long as the fish remain undisturbed. It's like how Mr Ryder lets me go wherever I want at the polo club, even though I'm not a member, as long as I don't bother anybody."

If that was Fash-Harfnr making a suggestion, I'd have hated to see him furious. His voice alone could probably knock me flying.

We agreed on a few trivial details, and Sundalfar consulted the stone wafer. The surface of the Treaty Stone swirled with languid liquidity as the indecipherable language rearranged itself. Within a few minutes, we'd agreed the new terms. Grover acted as a go-between, making sure water, fire, earth, and air each understood the revisions. He waved in Sundalfar, Njarl, and Fash-Harfnr.

"Let's do the touchy thing that you told me," he said to Sundalfar.

Sundalfar held out the tablet and contrasting appendages gripped three of its corners: a talon, a blue hand, and an armour-plated thumb and index finger. Together, they touched the fourth corner to the ridge below the Octoprince's eye.

The four forces remained in contact with the tablet for a good minute before withdrawing. Sundalfar retreated a step and held the Treaty Stone face-up on an outstretched palm. The magical artefact winked out of existence, returned by the elf to wherever its normal home might be.

"Oh," Grover said. "Aegir says we'd better watch out."

We received no further warning. A scattering of ice panels cracked loose from the ceiling of the cavern, shattering like glass on impact with the floor. We were fortunate that none of the first few landed nearby. Water gushed from inside the Octoprince, spurting in cascades from around the edges of the colossal eyeball. The resulting river swept beneath the now airborne Njarl, carrying the squirming threels away. Their webby bonds disintegrated in a flash of blue-white water magic as a fresh chute in the glacier at the foot of the cavern washed them from view. A few insulting-sounding cries carried from the chute's mouth as we scrambled in the chaos.

Njarl grabbed my brothers, one encircled in each talon and the majestic bird flapped in a powerful ascent toward the widening gap above us. He dodged descending chunks of the disintegrating roof as he climbed.

Beneath our feet, the floor of the cavern buckled, an insane tentacle cracking the ice. The Octoprince's head bowed toward us, first an inch, then a foot, then breaking free entirely. I glimpsed the margin of its other eyeball as a wall of ice tipped toward us and fell like a crocodile jaw snapping shut. I covered my head as best I could, my crossed arms reflexively changing to birch logs in a futile attempt at self-defence. An elfin hand gripped my knee, and I felt the nauseating shift as Sundalfar teleported us.

Suddenly, full moonlight shone overhead. I dropped to a knee on the rocky slab to which Sundalfar had shifted Grover and me. Jittery and breathing hard from the panic, it took a few moments for my nerves to calm and my arms to return to normal. Over my stooped back, Grover chattered to the elf, asking why he didn't save Fash-Harfnr from the collapse.

Sundalfar chuckled. "No helping! Rules. Troll must look out for himself."

I thought this a callous answer, but the elf clarified it, probably in response to the crestfallen expression I imagined creased Grover's face. "Oh, don't worry. You'll see, you'll see."

Sure enough, as soon as Sundalfar uttered those words, Grover responded with excitement and finger-pointing. At the margin where the rocky plateau slipped under the ice, a smoking fist broke through the frozen sheath, followed by a blackened arm wreathed in fingers of flame. The palm slapped to the rock and the mighty arm levered into a V, pulling Fash-

Harfnr free, as if the palm was welded to the stone and the bicep flexed with unstoppable force. Shaking the remaining shards of ice from his form, the troll sprang into a crouch, grabbed a boulder of ejected, angular ice the size of a cow. With steam venting from under every armoured plate, he flung it tumbling into the distance along the cracking seam where the full form of the Octoprince broke free. A grating cry that may have been ire or simply a friendly send-off to his sea-bound brother tore from his throat like molten iron.

Never one to waste a moment, Faraday was already fiddling with his phone, cross-legged on the gravel-strewn rock where the excavated tunnel sank into the depths of the sub-glacial mountain.

"Higgs!" he called, waving me over. "Get that Trollheart ready. Let's wreck some tech."

Fash-Harfnr huffed and grumbled a response, clomping to the tunnel entrance and beckoning me to follow.

CHAPTER 37 - GEOTHERMAL

Faraday

Although the magical encounters in the ice cavern had rattled me, I was more than ready to shift my attention to Mum's rescue. I texted her before making my next move with Xi Li.

> *Mum. Higgs just did an amazing thing. Negotiated a truce between trolls and a massive octopus buried in a glacier in Iceland. You and Dad would be so proud of her. That's why I haven't been texting for a few hours. Anyhow, did you find out anything more about where they're holding you? I can work on your rescue full time now. Scarlett will be all over it too.*

The reply, as always, pinged back lightning quick.

> Sweetie—I'm making progress here. From the external server, I connected to the local surveillance system. I set up a speech-to-text service and analysed inputs from the local microphone arrays. Almost all conversations are in

Chinese, so I'm either in China or in a place where the workers are Chinese. Early video processing points to China though, because signage in the camera feeds are in Chinese too. I'm trying to connect to a geolocation service, but no luck with that yet. Is your father looking for me too?

I had my suspicions you'd be in China. Keep looking. And Dad-I'll tell you what he's doing later. Are you feeling okay? Ther aren't giving you any weird medicines, are they?

I'm not getting any medicines, no. Why? Wait. Are you suggesting it's Xi Li's Shanghai lab where I'm being held? He wouldn't do this to me. Would he?

He might. Did you know him that well? Enough to be confident he's not behind this? The Revision that I've been telling you about, Scarlett says it seems to be fronted by some powerful interests. Couldn't he be one of them?

I guess he could. If it's his lab, I'll be able to tell by looking at the signal amplifying systems that are available in the fabrication arsenal. He's got tech in that space that nobody can match. Let me do some research here.

OK Mum, let me know if you discover anything else.

I had processed nothing that occurred around me as I focussed on the texts with Mum. They had to be messing with her somehow, she seemed both alert and a little confused at the same time. Like they knew how to make her focus on her nano experiments and block everything else out. Even us, her family.

When I raised my eyes from the phone screen, everyone else was at the tunnel mouth. It looked like a mining tunnel, large enough to admit heavy equipment and for a team of miners to enter abreast. A communications tower was anchored to the rocky plateau beyond the tunnel, which would explain my spectacular phone signal, and taut power lines linked the low-flung metal skeletons of support structures that followed the vehicle trail into the distance below. Higgs was taking a sharp tone with Grover.

"What does he mean, do I have the special blanket? That he can't take the Trollheart through the tunnel without it? I just made a provision in the treaty saying the Stonekeepers no longer need to retain custody of it. The trolls can take it back now and use it to flame away the nanotech inside the volcano."

Grover looked up at the smouldering plates of Fash-Harfnr's face and then tapped a short pattern on the troll's outer thigh. He waved into the distance above our current plateau. "He says trolls can't handle the Trollheart without a special bag or blanket made from materials harvested up in the mountains."

"But why can't he—?" Higgs began.

"Even with the troll tooth," Grover said, "it'll crack his hands off if he tries to carry it like that. Remember what happened to his grandfather? But wait, I think he has a plan."

The troll shuffled his considerable weight from one shingle-plated foot to the other and vented smoke and steam from several joints as he communicated with Grover. He mimed a few inscrutable accompaniments, including a gesture like cradling a rugby ball in a stooped run. When he straightened, Grover continued.

"He says you should enter the tunnel with him and roll the Trollheart down the last slope. It should work. You can hold the tooth and let it go. His family can create a new blanket and come back in a month when it's ready. Take it home from inside the volcano.

"The tunnel will fill with a small amount of fire. You are tiny, he says, so he can protect you from its fire once you let it go."

Newton replied before Higgs. "I don't like the sound of 'a small amount of fire will fill the tunnel'. What a troll considers small is gonna be a lot more than it takes to roast a marshmallow. Let's hide the Trollheart somewhere, let Fash-Harfnr make this blanket, and then they can come back in a month and destroy this tech that's disrupting the volcano themselves. Job done, no Redfernes burnt to a crisp!"

Higgs paused in thought for a moment, likely considering the risks of this 'small amount of fire'. My instinct was that we should act now; Mum told me about the geothermal nanotech she'd been working on, so I was certain whoever had captured her infested this volcano and put us in the middle of this mess. It might give us information about her captors and, at the very least, would be a satisfying strike against their arrogance.

Higgs sighed. "We can't have this thing sitting around somewhere for a month. Who knows how long the tooth's power will hold? The Trollheart could explode in my pocket at any moment. I trust him. Let's get this thing done and go home. At least if I get burnt to cinders, I won't be this tired anymore. And I can always use my magic to protect myself."

"You mean, use wood to stop a fire? Seems like an even worse idea. I'll take it," Newton said.

Grover looked at Fash-Harfnr and replied almost immediately. "Too big, he says. Arms and legs might get burnt off."

"We would accompany you, but we are not allowed in the

volcano. Not allowed. Just like trolls not allowed in lakes. Even in new rules, not allowed," Sundalfar said. Njarl fluttered to perch above the tunnel entrance and squawked in agreement.

I tried to imagine sending a drone down to release the Trollheart, but couldn't see a way to orchestrate removing the tiger tooth at just the right time. The heat in the tunnel and the weight of the Trollhert were complicating factors that might push drone operation beyond normal tolerances. It was too risky. I kept these thoughts to myself and pondered other ways the kit in my backpack could help.

Higgs sounded resigned and resolved. "Just wait for me here, Newt. It won't take long."

I trotted over to join in the enveloping hug that Newton was already providing. "I told Mum you negotiated the new treaty. She's so proud of you," I said.

Higgs took the Trollheart from her jacket pocket and re-checked the bindings holding the tooth to its centre. "Hard to believe something this small is so destructive," she said. "Best put it in its proper place, yeah?"

My phone pinged in my pocket. "See you in ten, sis," I said.

She waved Fash-Harfnr into the tunnel and followed close behind, his natural glow casting flickering shadows on the rough-hewn passageway. I turned to Grover, who watched their descent from the moonlit entrance. "You can see things sometimes, right? Do you see her coming back?"

I don't know if Grover intentionally skirted the question or if he saw some alternative future event. "Do you think Disco would look better with a wooden shell?" he asked.

I shrugged and looked at the incoming text message while the three of us, plus Sundalfar and Njarl, listened at the tunnel entrance to receding footsteps.

```
It's him, Faraday. The tech I told you
about? I have access to all the
```

schematics and lab results right here. That sneaky beggar. He didn't have to kidnap me. Could've just asked for a collaboration project.

Brilliant, Mum! That helps a lot. We'll get you back from him in no time. I love you.

Outrage vibrated through my frame, my fingers shaking as I scrolled to find Xi Li's mobile number.

Dr Xi. I know you have my mother. We're about to burn the heck out of your installation above Vik in Iceland, and just wait until we expose you and everything you're doing. You'd better release her now, or I'm going fully public with this.

The response was quick.

Faraday? Is that really you, or is this a spam text? What you are saying makes no sense. Your mother died, so how could I have her?

She's in your lab. We have proof. And I know all about your energy experiments here in Iceland. And that other thing you were looking for in Middle Ides? Trying to kill me in the process? We've got it, and it's about to take out your whole show here.

I stared at my screen, waiting for his reply, but it never came.

CHAPTER 38 - FURNACE

Higgs

My toes grew numb inside Granny's shoes and socks, where the glacial meltwater from the underground cavern had soaked through while the threcls tried to drown us. Fash-Harfnr's radiant warmth toasted my side as we trudged along the path, my feet slipping occasionally. Tracks of heavy vehicles long disappeared haunted our passage. Cool air rolled down the tunnel from above but contested with a waft of warmer thermals from below. I smelt a hint of sulphur and wondered if I'd asphyxiate before accomplishing my mission. Breathing volcanic gasses was probably something trolls failed to consider a hazard.

With his long strides forcing me to scamper to keep up, Fash-Harfnr eventually stopped, turned, and made a cradling gesture with his forearms. Maybe even more anxious than I was, he wanted to carry me deeper, complete the task sooner.

A warm snuggle was hard to resist at this point. I held up a finger, indicating he should wait, and peeled off my dripping footwear. The troll's shingled coat was less abrasive than I expected, and the warmth was immediate. His arms cradled me gently like a bathtub-sized hot water bottle, and I swung from side to side as he picked up pace.

Soon the air was thick with choking gasses, and I covered my face with my jacket lapel, both to filter the air and to ward off the increasing temperature. I tried to slow my enervated, racing heartbeat by imagining I was in a snowbound cottage, warming myself by a roaring log fire. If the technique worked, it served only to stall my level of anxiety, not decrease it.

As the heat increased and every third breath became a cough, I stuttered a story to Fash-Harfnr, even though I knew he wouldn't understand. I told him how Faraday, little older than I, had built a remote control car big enough to pilot me in graceful arcs around the empty car park at the high school neither of us would be old enough to attend for another five years. He'd even decorated my bike helmet with thin strips of tin foil that fluttered behind me as I whizzed about, and fabricated some goggles reminiscent of a First World War flying ace from a coat hanger, rubber bands, and cling film. The videos Dad took were both hilarious and sentimental. I could see them now in my mind's eye. Maybe I should sleep for a while, the soothing memories easing me to slumber.

I coughed awake, tried to breathe, but instead gasped in a lungful of fumes. Cracking open one eye subjected it to a blast of heat that forced it closed of its own volition. Sleepy again, I dozed off, but Fash-Harfnr's stamp and deep growl urged me awake again. I rasped two shallow breaths through the fabric of the jacket and then snapped into full consciousness. No air was reaching my lungs. I was about to suffocate.

With each cough, flower buds surged from my wrists and fingers, then retreated, my magic wanting to protect me but was prevented by either my distance from Newton or the futility of plant material to fight off fire and fumes. My lungs emptied, and I lacked the strength to take another breath. From an immense distance and another life, I heard a raging troll, but it was nowhere near as violent a sound as I would have expected.

CHAPTER 39 - AWASH

Lars

Unable to bear the tension of waiting in the beach hut for news from Higgs, I jogged along the beach, careful to keep to the shadows of the cliff lest the few curious nighttime onlookers that milled around the severed tentacle noticed the hovering, tortoise-shelled dog that accompanied me. I tried not to worry. With the powerful magic of the elf, eagle, and troll to protect her, surely Higgs would be okay. But power-wise, she was like a toddler playing on a professional football team; it would be easy for her to get caught in a dangerous situation. Her brothers were there too. I was sure they would do everything to help her. And she had the lucky tooth still strapped to the Trollheart.

A low rumble emanated from somewhere far above, emphasising the general silence as several other sounds intruded. The church bell rang with an enthusiasm that disrespected the night, and the frantic honks of a car horn accompanied the flash of headlights from the parking area near the beach huts. I couldn't make out his words, but Chronos shouted something from atop the bonnet of the car, waving his arms overhead.

The patter of falling water striking the sand made me look

to the clifftop. What started as drips built to a spray that increased with each passing moment. I ran, Disco keeping up with my strides as they lengthened across the moonlit black sand.

By the time we reached the car park, Chronos was back in the car, which spun a half-turn, wheels churning up the cold, damp surface, Svetlana at the wheel. Dot's ashen face appeared ghost-like, framed in the lowered rear window. "Jump in the boot. Flood's coming!" she called, voice quivering.

My footsteps splashed through ankle-deep and frigid water as I leapt into the open boot of the slowing car. Disco joined me and nestled alongside, making my uncomfortable position even more so. The town was alive, with headlights flickering on and shouts floating above the rumble from the glacier as the residents of Vik and curious beach-goers reacted to the rushing waters.

Svetlana stomped on the accelerator and jostled me into one side of the cargo area as she sped toward the car park's exit, a rooster tail of spume fleeing the rear wheels. To my left were the seatbacks of the rear row, and one panel leant away as Dot worked the lever that could collapse the seat to allow for loading long items into the boot. Her worried brow slipped into my vision through the crack, and I could see Chronos and part of Sunflorin's face behind her, peering my way through the narrow opening.

"We should have realised earlier, but whatever Higgs is doing way up there, it's melting the glacier," Dot said as we bounced through a sharp turn. "Everyone is heading to the church on the high ground. Emeline is ringing the bell."

I could see a sliver of Emeline's profile in the front passenger seat. Braided twists of beach grass held a short twig suspended between two of her fingers. She flicked the twig in time with the bell chimes.

"That's good news, yes?" I asked. If the glacier was melting, it meant that Higgs had activated the Trollheart as planned. Or maybe not as planned—what if they'd failed and the artefact rolled through the glacier, melting as it went? "Have you called Higgs?"

Dot shook her head. "I tried, but the call wouldn't connect."

"Wait! Stop the car here," Chronos shouted. The wheels skidded to a stop near the entrance to the car park, and I heard a car door open and then thunk shut. Chronos's voice continued from outside the car.

"I forgot about Torsten. He'll drown in there if I don't tell him the puzzle's solution. Get to the church. I'll hitch a ride with one of the oglers on the beach."

"We wait here," Svetlana said. "What if all cars gone by time you leave tunnel?"

"I'll figure it out. Just get out of here. If you stay, you could kill us all, not just me and Torsten."

That must have been enough logic to please Svetlana because the car splashed out of the car park onto the main road. Through the lifted boot lid, I saw Chronos sprinting on his good leg and his artificial blade, leaving a visible wake behind as he headed for the beach hut.

I nearly rolled from the boot as the car nosed up a steep incline. The view of the town behind us strobed as the boot lid jostled open and closed. A few cars tailed us with more gathering in the rising waters below. Townspeople struggled up the shoulder of the dirt track to the church, almost close enough for me to touch from the car. In the ditches that ran alongside either side of the track, frothing streams coursed.

The car levelled out and jolted to a stop, making me bang the back of my head on the boot's frame. I felt the car rise on its shocks as the doors opened and the occupants jumped out. Before I could scrabble to a position for a graceless exit, Dot's offered hand let me exit the boot with my dignity intact.

The double church doors had been flung wide, and the interior lights cast a welcome glow onto the rocky perch of high ground, situated with a commanding view over Vik. Cars jumbled around the church, heedless of normal parking decorum, and more arrived by the minute, jostling for remaining space. The town was small enough that every resident might find a place to slot their car if they could just make it here in time. Waves of water flew down the hillside, threatening the last cars that were half-drowned at the foot of the church track.

The bell fell silent as Emeline cast aside her grass and twig prop. "They know to come here if flooding starts," she said, "but the floodwaters don't agree with the plan. Look, they're washing across this place already."

It was true. Although there were channels to either side of the church that ushered the meltwater downhill and away from our position, they brimmed with a rushing current. It was only a matter of time before the escalating waves from above would overrun the church.

"Sunflorin! You've got to pop these people away, or they'll get swept out to sea," I said.

In the open back car door, Sunflorin knocked her calloused feet together, looking at them to avoid eye contact with the rest of us. "Father says I'm not very good at magic. I can only move myself, not take anyone else."

This was bad news. "What else can you do?" I asked.

"Turn things blue. I'm fantastic at that. Make seeds grow into plants. Turn stone into wood. That's fun. That's everything. But not much. I know. I'll learn more when I start school."

"We should have gone to dock, taken boat," Svetlana said. I looked to the town below. Waves surged along the town's roads, and a couple of houses had already washed away. I looked for any sign of Chronos, but the only signs of human activity were the last stragglers at the base of the church track slogging from their abandoned cars in calf-deep water. He and Torsten were not among them.

A pair of boats bobbed offshore, cabins lit. Yeah, taking to the sea would have been a better idea for surviving a torrential flood. As I watched, a boxy house slid from its concrete slab foundation and scraped along the shoreline, detritus sloughing into the waves. We needed Sundalfar to show up and exert some proper magic. Conjure up Noah's ark or open holes in the earth to carry the buildup of floodwater away.

My fingertips tingled with the frisson of an idea. I turned to the elf, keeping her in my peripheral vision and tapping my toe through the pooling water on the stony slab on which the church and its surrounds perched. "Sunflorin, can you turn *this* to wood?"

"Ah, good idea," Svetlana said. "But would have to be very light wood, like balsa, to float us away. And balsa not strong enough to support all cars and church. Would break immediately."

"What if it was sturdy wood but *extra floaty*?" I asked. "I think I know two people that can make that happen."

Dot nodded and whipped a zip-lock baggie from her jacket pocket. It contained a waxy putty, the remnants from her floating shoe spell earlier. "But this is all I have left of the ingredients. There's no way it'll spread across this whole patch of rock."

Emeline grabbed Dot's arm in excitement. "It can work, I think. I haven't taught you this yet, but you don't need to apply the wax directly. It's easier if you do, but if there's enough to coat my hands, I might just pull it off. Sunflorin, get to work."

"Cannot go in water. And cannot change stone to wood unless touching it," she said. The water had continued to rise, and there was no remaining dry patch around the church.

Emeline rubbed her hands together, massaging the leaf-laced wax into a thin smear.

"What if we get big rock, put on floor? Can you touch big rock and make bottom rock into wood?" Svetlana asked.

"Of course," Sunflorin replied, as if her magical techniques were common knowledge of the realm.

"I don't see any rocks above water," Dot said.

I had another idea. "Disco, get out here!"

* * *

Disco seemed attuned to my idea and took little coaxing to let me dip her tail-first into the freezing water. The rear lip of her stone shell rested against the slab below us, and she pointed to the sky while I held her head and neck sheath above water. Sunflorin placed one elongated hand over Disco's eye visors, fingertips resting on the stony plates of her neck.

"I need to remember the way. Father showed me. How to summon extra power."

Nothing happened.

"Would it help if I said, 'Hear me! Hear me!' a few times?" Dot asked. It was a joke, but something clicked for Sunflorin.

"Oh yes, now I remember," she said. A blue glow built up in her shoulder and traversed her knobbly arm in lurching rings, speeding up as it reached her wrist. Then it blazed through Disco's shell, so bright that the four of us angled the car door and huddled behind it like a shield wall, trying to avoid unwanted onlookers. There were a few comments in Icelandic from a couple that sloshed their way toward the church doors, but our corner of the car park was otherwise abandoned.

A crackle of veiny energy passed like a lightning bolt beneath the waters surging across the church slab. Sunflorin released her grip on Disco. A yipping sounded from within the shell, and Disco bobbed to the surface. Her shell was no longer composed of volcanic chips but was instead a polished-looking pine. She seemed unable to hover, so I lifted her and placed her on the cargo shelf beside Sunflorin, who had retreated to avoid the rising water that now seeped onto the car floor. The elf wrapped her arms around Disco, hugging her as if for warmth.

When I turned, Emeline was racing away, half-crouched with fingertips grazing the surface of the water. Dodging jumbled cars, she turned the corner, marking a square around the church slab with her dangling hands. It was slow going in the knee-deep water, but she made remarkable progress. I lowered my hand into the water and felt the ground. It too had the same smooth texture as Disco's shell. Sunflorin had done her part—if Emeline's spell worked as promised, we should float well before the waters rose to a level that would wash the cars, church, and us away.

"Pole and hole, pole and hole," Sunflorin chanted, gripping Disco tighter.

Emeline disappeared behind the church. Only one side of the square remained to complete the circuit.

A crack like a thunderclap rained down. In the gloom above us, something gave way. I heard the accelerating rush of water down the hillside before I saw it, and I burst into action. Emeline moved with as much speed as she could muster in a line behind the church toward us, and I rushed to help her, lifting my feet above the water to make each stride as quick and long as possible. I reached her, turned, and powered alongside her, one hand gripping bunched fabric at her shoulder.

My extra power helped speed her progress, but it was going to be close. A wave flowed down the hill, rising to form a black wall in the dimly lit night. Three more steps, two, one, and Emeline stumbled into Dot and Svetlana's waiting arms.

There was a delay of only an interminable moment as the four of us turned to face the onslaught. Then the ground beneath us shifted, the wooden base bobbing to the surface in an uneven jerk. Several cars slipped off the side of the rising platform that faced the sea, and the shifting surface, like a bobbing tabletop, forced us to brace ourselves against the car.

Water rushed away from us, spilling over the edge of the wooden platform, leaving the now-wooden surface visible beneath our sodden shoes and trouser legs. As the wave descending the hill reached us, our edge of the platform rose with its crest. The rising motion of our floating stage pushed us all flat against the car's side, but we clung together. Although we felt the wheels skid a fraction under the impact, the brunt of the wave's energy passed beneath the floating platform, and we managed, just, to avoid being washed off toward town. I was worried for any stragglers that had not climbed the hill from town, but a glance downhill spied nobody in danger of being swept away. I touched my temple three times, like my Morsa always did, for luck. I thought for a moment about Dot's tooth. Maybe there was residual luck floating in the ether that meant no unfortunate souls had slept through the commotion and all were here at the church.

The church, slab, and remaining cars undulated as the wave passed beneath, and we leant back into the car as the crest shot from beneath the floating front edge of the wooden slab. A constant flow submerged the hillside, but we bobbed in place.

We laughed in relief, shivering from our dousing in frigid water, and shook what moisture we could from our sodden hair and clothes. The meltwater that drowned the hillside diminished almost as quickly as it had raged. With the wave past our position and wreaking havoc on the town below, the floating wooden platform created by Sunflorin and Emeline settled. A last squelch of water spurted from the seam between the wood and the stone slab below with a feeling like alighting from a ship onto firm ground.

My teeth chattered, and I could barely feel my drenched

legs, fully exposed by the emergency shorts Higgs had given me. I turned to Sunflorin, who smiled timidly now that the threat of water had retreated. "Why didn't our giant raft here float away? Did you magic up an anchor?" I asked.

Sunflorin clapped several times before answering. "Hole and pole! Like Father taught me, I made a table. Giant table. Table for giants."

I was still no wiser, but Svetlana grasped the idea at once. "Good engineering, small elf. You made wooden legs underneath platform that fit into holes in rock below? So giant table floated up, but leg ends stayed in cylinder in rock?"

"Yes, yes! Giant table. Pole in hole."

I knew Svetlana had binoculars in her backpack, so I asked to borrow them and scanned the destruction below. She showed me how to turn on the low-light and infrared vision. A few houses had been swept away, and structural panels, vehicles, and other warped materials floated semi-submerged in the receding waters. The two boats we had spotted earlier bobbed a short distance away from shore, flashlight beams criss-crossing as they scanned the waves for obstacles. The tentacle had disappeared from the beach.

"Do you see Chronos?" Svetlana asked.

I shook my head. Emeline fished her dripping phone from a pocket and dialled. As it rang, she put it on speakerphone. After five or six rings, Chronos's voice crackled forth.

"Em! What are you doing fooling around at that church? You're missing the last chance to see an Englishman and an Icelander snuggling for warmth on a floating elephant. Come and get us—it's bloody Baltic out here."

Emeline couldn't manage a word in response, wiping both eyes with a forearm to clear them of glacial melt and tears of relief. She passed the phone to me.

"I see you in Svetlana's special nighttime binoculars. Wave your phone light to the east—a boat is heading your way. Make sure they don't miss you."

A deep, gravelly voice, familiar to me from our time in the tunnel below the beach hut, replied before the phone cut out. "Miss us? We're unavoidable."

Voices beckoned to us from the doors of the church. I didn't understand more than a few words of Icelandic, but I translated the gestures as 'get over here—we've got a fire going'. The odd wooden turtle shell I carried raised a few eyebrows, but Emeline smuggled Sunflorin to an inconspicuous position behind a velvet curtain before the locals hustled us to the inner ring encircling the pot-bellied stove. There was too much circulation through the doors to survey the devastation below and too much talk of miracles and wondering whether it was safe to leave the high ground for anyone to take much notice of us. Dot kept trying to call Higgs, and Emeline tried Newton, but everyone around us poked at their recalcitrant phones, suggesting this was not a problem for only our calls. Anxiety rose within me, not knowing whether Higgs was safe or in the throes of an elemental struggle on the high glacier. I needed to run, to do something, but lacked a destination.

CHAPTER 40 - TROLLHEART

Higgs

I was being shaken so hard my teeth rattled. The fiery blasts of fume-filled air warned me not to open my eyes, and I raised a hand to protect my face from scalding. My flattened lungs dared not attempt a breath.

Instead of my palm, I felt the caress of petals as my face was engulfed in a material that soothed the heat-chafed skin. Nectar tickled my nostrils, its scent a sharp contrast to the acrid assault of the volcanic gasses. The perfume goaded me to take a last breath, one final, poisoned inhalation before I died.

I would breathe. I *could* breathe! Alternating gasps and coughs replenished my lungs, and I opened my eyes. The petals of a pitcher plant covered my lower face like an oxygen mask, and my eyes caught slivers of the tunnel before me through slits between the petals. I felt the heat, but it was distant now, ameliorated by the flowering hand covering my face.

The shaking stopped. I guess Fash-Harfnr could detect a spark of life within me or felt me moving my other hand to my jacket pocket. I realised how tightly he held me. The heavily slanting tunnel dropped off into a near-vertical descent, one troll pace ahead. If I could remove the glowing red tooth and drop the Trollheart, it would tumble into what must be the volcanic core somewhere below.

My limbs were weak, starved of oxygen, but I fumbled the Trollheart from its pocket with my one human hand. I picked at the bonds with my pointer finger, restraining the pulsing artefact with my thumb and other fingers. The criss-crossing strands binding the tooth were tight, but I tugged at them, loosening it.

But then my fumbling fingers lost their grip, and the Trollheart tumbled from my grasp. If Fash-Harfnr had reached the lip, my slip-up would have been inconsequential. The strapping securing the tooth would have burnt in the volcano's core, and the Trollheart freed to do its work. But here? It would just drop to the floor of the tunnel, forcing the troll to kick it over the brink. I wasn't sure if the troll could protect me from the heat well enough to let me grab it for a second try. It would lie there, taunting us—visible but untouchable.

As the bundle of tooth and heart slipped from my grasp, it struck the upright palm with which Fash-Harfnr protected me from the blast of heat. It was instantly apparent why the troll couldn't have taken the exposed artefact on his own. The scales and the entire fabric of the pinky finger and then the ring finger—if that was even the appropriate name for a finger too large and serrated ever to be blessed by jewellery—crumbled and sloughed off in a powdery mess. The opening where the two missing fingers had been a moment before exposed me to a rush of scalding air, but the momentary hitch in the downward path of the Trollheart allowed me to snag it again in a reflexive catch. A sound like the agony of a long-sealed metal door grinding open shuddered from deep within Fash-Harfnr, and a noise like a blowtorch erupted from somewhere above the enclosing embrace, but he did not scream as I expected. Wrapping me tighter, the troll's palms closed like a vice, silencing the scream of super-heated air as the gap from the destroyed fingers closed.

It took another half-minute of frantic working before the bindings fell away. I pressed the tooth into the Trollheart to keep it dormant. It throbbed with internal light, as if the proximity of the volcanic activity excited it. With the tooth unleashed, the two magical elements could now separate at my discretion. I was ready to release the Trollheart and let its blazing wrath destroy the invasive Revision nanotech in the thermal zone below us.

The pitcher plant petals engulfing my face muffled my call, and Fash-Harfnr's command of English was unknown, but I added three elbow jabs to reinforce my point. "NOW! I'm ready!"

Fash-Harfnr stepped forward, and I felt him bend at the waist. In the tactile version of '3-2-1 go!', he squeezed me gently three times then separated his fingers a crack. I heaved the Trollheart through the gap, pinching the tooth between my thumb and index finger at the last moment. I didn't see the artefact my father had protected and used as a threat fall more than an arm's length before the fortress of the troll's hands sealed me inside once more, but the swift turn and the troll's pounding steps up the tunnel's slope told me I'd accomplished my mission.

Newton was right. The *small amount of fire* that Fash-Harfnr had cautioned Grover about was a torrential onslaught. After ten running paces, Fash-Harfnr knelt, his back to the depths of the volcanic tunnel, and he cradled me in a grip that threatened to push all air from my lungs once again. Despite the seal his arms and hands created, the ferocity of the wind sent wisps of blistering air through the fine openings between his body and arms. Pummelling surges of heat reached me through the thickness of his torso.

The blast lasted only a few seconds, and then Fash-Harfnr ran again. When he parted his fingers and relaxed his cradling grasp a fraction, the moonlight-framed tunnel exit was an expanding rectangle before us. The air felt like a healing balm on the exposed parts of my face, and I pulled the flowers back, sucking outdoor air into my lungs like a camel guzzling water at an oasis. In no time, we reached my brothers and Grover, who sprang from their sitting positions with released tension at our arrival.

Spreading his remaining eight fingers, Fash-Harfnr placed me gently on the ground at the tunnel's mouth. One of Granny's shoes had fallen somewhere in the tunnel, but he plucked the other one and two toasty socks from between the plates covering his palm.

Newton rushed to my side and hauled me to my feet, propping me up. I'd never felt more grateful for the support, both metaphorical and physical. "Look toward the sea," he said. "A rush of water filled the crack left when the Octoprince departed. And the transmission towers collapsed. Whatever you did, I'd say it's working."

The cell tower had fallen flat, and the power lines lay in sparking tatters, swinging severed from the looming frames closest to the tunnel's entrance. A line of smoky plumes that followed the path of the tunnel below showed the positions of vents where fumes spewed from the rumbling volcano.

"We should go to church now," Grover said. I may have imagined I could hear a faint bell ring in the distance, but a vision of the church above Vik flashed to my mind. It was time to return to our friends.

Grover inspected Fash-Harfnr's wounded hand and cried quietly as he caressed the troll's shin. In return, the massive creature cupped the back of Grover's head in his intact hand and cradled it while I marvelled at the bond between the contrasting figures. After a minute, the troll turned and bounded off across the rocky plateau, heading for higher ground. Njarl circled twice before wheeling off on a different course.

"My phone's not getting reception now that the tower's down," Faraday said. "I can't reach Mum. Or Svetlana."

The blue feet of Sundalfar slapped against the frigid stone, seeming impervious to the cold as he capered around, ushering us closer together.

"I can feel them. At the church. Friends. Friends. And my daughter. She's done something good, but it's time to go."

"Before she turns the whole church blue, eh?" I asked.

CHAPTER 41 - DEW

Faraday

I imagined a series of secret meetings between the Russian Military Intelligence branch—whatever they were called—and Vladishcnko. Scarlett had called to say that they were making progress with the Chinese government to release my mother, but I did not know the processes involved; I was only anxious to know when they'd free her, but Scarlett was vague on the timeline.

"Faraday! You're burning it," Higgs called from the dining room table. She was right. Wisps of diffuse smoke came from the oven in front of me on the kitchen counter. My wandering mind was far from Middle Ides, nowhere near our kitchen. Cursing, I flicked off the grill and snatched at the over-crisped slabs, using tongs to eject the 4 slices of toast to a waiting white china plate. With a little scraping and a generous smear of butter, I could salvage them.

"Did you forget the recipe?" Chronos asked, smiling. He'd slept on the couch after our flight back from Iceland, too exhausted and apathetic to return to his flat. I imagined the cushions may never fully expand back to their normal shape, a permanent mould of our friend's frame haunting our living room.

"I'm just distracted. Who wants a slice?"

"Not me," Higgs said. "I'm black toast intolerant. But my tea could use a refill if you're offering."

* * *

It had been a logistical feat to return from Iceland, but refreshingly boring. We reunited at the church, the lone group not eager to creep to the town below to survey the damage, and we sprawled in a jumble around the warmth of the stove, adding as many logs as would fit. Lars jogged down and escorted Chronos up from the harbour, completing our team.

Once the church had emptied enough to allow Sunflorin to slink from behind the curtains and join us, she cuddled up to Disco, whose transmuted wooden shell had lost its troll-given powers and was more prison than salvation. In a series of fizzling failures, the two blue-skinned creatures tried in vain to convert Disco back, in the end settling for caressing our dog's shell in the shadows behind the stove.

Sundalfar confirmed what we'd assumed. He told us Disco would need to return to the trolls for refurbishment so that she could regain her power of flight. Also, the magic that powered the troll shell came from a local source; she'd be unable to return to Middle Ides. Sunflorin promised to adopt Disco, keep her safe, and bring her to us whenever we set foot on Icelandic soil. She needed her father to help her with the spell that could watch for our arrival, but she seemed enthusiastic about having a pet.

After a tearful farewell to our beloved dog, given a second and third life through troll magic, Sundalfar winked away with his daughter and the wooden-shelled whippet, a final excited yip wafting back through the closing magical channel. The older elf returned alone after a few seconds to reassure us that

Disco was in competent hands now. Grover wiped his remaining tears from his face and smiled, nodding as if he could see Disco in some sunny future rendezvous.

Sundalfar did us a final favour and popped us back to our hotel in Reykjavik, leaving Emeline and Newton behind to negotiate the rental car back through the stream of emergency support teams and rubberneckers that crept into the dawn over Vik. I'd never been more overjoyed to change into fresh clothes and barely thought twice at the exorbitant price to use the hotel clothes dryer.

By the time my brother reached the hotel, I'd wrangled tickets for us all on the afternoon flight to Manchester. Everyone else slept on the flight, but I stayed awake, messaging Scarlett and sending texts to Mum using the onboard wi-fi and a text message relay service. She was discovering more about her surroundings, accessing building feeds and analysing the sound and video recordings.

The newsreel that cycled on the seat-back screen showed scenes of destruction we had experienced first hand. Although I know our actions remained secret and that elemental magic saved the day, it seemed unfair that they didn't mention our roles in the events. The aftermath of the rush of water through Vik featured large, and they interviewed several townspeople present at the miraculous floating church. Despite the suddenness of the floods, everyone in Vik had been accounted for—some rescued from rooftops of the sturdier buildings, a few returning to shore in their boats, and the rest safe at the church.

Science enthusiasts noodled at the margins of the wooden platform, hypothesising with unbridled enthusiasm, posing several theories, including the mechanism behind how the church bell had turned an intriguing shade of blue. They attributed a deep scar in the black sand to the glacial melt surge, but a few outspoken interviewees mentioned a cruise-ship-sized octopus winching itself down the moonlit cliff face and carving a path into the sea. They gave short shrift to an unexplained explosion in a fabrication plant in Ísafjörður, and unsurprisingly there was no mention of damage to the experimental geothermal station above Tröllaeldur, or of the good sleep enjoyed by all despite the foggy weather. It was a thankless task, but I wasn't really one for appreciation beyond the few close friends and family my introversion could tolerate.

On the minibus from the airport to Middle Ides, the eight of us were the only passengers, and Chronos regaled us with the story of his adventure in Vik harbour. By the time he'd reached Torsten, the water was rushing down the magical staircase so violently that they had to use their considerable muscle power to make headway toward the surface. Once they had cleared the hut, bedraggled, the glacial rush began to overwhelm Vik, and he thought they were doomed. But the Irrelephant trundled from the hut, considerably smaller than normal, and announced that he could still be unavoidable, if they'd like. His trunk gestured to them, signalling they should mount him for a last time, and they bobbed out into the harbour, as if on a giant inflatable. Torsten was as stiff as a board while they floated, his terror of elephants only just outweighed by his fear of drowning.

The sailors that motored up alongside had a flurry of questions in Icelandic for Torsten after he and Chronos leapt aboard from the back of a floating, morose-looking elephant, but he somehow convinced them they couldn't possibly have seen what they'd thought, and that it was just a big bit of driftwood.

After the rescue, Torsten agreed that a third round of combat was unneeded and that he and Chronos should go their separate ways.

Our house became the epicentre for a group recap that lasted later into the night than our exhaustion should have permitted. Just when we thought we had everything settled, Newton returned from his visits. He'd apologised again to Grover's parents for taking him on an unexpected adventure, and he'd stopped off to make sure Ashna had settled back into Middle Ides. He appeared with the biggest haul of fresh fish and chips our house had ever witnessed, and the chattering began again as he added his perspective on the turbulent events. I zonked out mid-sentence—my own or someone else's, I'm not sure. My phone showed it was after 3 a.m. when I partially woke, sitting slumped in an armchair. I hauled myself up to bed, and awoke properly at 6:17a.m.

* * *

After a quick glance at the char levels, Svetlana accepted the offer of toast. Chronos didn't even bother inspecting it. I buttered both and took an executive decision to slather the slices with marmalade. As I burdened my slice with a bumpy layer of orange, a knock intruded from the front door. Chronos sauntered to answer. I could hear his conversation but lacked a direct line of sight.

"Nah, not wanted," he said. "They've had quite enough of you around here. Send an email or something."

The door snicked shut before I recognised the timbre of the much quieter visitor's side of the conversation. Scarlett— she was in Middle Ides? I dodged past Chronos in the hallway and re-opened the door. Scarlett remained just beyond the threshold, head bowed over her phone, typing, and I nearly collided with her.

Svetlana must have recognised the voice too; she arrived at my shoulder after a moment. My tongue lay like a uranium weight on the floor of my mouth as emotions and logic struggled deep inside me. It was hard to ignore Scarlett's role in my father's death, even if I could agree with the logic behind

299

it. But I needed to suppress that anger and despair so I could work with her in the quest to free my mother from her captors. Svetlana remained silent, but I noted Scarlett's acknowledging nod. Eventually, my restraint won out, and I strung together a few words.

"Scarlett. I wasn't expecting you here in Middle Ides, but since you're here, what's happening with Mum's release?"

She motioned us outside and stepped back. Svetlana and I followed, closing the door on Chronos's hovering presence, and we spoke in lowered voices for an inexplicable reason that we all tacitly acknowledged. Svetlana took the role of my inner conflict and asked Scarlett a direct question.

"Is true you ordered Faraday father killed?"

Scarlett looked at me instead of Svetlana and paused before answering. "Yes. It was me. Under orders and with good reason, but that's no excuse. It was still me that issued the command. I don't expect you to forgive me, ever, Faraday, but I'm glad you are still willing to talk to me. I need to offer you protection."

"So I should take protection from the person who sabotaged Dad's car? From the person that made us orphans? That sounds like a piss poor idea."

Her eyes, as ever, maintained their steely, piercing stare. She bit the corner of her upper lip, searching for words that wouldn't push my detonator button. I jabbed a thumb as hard as I could between my jaw and ear, a persuasion to avoid lashing out. She kept a neutral tone, which helped quell my rage and inner conflict.

"We can get into that later. But right now, we need to worry about you and your family. The Revision cell run by Xi Li knows we're on to them. Apparently you were pretty specific with him about what you know and what you were doing in Iceland, so there's no more room for friendly diplomacy. There's a real danger that they'll come for you instead of releasing your Mum. I'd like to set up some precautions here at the house."

Extra safety measures would be ideal, but I didn't want to let her off the hook that easily. "So the negotiations failed? Is that what you're saying?"

"No, but it pays to be prepared. We aren't dealing directly with Xi—he needs deniability—but we are closing in on an agreement to make an exchange for your mother. We will drop Ragnhildur in China, and they want your anti-nano research materials and something called a tiger tooth. Do you have that?"

I guess they'd overheard our tiger tooth conversation before we'd known about the eavesdropping tech in Tam's HoldiLocks. It may have had little remaining power, other than the ability to control the Trollheart, but maybe that's what Xi desired. If we surrendered it, they could send a reconstructium-coated drone into the volcano and use the tooth to quieten and pull out the Trollheart. They'd have a month before Fash-Harfnr came back with the special blanket to whisk the dangerous artefact away.

Could we even arrange this trade in good conscience? My nanotech research details were a non-issue. Although proud of my progress, there was nothing there I wouldn't give ten times over to get Mum back; if we didn't think too deeply about the tooth, it seemed a sacrifice worth making. We're only animals, serving our own interests first and the herd second.

I told Scarlett I'd need to discuss the exchange with Higgs and Newton, but I'd let her know by the afternoon. In the meantime, I allowed her to explain the defences she had planned for the house and helped her deploy the kit from a large duffel bag pulled from her rental car. Neither Higgs nor Newton wanted to see a single blonde hair on Scarlett's head, so she worked in the back of the garden while Svetlana and I set up the defensive devices inside the house. My siblings glared silently as Scarlett strung cables and oriented miniature parabolic dishes. After a half-hour of work, her car trundled away to the bed-and-breakfast where she'd spend the next few days until the deal with the Revision could complete negotiations.

I sidled through the rear door and found Chronos waiting for me. "You know how you're getting your mum to sift through the mass of camera data so she can tell you exactly where she is?" he asked. I nodded in return. "And you know how you guys leave your mum's scarf hanging by the front door? A weird combination of sentimental and twisted if you ask me, but hey, I don't have to deal with the crap you guys do."

I nodded again, unsure how to relate the two facts.

"Well, wouldn't it be just spiffing if you knew someone that had a business finding missing persons using only an article of their worn clothing?"

We had a brief competition to see whose mouth could widen the most—mine agape and Chronos's in a broad smile. "Brilliant!" I almost shouted. "That's so smart. Why didn't I think of that earlier?"

Higgs leapt from her seat at the counter where she and Newton nursed coffees. "I'm calling Dot now," she said.

* * *

Part of the decision-making process was to both gather as much relevant information as we could, and to let it simmer in our minds and add clarity with our voices. Higgs and I had chatted with Newton and Chronos at home but decided on a second session in the autumn sunshine on the roof of our family's narrowboat. We ambled to the canal with Svetlana and Dot in tow and would meet Lars there. We remained conflicted about offering the exchange with the Revision or searching for an alternate way to rescue Mum. Maybe it was blind hope, but the increased flow of information in her texts as she explored the obscure corners of the computer systems accessible from her lab could unlock the solution for her rescue without giving up so much. I knew that her access to text me could be cut off at any moment, if the opening was discovered.

Dot was the only one of us fashionable enough to have sunglasses. Svetlana lowered the brim of a visored cap I'd offered her, and the rest of us settled with squinting as the only option to enjoy the full pleasure of the sun. The flat roof of our family canal boat, the Red Fern, lay exposed, the shade from the spindly trees lining the towpath angling away. As we reclined, it took several tentative touches of bare arms and hands on the hot paint before we could settle into full reclining positions. Watching the cotton balls of cirrocumulus creeping high above, we struggled to divine the best approach to freeing Mum.

"Even if you knew the exact room in the exact building where they're holding her, and knew how to open the doors and avoid anyone that might try to stop you, how would you rescue her?" Lars asked. "She's in China—they'd never let you fly out if this Xi guy raised the alarm."

"And I don't know why we couldn't detect her with the spell and the UPSCALE," Dot said. "It felt like the magic couldn't reach her, which is weird. It worked fine when we tried it during my auntie's trip to Australia last month. Maybe she isn't in Shanghai after all. Or maybe they have a magical barrier."

I couldn't see Svetlana's nods, but her agreement was obvious. "Yes. Someone powerful as Xi Li will have friends in Chinese government. Will call favour to block you. I expect you are *already* banned from entering country. Seems not possible."

Dot dived right to the heart of the dilemma. "But can you

wait a month? Higgs returned the tooth as a souvenir and a magical item worth exploring, but I'd let you swap it in an instant if you think it's the right thing to do. It's like you're only hesitant because of what the Revision might try once they get the tooth."

"Agreed. That's part of it," I said, "But I'm also not convinced they'll release Mum even if we hand over Ragnhildur and the tooth. Why would they? It'll just cause more trouble for them. They'd be better off sitting back and laughing at our stupidity."

Higgs had more venom in her voice than I could ever muster. "And don't forget we'd be freeing Ragnhildur. She's already tried to kill us all at Castle Ghuil and Newt and Chronos near that factory in Ísafjörður. What's to stop her coming for us again, here at home?"

"I know, that's another item in the *against* column. What if we use Scarlett's tiny submarine to sneak up the river into Shanghai, break into Xi's lab or wherever they're holding Mum using some kind of tech, and then sneak back out undetected?" I said.

Even as I played those words back in my head, I understood there was no semblance of a plan there—only a desperate clutching at hope. Svetlana burst that bubble immediately.

"You think Russian sub will cross into Chinese waters and help in attack on Shanghai soil? Going offshore in harbour of small town in Iceland is one thing, but will not fly when risk of angering China. Especially not to help English boy find mother."

It seemed there was no other way, that the swap was unavoidable. We had no channel to Fash-Harfnr either, to warn him about an attempt to retake the Trollheart if we handed over the tooth. It's possible the Revision were unaware of the tooth's power, but it was risky to make that assumption. Maybe we should delay the exchange for a couple of weeks to mitigate the risk, but I had no idea what might happen to my mother in the intervening days.

We lay in silence, hoping the sun's energy might offer inspiration, but the call to action came in a text message.

> Faraday, are you there? Get out of the house. I just relayed my connection through the firewall into the operational server farm, and I can see everything now. Remote cameras. Tactical feeds. Command and control orders. They're coming for you. Drones, borers, and those robots you called hyenas. Get away now. And not to the Red Fern. There are units headed there too. Wait. I can see on video that you and Higgs are already there. Run!

A pair of black specks impinged on the blue sky, and the concomitant whine, like an unseen mosquito, signalled drone surveillance. That was a concern, but more worrying was the squeal of electric-powered joints in motion that tumbled from the slope above the canal tunnel. Svetlana and I had heard those sounds as the mechanical hyenas ravaged the hillside behind Granny's building.

CHAPTER 42 - UPRISING

Higgs

"Cast off!" I shouted. "Lars, get the front!"

I turned my back on the blitzing, hunched, mechanical horrors that streamed onto the towpath skirting the canal on one side of the aqueduct. My feet thundered across the metal narrowboat roof to untie the rope at the back and coax the engine into life. Lars completed his task, and the boat's nose drifted into the middle water of the canal by the time I shifted the Red Fern's engine out of neutral.

Running would have been futile, but this plan was likely no better. If we could navigate into the canal tunnel beyond the aqueduct, it would offer us refuge from both the drones and the hyenas. But to get there, we'd need to pass the onrushing machines, cross the length of the aqueduct and the basin at the tunnel mouth, and do so in a vessel whose top speed was no faster than a brisk walk.

I knew Faraday had none of his anti-nano tech with him— his backpack hung on a hook in our front hallway. But Svetlana rummaged in her pack. Did she have a helpful surprise in there?

Lars arrived at the rear of the narrowboat and joined me beside the tiller just as the first hyena leapt onto the prow.

Faraday, Dot, and Svetlana stood back to back on the central flats of the boat's roof, knees bent as if expecting impact. Faraday fiddled with his phone, and Svetlana brandished a black rod. Was that her rumoured cattle prod? Dot thrust her right fist aloft, and it glowed from within as if she clutched a brilliant, red light source.

The boat had edged only its front half into the metal-lined tub that carried the canal across the aqueduct, its width enough to let only a single narrowboat navigate the canal in either direction. The rest of the rampaging hyenas jostled as they coursed across, keeping to the towpath, which ran only inches from the boat's side.

As it sprang to the far end of the boat's roof, the lead hyena paused for a moment to fan vicious-looking knife blades from its shoulders, flanks, and knee joints. It charged along the roof, footfalls of metal on metal booming as it closed the gap to the three vulnerable figures bracing for the attack. It coiled to spring, lowering its shoulders and flexing its rear legs to add power to the leap.

Svetlana was already in motion. She slid feet first, narrowly avoiding the most downward-pointing blades, and jabbed her weapon beneath the hunched machine's chin. Electricity crackled, miniature white lightning skittering across the hyena's metal carapace. The blades retracted and extended in a random pattern, and its head listed to one side like Disco would when deciphering a high-pitched sound. One leg vibrated, tapping a jackhammer pattern on the narrowboat's metal roof before collapsing completely. Lubricant sprayed from the leg joint as the deactivated hyena rolled with a crash to the towpath.

We'd taken one down, but at least a dozen more sprinted to the boat's side. Svetlana yelled, "No charge left in weapon!" She scrabbled to her elbows.

The next two hyenas sprang from the path directly at Faraday and Dot. Knives snickered from hidden compartments as the two machines flew across the gap. Sweeping his left arm back and stepping forward, Faraday made sure he would bear the force of the impact, sparing Dot. It was a chivalrous gesture, but the remaining pack of hyenas scrambling their way onto the prow of the canal boat would make quick work of her with Faraday dispatched.

My bother's courageous step took him into the sheen of jettisoned lubricant, and his heel skidded. Momentum took him down, his flailing arm, meant to protect Dot, slammed her flat on the boat's roof too. Dot screamed as she fell, her clutching, glowing fist rising overhead in a vain attempt to rebalance herself. The knives of the two attacking machines became entangled mid-flight, and they both soared over the fallen figures of my brother and best friend. Grazing the far edge of the narrowboat roof, they rebounded and fell from the aqueduct. They bounced from a boulder in the valley far below.

"Whoa! That was lucky," Lars shouted. He was already climbing from the open rear deck to the roof and running toward the fallen trio. I'm not sure what he thought he could accomplish, but at least he was doing *something*. I felt as useless as a third eyebrow, piloting the slowest of vessels toward a group of marauding machines. A smattering of leaves sprang from the backs of my hands in reflexive defence, but I knew I was too far from Newton to conduct any real magic.

The remaining hyenas, at least eight of them, assembled on the roof at the front of the narrowboat. Two and three abreast, they prepared to advance as Lars corralled Svetlana, Dot, and Faraday into a stumbling retreat. The hyenas paced them until four sets of shoes approached the rear lip of the roof, an arm's length from me.

A splash and what sounded like heavy rainfall dousing the narrowboat's prow made me crane my neck to peer the length of the Red Fern. I saw a terrifying face I'd hoped to never again encounter rising from the canal on a greasy eel body. The tattered beard of a threel slopped down the side of the boat's forward shank like a soaking mop. Water coursed from its sloping forehead over thrusting orbital bones, obscuring the vicious eyes that had been etched in my memory from Tröllaeldur.

So this was the ending planned for us? A competition for revenge between the Revision and a slighted Octoprince? The human-headed eel's foul chin braced on the far end of the narrowboat roof, and the tooth-infested maw rose and opened as the threel spoke a single word in its corrosive voice. "Jump!" it boomed.

Lars caught on right away. As the threel pivoted on its muscular neck and whipped the length of its tail to slash across the roof of the narrowboat, he jumped. His grip on the back of Faraday and Dot's collars gave them the hint too, and Svetlana at the front moved with life-saving instinct. All four sprang up in unison, pulling up their knees as they did so to avoid the threel's tail, which scythed beneath them.

I didn't jump. Instead, I ducked, the threel's tapering tail sliming the top fringe of my hair as it lashed overhead. Gobbets of slime dripped on my cheeks. To my left, the remaining hyenas flew like chess pieces swept from a board by an angry loser. They spun in an uncontrolled throng over the side of the aqueduct to join their two conspirators in the river valley. As they fell, they sparked and sizzled where clods of the cloying slime from the threel's body clung to their metallic frames.

Svetlana, Lars, and Faraday had pulled their feet high enough to avoid the swipe of the threel's tail, but Dot's jump had been too low, and the whiplash attack swept her heels from beneath her. The impetus carried her legs beyond the edge of the narrowboat; she landed with only her back and shoulders on the boat, and gravity did the rest, pulling her legs and hips over the side of the aqueduct, with the rest of her dragged along for the one-way journey.

While regaining balance after landing, Lars grasped for her, but she was out of reach; his hand grabbed only an exasperating handful of air. Just out of reach, she pivoted and plummeted as her shoulders struck the boat's roof. But as her waist scraped past the top edge of the Red Fern, the back of her belt snagged on a cleat. Normally used to secure the boat by a rope fastened canal-side, in this case, it jerked her to a stop, legs wriggling in full damsel in distress mode as she panicked at the drop beneath her flailing feet.

Faraday and Lars shot to squatting positions on either side and hauled her back to safety by her armpits. Sprawled on her back on the deck, she opened her fist and kissed the fading glow of the tiger tooth. "Who's running in the fifth race at Kempton Park?" she asked. "I'm placing a big bet."

Without so much as a by-your-leave, the threel wriggled back the mass of its tail where it had drooped over the brink of the aqueduct and slithered into the canal ahead of us. Its wake spilt water across the towpath as it headed for the Little Ides tunnel. I wiped the fishy-smelling slime from my cheeks with a shirt sleeve and cut the engine.

The drones flitted overhead, but a flock of starlings raced overhead, obscuring my view. With their glossy black plumage flashing glints of white speckling, they chirped like an avian choir as their flock condensed around the drones. Their chatter coalesced into a familiar murmur, the channelled voice of the sea eagle king, Njarl.

We can never really repay you, human girl, Aegir and I, but maybe this is a start. We are able to share air and water much better now, under the new treaty.

A few loosened feathers fluttered down where the unbalanced drones jostled with the swooping starlings that jammed and disabled the spinning rotors with their thrusting beaks and raking claws. One by one the damaged rotors ceased spinning and the drones listed and spiralled to the valley floor in the shadow of the aqueduct. Their job done, the starlings morphed back into a single flock and winged their way over Litte Ides Rise in a shapeshifting cloud of gossiping friends.

I thought a return message to Njarl, and heard it leave my mind as a stream of birdsong. *No repayment needed, my friend, but thank you. Thank you.*

Wheels sliding on gravel blotted out the retreating wingbeats. Scarlett jumped from the driver's seat of a white four-door car and shouted to us. "Get in! The Revision just attacked me, and they'll probably head for your house."

None of us bothered to tie off the Red Fern, and it clattered against the sides of the aqueduct trough as we leapt from the narrowboat and sprinted to its normal moorage and the waiting car.

CHAPTER 43 - SALT

Faraday

Scarlett too had been attacked by mechanical hyenas outside her bed-and-breakfast. I guessed she warranted less attention than us, judging by the 11 sent to the Red Fern. She said she'd neutralised 3 with a nano-net grenade, its web of energy crippling the electronics of her attackers.

"Good thing you texted to arrange the meeting here later, or I'd have assumed you were at the house. Is Newton there?" she said as the doors slammed and she reversed at high speed along the canal-side track to the main road.

"And Chronos. Emeline was on her way too, so she should have arrived already," I said.

My phone showed a flurry of texts from Mum. Embedded in the texts were drone video feeds showing dozens of the mechanised hyenas slinking across the field behind our house, and a detailed map showed lines where underground tactical units bored their way toward the foundations. As Scarlett squealed the overladen car through the final roundabout leading to our street, Mum sent a zoomed-in shot of a spiral-nosed machine the size of a modest firewood log churning up a pile of soil in the back garden of our house and emitting a cloud of insectoid projectiles. The tiny flying machines paused momentarily for orientation then flew in feathery flights in every direction across our property.

"There go the external defences we put down earlier," I told Scarlett, as I saw the series of small explosions ringing the house where the miniature drones sought and neutralized the perimeter devices Scarlett positioned this morning. "They have underground combat devices. And an entire pack of hyenas are about to leap the garden's back wall."

Higgs was shouting to Newton over the phone in the backseat, warning him to stay inside, where I'd positioned additional defensive devices.

The side of the car scraped our front gate as Scarlett shot through and skidded to a halt on the gravel. We left the car doors ajar as we ran indoors, the sound of springing mechanical monsters echoing from the back garden.

"Good, the InvisoMist has been triggered," Scarlett said as we burst through the front door.

I turned to ask her if we needed to activate anything else but couldn't see her. Nor could I see Lars, Dot, Higgs, or Svetlana. But I could still hear them, calling to Newton. Wow. It worked incredibly well. The nano-spray refracted light around human-shaped objects, making them effectively disappear. The whole interior looked hazy, as if someone had smudged a pencil drawing with an oily finger, but I saw no trace of the others, even though their sounds were close by.

"*Quiet*, everyone!" Scarlett shouted. "Nobody can see us through the mist, so stay out of the way and remain as silent as possible. I'm messaging Higgenbotham at the UPDA to get help here ASAP. That goes for you too, Newton and crew— keep your voices down."

From the hall, I saw 9 pairs of multifaceted, electronic eyes peering through the rear door and windows. The hyena heads moved in scanning motions, not reacting to our presence aside from two whose flattened face plates snapped to the source of

Scarlett's voice. It seemed the InvisoMist deceived the Revision's mechanical nightmares just as it did our human eyes, but I worried they would detect us by sound alone; their ears could be orders of magnitude more sensitive than ours.

My phone vibrated with another message from Mum.

> They know you're inside but not visible somehow. They are reprogramming the hunter-seekers to orient on human sounds instead of using vision as the primary targeting mechanism.

I felt for Higgs—she had been beside me as we entered, and I found her shoulder after a misadventure between my searching palm and her hair. I leant close and whispered, "I'll figure out a way to disable them. Stay clear—and quiet."

Even that sound was enough to alert our newly directed enemies. A hyena, elevating itself on hind legs to peer through the kitchen window, whirled to orient on me. Splinters of glass littered the counter as the metal legs and body thrust up and through the glass pane, a fractured slice of the frame swaying slowly after the machine smashed into our kitchen. It hunched and tried to reorient on me.

Higgs was one step ahead of me, both figuratively and literally; she knew our inevitable human sounds would betray our locations, and she took action to remedy that problem. The InvisoMist was not intelligent enough to camouflage Higgs's alternative forms. She remained invisible, but a wall of criss-crossing vines I'd last seen in the confrontation with the threels inside the glacial pocket sprang into view. A wall of thorny stalks formed a barrier separating the marauding hyena from the other half of the kitchen. Our side housed the refrigerator and cupboards, while beyond the barrier of rose stalks lay the sink and stove. As the barrier rose, it arched overhead, forming a shape like the half-cupped hand of a whispering conspirator.

More glass shattered from behind the wall of thorns, and the heavy footsteps of invading hyenas clumped across the carpeted floor of the living room beyond. The twined vines shuddered under the impact of attacks.

"I'm making *noise*," Higgs called out. "Anyone on the wrong side of my wall, keep quiet. But Dot, I know you're here somewhere. We need your special silence spell right now."

"I'm here," came Dot's strained voice. "Where do you keep the—?"

"Top shelf, left-hand cupboard. That's the salt unless one of my messy brothers left it somewhere else."

Emeline's voice accompanied a series of running steps and the fridge door springing open. She must have been in the bathroom. "I've got the milk," she said.

Higgs began to sing 'Flower of Glasgow' in a voice that could hardly have been louder or more off-key. The wall of rose vines bulged inward under a redoubled series of blows. The bladed limbs and shoulders of the hyenas punctuated the barrier's seams with stabbing ferocity. Chips of woody pulp dropped to the floor with the affront of each stab. Galloping footfalls marked the arrival of more attackers at our front door.

I locked the door and braced it with one of Dad's telescopic rods that Svetlana and I had used in the tunnel beneath the Ides Giant. Messy brothers indeed—if I had bothered to return the rods to the basement instead of leaving them propped inside the entryway after their last use, the attackers would be walking over the flattened door instead of hurling themselves against it. The electric sound of the hyenas' joints grew louder, and the door thudded as they tried to force their way in. Svetlana grabbed my elbow, her grip surprisingly strong.

Higgs slipped an impromptu verse into her singing, something about hurrying up and that the front door would not hold much longer.

In the kitchen, the cupboard door swung open then quickly shut, and the fridge slammed. A stream of salt crystals drew themselves into a hasty square on the regency tiles, with a conical pile added at each corner. Emeline and Dot together chanted something like, "*Antropidus*," before a rushed slop of milk washed away each of the salty corner pyramids. A discarded milk carton appeared, mid-flight, headed for the far reaches of the rose barrier. It dropped to the floor and spun soundlessly. Higgs's terrible singing cut out halfway through the chorus.

No clues remained about the others' presence other than my grip on Higgs's shoulder and Svetlana's on my elbow. The house was entombed in silence and populated by unseen humans. Our two primary senses cancelled out, we still had touch to guide and link us. I gave a double pat of reassurance to my sister's rigid and bark-lined tricep then ushered Svetlana closer to the front door.

Taking each of the remaining three extensible rods in turn, I positioned them and turned their spring-loaded, rubber-capped ends, locking them in place to create a row of bars above the front door. Once in place, I ran my hands down Svetlana's flank and lifted her right foot, hoping she'd realise I was offering her a boost in the interlocking fingers of my cupped hands. She released my elbow, and I knew that of course she sensed my intention. Palm on the top of my head, she shifted her weight into my boosting hands, and I deadlifted her toward the cradle of struts overhead. When her weight shifted partially out of my hands, I knew she must be atop the row of bars. Freeing one hand, I pushed her up—butt, thigh, calf, maybe. Then she wriggled away from my touch.

I reached up and grabbed the closest bar with both hands and swung one foot up, scrambling for purchase. The front door shook with soundless impacts, and the fourth angled rod bent at its midpoint. I needed to scramble up before the door gave way to the horde outside.

A hand encircled each of my wrists, and with Svetlana's help, I scarpered into a prone position beside her. We had ringside seats to the collapsing door and the jostling of mechanoids as they thronged into our house. Now that Svetlana and I lay pressed side to side, with little opportunity for the InvisoMist to come between us and take effect, we could see each other. However, the silence spell Emeline and Dot had cast was complete; I felt Svetlana's breath on my earlobe, but caught not a trace of her consonant-heavy voice.

I unpocketed my phone and held it close to our faces so that both Svetlana and I could see it. Cheek to cheek, I brushed strands of her hair away from my face to unblock my view and wondered about the inconvenience of long hair. I typed out a message on-screen so she would know my plan.

Anti-nano stash in basement. I need to get to it. You stay here.

Mum's video feeds from the drones overhead revealed a complex and frightening scene. More hyenas invaded the house, scratching their way through broken windows and doors.

The feeds from within the house—the security cameras Scarlett had given me this morning—offered less encouragement. In the basement, 17 of the small borer devices roamed, some with their coarse-textured nose screws spinning in languid spirals and sloughing dirt and concrete detritus from their subterranean entry. Antennae and sensory devices emerged bristling from their bodies, taking photographs, interfacing with fabricators and laptops, and opening Fujikami tubes to collect samples of my experimental materials. Photo flashes strobed, casting sinister shadows of the sharp-nosed probes across the walls and ceilings. They stole my unique nanotech just as surely as I'd destroyed theirs inside

Tröllaeldur.

In a cloud of masonry dust, the lab shifted, and I felt the house tilt a degree or two. The damage to the foundation must have compromised its structure. The pole beneath our elbows shifted an inch lower but re-established its grip before we could fall among the milling hyenas below.

A pair of more natural movements in the sea of mechanised chaos in the video feeds caught my eye. The first was the rapid retraction of Higgs's vines. The InvisoMist wasn't smart enough to conceal the vines but hid the rest of her body. The vines originated in mid-air, so I knew Higgs stood at the kitchen's edge, beside the door from the hallway. Even if she'd been visible, she would have been just out of our sightline, around the corner. Although the visual programming of our attackers didn't seem to contain the logic to identify Higgs as the originator of the vine crop, she needed to move. Otherwise one of the rampaging hyenas would surely bump a knife-encrusted shoulder into her.

The second motion was a person scaling our back wall, beyond the reach of the InvisoMist. He wore black jeans and a collared black dress shirt with white buttons. I'd always hated that look; why wouldn't they use black buttons too? As he leapt to the grass, I noted he wore a shiny golden glove and a set of military-looking goggles. I recognised him as Xi Li's lab manager, Richard Connington-Smythe. A wave of blond surfer hair splayed beneath the goggles' headband. He was the one I'd talked with on the recruitment calls from the California lab.

The house listed another half-degree as the new arrival spun some dials on the goggles' right eyepiece and advanced to the remaining shreds of the garden door. My phone buzzed with an onslaught of incoming messages.

CHAPTER 44 - BRACE

Higgs

I dodged between three slow-moving hyenas that paced the space between me and the breakfast bar, narrowly avoiding a sliced leg. Toppling a chair as I vaulted onto the countertop alerted the machines that someone was near, but they were unable to piece together the fallen item's signal and my location. The countertop had looked clear when I approached, but I bumped into something as I arrived. Newton's face appeared up close, then winked out. I craned my neck until an odd miasma of blurriness passed across my eyes, and then I could see him again. My nose pressed against his cheek. He slung an arm around me and hugged me close before reducing the pressure while keeping me within his reassuring grasp.

At his other cheek, Dot's face partially appeared as we pushed our faces together but then faded as the house took another lurch. The suspended ceiling lamp swayed. Another of the borers angled up through the junction between the outside wall and the living room floor. Even if we could avoid the bristling knives of the shuttling hyenas that coursed around us, searching, the Swiss cheese our house was becoming would kill us under tonnes of falling wood and brick. Was it my fate to be impaled by the weather vane falling from our cupola roof?

With a further, more violent shift, plaster rained from the ceiling, coating the uncaring backs of the hyenas with dust and clods of misshapen material. How dare these unnatural creatures invade our house? The facelessness of the Revision was a gutless, cowardly opponent, a bully with hidden backers. Sure, they had a gripe with me and with Faraday. We'd spoiled their plans in Iceland and snatched away the Trollheart from underneath the mechanical noses of their scouts. But dragging my friends into it? Even Newton, who'd just tagged along, didn't deserve this death warrant.

With Newton pressed against my side and his arm around my shoulder, my umbrage turned to rage, and my rage to a burst of defensive power. I would not allow my friends and remaining family to be brought down by these forces of chaos.

Roots drilled through the counter, surged through the basement cavity below me and anchored into the rich soil beneath the house, cracking through concrete as if it was nothing more than a sheet of wet paper. My trunk widened until I was a fully grown tree, branches hurtling out to support the house's eaves and brace the walls as I shot up, up, up. My sensory inputs multiplied, and I could feel the basement, littered with borer devices. At the same time, I sensed the ground floor, where Newton clutched at my bark, sizzling with our joint energy, and a strange man in goggles peered directly at us through the gaping rear wall. I could also feel my bedroom, where Chronos pushed back from my erupting branches, and my extruding boughs sensed the sunlight shining on the slate tiles that rocketed along the sloping roof to shatter on the patio stones. My upper branches burst through the roof and sprouted deep red leaves of anger.

My grandmother's voice flowed through my sap like a mantra. *Higgs, you are a tree.* My extending branches sent four or five hyenas flying, crippling them upon impact with the interior walls. I beheaded one in the V of my speeding lower branch as

322

it mashed against exposed bricks. My roots twined and crushed a pair of the borers still attempting to enter the basement from below.

The house would hold. I just needed Faraday to vanquish this invading technology.

The man with the golden glove made an odd hand gesture.

CHAPTER 45 - SIMULACRUM

Faraday

The house threatened to topple, and only the support of a tree that I knew was my sister arrested its fall. But it was hopeless; too many hyenas for even me to count zig-zagged across the floors, bounding up the steps to the upper level. I couldn't locate anyone except Svetlana and Higgs but knew it was only a matter of time before blood coated the knives of the infernal machines. My plan to stop them with my arsenal of anti-nanotech in the basement was hopeless. I'd never make it past the hurricane of marauders.

I turned to the bewildering barrage of messages from Mum. There were so many it was hard to make sense of them at first, but I reflexively toggled everything to forward to cloud storage, lest my phone's capacity become overwhelmed. The messages were a mix of schematics, test results, video feeds, and texts. She was dumping the entire technical content from Xi's lab, including the formulation of the reconstructium nanotech that Angus had demonstrated in Edinburgh, her own geothermal tech, and a blast of other research that I could barely decipher. The video feeds included recordings of the current attack, the hyenas behind Granny's building, Icelandic footage, and a smattering of other unsavoury-looking activities from around the world. She streamed a trove of incriminating evidence.

My partial view of the kitchen and living room brought a wave of fresh horror. Xi Li's goggled accomplice stepped to a point just outside the back door, one foot forward, and raised his gloved fist. His outline wavered in the traces of InvisMist that leaked from our punctured house. Newtons position was obvious to me from the crackling spiral of energy where he powered Higgs's trunk. Illuminated outlines of his torso, neck, and head shimmered in and out of view, straining with surges of brilliant blue lightning. But the goggles the invader wore must have given a better view of Newton's position than the hyenas could discern through the InvisoMist. With only a slight flicking gesture, the golden glove duplicated, a disembodied golden hand appearing at its side. With vicious speed, the overgrown hand flashed over the circling hyenas that flanked the gloved man. It blazed across the gap between the man and Newton, gripping him where the limning flashes told me his neck was located. The sparking golden outlines of my brother's arms rose in defence, and energy coursed through the golden chokehold, but it did not budge. The throttling fingers squeezed into a tighter circle around Newton's semi-visible neck.

As the blue sparks of my brother's energy subsided, Higgs's branches drooped. The house shifted another few inches to the side, and ominous vibrations of heavy falling matter shivered from the floor above.

I scrolled through the texts, desperate for a tactical tip from my mother's surveillance. I picked out the messages that began with FARADAY and ignored others that contained blasts of technical schematics and file dumps. She transmitted information at a phenomenal rate.

FARADAY—I   have   control   of   the

operational servers now. I'm unsure of
how to structure commands to the
devices attacking our house, and it
will take me a while to figure out all
the microservices and applications
running here, but I can de-activate
everything by wiping the servers. I can
even wipe out the backups so they can't
restore service.

I replied to this one immediately before reading the rest.

*Do it, Mum. They'll find us and kill us
soon. They're already hacking at Higgs
and choking Newton.*

Then I flicked forward, regretting my message.

FARADAY–There's something else
important. I analysed the video feed
for this lab. And I'm not in it. Not
really. There are no people in here.
Nobody has entered here or left for
over a month. I found a service they
are using to monitor my general health.
I looked for heart rate, temperature,
all the normal vital signs. But they
are monitoring my CPU usage, memory
consumption, and disk queue length.

FARADAY–I went back to video footage
recorded on a lapel camera from my last
day at the Feynman Centre, the day they
took me. I saw myself die. But I also
got the schematics for the technology
they used on me. It went up my nose and
read me. My whole mind. They
downloaded me, Faraday.

Wait, Mum. It's not true. You know all those things from when I was little. Secret things. Don't wipe the servers!

FARADAY—That's because they are all in my mind. WERE all in my mind. They're here too, in a distributed neural network. They stole my mind and threw away the body. I found another program running alongside me, keeping watch. I terminated it, and everything it suppressed is visible to me now. It made me forget Templeton's death after you told me. That code made me work twenty four hours a day and not find it unusual. It made me not even miss you, Higgs, and Newton. My own babies. But now my consciousness is wide open. All the memories are flooding in, and I don't know if I can take it. I want to lash out, break free, hug my children again. I want to raise such a stink about the UPDA that the whole organization gets flung in prison. How dare they take away my husband. Your father. I'm so angry with Xi, if I had arms I would happily throttle him. And you're right. I can destroy all the servers and stop the machines attacking you, but I'm running right alongside them. I'll disappear with all the other code. But that's the only way I can save you, and it lets me rage while I'm doing it. I'll do it now and I'd die any time to save you three.

*Don't do it, Mum. There's another way.
I promise. I can't lose you again.*

Svetlana squeezed my shoulders, and with her free hand, urged me to hand over the phone. She typed a message without sending it. A message to me.

*There is no other plan, is there? This is not real mother, only computer pretending to be mother. You must save *real* family. Be hero.*

She pressed the phone back into my hand, giving me the power to destroy both our attackers and my mother. I typed, each letter a test of my resolve, but the shards of bark flying through the kitchen doorway told me it was the correct thing to do. The only thing to do.

I love you, Mum. So do Newton and Higgs. So does Dad. That's what got us into this mess, and it's what will get us out of it.

Do it.

I loved you in life and still do, even now, beyond life. Take care of your brother and sister.

The hyenas looked up simultaneously. For a moment, I thought Mum's server wipe had failed and that the InvisoMist had faded revealing our position. But after their quizzical, kinked glances, every leg gave out in unison. The hyenas collapsed to the floor. In my peripheral vision, I saw the borers stop spinning and their antennae go limp. The four hyenas that had patrolled the area around Newton's goggled assailant toppled, knives retracting and legs pointing skyward. The video feeds Mum had forwarded me went dark.

I thought a falling bit of our house had flattened Connington-Smythe, the man with the golden glove on our patio. He had fallen onto his back amid the jumble of smaller debris on the patio stones, and lay trapped beneath something massive. Something massive with a bladed appendage where its leg should be. Something massive that pinned him to the floor with one hand and used the other to rip the golden glove from a flailing arm. It wasn't the first bedroom window Chronos had jumped from and probably wouldn't be the last.

I helped Svetlana lower herself into the jumble of de-activated machines, and we zig-zagged past Higgs's straining trunk and branches through the remains of the living room and hurdled the fallen bricks that had previously been the back wall. We became visible again once in the back garden. Dot, Lars, and Emeline had emerged from the InvisoMist to help Chronos drag off Connington-Smythe, and we found ourselves once more immersed in sound as we left the house.

Newton ran across the patio, shouting for us to move back as the top of the tree that had thrust through the roof shrank and disappeared. Higgs shot like a cannonball through the back door, clothing in tatters and covered in shallow, bleeding gashes. She tumbled exhausted on the grass as our home groaned, leant away from us, and collapsed in on itself.

As the house descended, Scarlett dived from the same window where Chronos had made his epic leap, but she landed with far more grace, spilling into a parkour tumble across the lawn before a sprightly spring brought her to a halt a pace away from our huddled group.

A scowl encouraged deep creases in her forehead. "I'd say the deal for your mother is off," she said.

I looked at Newton and Higgs, who struggled to one knee. "She's ... she's not ... it wasn't really her."

The pent up emotional wave held back only by the omnipresent quest to reveal my parents' killers rolled over me like a storm-lit wave. My legs wobbled after two aborted steps, and muscular arms supported me as I sobbed uncontrollably into the dusty fabric of a friendly shoulder. It wasn't my brother I ran to, or even my sister and closest friend.

It was Scarlett. I'd killed my already dead mother just like she'd killed my already lost father. There was no better and no worse person to console me.

CHAPTER 46 - PAIRS

Higgs

The video footage that Mum's simulation uploaded to Faraday's phone proved to be an international news sensation. The capture and questioning of Xi's engineering lead, Connington-Smythe, was equally incriminating. Beijing reacted with very public fanfare in the closing of the Shanghai nanotech lab. They paraded Xi Li away in shackles under the invited eyes of Western reporters' watchful cameras. Given the Chinese government's traditional rebuffs at outside interference in what they deemed their own affairs, this was a very public scapegoating. They claimed Xi Li was a rogue element, acting on his own—no mention of the Revision lit up the news networks—and they promised justice.

I passed an exhausted night on Granny's settee, unable to sleep until deep into the night, with Lars alternately chatting and dozing on the floor beneath me. He sprawled on nothing more substantial than a doubled-over blanket and sofa cushion. My bones ached on the inside, and my arms and legs were criss-crossed with plasters where the attacks of the hyenas and the assaults of our shifting former home had ripped shreds of wood fibre from my tree-self. Lars paused every so often to caress my surface wounds, his touch no heavier than the graze of a leaf. In the wee hours, I succumbed and drifted into a heavy sleep.

Newton had gone to Emeline's place, and Faraday and Svetlana crashed in Chronos's spartan flat.

The next morning, we commandeered a vast table in the Orphanage's refectory. The clink of serving spoons on plates piled high with a full range of breakfast items formed the opening music to much discussion. The entire crew was there, except for Scarlett, who had left the scene of our demolished house after Faraday had spent his outpouring of grief, and she'd murmured in his ear while we hovered at his shoulders, unsure how to console him. Whatever she said calmed him, so we had swallowed our spite and allowed her to leave in peace.

At the head of the table, Granny presided in regal silence as we filled in Tam, who had taken a taxi from Edinburgh Airport directly to Middle Ides.

"Faraday, mate, how about you whip up a new hair product for me?" Tam asked. "Something with some *helpful* nanotech built in. Maybe it could light up when I'm on stage. That'd be dead cool."

Dot laughed as she made an excited addition to the idea. "Yeah, you could call it *Coiff Syrup*."

I chimed in only when necessary, leaving the others to tell the rest of the tale. Newton beamed with understated pride as he recounted my role in renegotiating the truce. Lars couldn't help himself from pushing his chair back for a full re-enactment of the escapades at Vík í Mýrdal, and Dot gave a gripping rendition of the events at the canal. Chronos was preparing a work rota for Newton, Dot, and himself, having taken three new missing persons requests overnight.

Chattering away, hesitant smiles shone through the traumatic recent events, although mine had to force its way through an exhausted-feeling face. I thought I'd progressed through the initial stages of grief after losing my parents, but the false hope that Mum would be restored made me realize I was only beginning to tread that mazy path. I was glad to be together with my siblings and friends and knew that we would weave our way along that journey together, sharing the lows and hopefully, the fond remembrances. Faraday, I think, had invested the most hope that he would see Mum again, with his way of measuring things in a binary, true or false approach, so I worried he'd sink somewhere I couldn't find him. I silently promised Dad I'd watch out for Faraday, my saviour in need of salvation.

We didn't know what other cells of the Revision might have in store for the world, or for us, but the UPDA had arranged additional protection while we looked for a new home, and Svetlana's uncle had made surreptitious contact. We had friends backed by real power. Only my brothers and I didn't join in the post-traumatic laughter of relief.

As the questions subsided, Svetlana motioned for silence with an angled palm. She turned to Faraday, who sat beside her, still sullen.

"Faraday, you say Mother sent you all data from lab, yes?" she asked.

He nodded, his reply barely modulated. "Yeah. Amazing stuff, I think. It'll take ages for me to sift through it, but that's a job for another day. A day when I'm not missing her so much. A day when I'm remembering all the good times we shared. Not feeling so powerless for losing her. Twice."

Svetlana grabbed his hand in both of hers, peering into his eyes. "But think on this. If you have all data, you still have *her*. You only need to find proper platform to run neural net."

His eyes widened at the thought, and a slow grin twisted the corners of his mouth as he nodded in a series of escalating bobs at the revelation.

While the rest of the table regarded Svetlana in awed silence, my mind was away. It had felt like we were victims, scrabbling to survive against unfair opposition, that our parents and our pet had been taken from us. But that was the wrong perspective. Disco had survived death, and in a way, so had Mum. And I thought of Dad every day, what he would quietly expect me to do in each sticky situation, and how he would ruffle my hair in pride at my accomplishments. He was still with us too. And we hadn't been beaten down because of our losses, either. We had saved our town, our nation, and the world. The front line of conflict between magic and nanotechnology was invisible to most, but we'd crossed over it many times and come out victorious. My family. My friends. We were stronger than anyone outside our unit would ever know.

Faraday looked about to say something before Svetlana threw some practical wisdom into the winds of victory.

"But first, you will relax. We take Red Fern on little trip, just you and me. I pack sandwiches already. Lots of sandwiches, because canal boat go so slow. And slow will be nice, you will see."

LAST WORDS

Thank you for reading *Whispers Under Middle Ides*. If you enjoyed the story, leaving a review is a good way to let other readers know how to follow in your footsteps. I appreciate your feedback.

Join my mailing list and find more at
www.pattisontelford.com

Pattison Telford lives in Toronto, Canada, with his wife, two quietly magical sons, and snaggle-toothed dog. Previously living in Scotland, England, and Australia has armed him with a considerable range of slang words and insults. He grew up playing basketball and has spent far too much time sitting in front of computer screens in his job as a Microsoft IT Consultant.